Sir Arthur Conan Doyle (1859-1930), was born in Edinburgh, where his father, of Irish parentage, was a clerk of works for the government. Educated by the Jesuits at Stonyhurst, Doyle entered the medical school at Edinburgh University in 1876, working as a doctor's assistant at times to help pay the fees. He graduated in 1881 and, after Greenland and African voyages as a ship's doctor, went into practice at Southsea, Portsmouth.

Conan Doyle had started to write while he was a medical student, and at 20 had a story published in *Chambers' Journal*. Sherlock Holmes first appeared in *A Study in Scarlet* (1887), and from 1891 he featured regularly in stories for *Strand* magazine. Killed-off in 1893 ('The Final Problem'), Holmes was brought back by popular demand, in *The Hound of the Baskervilles* (1902) and four further collections, from *The Return of Sherlock Holmes* (1905), to *The Case-Book of Sherlock Holmes* (1927).

To replace Holmes, Conan Doyle created Etienne Gerard, a young French cavalry officer from the time of the Napoleonic wars, endearing, ludicrous and heroic, whose memoirs were collected as *The Exploits of Brigadier Gerard* (1896) and its sequel *Adventures of Gerard* (1903). Together they form a miniature epic triumphantly reviving the spirit of Napoleon's armies and of the nations aroused against them. After Gerard there came Professor Challenger, the scientist and explorer of *The Lost World* (1912) and *The Poison Belt* (1913).

Knighted in 1902, Conan Doyle produced more than 60 books in the course of his career, including songs, poetry and historical fiction in the spirit of Scott, including *Micah Clarke* (1889), and *The White Company* (1891). But his greatest literary achievement lay in his short stories, unrivalled in the mingling of character, action and atmosphere, whether Holmesian, Gerardine or self-standing.

Arthur Conan Doyle

THE EXPLOITS
OF BRIGADIER GERARD

Edited & Introduced by
Owen Dudley Edwards

CANONGATE
CLASSICS
38

This edition first published as a Canongate Classic in 1991 by Canongate Press, 14 Frederick Street, Edinburgh EH2 2HB. Introduction copyright © Owen Dudley Edwards 1991.

The publishers gratefully acknowledge general subsidy from the Scottish Arts Council towards the Canongate Classics series and a specific grant towards the publication of this title.

Set in 10pt Plantin by Falcon Typographic Art Ltd, Edinburgh & London. Printed and bound in Great Britain by Cox & Wyman Ltd, Reading, Berkshire.

Canongate Classics
Series Editor: Roderick Watson
Editorial Board: Tom Crawford, John Pick
British Library Cataloguing in Publication Data
Doyle, *Sir* Arthur Conan, 1859-1930
The exploits of Brigadier Gerard
I. Title
823,912[F]

ISBN 0862413419

Contents

EDITOR'S NOTE

The text of this volume in the main is that originally passed by Arthur Conan Doyle for publication in the *Strand* where these stories appeared in the order assigned here: the first in the issue for December 1894, the next six in those for April to September 1895 inclusive, the last in that for December 1895. The reader thus can conveniently judge how Conan Doyle initially conceived his Brigadier, and how he developed the creation and his world with increasing sophistication and historical craft. Gerard evidently narrates the events of the first story during Napoleon's lifetime, probably before his abdication in April 1814 or possibly between his return and Waterloo, whereas the other stories are supposedly delivered at a much later date (the 1840s for the rest of the *Exploits*, the 1850s and perhaps later for the *Adventures*), *The Exploits of Brigadier Gerard* was originally published in book form by George Newnes, publisher of the *Strand*, on 15 February 1896, with its stories reordered in historical sequence, thus necessitating a few deletions, notably the first sentence on p. 26, and the first five sentences on p. 74 (the loss of the latter eliminating a comic gem). I have retained some minor revisions in the book-text.

I have added head-notes to each of the stories, to supply the chronology of the *Exploits* and add an additional whiff of historical context.

O.D.E.

Introduction

Readers of Marbot, de Gonneville, Coignet, de Fezensac, Bourgogne, and the other French soldiers who have recorded their reminiscences of the Napoleonic campaigns, will recognise the fountain from which I have drawn the adventures of Etienne Gerard. It was an extraordinary age and produced extraordinary types. For twenty-three years France was at war, with one short breathing space of a few months. To Frenchmen war had become the normal and natural state. Children were born in war, grew up in war, fought in the war, and died in the same endless war without ever knowing what peace was like. Yet, as we read the memoirs of these fighting men, or if we consult the descriptions left by those who, like our own Napier, had met them in the field, we find that they were by no means brutalised by this strange experience, and that among them were knightly and gentle souls, playfully gallant, whose actions recall the very spirit of chivalry. A better knight than Marbot never rode in the lists, and what shall we say of that dragoon, described by Napier, who raised his sword, saluted and passed, on perceiving that his English antagonist in a fierce *mêlée* had only one arm, or that madcap officer of cavalry who charged the whole English army single-handed. These are the men, glorious in their youth, and pathetic in their useless and poverty-stricken old age, of whom I desired to draw a type, noble, *débonnaire*, capable, self-sufficient, human, and garrulous. I may add that, light as the sketches are, there has been some attempt to keep the military and historical detail correct.

This was Arthur Conan Doyle's preface to *The Exploits of Brigadier Gerard*, when the Author's Edition of his works was published on 16 November 1903. The first book publication, from George Newnes, had been on 15 February 1896, following the appearance of individual exploits in Newnes's *Strand* magazine for December 1894, April through September 1895, and December 1895. Ironically the Author's Edition *Exploits* emerged two months after Newnes's book publication of the only other collection of Gerard stories, *The Adventures of Gerard*, but this was far too short an interval to permit its inclusion (save for one story) in the Author's Edition. The *Adventures*, fresher in the author's mind as he was writing his preface, accounts for his inclusion of a source not available for the *Exploits*, the *Mémoires* of Sergeant Adrien Jean Baptiste François Bourgogne, published in Paris in 1898. Bourgogne (1785–1867) was in any case purely concerned with the Russian Campaign of 1812, which is only glancingly noticed in its conclusion in the *Exploits*, and while ACD drew important lessons from the *Journal de la Campagne de Russie* by Raymond Aymery Philippe Joseph, Duc de Montesquiou-Fezensac (1784–1867), its preoccupations were likewise peripheral to the *Exploits* though vital to the *Adventures*. What had launched Conan Doyle's first series of Napoleonic short stories supposedly narrated by his Gerard, were primarily the recollections of Jean Baptiste Antoine Marcellin, Baron de Marbot (1782–1854), of Aymar Olivier Le Harivel de Gonneville (1783–1872), and of Jean-Roch Coignet (1776–1860?).

ACD's *Through the Magic Door*, published in 1907, is a seminal positive criticism and celebration of his favourite works (some of its material reworked from articles in 1894, the year of Gerard's serialised *Exploits*). The reader is supposedly standing with the enthusiastic author before one of his bookshelves:

> Here is Marbot at this end—the first of all soldier books in the world. This is the complete three-volume French edition, with red and gold cover, smart and *débonnaire* like its author. Here he is in one frontispiece with his pleasant, round, boyish face, as a Captain of his beloved Chasseurs. And here in the other is the grizzled old bull-dog as a full general, looking as full of fight as ever. . . . the human, the gallant, the inimitable Marbot! His book is that which gives us the best picture by far of the Napoleonic soldiers,

and to me they are even more interesting than their great leader, though his must ever be the most singular figure in history. But those soldiers, with their huge shakeos, their hairy knapsacks, and their hearts of steel—what men they were! . . .

It must be confessed that Marbot's details are occasionally a little hard to believe. Never in the pages of Lever has there been such a series of hairbreadth escapes and dare-devil exploits. Surely he stretched it a little sometimes. You may remember his adventure at Eylau . . . how a cannon-ball, striking the top of his helmet, paralyzed him by the concussion of his spine; and how, on a Russian officer running forward to cut him down, his horse bit the man's face nearly off. This was the famous charger which savaged everything until Marbot, having bought it for next to nothing, cured it by thrusting a boiling leg of mutton into its mouth when it tried to bite him. It certainly does need a robust faith to get over these incidents. And yet, when one reflects upon the hundreds of battles and skirmishes which a Napoleonic officer must have endured—how they must have been the uninterrupted routine of his life from the first dark hair upon his lip to the first grey one upon his head, it is presumptuous to say what may or may not have been possible in such unparalleled careers. At any rate, be it fact or fiction—fact it is, in my opinion, with some artistic touching up of the highlights—there are few books which I could not spare from my shelves better than the memoirs of the gallant Marbot.

I dwell upon this particular book because it is the best; but take the whole line, and there is not one which is not full of interest. Marbot gives you the point of view of the officer. So does De Ségur and De Fezensac and Colonel Gonville, each in some different branch of the service. But some are from the pens of the men in the ranks, and they are even more graphic than the others. Here, for example, are the papers of good old Coignet, who was a grenadier of the Guard, and could neither read nor write until after the great wars were over. A tougher soldier never went into battle.

In 1948 there was published a little biography of Marbot by Vyvyan Ferrers. It shares with John Bunyan's *Pilgrim's Progress*, Oscar Wilde's *De Profundis* and P. G. Wodehouse's *Money in the Bank* the distinction of having been written in prison, for Ferrers had been British Consul at St Malo when the Nazis took it. Before his imprisonment, Ferrers had been reading the Marbot *Mémoires*. Now he based his book on its memory. His manuscript was rescued after the war and returned to him. He called it *The Brigadier* and this was how the imprisoned consul began his book:

> Conan Doyle has written a series of entertaining short stories of which the central figure is a dashing young French hussar, who, in the course of the Napoleonic Wars goes through a number of hair-raising adventures in every part of Europe. The hero is both lovable and laughable. Gallant and gay, valiant and vain, he combines two characters which are sometimes supposed to be incompatible. He is both a braggart and a brave man. . . .
>
> It is evident that by the word 'brigadier' the author intended to signify the rank which the French call *général de brigade*. Unfortunately, there is also in the French service a rank which bears the designation *brigadier*. It is a very lowly rank indeed: it is approximately equivalent to 'lance-corporal'. This must have been pointed out to the author while the stories were appearing one by one. When they were collected and republished in book form an explanatory footnote was added. The word 'brigadier' is to be understood (it says) in the English sense. This is all very well, but the reader must be permitted to wonder whether the writer, when he conferred that rank upon his hero, was aware that it has a French sense also, and what that sense is.

And Ferrers then introduces his own subject, Marcellin Marbot, 'a real officer who was undoubtedly the author's model'. He was not alone in this identification. Andrew Lang, reviewing the Author's Edition anonymously in the *Quarterly Review* (vol. 200, July 1904), wrote that

> Brigadier Gerard is Sir Arthur's masterpiece; we never weary of that brave, stupid, vain, chivalrous being, who hovers between General Marbot and Thackeray's Major Geoghegan, with all the merits of both, and with others of his own.

We may grant 'Geoghegan'—Conan Doyle was proud that Thackeray had been a friend of his father's family, deeply respected the campaign in the Lowlands in *Henry*

Esmond and thought *Vanity Fair* one of the three greatest novels of the nineteenth century, and these no less
than Thackeray's swashbuckling pastiche *The Tremendous
Adventures of Major Gahagan* must be included among
the sources of Gerard—with the reservation that Gahagan
recounts impossible exploits, while Gerard, no less than
Marbot, prefers and reminisces in ambiguous inclination
towards an adorned truth.

But there is more to Gerard than an imitation of Marbot,
albeit Marbot was the initial inspiration. The *Mémoires* in
the edition Conan Doyle prized was published in 1891, and
this French text integrated the fire, and dash, and vivid
sense of landscape and action, with subtleties, and of this
example Conan Doyle made good use. But he used it in
a fashion entirely his own. Marbot tells one story of how
the elder of two Cossack prisoners attempted to assassinate
him and succeeded in killing a beloved friend, whereupon
Marbot shot him, but his furious intention to slaughter the
murderer's brother with his next bullet was stopped by
the Cossacks' tutor who begged him to think of his own
mother and spare the innocent. Conan Doyle combined a
remarkable mastery of the mingling of pathos and comedy,
and one can see him simultaneously moved by the episode
and thoughtfully aware of its unintended comic possibilities.
So in 'The Medal of Brigadier Gerard' this becomes an
encounter with a youth who challenges pistol with sword:

> 'Rendez-vous!' he yelled.
> 'I must compliment monsieur upon his French', said I,
> resting the barrel of my pistol upon my bridle arm, which
> I have always found best when shooting from the saddle. I
> aimed at his face, and could see, even in the moonlight, how
> white he grew when he understood that it was all up with
> him. But even as my finger pressed the trigger I thought of
> his mother, and put my ball through his horse's shoulder.

It neatly makes its point about French chivalry towards a
disadvantaged opponent, which deduction ACD had drawn
from several sources other than Marbot. But intricate and
implicit in the chivalry is the glorious laughter of 'I thought
of his mother and shot the horse'. The chivalry, and the
momentary fear transmitted to the reader on the boy's

behalf, are the greater because of the delicious infelicity of the association of images, and Gerard is all the more lovable because he so blatantly and unwittingly makes such a ham-fisted business of recording his unquestionable nobility. Wilde, with whom Conan Doyle had conversed with such interest at the famous meeting which set on foot *The Sign of Four* and *The Picture of Dorian Gray*, had once termed a bad stage version of *The Three Musketeers* 'Athos, Pathos and Bathos'. Whether he repeated his remark to ACD or not, his interlocutor showed his capacity for using that formula to excellent (in place of execrable) effect. And if Gerard unconsciously sacrifices tact, thereby he retains his vital narrative pace.

One of the strongest points of difference between Marbot and Gerard lies in their relationship to Napoleon. Marbot, confronted by Napoleon's Machiavellian encouragement of hostility between Charles IV of Spain and his son Ferdinand, the better to instal Joseph Bonaparte on the Spanish throne, was disgusted:

> . . . *mais disons-le sincèrement, la conduite de Napoléon dans cette scandaleuse affaire fut indigne d'un grand homme tel que lui. S'offrir comme médiateur entre le père et le fils pour les attirer dans un piège, les dépouiller ensuite l'un et l'autre . . . ce fut une atrocité, un acte odieux, que l'histoire a flétri et que la Providence ne tarda pas à punir, car ce fut la guerre d'Espagne qui prépara et amena la chute de Napoléon.*

The farthest Gerard will go in criticism of his great man is to deplore Napoleon's insistence that Gerard has the thickest head in his army. Of Marbot's sense of the great diplomatic games afoot behind the battles and occupations, Gerard (unless directly informed) has hardly the slightest inkling. Beyond his own immediate experience he knows very little, and his Emperor is unquestionable save where he acts unfairly to Gerard. There are moments of similarity in their confrontations: when Napoleon is pleased with Gerard, he pulls Gerard's ear as in reality he pulled Marbot's, but then he also pulled Coignet's.

Conan Doyle has given us the clue: Marbot was an officer, and an officer's son. De Gonville was an aristocrat: he supplies something of Gerard too, notably in his intoxication with chivalry and its ancient French traditions, but these he says came from his boyhood reading while to Gerard his own place in the tradition is instinctive and unliterary. It is to Coignet, the illiterate soldier, that we must turn for many of Gerard's qualities and situations. Coignet had been promoted, as *Les cahiers du capitaine Coignet* proudly asserts, but he started as a private. Gerard we know as an officer, but he shares with Coignet his creation as a soldier by the Napoleonic wars. Of Gerard's family we know little, save that he loved them, a quality he holds in common with many Napoleonic soldier memorialists—Coignet is an exception here, saying much of his hatred of his stepmother and of the father who sired 45 children (Marbot is far from the least credible of these *raconteurs*) and abandoned his legitimate offspring to misery and illiteracy and possible death. But Coignet's harsh background led him into more detail than Marbot on the savagery, and treachery of Spanish guerilla warfare, and Gerard's adventures in Spain can recall this horrific undertone of Coignet's *Cahiers*, however different the actual episodes. It is Coignet who at the end of the war is sent to plant cabbages like Gerard, unlike the officer aristocrats who continue with military careers. It is Coignet who goes to the Café Milon after the war, thus supplying the location where Gerard tells his stories. What Conan Doyle had produced was a hero who moved between the harshly divided classes, and who reflected some of the attitudes of each. His experiences are those of an officer; his circumstances have more in common with the soldiers who originated without family advantages. Ferrers was shrewder than he realised in raising the question of a brigadier's being a lance-corporal: the aged soldier whose life has been meaningless other than during his Napoleonic experiences has as his counterpart in Conan Doyle's English fictions the nonagenarian Corporal Brewster in 'A Straggler of '15' still absolutely dominated by his moment of glory at Waterloo. In real life it was this kind of veteran whom ACD would have most naturally encountered as a Portsmouth doctor. And Brewster sees nothing later or greater than his 'Dook', Wellington, much as Gerard has no horizons

beyond Napoleon. Coignet gives the soldiers' heartbreak
at Napoleon's abdication, and behind all the laughter and
thrilling involvement in each episode, the heartbreak is
fundamental to Gerard's narratives.

Gerard, however many influences he reflected from the
literature of Napoleonic veterans, was Conan Doyle's own
creation, and no warmed-over fictionalisation of Marbot,
Coignet, or anyone else. In saluting Marbot as 'inimitable',
ACD quietly served notice that he was not imitating him.
His declaration of 'attempt to keep the military and historical detail correct' intermingled humour with modesty,
for the stories followed a massive absorption in the sources.
But when all is said Gerard is not writing or dictating his
memoirs: he is giving a series of oral reminiscences to buyers
of drinks in his chosen *café*. His obvious emulator is Bertie
Wooster in the work of Conan Doyle's most impressive
disciple, Wodehouse, whose oral narratives are presumably delivered to Drones Club or country-house audiences.
Like Bertie, Gerard is literate (and thus lacks Coignet's
ambition to master the education of which he had been
deprived), but he wears what little non-military education
he had assimilated very lightly. Their breezy indifference
to conventions of art appreciation (more evident in the
Adventures of Gerard than the *Exploits*) is but one aspect of a
Gerard-Wooster affinity: neither are absolute Philistines, for
both can warm to some aesthetic epiphany entirely in terms
of their own personal reactions. And both creations make
masterly use of narrative to reveal the narrator's absurdity
all the more clearly in the conviction of their own profun-
dity. Simultaneously the narrators' gallantry, good humour,
altruism, loyalty and sense of code invite the admiration their
declarations of intelligence so seldom obtain. On the other
hand within their own limited area of special knowledge each
has a startling shrewdness: Gerard can predict a soldier's
tactical reaction in an immediate military situation, Bertie
can foretell a woman's fury if deprived of her afternoon
tea. The all-revealing military narrator reappears in George
MacDonald Fraser's Flashman, but the work here is much
less subtle: Flashman is a coward and a fraud, while
Gerard is neither, nor, fundamentally, is Bertie, however

much circumstances force them into ludicrous attempts at disguise from time to time—and Flashman's unintentional revelations are to the depth of his depravity, not to its existence. The frank poltroon is easier to draw than the thickhead stoutheart, who must feed audience irony while warming emotions.

Conan Doyle tells us in *Memories and Adventures* (1923, 1930) that he 'began the Brigadier Gerard series of stories' in Davos where he had gone to do what might be possible to save his wife whose health had collapsed from tuberculosis. So 'The Medal of Brigadier Gerard', published well in advance of the rest, was written there early in 1894. There were excellent reasons for it. Convinced that he was being mercilessly tagged as the Sherlock Holmes man at the expense of all of his other literary work, ACD had resolved on ending the Holmes series. But with 'the death of Sherlock Holmes', emblazoned on the frontispiece of the *Strand* for December 1893, ACD had to provide a new character or characters for a short story series, having established so well the public appetite for his innovation of two interacting characters in otherwise unrelated episodes. If Holmes supposedly met his death in order to destroy 'the Napoleon of Crime', Professor Moriarty, it was what Holmes would call an obvious chain of reasoning that his own place should be taken by a creation dominated by Napoleon himself. There were decided risks. Holmes was the author's to do with as he wished, as he so drastically showed in 'The Final Problem'; Napoleon would be absolutely circumscribed by what was known about him, and it was a great deal. Hence the Napoleon-Gerard association became the natural partnership with which to succeed Holmes and Watson, but Gerard, while a very well worked-out character, is also symbolic of countless French soldiers, and Napoleon was too much occupied to play a part in each instalment. Gerard, therefore, does all that he does in the cause of a Napoleon constantly in his mind, but we seldom see Napoleon—he enters only three Exploits. Naturally Napoleon had to make a personal appearance in the 'Medal', as the pilot story to launch the series, so neatly accomplished in the *Strand* of December 1894, exactly a year after it had carried 'The

Final Problem'. ACD had found the formula with which to mollify, though not to silence, his devoted and infuriated readers.

'The Medal of Brigadier Gerard' was an excellent pilot for the series, but it has some instructive points of difference from what was to follow. As a story it is very much a unity, with everything subordinated to its beginning and end, an ironic though intensely thrilling Odyssey with a decidedly mixed reception for the returned Odysseus. It reflects the speed and isolation in which it was written, and it makes magnificent reading aloud as the author proved on his American tour late in 1894 when, in the Homeric tradition, he delivered it to lecture audiences. The main body of the *Exploits* indicates the renewed accessibility of his mass of source-material for ACD, beginning with 'How the Brigadier Held the King', an Aeneid rather than an Odyssey whose ultimate destination, let alone adventures *en route*, is unknown to Gerard and to his audience, whereas the reader of the 'Medal' may sense or deduce the true nature of the mission which Gerard will only discover at its conclusion. 'How the Brigadier Held the King' maintains its ironies while piling twist upon turn as the hero is moved by forces outside his control through events and characters of dizzying but sharply-etched contrasting individualities. The brigand chief so powerfully struck the imagination that he was appropriated by Conan Doyle's iconoclastic neighbour at Hindhead, George Bernard Shaw, for his Mendoza in *Man and Superman*, with some additional blooms purloined from the Marshal Millefleurs. 'The theft of the brigand-poetaster from Sir Arthur Conan Doyle is deliberate', declared Shaw in the Epistle Dedicatory prefacing his published play. Napoleon and his romantic, thick-headed lieutenant in Shaw's earlier *The Man of Destiny* also have obvious Gerardine origins.

Andrew Lang commented in his *Quarterly Review* essay of 1904:

> The vanity of the Brigadier and his extreme simplicity are a little exaggerated; perhaps the author did not know at first how dear Gerard was to grow to himself and to his readers.

This was written after publication of *The Adventures of Gerard*, which ends with the Brigadier in supreme command of the reader's affections and loyalties as he looks on the face of his dead Napoleon. But he had grown dear to Lang from the first, witness the notice of the *Exploits* in *Longman's* (vol. XXVII, April 1896), in Lang's column 'At the Sign of the Ship':

> He is an absolutely delightful brigadier—brave, vain, not too clever. . . . For humour, excitement, adventure, and manly feeling Mr Doyle has never excelled this new work, which is a thing of the open air, and much superior to (as I trust it will be even more popular than) *Sherlock Holmes*. 'Mair meat', we say, as the ghost said to King Jamie, more Brigadier, please, Mr Doyle, when your leisure serves!

This brings the realisation that it is in Brigadier Gerard we meet the true rival of Sherlock Holmes. Conan Doyle had not realised it when he made Dr Watson 'take up my pen to write these the last words in which I shall ever record the singular gifts by which my friend Mr Sherlock Homes was distinguished', but it was to bring Gerard to life that Holmes had 'died', and Lang, for one, thought the contrivance of the linked short story series had now been given a more worthy protagonist. Lang's reservations on Holmes were not, perhaps, entirely divorced from the ill-success of his own murder story *The Mark of Cain* (published in 1886, a year before *A Study in Scarlet*), but his verdict must have been a relief to Conan Doyle after inevitable gnawing doubts as to the wisdom of Holmes's sacrifice. Reviewers were so ready to insist one's true métier had been found in the literary form one had just abandoned, and indeed the *Athenaeum* on 4 April 1896 had welcomed Gerard bleakly enough:

> Sherlock Holmes was a considerable creation, and none can write a better detective story than Dr Conan Doyle; but Sherlock Holmes is dead, and the tangled tales of crime and the avengers of crime are replaced by the exploits of a veteran warrior moulded on the lines at present popular. . . . No doubt a novel of this sort will meet with a hearty reception from those who like tales full of stir and movement.

The reviewer called Gerard a 'fine old fellow', but ACD had hopes of a somewhat younger audience than would be induced to spring to the bookseller on that information. The *Bookman* (April, 1896), reviewing the *Exploits*, was a comparable relief:

> Mr Conan Doyle has never done anything better than this—and, remembering the good things he has already given us, this is saying a good deal. If this book had appeared ten years ago it would have made a great impression. But it is the fate of a novelist who has made a new departure to be quickly followed by a score of imitators, and only the sifting power of time can give him the distinction he deserves. Mr Conan Doyle's work will *keep*. It has the salt of an excellent style; and when a score of books of a like kind are dead and forgotten, his will be read.

The *Bookman* judged the critical market well. *The Exploits of Brigadier Gerard* won many friends and made many other reviewers very happy, bringing favourable reports first from the *Scotsman*, on 17 February 1896, a mere two days after publication; followed by *The Speaker* which paid tribute to the scholarship of the book, and the *Spectator* (both on 25 April), which responded as so many did, to what it saw as the Brigadier's childlike or schoolboy qualities.

It was, no doubt, to be expected that the reviewers' chief reaction should be one of some satisfaction at their own intellectual superiority to Etienne Gerard. And this certainly helped to make him a favourite. Indeed, the reviewers seem to have agreed in seeing Gerard as appropriate to their notion of a Napoleonic officer, stage-French above all in his un-British self-admiration. Yet there was real historical insight here, too, for to read 'How the Brigadier Played for a Kingdom', for example, is to gain purchase on the awakening of German romantic nationalism in a form the cold print of scientific history cannot supply. The measure of Arthur Conan Doyle's success may be shown by the final passage in which Gerard for once shows himself a visionary of the *Zeitgeist*, and with nothing incongruous about his understanding having for once transcended the limits of Napoleon's.

The quality which enabled Conan Doyle to strike so hard and so acutely in the furtherance of historical understanding was in itself a highly scientific one. He had followed the principle Sir Herbert Butterfield was to single out as essential for the historian, that of considering the problem from a reversal of the loyalties the historian discovered in himself. The Gerard stories themselves are such an attempt: his *The Great Shadow* (1892) had looked on Napoleon with a sense of the menace indicated by its title which he posed to Britain, specifically to a Scots boy, and 'A Straggler of '15' had given a memory of the struggle through the dying eyes of an aged British soldier, transformed to his old force at the moment of death. And in 'The Lord of Chateau Noir', published in the *Strand*, in July of the year whose December saw the first Gerard exploit in that periodical, ACD had produced a haunting work of power and anger on the German occupation of France during the Franco-Prussian War of 1870, ominously detailing the intransigence of French revenge. For all of his charm, Gerard is the patriot transformed into the aggressor, and the nationalism his master's aggression calls forth in Germany was to become aggression in its turn with comparable responses.

As the United Kingdom enters on its new destiny in deeper involvement with the European continent, it is still faced by the difficulty that ailed Conan Doyle's reviewers: how to think European. It is all the more appropriate, then, to turn to a delightful but instructive group of stories from a Scotsman dismayed at the isolation which led his fellow-British to devalue and to miss the realities of the European continental peoples. Of that dismay he gave frank testimony in *Through the Magic Door*. Of his attempts to counter its causes few are so timely for our needs today as the fascinating panorama of European identities first put before the world in *The Exploits of Brigadier Gerard*.

Owen Dudley Edwards

ONE

The Medal of Brigadier Gerard

1814, and, as stated, 14 March, a month before Napoleon's abdication and retirement to Elba. Despite facing several foreign armies on French soil, confidence among Napoleon's soldiers was running high, having just scattered the Russians from Rheims with 6000 enemy casualties and less than 700 French. Napoleon had now to decide between three different routes to reach Paris.

The Duke of Tarentum, or Macdonald, as his old comrades prefer to call him, was, as I could perceive, in the vilest of tempers. His grim Scotch face was like one of those grotesque door-knockers which one sees in the Faubourg St Germain. We heard afterwards that the Emperor had said in jest that he would have sent him against Wellington in the South, but that he was afraid to trust him within the sound of the pipes. Major Charpentier and I could plainly see that he was smouldering with anger.

'Brigadier Gerard of the Hussars,' said he, with the air of the corporal with the recruit.

I saluted.

'Major Charpentier of the Horse Grenadiers.'

My companion answered to his name.

'The Emperor has a mission for you.'

Without more ado he flung open the door and announced us.

I have seen Napoleon ten times on horseback to once on foot, and I think that he does wisely to show himself to the troops in this fashion, for he cuts a very good figure in the saddle. As we saw him now he was the shortest man out of six by a good hand's breadth, and yet I am no very big man myself, though I ride quite heavy enough for a hussar. It is evident, too, that his body is too long for his legs. With his big round head, his curved shoulders, and his clean-shaven face, he is more like a Professor at the Sorbonne than the first soldier in France. Every man to his taste, but it seems to me that, if I could clap a pair of fine light cavalry whiskers, like my own, on to him, it would do him no harm. He has a firm mouth, however, and his eyes are remarkable. I have seen them once turned on me in anger, and I had rather ride at a square on a spent horse than face them again. I am not a man who is easily daunted, either.

He was standing at the side of the room, away from the window, looking up at a great map of the country which was hung upon the wall. Berthier stood beside him, trying to look wise, and just as we entered, Napoleon snatched his sword impatiently from him and pointed with it on the map. He was talking fast and low, but I heard him say, 'The valley of the Meuse,' and twice he repeated 'Berlin.' As we entered, his aide-de-camp advanced to us, but the Emperor stopped him and beckoned us to his side.

'You have not yet received the cross of honour, Brigadier Gerard?' he asked.

I replied that I had not, and was about to add that it was not for want of having deserved it, when he cut me short in his decided fashion.

'And you, Major?' he asked.

'No, sire.'

'Then you shall both have your opportunity now.'

He led us to the great map upon the wall and placed the tip of Berthier's sword on Rheims.

'I will be frank with you, gentlemen, as with two comrades. You have both been with me since Marengo, I believe?' He had a strangely pleasant smile, which used to light up his pale face with a kind of cold sunshine. 'Here at Rheims are our present headquarters on this the 14th of March. Very good. Here is Paris, distant by road a good twenty-five leagues. Blucher lies to the north, Schwarzenberg to the south.' He prodded at the map with the sword as he spoke.

'Now,' said he, 'the further into the country these people march, the more completely I shall crush them. They are about to advance upon Paris. Very good. Let them do so. My brother, the King of Spain, will be there with a hundred

thousand men. It is to him that I send you. You will hand
him this letter, a copy of which I confide to each of you. It
is to tell him that I am coming at once, in two days' time,
with every man and horse and gun to his relief. I must give
them forty-eight hours to recover. Then straight to Paris!
You understand me, gentlemen?'

Ah, if I could tell you the glow of pride which it gave me
to be taken into the great man's confidence in this way. As
he handed our letters to us I clicked my spurs and threw
out my chest, smiling and nodding to let him know that I
saw what he would be after. He smiled also, and rested his
hand for a moment upon the cape of my dolman. I would
have given half my arrears of pay if my mother could have
seen me at that instant.

'I will show you your route,' said he, turning back to the
map. 'Your orders are to ride together as far as Bazoches.
You will then separate, the one making for Paris by Oulchy
and Neuilly, and the other to the north by Braine, Soissons,
and Senlis. Have you anything to say, Brigadier Gerard?'

I am a rough soldier, but I have words and ideas. I had
begun to speak about glory and the peril of France when he
cut me short.

'And you, Major Charpentier?'

'If we find our route unsafe, are we at liberty to choose
another?' said he.

'Soldiers do not choose, they obey.' He inclined his
head to show that we were dismissed, and turned round
to Berthier. I do not know what he said, but I heard them
both laughing.

Well, as you may think, we lost little time in getting upon
our way. In half an hour we were riding down the High
Street of Rheims, and it struck twelve o'clock as we passed
the cathedral. I had my little grey mare, Violette, the one
which Sebastiani had wished to buy after Dresden. It is the
fastest horse in the six brigades of light cavalry, and was
only beaten by the Duke of Rovigo's racer from England.
As to Charpentier, he had the kind of horse which a horse
grenadier or a cuirassier would be likely to ride: a back like
a bedstead, you understand, and legs like the posts. He is a
hulking fellow himself, so that they looked a singular pair.

And yet in his insane conceit he ogled the girls as they waved their handkerchiefs to me from the windows, and he twirled his ugly red moustache up into his eyes, just as if it were to him that their attention was addressed.

When we came out of the town we passed through the French camp, and then across the battle-field of yesterday, which was still covered both by our own poor fellows and by the Russians. But of the two the camp was the sadder sight. Our army was thawing away. The Guards were all right, though the young guard was full of conscripts. The artillery and the heavy cavalry were also good if there were more of them, but the infantry privates with their under-officers looked like schoolboys with their masters. And we had no reserves. When one considered that there were 80,000 Russians to the north and 150,000 Russians and Austrians to the south, it might make even the bravest man grave.

For my own part, I confess that I shed a tear until the thought came that the Emperor was still with us, and that on that very morning he had placed his hand upon my dolman and had promised me a medal of honour. This set me singing, and I spurred Violette on, until Charpentier had to beg me to have mercy on his great, snorting, panting camel. The road was beaten into paste and rutted 2ft deep by the artillery, so that he was right in saying that it was not the place for a gallop.

I have never been very friendly with this Charpentier; and now for twenty miles of the way I could not draw a word from him. He rode with his brows puckered and his chin upon his breast, like a man who is heavy with thought. More than once I asked him what was on his mind, thinking that, perhaps, with my quicker intelligence I might set the matter straight. His answer always was that it was his mission of which he was thinking, which surprised me, because, although I had never thought much of his intelligence, still it seemed to me to be impossible that anyone could be puzzled by so simple and soldierly a task.

Well, we came at last to Bazoches, where he was to take the southern road and I the northern. He half turned in his saddle before he left me, and he looked at me with a singular expression of inquiry in his face.

'What do you make of it, Brigadier?' he asked.

'Of what?'

'Of our mission.'

'Surely it is plain enough.'

'You think so? Why should the Emperor tell us his plans?'

'Because he recognised our intelligence.'

My companion laughed in a manner which I found annoying.

'May I ask what you intend to do if you find these villages full of Prussians?' he asked.

'I shall obey my orders.'

'But you will be killed.'

'Very possibly.'

He laughed again, and so offensively that I clapped my hand to my sword. But before I could tell him what I thought of his stupidity and rudeness he had wheeled his horse, and was lumbering away down the other road. I saw his big fur cap vanish over the brow of the hill, and then I rode upon my way, wondering at his conduct. From time to time I put my hand to the breast of my tunic and felt the paper crackle beneath my fingers. Ah, my precious paper, which should be turned into the little silver medal for which I had yearned so long. All the way from Braine to Sermoise I was thinking of what my mother would say when she saw it.

I stopped to give Violette a meal at a wayside auberge on the side of a hill not far from Soissons—a place surrounded by old oaks, and with so many crows that one could scarce hear one's own voice. It was from the innkeeper that I learned that Marmont had fallen back two days before, and that the Prussians were over the Aisne. An hour later, in the fading light, I saw two of their vedettes upon the hill to the right, and then, as darkness gathered, the heavens to the north were all glimmering from the lights of a bivouac.

When I heard that Blucher had been there for two days, I was much surprised that the Emperor should not have known that the country through which he had ordered me to carry my precious letter was already occupied by the enemy. Still, I thought of the tone of his voice when he said to Charpentier that a soldier must not choose, but must obey. I should follow the route he had laid down for me as long as Violette could move a hoof or I a finger upon her bridle. All the way from Sermoise to Soissons, where the road dips up and down, curving among fir-woods, I kept my pistol ready and my swordbelt braced, pushing on swiftly where the path was straight, and then coming slowly round the corners in the way we learned in Spain.

When I came to the farmhouse which lies to the right of the road just after you cross the wooden bridge over the Crise, near where the great statue of the Virgin stands, a woman cried to me from the field saying that the Prussians were in Soissons. A small party of their lancers, she said, had come in that very afternoon, and a whole division was expected before midnight. I did not wait to hear the end of her tale, but clapped spurs into Violette, and in five minutes was galloping her into the town.

Three Uhlans were at the mouth of the main street, their horses tethered, and they gossiping together, each with a pipe as long as my sabre. I saw them well in the light of an open door, but of me they could have seen only the flash of Violette's grey side and the black flutter of my cloak. A moment later I flew through a stream of them rushing from an open gateway. Violette's shoulder sent one of them reeling, and I stabbed at another but missed him. Pang, pang, went two carbines, but I had flown round the curve of the street and never so much as heard the hiss of the balls. Ah, we were great, both Violette and I. She lay down to it like a coursed hare, the fire flying from her hoofs. I stood in my stirrups and brandished my sword. Someone sprang for my bridle. I sliced him through the arm, and I heard him howling behind me. Two horsemen closed upon me, I cut one down and outpaced the other. A minute later I was clear of the town and flying down a broad white road with the black poplars on either side. For a time I heard the rattle of hoofs behind me, but they died and died until I could not tell them from the throbbing of my own heart. Soon I pulled up and listened, but all was silent. They had given up the chase.

Well, the first thing that I did was to dismount and to lead my mare into a small wood through which a stream ran. There I watered her and rubbed her down, giving her two pieces of sugar soaked in cognac from my flask. She was spent from the sharp chase, but it was wonderful to see how she came round with a half-hour's rest. When my thighs closed upon her again, I could tell by the spring and the swing of her that it would not be her fault if I did not win my way safe to Paris.

I must have been well within the enemy's lines now, for I heard a number of them shouting one of their rough drinking songs out of a house by the roadside, and I went round by the fields to avoid it. At another time two men came out into the moonlight (for by this time it was a cloudless night) and shouted something in German; but I galloped on without heeding them, and they were afraid to fire, for their own hussars are dressed exactly as I was. It is best to take no notice at these times, and then they put you down as a deaf man.

It was a lovely moon, and every tree threw a black bar across the road. I could see the country side just as if it were daytime, and very peaceful it looked, save that there was a great fire raging somewhere in the north. In the silence of the night-time, and with the knowledge that danger was in front and behind me, the sight of that great distant fire was very striking and awesome. But I am not easily clouded, for I have seen too many singular things, so I hummed a tune between my teeth and thought of little Lisette, whom I might see in Paris. My mind was full of her when, trotting round a corner, I came straight upon half-a-dozen German dragoons, who were sitting round a brushwood fire by the roadside.

I am an excellent soldier. I do not say this because I am prejudiced in my own favour, but because I really am so. I can weigh every chance in a moment, and decide with as much certainty as though I had brooded for a week. Now I saw like a flash that, come what might, I should be chased, and on a horse which had already done a long twelve leagues. But it was better to be chased onwards than to be chased back. On this moonlit night, with fresh horses behind me, I must take my risk in either case; but if I were to shake them off, I preferred that it should be near Senlis than near Soissons. All this flashed on me as if by instinct, you understand. My eyes had hardly rested on the bearded faces under the brass helmets before my rowels were up to the bosses in Violette's side, and she off with a rattle like a *pas-de-charge*. Oh, the shouting and rushing and stamping from behind us! Three of them fired and three swung themselves on to their horses. A bullet rapped on the crupper of my saddle with a noise like a stick on a door. Violette sprang madly forward, and I thought she had been wounded, but it was only a graze above the near-fetlock. Ah, the dear little mare, how I loved her when I felt her settle down into that long, easy gallop of hers, her hoofs going like a Spanish girl's castanets. I could not hold myself. I turned on my saddle and shouted and raved, 'Vive l'Empereur!' I screamed and laughed at the gust of oaths that came back to me.

But it was not over yet. If she had been fresh she might have gained a mile in five. Now she could only hold her own with a very little over. There was one of them, a young boy of an officer, who was better mounted than the others. He drew ahead with every stride. Two hundred yards behind him were two troopers, but I saw every time that I glanced round, that the distance between them was increasing. The other three who had waited to shoot were a long way in the rear. The officer's mount was a bay, a fine horse, though not to be spoken of with Violette. Yet it was a powerful brute, and it seemed to me that in a few miles its freshness might tell. I waited until the lad was a long way in front of his comrades, and then I eased my mare down a little—a very, very little, so that he might think he was really catching me. When he came within pistol shot of me I drew and cocked my own pistol, and laid my chin upon my shoulder to see what he would do. He did not offer to fire, and I soon discerned the cause. The silly boy had taken his pistols from his holsters when he had camped for the night. He wagged his sword at me now and roared some of his gibberish. He did not seem to understand that he was at my mercy. I eased Violette down until there was not the length of a long lance between the grey tail and the bay muzzle.

'Rendez-vous!' he yelled.

'I must compliment monsieur upon his French,' said I, resting the barrel of my pistol upon my bridle arm, which I have always found best when shooting from the saddle. I aimed at his face, and could see, even in the moonlight, how white he grew when he understood that it was all up with him. But even as my finger pressed the trigger I thought of his mother, and I put my ball through his horse's shoulder. I fear he hurt himself in the fall, for it was a fearful crash, but I had my letter to think of, so I stretched the mare into a gallop once more.

But they were not so easily shaken off, these brigands. The two troopers thought no more of their young officer than if he had been a recruit thrown in the riding-school. They left him to the others and thundered on after me. I had pulled up on the brow of a hill, thinking that I had heard the last of them; but, my faith, I soon saw there was no time for loitering, so away we went, the mare tossing her head and I my busby, to show what we thought of two dragoons who tried to catch a hussar. But at this moment, even while I laughed at the thought, my heart stood still within me, for there at the end of the long white road was a black patch of cavalry waiting to receive me. To a young soldier it might have seemed the shadow of the trees, but to me it was a troop of hussars, and, turn where I could, death seemed to be waiting for me.

Well, I had the dragoons behind me and the hussars in front. Never since Moscow have I seemed to be in such peril. But for the honour of the brigade I had rather be cut down by a light cavalryman than by a heavy. I never drew bridle, therefore, or hesitated for an instant, but I let Violette have her head. I remember that I tried to pray as I rode, but I am a little out of practice at such things, and the only words I could remember were the prayer for fine weather which we used at the school on the evening before holidays. Even this seemed better than nothing, and I was pattering it out, when suddenly I heard French voices in front of me. Ah, mon Dieu, but the joy went through my heart like a musket-ball. They were ours—our own dear little rascals from the corps of Marmont. Round whisked my two dragoons and galloped for their lives, with the moon gleaming on their brass helmets, while I trotted up to my friends with no undue haste, for I would have them understand that though a hussar may fly, it is not in his nature to fly very fast. Yet I fear that Violette's heaving flanks and foam-spattered muzzle gave the lie to my careless bearing.

Who should be at the head of the troop but old Bouvet, whom I saved at Leipzig! When he saw me his little pink eyes filled with tears, and, indeed, I could not but shed a few myself at the sight of his joy. I told him of my mission, but he laughed when I said that I must pass through Senlis.

'The enemy is there,' said he. 'You cannot go.'

'I prefer to go where the enemy is,' I answered. 'I would ride through Berlin if I had the Emperor's orders.'

'But why not go straight to Paris with your despatch? Why should you choose to pass through the one place where you are almost sure to be taken or killed?'

'A soldier does not choose—he obeys,' said I, just as I had heard Napoleon say it.

Old Bouvet laughed in his wheezy way, until I had to give my moustachios a twirl and look him up and down in a manner which brought him to reason.

'Well,' said he, 'you had best come along with us, for we are all bound for Senlis. Our orders are to reconnoitre the place. A squadron of Poniatowski's Polish lancers are in front of us. If you must ride through it, it is possible that we may be able to go with you.'

So away we went, jingling and clanking through the quiet night until we came up with the Poles—fine old soldiers all of them, though a trifle heavy for their horses. It was a treat to see them, for they could not have carried themselves better if they had belonged to my own brigade. We rode together, until in the early morning we saw the lights of Senlis. A peasant was coming along with a cart, and from him we learned how things were going there.

His information was certain, for his brother was the Mayor's coachman, and he had spoken with him late the night before. There was a single squadron of Cossacks—or a polk, as they call it in their frightful language—quartered upon the Mayor's house which stands at the corner of the marketplace, and is the largest building in the town. A whole division of Prussian infantry was encamped in the woods to the north, but only the Cossacks were in Senlis. Ah, what a chance to avenge ourselves upon these barbarians, whose cruelty to our poor country-folk was the talk at every camp fire.

We were into the town like a torrent, hacked down the vedettes, rode over the guard, and were smashing in the doors of the Mayor's house before they understood that there was a Frenchman within twenty miles of them. We saw horrid heads at the windows, heads bearded to the temples, with tangled hair and sheepskin caps, and silly, gaping mouths. 'Hourra! Hourra!' they shrieked, and fired with their carbines, but our fellows were into the house and at their throats before they had wiped the sleep out of their eyes. It was dreadful to see how the Poles flung themselves upon them, like starving wolves upon a herd of fat bucks—for, as you know, the Poles have a blood feud against the Cossacks. The most were killed in the upper rooms, whither they had fled for shelter, and the blood was pouring down into the hall like rain from a roof. They are terrible soldiers, these Poles, though I think they are a trifle heavy for their horses. Man for man, they are as big as Kellermann's cuirassiers. Their equipment is, of course, much lighter, since they are without the cuirass, back-plate, and helmet.

Well, it was at this point that I made an error—a very serious error it must be admitted. Up to this moment I had carried out my mission in a manner which only my modesty prevents me from describing as remarkable. But now I did that which an official would condemn and a soldier excuse.

There is no doubt that the mare was spent, but still it is true that I might have galloped on through Senlis and reached the country, where I should have had no enemy between me and Paris. But what hussar can ride past a fight and never draw rein? It is to ask too much of him. Besides, I thought that if Violette had an hour of rest I might have three hours the better at the other end. Then on the top of it came those heads at the windows, with their sheepskin hats and their barbarous cries. I sprang from my saddle, threw Violette's bridle over a rail-post, and ran into the house with the rest. It is true that I was too late to be of service, and that I was nearly wounded by a lance-thrust from one of these dying savages. Still, it is a pity to miss even the smallest affair, for one never knows what opportunity for advancement may present itself. I have seen more soldierly work in out-post skirmishes and little gallop-and-hack affairs of the kind than in any of the Emperor's big battles.

When the house was cleared I took a bucket of water out for Violette, and our peasant guide showed me where the good Mayor kept his fodder. My faith, but the little sweetheart was ready for it. Then I sponged down her legs, and leaving her still tethered I went back into the house to find a mouthful for myself, so that I should not need to halt again until I was in Paris.

And now I come to the part of my story which may seem singular to you although I could tell you at least ten things every bit as queer which have happened to me in my lifetime. You can understand that, to a man who spends his lifetime in scouting and vedette duties on the bloody ground which lies between two great armies, there are many chances of strange experiences. I'll tell you, however, exactly what occurred.

Old Bouvet was waiting in the passage when I entered, and he asked me whether we might not crack a bottle of wine together. 'My faith, we must not be long,' said he. 'There are ten thousand of Theilmann's Prussians in the woods up yonder.'

'Where is the wine?' I asked.

'Ah, you may trust two hussars to find where the wine is,' said he, and taking a candle in his hand, he led the way down the stone stairs into the kitchen.

When we got there we found another door, which opened on to a winding stair with the cellar at the bottom. The Cossacks had been there before us, as was easily seen by the broken bottles littered all over it. However, the Mayor was a *bon-vivant*, and I do not wish to have a better set of bins to pick from. Chambertin, Graves, Alicant, white wine and red, sparkling and still, they lay in pyramids peeping coyly out of the sawdust. Old Bouvet stood with his candle, looking here and peeping there, purring in his throat like a cat before a milk-pail. He had picked upon a Burgundy at last, and had his hand outstretched to the bottle, when there came a roar of musketry from above us, a rush of feet, and such a yelping and screaming as I have never listened to. The Prussians were upon us.

Bouvet is a brave man: I will say that for him. He flashed out his sword and away he clattered up the stone steps, his spurs clinking as he ran. I followed him, but just as we came out into the kitchen passage a tremendous shout told us that the house had been recaptured.

'It is all over,' I cried, grasping at Bouvet's sleeve.

'There is one more to die,' he shouted, and away he went like a madman up the second stair. In effect, I should have gone to my death also had I been in his place, for he had done very wrong in not throwing out his scouts to warn him if the Germans advanced upon him. For an instant I was about to rush up with him, and then I bethought myself that, after all, I had my own mission to think of, and that if I were taken the important letter of the Emperor would be sacrificed. I let Bouvet die alone, therefore, and I went down into the cellar again, closing the door behind me.

Well, it was not a very rosy prospect down there either. Bouvet had dropped the candle when the alarm came, and I, pawing about in the darkness, could find nothing but broken bottles. At last I came upon the candle, which had rolled under the curve of a cask, but, try as I would with my tinderbox, I could not light it. The reason was that the wick had been wet in a puddle of wine, so suspecting that this might be the case, I cut the end off with my sword. Then I found that it lighted easily enough. But what to do I could not imagine. The scoundrels upstairs were shouting themselves hoarse, several hundred of them from the sound, and it was clear that some of them would soon want to moisten their throats. There would be an end to a dashing soldier, and of the mission and of the medal. I thought of my mother and I thought of the Emperor. It made me weep to think that the one would lose so excellent a son and the other the best light cavalry officer he ever had since Lasalle's time. But presently I dashed the tears from my eyes. 'Courage!' I cried, striking myself upon the chest. 'Courage, my brave boy! Is it possible that one who has come safely from Moscow without so much as a frost-bite will die in a French wine-cellar?' At the thought I was up on my feet and clutching at the letter in my tunic, for the crackle of it gave me courage.

My first plan was to set fire to the house, in the hope of escaping in the confusion. My second, to get into an empty wine-cask. I was looking round to see if I could find one, when suddenly, in the corner, I espied a little low door, painted of the same grey colour as the wall, so that it was only a man with quick sight who would have noticed it. I pushed against it, and at first I imagined that it was locked. Presently, however it gave a little, and then I understood that it was held by the pressure of something on the other side. I put my feet against a hogshead of wine, and I gave such a push that the door flew open and I came down with a crash upon my back, the candle flying out of my hands, so that I found myself in darkness once more. I picked myself up and stared through the black archway into the gloom beyond.

There was a slight ray of light coming from some slit or grating. The dawn had broken outside, and I could dimly see the long curving sides of several huge casks, which made me think that perhaps this was where the Mayor kept his reserves of wine while they were maturing. At any rate, it seemed to be a safer hiding-place than the outer cellar, so gathering up my candle, I was just closing the door behind me, when I suddenly saw something which filled me with amazement, and even, I confess, with the smallest little touch of fear.

I have said that at the further end of the cellar there was a dim grey fan of light striking downwards from somewhere near the roof. Well, as I peered through the darkness, I suddenly saw a great, tall man skip into this belt of daylight, and then out again into the darkness at the further end. My word, I gave such a start that my busby nearly broke its chin-strap! It was only a glance, but, none the less, I had time to see that the fellow had a hairy Cossack cap on his head, and that he was a great, long-legged, broad-shouldered brigand, with a sabre at his waist. My faith, even Etienne

Gerard was a little staggered at being left alone with such a creature in the dark.

But only for a moment. 'Courage!' I thought. 'Am I not a hussar, a brigadier, too, at the age of thirty-one, and the chosen messenger of the Emperor?' After all, this skulker had more cause to be afraid of me than I of him. And then suddenly I understood that he was afraid—horribly afraid. I could read it from his quick step and his bent shoulders as he ran among the barrels, like a rat making for its hole. And, of course, it must have been he who had held the door against me, and not some packing-case or wine-cask as I had imagined. He was the pursued then, and I the pursuer. Aha, I felt my whiskers bristle as I advanced upon him through the darkness! He would find that he had no chicken to deal with, this robber from the North. For the moment I was magnificent.

At first I had feared to light my candle lest I should make a mark of myself, but now, after cracking my shin over a box, and catching my spurs in some canvas, I thought the bolder course the wiser. I lit it therefore, and then I advanced with long strides, my sword in my hand. 'Come out, you rascal!' I cried. 'Nothing can save you. You will at last meet with your deserts.'

I held my candle high, and presently I caught a glimpse of the man's head staring at me over a barrel. He had a gold chevron on his black cap, and the expression of his face told me in an instant that he was an officer and a man of refinement.

'Monsieur,' he cried in excellent French, 'I surrender myself on a promise of quarter. But if I do not have your promise, I will then sell my life as dearly as I can.'

'Sir,' said I, 'a Frenchman knows how to treat an unfortunate enemy. Your life is safe.' With that he handed his sword over the top of the barrel, and I bowed with the candle on my heart. 'Whom have I the honour of capturing?' I asked.

'I am the Count Boutkine, of the Emperor's own Don Cossacks,' said he. 'I came out with my troop to reconnoitre Senlis, and as we found no sign of your people we determined to spend the night here.'

'And would it be an indiscretion,' I asked, 'if I were to inquire how you came into the back cellar?'

'Nothing more simple,' said he. 'It was our intention to start at early dawn. Feeling chilled after dressing, I thought that a cup of wine would do me no harm, so I came down to see what I could find. As I was rummaging about, the house was suddenly carried by assault so rapidly that by the time I had climbed the stairs it was all over. It only remained for me to save myself, so I came down here and hid myself in the back cellar, where you have found me.'

I thought of how old Bouvet had behaved under the same conditions, and the tears sprang to my eyes as I contemplated the glory of France. Then I had to consider what I should do next. It was clear that this Russian Count, being in the back cellar while we were in the front one, had not heard the sounds which would have told him that the house was once again in the hands of his own allies. If he should once understand this the tables would be turned, and I should be his prisoner instead of he being mine. What was I to do? I was at my wits' end, when suddenly there came to me an idea so brilliant that I could not but be amazed at my own invention.

'Count Boutkine,' said I, 'I find myself in a most difficult position.'

'And why?' he asked.

'Because I have promised you your life.' His jaw dropped a little.

'You would not withdraw your promise?' he cried.

'If the worst comes to the worst I can die in your defence,' said I; 'but the difficulties are great.'

'What is it, then?' he asked.

'I will be frank with you,' said I. 'You must know that our fellows, and especially the Poles, are so incensed against the Cossacks that the mere sight of the uniform drives them mad. They precipitate themselves instantly upon the wearer and tear him limb from limb. Even their officers cannot restrain them.'

The Russian grew pale at my words and the way in which I said them.

'But this is terrible,' said he.

'Horrible!' said I. 'If we were to go up together at this moment I cannot promise how far I could protect you.'

'I am in your hands,' he cried. 'what would you suggest that we should do? Would it not be best that I should remain here?'

'That worst of all.'

'And why?'

'Because our fellows will ransack the house presently, and then you would be cut to pieces. No, no, I must go up and break it to them. But even then, when once they see that accursed uniform, I do not know what may happen.'

'Should I then take the uniform off?'

'Excellent!' I cried. 'Hold, we have it! You will take your uniform off and put on mine. That will make you sacred to every French soldier.'

'It is not the French I fear so much as the Poles.'

'But my uniform will be a safeguard against either.'

'How can I thank you?' he cried. 'But you—what are you to wear?'

'I will wear yours.'

'And perhaps fall a victim to your generosity?'

'It is my duty to take the risk,' I answered, 'but I have no fears. I will ascend in your uniform. A hundred swords will be turned upon me. "Hold!" I will shout, "I am the Brigadier Gerard!" Then they will see my face. They will know me. And I will tell them about you. Under the shield of these clothes you will be sacred.'

His fingers trembled with eagerness as he tore off his tunic. His boots and breeches were much like my own, so there was no need to change them, but I gave him my hussar jacket, my dolman, my busby, my sword-belt, and my sabre-tasche, while I took in exchange his high sheepskin cap with the gold chevron, his fur-trimmed coat, and his crooked sword. Be it well understood that in changing the tunics I did not forget to change my thrice-precious letter also from my old one to my new.

'With your leave,' said I, 'I shall now bind you to a barrel.'

He made a great fuss over this, but I have learned in my soldiering never to throw away chances, and how could I tell that he might not, when my back was turned, see how the matter really stood and break in upon my plans? He was leaning against a barrel at the time, so I ran six times round it with a rope, and then tied it with a big knot behind. If he wished to come upstairs he would, at least, have to carry a thousand litres of good French wine for a knapsack. I then shut the door of the back cellar behind me, so that he might not hear what was going forward, and tossing the candle away I ascended the kitchen stair.

There were only about twenty steps, and yet, while I came up them, I seemed to have time to think of everything that I had ever hoped to do. It was the same feeling that I had at Eylau when I lay with my broken leg and saw the horse artillery galloping down upon me. Of course, I knew that if I were taken I should be shot instantly as being disguised within the enemy's lines. Still, it was a glorious death—in the direct service of the Emperor – and I reflected that there could not be less than five lines, and perhaps seven, in the *Moniteur* about me. Palaret had eight lines, and I am sure that he had not so fine a career.

When I made my way out into the hall, with all the nonchalance in my face and manner that I could assume, the very first thing that I saw was Bouvet's dead body, with his legs drawn up and a broken sword in his hand. I could see by the black smudge that he had been shot at close quarters. I should have wished to salute as I went by, for he was a gallant man, but I feared lest I should be seen, and so I passed on.

The front of the hall was full of Prussian infantry, who were knocking loopholes in the wall, as though they expected that there might be yet another attack. Their officer, a little rat of a man, was running about giving directions. They were all too busy to take much notice of me, but another officer, who was standing by the door with a long pipe in his mouth, strode across and clapped me on the shoulder, pointing to the dead bodies of our poor hussars, and saying something which was meant for a jest, for his long beard opened and showed every fang in his head. I laughed heartily also, and said the only Russian words that I knew. I learned them from little Sophia, at Wilna, and they meant: 'If the night is fine we shall meet under the oak tree, and if it rains we shall meet in the byre.' It was all the same to this German, however, and I have no doubt that he gave me credit for saying something very witty indeed, for he roared laughing, and slapped me on my shoulder again. I nodded to him and marched out of the hall-door as coolly as if I were the commandant of the garrison.

There were a hundred horses tethered about outside, most of them belonging to the Poles and hussars. Good little Violette was waiting with the others, and she whinnied when she saw me coming towards her. But I would not mount her. No. I was much too cunning for that. On the contrary, I chose the most shaggy little Cossack horse that I could see, and I sprang upon it with as much assurance as though it had belonged to my father before me. It had a great bag of plunder slung over its neck, and this I laid upon Violette's back, and led her along beside me. Never have you seen such a picture of the Cossack returning from the foray. It was superb.

Well, the town was full of Prussians by this time. They lined the side-walks and pointed me out to each other, saying, as I could judge from their gestures, 'There goes one of those devils of Cossacks. They are the boys for foraging and plunder.'

One or two officers spoke to me with an air of authority, but I shook my head and smiled, and said, 'If the night is fine we shall meet under the oak tree, but if it rains we shall meet in the byre,' at which they shrugged their shoulders and gave the matter up. In this way I worked along until I was beyond the northern outskirts of the town. I could see in the roadway two lancer vendettes with their black and white pennons, and I knew that when I was once past these I should be a free man once more. I made my pony trot, therefore, Violette rubbing her nose against my knee all the time, and looking up at me to ask how she had deserved that this hairy doormat of a creature should be preferred to her. I was not more than a hundred yards from the Uhlans, when suddenly, you can imagine my feelings when I saw a real Cossack coming galloping along the roadway towards me.

Ah, my friend, you who read this, if you have any heart,

you will feel for a man like me, who had gone through so many dangers and trials, only at this very last moment to be confronted with one which appeared to put an end to everything. I will confess that for a moment I lost heart, and was inclined to throw myself down in my despair, and to cry out that I had been betrayed. But, no; I was not beaten even now. I opened two buttons of my tunic so that I might get easily at the Emperor's message, for it was my fixed determination when all hope was gone to swallow the letter and then die sword in hand. Then I felt that my little crooked sword was loose in its sheath, and I trotted on to where the vedettes were waiting. They seemed inclined to stop me, but I pointed to the other Cossack, who was still a couple of hundred yards off, and they, understanding that I merely wished to meet him, let me pass with a salute.

I dug my spurs into my pony then, for if I were only far enough from the lancers I thought I might manage the Cossack without much difficulty. He was an officer, a large, bearded man, with a gold chevron in his cap, just the same as mine. As I advanced he unconsciously aided me by pulling up his horse, so that I had a fine start of the vedettes. On I came for him, and I could see wonder changing to suspicion in his brown eyes as he looked at me and at my pony, and at my equipment. I do not know what it was that was wrong, but he saw something which was as it should not be. He shouted out a question, and then when I gave no answer he pulled out his sword. I was glad in my heart to see him do so, for I had always rather fight than cut down an unsuspecting enemy. Now I made at him full tilt, and, parrying his cut, I got my point in just under the fourth button of his tunic. Down he went, and the weight of him nearly took me off my horse before I could disengage. I never glanced at him to see if he were living or dead, for I sprang off my pony and onto Violette, with a shake of my bridle and a kiss of my hand to the two Uhlans behind me. They galloped after me, shouting, but Violette had had her rest and was just as fresh as when she started. I took the first side road to the west and then the first to the south, which would take me away from the enemy's country. On we went and on, every stride taking me further from my foes and nearer to my friends.

At last, when I reached the end of a long stretch of road, and looking back from it could see no sign of any pursuers, I understood that my troubles were over.

And it gave me a glow of happiness, as I rode, to think that I had done to the letter what the Emperor had ordered. What would he say when he saw me? What could he say which would do justice to the incredible way in which I had risen above every danger? He had ordered me to go through Sermoise, Soissons, and Senlis, little dreaming that they were all three occupied by the enemy. And yet I had done it. I had borne his letter in safety through each of these towns. Hussars, dragoons, lancers, Cossacks, and infantry—I had run the gauntlet of all of them, and had come out unharmed.

When I had got as far as Dammartin I caught a first glimpse of our own outposts. There was a troop of dragoons in a field, and of course I could see from the horsehair crests that they were French. I galloped towards them in order to ask them if all was safe between there and Paris, and as I rode I felt such a pride at having won my way back to my friends again, that I could not refrain from waving my sword in the air.

At this a young officer galloped out from among the dragoons, also brandishing his sword, and it warmed my heart to think that he should come riding with such ardour and enthusiasm to greet me. I made Violette caracole, and as we came together I brandished my sword more gallantly than ever, but you can imagine my feelings when he suddenly made a cut at me which would certainly have taken my head off if I had not fallen forward with my nose in Violette's mane. My faith, it whistled just over my cap like an east wind. Of course, it came from this accursed Cossack uniform which, in my excitement, I had forgotten all about, and this young dragoon had imagined that I was some Russian champion who was challenging the French cavalry. My word, he was a frightened man when he understood how near he had been to killing the celebrated Brigadier Gerard.

Well, the road was clear, and about three o'clock in the afternoon I was at St Denis, though it took me a long two hours to get from there to Paris, for the road was blocked with commissariat waggons and guns of the artillery reserve, which was going north to Marmont and Mortier. You cannot conceive the excitement which my appearance in such costume made in Paris, and when I came to the Rue de Rivoli I should think I had a quarter of a mile of folk riding or running behind me. Word had got about from the dragoons (two of whom had come with me), and everybody knew about my adventures and how I had come by my uniform. It was a triumph—men shouting and women waving their handkerchiefs and blowing kisses from the windows.

Although I am a man singularly free from conceit, still I must confess that, on this one occasion, I could not restrain myself from showing that this reception gratified me. The Russian's coat had hung very loose upon me, but now I threw out my chest until it was as tight as a sausage-skin. And my little sweetheart of a mare tossed her mane and pawed with her front hoofs, frisking her tail as though she said, 'We've done it together this time. It is to us that commissions should be intrusted.' When I kissed her between the nostrils as I dismounted at the gate of the Tuileries there was as much shouting as if a bulletin had been read from the Grand Army.

I was hardly in costume to visit a king; but, after all, if one has a soldierly figure one can do without that. I was shown up straight away to Joseph, whom I had often seen in Spain. He seemed as stout, as quiet, and as amiable as ever. Talleyrand was in the room with him, or I suppose I should call him the Duke of Benevento, but I confess that I like old names best. He read my letter when Joseph Buonaparte handed it to him, and then he looked at me with the strangest expression in those funny little, twinkling eyes of his.

'Were you the only messenger?' he asked.

'There was one other, sire,' said I. 'Major Charpentier, of the Horse Grenadiers.'

'He has not yet arrived,' said the King of Spain.

'If you had seen the legs of his horse, sire, you would not wonder at it,' I remarked.

'There may be other reasons,' said Talleyrand, and he gave that singular smile of his.

Well, they paid me a compliment or two, though they might have said a good deal more and yet have said too little. I bowed myself out, and very glad I was to get away, for I hate a court as much as I love a camp. Away I went to my old friend Chaubert, in the Rue Miromesnil, and there I got his hussar uniform, which fitted me very well. He and Lisette and I supped together in his rooms, and all my dangers were forgotten. In the morning I found Violette ready for another twenty-league stretch. It was my intention to return instantly to the Emperor's headquarters, for I was, as you may well imagine, impatient to hear his words of praise, and to receive my reward.

I need not say that I rode back by a safe route, for I had seen quite enough of Uhlans and Cossacks. I passed through Meaux and Château Thierry, and so in the evening I arrived at Rheims, where Napoleon was still lying. The bodies of our fellows and of St Prest's Russians had all been buried, and I could see changes in the camp also. The soldiers looked better cared for; some of the cavalry had received remounts, and everything was in excellent order. It is wonderful what a good general can effect in a couple of days.

When I came to the headquarters I was shown straight into the Emperor's room. He was drinking coffee at a writing-table, with a big plan drawn out on paper in front of him. Berthier and Macdonald were leaning, one over each shoulder, and he was talking so quickly that I don't believe that either of them could catch a half of what he was saying. But when his eyes fell upon me he dropped the pen on to the chart, and he sprang up with a look in his pale face which struck me cold.

'What the deuce are you doing here?' he shouted. When he was angry he had a voice like a peacock.

'I have the honour to report to you, sire,' said I, 'that I have delivered your despatch safely to the King of Spain.'

'What!' he yelled, and his two eyes transfixed me like bayonets. Oh, those dreadful eyes, shifting from grey to blue, like steel in the sunshine. I can see them now when I have a bad dream.

'What has become of Charpentier?' he asked.

'He is captured,' said Macdonald.

'By whom?'

'The Russians.'

'The Cossacks?'

'No, a single Cossack.'

'He gave himself up?'

'Without resistance.'

'He is an intelligent officer. You will see that the medal of honour is awarded to him.'

When I heard those words I had to rub my eyes to make sure that I was awake.

'As to you,' cried the Emperor, taking a step forward as if he would have struck me, 'you brain of a hare, what do you think that you were sent upon this mission for? Do you conceive that I would send a really important message by such a hand as yours, and through every village which the enemy holds? How you came through them passes my comprehension; but if your fellow messenger had had but as little sense as you, my whole plan of campaign would have been ruined. Can you not see, coglione, that this message contained false news, and that it was intended to deceive the enemy whilst I put a very different scheme into execution?'

When I heard those cruel words and saw the angry, white face which glared at me, I had to hold the back of a chair, for my mind was failing me and my knees would hardly bear me up. But then I took courage as I reflected that I was an honourable gentleman, and that my whole life had been spent in toiling for this man and for my beloved country.

'Sire,' said I, and the tears would trickle down my cheeks whilst I spoke, 'when you are dealing with a man like me you would find it wiser to deal openly. Had I known that you had wished the despatch to fall into the hands of the enemy, I would have seen that it came there. As I believed that I was to guard it, I was prepared to sacrifice my life for it. I do not believe, sire, that any man in the world ever met with more toils and perils than I have done in trying to carry out what I thought was your will.'

I dashed the tears from my eyes as I spoke, and with such

fire and spirit as I could command I gave him an account of it all, of my dash through Soissons, my brush with the dragoons, my adventure in Senlis, my rencontre with Count Boutkine in the cellar, my disguise, my meeting with the Cossack officer, my flight, and how at the last moment I was nearly cut down by a French dragoon. The Emperor, Berthier, and Macdonald listened with astonishment on their faces. When I had finished Napoleon stepped forward and he pinched me by the ear.

'There, there!' said he. 'Forget anything which I may have said. I would have done better to trust you. You may go.'

I turned to the door, and my hand was upon the handle, when the Emperor called upon me to stop.

'You will see,' said he, turning to the Duke of Tarentum, 'that Brigadier Gerard has the special medal of honour, for I believe that if he has the thickest head he has also the stoutest heart in my army.'

TWO

How the Brigadier Held the King

1 and 2 July 1810, as stated. Marshal Ney began his siege of Ciudad Rodrigo on 2 July and captured it from the British on 10 July. The then Viscount Wellington was still unable to risk his raw recruits against the French veterans, in addition to being somewhat embarrassed by the indisciplined forays of General Robert ('Black Bob') Crauford.

I believe that the last story which I told you, my friends, was about how I received at the bidding of the Emperor the cross for valour which I had, if I may be allowed to say so, so long deserved.* Here upon the lapel of my coat you may see the ribbon, but the medal itself I keep in a leathern pouch at home, and I never venture to take it out unless one of the modern peace generals, or some foreigner of distinction who finds himself in our little town, takes advantage of the opportunity to pay his respects to the well-known Brigadier Gerard. Then I place it upon my breast, and I give my moustache the old Marengo twist which brings a grey point into either eye. Yet with it all I fear that neither they, nor you either, my friends, will ever realize the man that I was. You know me only as a civilian—with an air and a manner, it is true—but still merely as a civilian. Had you seen me as I stood in the doorway of the inn at Alamo, on the 1st of July, in the year 1810, you would then have known what the hussar may attain to.

For a month I had lingered in that accursed village, and all on account of a lance thrust in my ankle, which made it impossible for me to put my foot to the ground. There were three of us at first: old Bouvet, of the Hussars of Bercheny, Jacques Regnier, of the Cuirassiers, and a funny

* December, 1894.

little voltigeur captain whose name I forget; but they all got well and hurried on to the front, while I sat gnawing my fingers and tearing my hair, and even, I must confess, weeping from time to time as I thought of my Hussars of Conflans, and the deplorable condition in which they must find themselves when deprived of their colonel. I was not a chief of brigade yet, you understand, although I already carried myself like one, but I was the youngest colonel in the whole service, and my regiment was wife and children to me. It went to my heart that they should be so bereaved. It is true that Villaret, the senior major, was an excellent soldier; but still, even among the best there are degrees of merit.

Ah, that happy July day of which I speak, when first I limped to the door and stood in the golden Spanish sunshine! It was but the evening before that I had heard from the regiment. They were at Pastores, on the other side of the mountains, face to face with the English—not forty miles from me by road. But how was I to get to them? The same thrust which had pierced my ankle had slain my charger. I took advice both from Gomez, the landlord, and from an old priest who had slept that night in the inn, but neither of them could do more than assure me that there was not so much as a colt left upon the whole country side. The landlord would not hear of my crossing the mountains without an escort, for he assured me that El Cuchillo, the Spanish guerilla chief, was out that way with his band, and that it meant a death by torture to fall into his hands. The old priest observed, however, that he did not think a French hussar would be deterred by that, and if I had had any doubts, they would of course have been decided by his remark.

But a horse! How was I to get one? I was standing in the doorway, plotting and planning, when I heard the clink of shoes, and, looking up, I saw a great bearded man, with a blue cloak frogged across in military fashion, coming towards me. He was riding a big black horse with one white stocking on his near fore-leg.

'Halloa, comrade!' said I, as he came up to me.

'Halloa!' said he.

'I am Colonel Gerard, of the Hussars,' said I. 'I have lain

here wounded for a month, and I am now ready to rejoin my regiment at Pastores.'

'I am Monsieur Vidal, of the commissariat,' he answered, 'and I am myself upon my way to Pastores. I should be glad to have your company, colonel, for I hear that the mountains are far from safe.'

'Alas,' said I, 'I have no horse. But if you will sell me yours, I will promise that an escort of hussars shall be sent back for you.'

He would not hear of it, and it was in vain that the landlord told him dreadful stories of the doings of El Cuchillo, and that I pointed out the duty which he owed to the army and to the country. He would not even argue, but called loudly for a cup of wine. I craftily asked him to dismount and to drink with me, but he must have seen something in my face for he shook his head; and then, as I approached him with some thought of seizing him by the leg, he jerked his heels into his horse's flanks, and was off in a cloud of dust.

My faith! it was enough to make a man mad to see this fellow riding away so gaily to join his beef-barrels, and his brandy-casks, and then to think of my five hundred beautiful hussars without their leader. I was gazing after him with bitter thoughts in my mind, when who should touch me on the elbow but the little priest whom I have mentioned.

'It is I who can help you,' he said. 'I am myself travelling south.'

I put my arms about him and, as my ankle gave way at the same moment, we nearly rolled upon the ground together.

'Get me to Pastores,' I cried, 'and you shall have a rosary of golden beads.' I had taken one from the Convent of Spiritu Santo. It shows how necessary it is to take what you can when you are upon a campaign, and how the most unlikely things may become useful.

'I will take you,' he said, in very excellent French, 'not because I hope for any reward, but because it is my way always to do what I can to serve my fellow-man, and that is why I am so beloved wherever I go.'

With that he led me down the village to an old cow-house,

in which we found a tumble-down sort of diligence, such as they used to run early in this century, between some of our remote villages. There were three old mules, too, none of which were strong enough to carry a man, but together they might draw the coach. The sight of their gaunt ribs and spavined legs gave me more delight than the whole two hundred and twenty hunters of the Emperor which I have seen in their stalls at Fontainebleau. In ten minutes the owner was harnessing them into the coach, with no very good will, however, for he was in mortal dread of this terrible Cuchillo. It was only by promising him riches in this world, while the priest threatened him with perdition in the next, that we at last got him safely upon the box with the reins between his fingers. Then he was in such a hurry to get off, out of fear lest we should find ourselves in the dark in the passes, that he hardly gave me time to renew my vows to the innkeeper's daughter. I cannot at this moment recall her name, but we wept together as we parted, and I can remember that she was a very beautiful woman. You will understand, my friends, that when a man like me, who has fought the men and kissed the women in fourteen separate kingdoms, gives a word of praise to the one or the other, it has a little meaning of its own.

The little priest had seemed a trifle grave when we kissed good-bye, but he soon proved himself the best of companions in the diligence. All the way he amused me with tales of his little parish up in the mountains, and I in my turn told him stories about my camp; but, my faith, I had to pick my steps, for when I said a word too much he would fidget in his seat and his face would show the pain that I had given him. And of course it is not the act of a gentleman to talk in anything but a proper manner to a religious man, though, with all the care in the world, one's words may get out of hand sometimes.

He had come from the North of Spain, as he told me, and was going to see his mother in a village of Estremadura, and as he spoke about her little peasant home, and her joy in seeing him, it brought my own mother so vividly to my thought that the tears started to my eyes. In his simplicity he showed me the little gifts which he was taking to her, and so kindly was his manner that I could readily believe him when he said that he was loved wherever he went. He examined my own uniform with as much curiosity as a child, admiring the plume of my busby, and passing his fingers through the sable with which my dolman was trimmed. He drew my sword, too, and then when I told him how many men I had cut down with it, and set my finger on the notch made by the shoulder-bone of the Russian Emperor's aide-de-camp, he shuddered and placed the weapon under the leathern cushion, declaring that it made him sick to look at it.

Well, we had been rolling and creaking on our way whilst this talk had been going forward, and as we reached the base of the mountains we could hear the rumbling of cannon far away upon the right. This came from Massena, who was, as I knew, besieging Ciudad Rodrigo. There was nothing I should have wished better than to have gone straight to him, for if, as some said, he had Jewish blood in his veins, he was the best Jew that I have heard of since Joshua's time. If you are in sight of his beaky nose and bold, black eyes, you are not likely to miss much of what is going on. Still, a siege is always a poor sort of a pick-and-shovel business, and there were better prospects with my hussars in front of the English. Every mile that passed, my heart grew lighter and lighter, until I found myself shouting and singing like a young ensign fresh from Saint Cyr, just to think of seeing all my fine horses and my gallant fellows once more.

As we penetrated the mountains the road grew rougher and the pass more savage. At first we had met a few muleteers, but now the whole country seemed deserted, which is not to be wondered at when you think that the French, the English, and the guerillas had each in turn had command over it. So bleak and wild was it, one great brown wrinkled cliff succeeding another, and the pass growing narrower and narrower, that I ceased to look out, but sat in silence, thinking of this and that, of women whom I had loved and of horses which I had handled. I was suddenly brought back from my dreams, however, by observing the difficulties of my companion, who was trying with a sort of brad-awl, which he had drawn out, to bore a hole through the leathern strap which held up his water-flask. As he worked with twitching fingers the strap escaped his grasp, and the wooden bottle fell at my feet. I stooped to pick it up, and as I did so the priest silently leaped upon my shoulders and drove his brad-awl into my eye!

My friends, I am, as you know, a man steeled to face every danger. When one has served from the affair of Zurich to that last fatal day of Waterloo, and has had the special medal, which I keep at home in a leathern pouch, one can afford to confess when one is frightened. It may console some of you, when your own nerves play you tricks, to remember that you have heard even me, Brigadier Gerard, say that I have been scared. And besides my terror at this horrible attack, and the maddening pain of my wound, there was a sudden feeling of loathing such as you might feel were some filthy tarantula to strike its fangs into you.

I clutched the creature in both hands, and, hurling him on to the floor of the coach, I stamped on him with my heavy boots. He had drawn a pistol from the front of his soutane, but I kicked it out of his hand, and again I fell with my knees upon his chest. Then, for the first time, he screamed horribly, while I, half blinded, felt about for the sword which he had so cunningly concealed. My hand had just lighted upon it, and I was dashing the blood from my face to see where he lay that I might transfix him, when the whole coach turned partly over upon its side, and my weapon was jerked out of my grasp by the shock. Before I could recover myself the door was burst open, and I was dragged by the heels on to the road. But even as I was torn out on to the flint stones and realized that thirty ruffians were standing around me, I was filled with joy, for my pelisse had been pulled over my head in the struggle and was covering one of my eyes, and it was with my wounded eye that I was seeing this gang of brigands. You see for yourself by this pucker and scar how the thin blade passed between socket and ball, but it was only at that moment, when I was dragged from the coach, that I understood that my sight was not gone for ever. The creature's intention doubtless, was to drive it through into my brain, and indeed he loosened some portion of the inner bone of my head, so that I afterwards had more trouble from

that wound than from any one of the seventeen which I have
received.

They dragged me out, these sons of dogs, with curses
and execrations, beating me with their fists and kicking me
as I lay upon the ground. I had frequently observed that
the mountaineers wore cloth swathed round their feet, but
never did I imagine that I should have so much cause to be
thankful for it. Presently, seeing the blood upon my head,
and that I lay quiet, they thought that I was unconscious,
whereas I was storing every ugly face among them into
my memory, so that I might see them all safely hanged
if ever my chance came round. Brawny rascals they were,
with yellow handkerchiefs round their heads, and great red
sashes stuffed with weapons. They had rolled two rocks
across the path, where it took a sharp turn, and it was
these which had torn off one of the wheels of the coach
and upset us. As to this reptile, who had acted the priest
so cleverly and had told me so much of his parish and his
mother, he, of course, had known where the ambuscade was
laid, and had attempted to put me beyond all resistance at
the moment when we reached it.

I cannot tell you how frantic their rage was when they
drew him out of the coach and saw the state to which I had
reduced him. If he had not got all his deserts, he had, at
least, something as a souvenir of his meeting with Etienne
Gerard, for his legs dangled aimlessly about, and though the
upper part of his body was convulsed with rage and pain, he
sat straight down upon his feet when they tried to set him
upright. But all the time his two little black eyes, which had
seemed so kindly and so innocent in the coach, were glaring
at me like a wounded cat, and he spat, and spat, and spat
in my direction. My faith! when the wretches jerked me on
to my feet again, and when I was dragged off up one of the
mountain paths, I understood that a time was coming when
I was to need all my courage and resource. My enemy was
carried upon the shoulders of two men behind me, and I
could hear his hissing and his reviling, first in one ear and
then in the other, as I was hurried up the winding track.

I suppose that it must have been for an hour that we
ascended, and what with my wounded ankle and the pain

from my eye, and the fear lest this wound should have spoiled my appearance, I have made no journey to which I look back with less pleasure. I have never been a good climber at any time, but it is astonishing what you can do, even with a stiff ankle, when you have a copper-coloured brigand at each elbow and a nine-inch blade within touch of your whiskers.

We came at last to a place where the path wound over a ridge, and descended upon the other side through thick pine trees into a valley which opened to the south. In time of peace I have little doubt that the villains were all smugglers, and that these were the secret paths by which they crossed the Portuguese frontier. There were many mule tracks, and once I was surprised to see the marks of a large horse where a stream had softened the track. These were explained when, on reaching a place where there was a clearing in the fir wood, I saw the animal itself haltered to a fallen tree. My eyes had hardly rested upon it, when I recognised the great black limbs and the white near fore-leg. It was the very horse which I had begged for in the morning.

What, then, had become of Commissariat Vidal? Was it possible that there was another Frenchman in as perilous a plight as myself? The thought had hardly entered my head when our party stopped and one of them uttered a peculiar cry. It was answered from among the brambles which lined the base of a cliff at one side of a clearing, and an instant later ten or a dozen more brigands came out from amongst them, and the two parties greeted each other. The new-comers surrounded my friend of the brad-awl with cries of grief and sympathy, and then turning upon me they brandished their knives and howled at me like the gang of assassins that they were. So frantic were their gestures that I was convinced that my end had come, and was just bracing myself to meet it in a manner which should be worthy of my past reputation, when one of them gave an order and I was dragged roughly across the little glade to the brambles from which this new band had emerged.

A narrow pathway led through them to a deep grotto in the side of the cliff. The sun was already setting outside, and in the cave itself it would have been quite dark but for a pair of torches which blazed from a socket on either side. Between them there was sitting at a rude table a very singular-looking person, whom I saw instantly, from the respect with which the others addressed him, could be none other than the brigand chief who had received, on account of his dreadful character, the sinister name of El Cuchillo.

The man whom I had injured had been carried in and placed upon the top of a barrel, his helpless legs dangling about in front of him, and his cat's eyes still darting glances of hatred at me. I understood from the snatches of talk which I could follow between the chief and him, that he was the lieutenant of the band, and that part of his duties was to lie in wait with his smooth tongue and his peaceful garb for travellers like myself. When I thought of how many gallant officers may have been lured to their death by this monster of hypocrisy, it gave me a glow of pleasure to think that I had brought his villainies to an end—though I feared that it would be at the price of a life which neither the Emperor nor the army could well spare.

As the injured man, still supported upon the barrel by two comrades, was explaining in Spanish all that had befallen him, I was held by several of the villains in front of the table at which the chief was seated, and had an excellent opportunity of observing him. I have seldom seen any man who was less like my idea of a brigand, and especially of a brigand with such a reputation that in a land of cruelty he had earned so dark a nickname. His face was bluff and broad and bland, with ruddy cheeks and comfortable little tufts of side-whiskers, which gave him the appearance of a well-to-do grocer of the Rue St Antoine. He had not any of those flaring sashes or gleaming weapons which distinguished his followers, but on the contrary he wore a good broad-cloth coat like a respectable father of a family, and save for his brown leggings there was nothing to indicate a life among the mountains. His surroundings, too, corresponded with himself, and beside his snuff-box upon the table there stood a great brown book, which looked like a commercial ledger. Many other books were ranged along a plank between two powder casks, and there was a great litter of papers, some of which had verses scribbled upon them. All this I took in while he, leaning indolently back in his chair, was listening to the report of his lieutenant. Having heard everything, he ordered the cripple to be carried out again, and I was left with my three guards, waiting to hear my fate. He took up his pen, and, tapping his forehead with the handle of it, he pursed up his lips and looked out of the corner of his eyes at the roof of the grotto.

'I suppose,' said he, at last, speaking very excellent French, 'that you are not able to suggest a rhyme for the word Covilha.'

I answered him that my acquaintance with the Spanish language was so limited that I was unable to oblige him.

'It is a rich language,' said he, 'but less prolific in rhymes than either the German or the English. That is why our best work has been done in blank verse, a form of composition which, though hardly known in your literature, is capable of reaching great heights. But I fear that such subjects are somewhat outside the range of a hussar.'

I was about to answer that if they were good enough for a guerilla, they could not be too much for the light cavalry, but he was already stooping over his half-finished verse. Presently he threw down the pen with an exclamation of satisfaction, and declaimed a few lines which drew a cry of approval from the three ruffians who held me. His broad face blushed like a young girl who receives her first compliment.

'The critics are in my favour, it appears,' said he; 'we amuse ourselves in our long evenings by singing our own ballads, you understand. I have some little facility in that direction, and I do not at all despair of seeing some of my poor efforts in print before long, and with "Madrid" upon the title page, too. But we must get back to business. May I ask what your name is?'

'Etienne Gerard.'

'Rank?'

'Colonel.'

'Corps?'

'The Third Hussars of Conflans.'

'You are young for a colonel.'

'My career has been an eventful one.'

'Tut, that makes it the sadder,' said he, with his bland smile.

I made no answer to that, but I tried to show him by my bearing that I was ready for the worst which could befall me.

'By the way, I rather fancy that we have had some of your corps here.' said he, turning over the pages of his big brown register. 'We endeavour to keep a record of our operations. Here is a heading under June 24th. Have you not a young officer named Soubiron, a tall, slight youth with light hair?'

'Certainly.'

'I see that we buried him upon that date.'

'Poor lad!' I cried. 'And how did he die?'

'We buried him.'

'But before you buried him?'

'You misunderstand me, Colonel. He was not dead before we buried him.'

'You buried him alive!'

For a moment I was too stunned to act. Then I hurled myself upon the man, as he sat with that placid smile of his upon his lips, and I would have torn his throat out had the three wretches not dragged me away from him. Again and again I made for him, panting and cursing, shaking off this man and that, straining and wrenching, but never quite free. At last, with my jacket torn nearly off my back and blood dripping from my wrists, I was hauled backwards in the bight of a rope and cords passed round my ankles and my arms.

'You sleek hound,' I cried. 'If ever I have you at my sword's point, I will teach you to maltreat one of my lads. You will find, you blood-thirsty beast, that my Emperor has long arms, and though you lie here like a rat in its hole, the time will come when he will tear you out of it, and you and your vermin will perish together.'

My faith, I have a rough side to my tongue, and there was not a hard word that I had learned in fourteen campaigns which I did not let fly at him, but he sat with the handle of his pen tapping against his forehead and his eyes squinting up at the roof as if he had conceived the idea of some new stanza. It was this occupation of his which showed me how I might get my point into him.

'You spawn!' said I; 'you think that you are safe here, but your life may be as short as that of your absurd verses, and God knows it could not be shorter than that.'

Ah, you should have seen him bound from his chair when I said the words. This vile monster, who dispensed death and torture as a grocer serves out his figs, had one raw nerve then which I could prod at pleasure. His face grew livid, and those little bourgeois side-whiskers quivered and thrilled with passion.

'Very good, Colonel. You have said enough,' he cried, in a choking voice. 'You say that you have had a very distinguished career. I promise you also a very distinguished ending. Colonel Etienne Gerard of the Third Hussars shall have a death of his own.'

'And I only beg,' said I, 'that you will not commemorate it in verse.' I had one or two little ironies to utter, but he cut me short by a furious gesture which caused my three guards to drag me from the cave.

Our interview, which I have told you as nearly as I can remember it, must have lasted some time, for it was quite dark when we came out, and the moon was shining very clearly in the heavens. The brigands had lighted a great fire of the dried branches of the fir trees; not, of course, for warmth, since the night was already very sultry, but to cook their evening meal. A huge copper pot hung over the blaze, and the rascals were lying all round in the yellow glare, so that the scene looked like one of those pictures which Junot stole out of Madrid. There are some soldiers who profess to care nothing for art and the like, but I have always been drawn towards it myself, in which respect I show my good taste and my breeding. I remember, for example, that when Lefebvre was selling the plunder after the fall of Danzig, I bought a very fine picture, called 'Nymphs Surprised in a Wood,' and I carried it with me through two campaigns, until my charger had the misfortune to put his hoof through it.

I only tell you this, however, to show you that I was never a mere rough soldier like Rapp or Ney. As I lay in that brigand's camp, I had little time or inclination to think about such matters. They had thrown me down under a tree, the three villains squatting round and smoking their cigarettes within hands' touch of me. What to do I could not imagine. In my whole career I do not suppose that I have ten times been in as hopeless a situation. 'But courage,' thought I. 'Courage, my brave boy! You were not made a Colonel of Hussars at twenty-eight because you could dance a cotillon. You are a picked man, Etienne; a man who has come through more than two hundred affairs, and this little one is surely not going to be the last.' I began eagerly to glance about for some chance of escape, and as I did so I saw something which filled me with great astonishment.

I have already told you that a large fire was burning in the centre of the glade. What with its glare, and what with the moonlight, everything was as clear as possible. On the other side of the glade there was a single tall fir tree which attracted my attention because its trunk and lower branches were discoloured, as if a large fire had recently been lit underneath it. A clump of bushes grew in front of it which concealed the base. Well, as I looked towards it, I was surprised to see projecting above the bush, and fastened apparently to the tree, a pair of fine riding boots with the toes upwards. At first I thought that they were tied there, but as I looked harder I saw that they were secured by a great nail which was hammered through the foot of each. And then, suddenly, with a thrill of horror, I understood that these were not empty boots; and moving my head a little to the right, I was able to see who it was that had been fastened there, and why a fire had been lit beneath the tree. It is not pleasant to speak or to think of horrors, my friends, and I do not wish to give any of you bad dreams to-night—but I cannot take you among the Spanish guerillas without showing you what kind of men they were, and the sort of warfare that they waged. I will only say that I understood why Monsieur Vidal's horse was waiting masterless in the grove, and that I hoped he had met this terrible fate with sprightliness and courage, as a good Frenchman ought.

It was not a very cheering sight for me, as you can imagine. When I had been with their chief in the grotto

I had been so carried away by my rage at the cruel death of young Soubiron, who was one of the brightest lads who ever threw his thigh over a charger, that I had never given a thought to my own position. Perhaps it would have been more politic had I spoken the ruffian fair, but it was too late now. The cork was drawn, and I must drain the wine. Besides, if the harmless commissariat man were put to such a death, what hope was there for me, who had snapped the spine of their lieutenant. No, I was doomed in any case, so it was as well perhaps that I should have put the best face on the matter. This beast could bear witness that Etienne Gerard had died as he had lived, and that one prisoner at least had not quailed before him. I lay there thinking of the various girls who would mourn for me, and of my dear old mother, and of the deplorable loss which I should be both to my regiment and to the Emperor, and I am not ashamed to confess to you that I shed tears as I thought of the general consternation which my premature end would give rise to.

But all the time I was taking the very keenest notice of everything which might possibly help me. I am not a man who would lie like a sick horse waiting for the farrier sergeant and the pole-axe. First I would give a little tug at my ankle cords, and then another at those which were round my wrists, and all the time that I was trying to loosen them I was peering round to see if I could find something which was in my favour. There was one thing which was very evident. A hussar is but half formed without a horse, and there was my other half quietly grazing within thirty yards of me. Then I observed yet another thing. The path by which we had come over the mountains was so steep that a horse could only be led across it slowly and with difficulty, but in the other direction the ground appeared to be more open, and to lead straight down into a gently-sloping valley. Had I but my feet in yonder stirrups and my sabre in my hand, a single bold dash might take me out of the power of these vermin of the rocks.

I was still thinking it over and straining with my wrists and my ankles, when their chief came out from his grotto, and after some talk with his lieutenant, who lay groaning near the fire, they both nodded their heads and looked across at me.

He then said some few words to the band, who clapped their hands and laughed uproariously. Things looked ominous, and I was delighted to feel that my hands were so far free that I could easily slip them through the cords if I wished. But with my ankles, I feared that I could do nothing, for when I strained it brought such pain into my lance wound, that I had to gnaw my moustache to keep from crying out. I could only lie still, half free and half bound, and see what turn things were likely to take.

For a little I could not make out what they were after. One of the rascals climbed up a well-grown fir-tree upon one side of the glade, and tied a rope round the top of the trunk. He then fastened another rope in the same fashion to a similar tree upon the other side. The two loose ends were now dangling down, and I waited with some curiosity, and just a little trepidation also, to see what they would do next. The whole band pulled upon one of the ropes until they had bent the strong young tree down into a semi-circle, and they then fastened it to a stump, so as to hold it so. When they had bent the other tree down in a similar fashion, the two summits were within a few feet of each other, though, as you understand, they would each spring back into their original position the instant that they were released. I already saw the diabolical plan which these miscreants had formed.

'I presume that you are a strong man, Colonel,' said the chief, coming towards me with his hateful smile.

'If you will have the kindness to loosen these cords,' I answered, 'I will show you how strong I am.'

'We were all interested to see whether you were as strong as these two young saplings,' said he. 'It is our intention, you see, to tie one end of each rope round your ankles and then to let the trees go. If you are stronger than the trees, then, of course, no harm would be done; if, on the other hand, the trees are stronger than you, why, in that case, Colonel, we may have a souvenir of you upon each side of our little glade.'

He laughed as he spoke, and at the sight of it the whole forty of them laughed also. Even now if I am in my darker humour, or if I have a touch of my old Lithuanian ague, I see in my sleep that ring of dark savage faces, with their cruel eyes, and the firelight flashing upon their strong white teeth.

It is astonishing—and I have heard many make the same remark—how acute one's senses become at such a crisis as this. I am convinced that at no moment is one living so vividly, so acutely, as at the instant when a violent and foreseen death overtakes one. I could smell the resinous fagots, I could see every twig upon the ground, I could hear every rustle of the branches, as I have never smelled or seen or heard save at such times of danger. And so it was that long before anyone else, before even the time when the chief had addressed me, I had heard a low, monotonous sound, far away indeed, and yet coming nearer at every instant. At first it was but a murmur, a rumble, but by the time he had finished speaking, while the assassins were untying my ankles in order to lead me to the scene of my murder, I heard, as plainly as ever I heard anything in my life, the clinking of horseshoes and the jingling of bridle chains, with the clank of sabres against stirrup-irons. Is it likely that I, who had lived with the light cavalry since the first hair shaded my lip, would mistake the sound of troopers on the march?

'Help, comrades, help!' I shrieked, and though they struck me across the mouth and tried to drag me up to the trees I kept on yelling. 'Help me, my brave boys! Help me, my children! They are murdering your colonel!'

For the moment my wounds and my troubles had brought on a delirium, and I looked for nothing less than my five hundred hussars, kettle-drums and all, to appear at the opening of the glade.

But that which really appeared was very different to anything which I had conceived. Into the clear space there came galloping a fine young man upon a most beautiful roan horse. He was fresh-faced and pleasant looking, with the most debonair bearing in the world and the most gallant way of carrying himself—a way which reminded me somewhat of my own. He wore a singular coat which had once been red all over, but which was now stained to the colour of a withered oak leaf wherever the weather could reach it. His shoulder-straps, however, were of golden lace, and he had a bright metal helmet upon his head, with a coquettish white plume upon one side of its crest. He trotted his horse up the glade, while behind him rode four cavaliers in the same dress—all clean-shaven, with round, comely faces, looking to me more like monks than dragoons. At a short, gruff order they halted with a rattle of arms, while their leader cantered forward, the fire beating upon his eager face and the beautiful head of his charger. I knew, of course, by the strange coats that they were English. It was the first sight that I had ever had of them, but from their stout bearing and their masterful way I could see at a glance that what I had always been told was true, and that they were excellent people to fight against.

'Well, well, well!' cried the young officer, in sufficiently bad French, 'what game are you up to here? Who was that who was yelling for help, and what are you trying to do to him?'

It was at that moment that I learned to bless those months which Obriant, the descendant of the Irish kings, had spent in teaching me the tongue of the English. My ankles had just been freed, so that I had only to slip my hands out of the cords, and with a single rush I had flown across, picked up my sabre where it lay by the fire, and hurled myself on to the saddle of poor Vidal's horse. Yes, for all my wounded ankle, I never put foot to stirrup, but was in the seat in a single bound. I tore the halter from the tree, and before these villains could so much as snap a pistol at me I was beside the English officer.

'I surrender to you, sir,' I cried; though I daresay my English was not very much better than his French. 'If you will look at that tree to the left you will see what these villains do to the honourable gentlemen who fall into their hands.'

The fire had flared up at that moment, and there was poor Vidal exposed before them, as horrible an object as one could see in a nightmare. 'Godam!' cried the officer, and 'Godam!' cried each of the four troopers, which is the same as with us when we cry 'Mon Dieu!' Out rasped the five swords, and the four men closed up. One, who wore a sergeant's chevrons, laughed and clapped me on the shoulder.

'Fight for your skin, froggy,' said he.

Ah, it was so fine to have a horse between my thighs and weapon in my grip. I waved it above my head and shouted in my exultation. The chief had come forward with that odious smiling face of his.

'Your excellency will observe that this Frenchman is our prisoner,' said he.

'You are a rascally robber,' said the Englishman, shaking his sword at him. 'It is a disgrace to us to have such allies. By my faith, if Lord Wellington were of my mind we would swing you up on the nearest tree.'

'But my prisoner?' said the brigand, in his suave voice.

'He shall come with us to the British camp.'

'Just a word in your ear before you take him.'

He approached the young officer, and then, turning as quick as a flash, he fired his pistol in my face. The bullet scored its way through my hair and burst a hole on each side of my busby. Seeing that he had missed me, he raised the pistol and was about to hurl it at me when the English sergeant, with a single back-handed cut, nearly severed his head from his body. His blood had not reached the ground, nor the last curse died on his lips, before the whole horde was upon us, but with a dozen bounds and as many slashes we were all safely out of the glade, and galloping down the winding track which led to the valley.

It was not until we had left the ravine far behind us and were right out in the open fields that we ventured to halt, and to see what injuries we had sustained. For me, wounded and weary as I was, my heart was beating proudly, and my chest was nearly bursting my tunic to think that I, Etienne Gerard, had left this gang of murderers so much by which to remember me. My faith, they would think twice before they ventured to lay hands upon one of the Third Hussars. So carried away was I that I made a small oration to these brave Englishmen, and told them who it was that they had helped to rescue. I would have spoken of glory also, and of the sympathies of brave men, but the officer cut me short.

'That's all right,' said he. 'Any injuries, Sergeant?'

'Trooper Jones's horse hit with a pistol bullet on the fetlock.'

'Trooper Jones to go with us. Sergeant Halliday, with

troopers Harvey and Smith, to keep to the right until they touch the vedettes of the German Hussars.'

So these three jingled away together, while the officer and I, followed at some distance by the trooper whose horse had been wounded, rode straight down in the direction of the English camp. Very soon we had opened our hearts, for we each liked the look of the other from the beginning. He was of the nobility, this brave lad, and he had been sent out scouting by Lord Wellington to see if there were any signs of our advancing through the mountains. It is one advantage of a wandering life like mine, that you learn to pick up those bits of knowledge which distinguish the man of the world. I have, for example, hardly ever met a Frenchman who could repeat an English title correctly. If I had not travelled I should not be able to say with confidence that this young man's real name was Milor the Hon. Sir Russell, Bart., this last being an honourable distinction, so that it was as the Bart that I usually addressed him, just as in Spanish one might say 'the Don.'

As we rode beneath the moonlight in the lovely Spanish night, we spoke our minds to each other, as if we were brothers. We were both of an age, you see, both of the light cavalry also (the Sixteenth Light Dragoons was his regiment), and both with the same hopes and ambitions. Never have I learned to know a man so quickly as I did the Bart. He gave me the name of a girl whom he had loved at a garden called Vauxhall, and, for my own part, I spoke to him of little Coralie, of the Opera. He took a lock of hair from his bosom, and I a garter. Then we nearly quarrelled over hussar and dragoon, for he was absurdly proud of his regiment, and you should have seen him curl his lip and clap his hand to his hilt when I said that I hoped it might never be its misfortune to come in the way of the Third. Finally, he began to speak about what the English call sport, and he told such stories of the money which he had lost over which of two cocks could kill the other, or which of two men could strike the other the most in a fight for a prize, that I was filled with astonishment. He was ready to bet upon anything in the most wonderful manner, and when I chanced to see a shooting star he was anxious to bet that he would see more than me, twenty-five francs a star, and it was only when I explained that my purse was in the hands of the brigands that he would give over the idea.

Well, we chatted away in this very amiable fashion until the day began to break, when suddenly we heard a great volley of musketry from somewhere in the front of us. It was very rocky and broken ground, and I thought, although I could see nothing, that a general engagement had broken out. The Bart laughed at my idea, however, and explained that the sound came from the English camp, where every man emptied his piece each morning so as to make sure of having a dry priming.

'In another mile we shall be up with the outposts,' said he.

I glanced round at this, and I perceived that we had trotted along at so good a pace during the time that we were keeping up our pleasant chat that the dragoon with the lame horse was altogether out of sight. I looked on every side, but in the whole of that vast rocky valley there was no one save only the Bart and I—both of us armed, you understand, and both of us well mounted. I began to ask myself whether after all it was quite necessary that I should ride that mile which would bring me to the British outposts.

Now, I wish to be very clear with you on this point, my friends, for I would not have you think that I was acting dishonourably or ungratefully to the man who had helped me away from the brigands. You must remember that of all duties the strongest is that which a commanding officer owes to his men. You must also bear in mind that war is a game which is played under fixed rules, and when these rules are broken one must at once claim the forfeit. If, for example, I had given a parole, then I should have been an infamous wretch had I dreamed of escaping. But no parole had been asked of me. Out of over-confidence, and the chance of the lame horse dropping behind, the Bart had permitted me to get up on equal terms with him. Had it been I who had taken him, I should have used him as courteously as he had me, but, at the same time, I should have respected his enterprise so far as to have deprived him of his sword, and seen that I had at least one guard beside myself. I reined up my horse and explained this to him, asking him at the same time whether he saw any breach of honour in my leaving him.

He thought about it, and several times repeated that which the English say when they mean 'Mon Dieu!'

'You would give me the slip, would you?' said he.

'If you can give no reason against it.'

'The only reason that I can think of,' said the Bart, 'is that I should instantly cut your head off if you were to attempt it.'

'Two can play at that game, my dear Bart,' said I.

'Then we'll see who can play at it best,' he cried, pulling out his sword.

I had drawn mine also, but I was quite determined not to hurt this admirable young man who had been my benefactor.

'Consider,' said I, 'you say that I am your prisoner. I might with equal reason say that you are mine. We are alone here, and though I have no doubt that you are an excellent swordsman, you can hardly hope to hold your own against the best blade in the six light cavalry brigades.'

His answer was a cut at my head. I parried and shore off half of his white plume. He thrust at my breast. I turned his point and cut away the other half of his cockade.

'Curse your monkey tricks!' he cried, as I wheeled my horse away from him.

'Why should you strike at me?' said I. 'You see that I will not strike back.'

'That's all very well,' said he; 'but you've got to come along with me to the camp.'

'I shall never see the camp,' said I.

'I'll lay you nine to four you do,' he cried, as he made at me, sword in hand.

But those words of his put something new into my head. Could we not decide the matter in some better way than by fighting? The Bart was placing me in such a position that I should have to hurt him, or he would certainly hurt me. I avoided his rush, though his sword point was within an inch of my neck.

'I have a proposal,' I cried. 'We shall throw dice as to which is the prisoner of the other.'

He smiled at this. It appealed to his love of sport.

'Where are your dice?' he cried.

'I have none.'

'Nor I. But I have cards.'

'Cards let it be,' said I.

'And the game?'

'I leave it to you.'

'Écarté, then—the best of three.'

I could not help smiling as I agreed, for I do not suppose that there were three men in France who were my masters at the game. I told the Bart as much as we dismounted. He smiled also as he listened.

'I was counted the best player at Watier's,' said he. 'With even luck you deserve to get off if you beat me.'

So we tethered our two horses and sat down one on either side of a great flat rock. The Bart took a pack of cards out of his tunic, and I had only to see him shuffle to convince me that I had no novice to deal with. We cut, and the deal fell to him.

My faith, it was a stake worth playing for. He wished to add a hundred gold pieces a game, but what was money when the fate of Colonel Etienne Gerard hung upon the cards? I felt as though all those who had reason to be interested in the game: my mother, my hussars, the Sixth Corps d'Armée, Ney, Massena, even the Emperor himself, were forming a ring round us in that desolate valley. Heavens, what a blow to one and all of them should the cards go against me! But I was confident, for my écarté play was as famous as my swordsmanship, and save old Bouvet of the Hussars of Bercheny, who won seventy-six out of one hundred and fifty games off me, I have always had the best of a series.

The first game I won right off, though I must confess that the cards were with me, and that my adversary could have done no more. In the second, I never played better and saved a trick by a finesse, but the Bart voled me once, marked the king, and ran out in the second hand. My faith, we were so excited that he laid his helmet down beside him and I my busby.

'I'll lay my roan mare against your black horse,' said he.

'Done!' said I.

'Sword against sword.'

'Done!' said I.

'Saddle, bridle, and stirrups!' he cried.

'Done!' I shouted.

I had caught this spirit of sport from him. I would have laid my hussars against his dragoons had they been ours to pledge.

And then began the game of games. Oh, he played, this Englishman—he played in a way that was worthy of such a stake. But I, my friends, I was superb! Of the five which I had to make to win, I gained three on the first hand. The Bart bit his moustache and drummed his hands, while I already felt myself at the head of my dear little rascals. On the second, I turned the king, but lost two tricks—and my score was four to his two. When I saw my next hand I could not but give a cry of delight. 'If I cannot gain my freedom on this,' thought I, 'I deserve to remain for ever in chains.'

Give me the cards, landlord, and I will lay them out on the table for you.

Here was my hand: knave and ace of clubs, queen and knave of diamonds, and king of hearts. Clubs were trumps, mark you, and I had but one point between me and freedom. As you may think, I declined his proposal. He knew that it was the crisis and he undid his tunic. I threw my dolman on the ground. He led the ten of spades. I took it with my ace of trumps. One point in my favour. The correct play was to clear the trumps, and I led the knave. Down came the queen upon it, and the game was equal. He led the eight of spades, and I could only discard my queen of diamonds. Then came the seven of spades, and the hair stood straight up on my head. We each threw down a king at the final. He had won two points, and my beautiful hand had been mastered by his inferior one. I could have rolled on the ground as I thought of it. They used to play very good écarté at Watier's in the year '10. I say it—I, Brigadier Gerard.

The last game was now four all. This next hand must settle it one way or the other. He undid his sash, and I put away my sword belt. He was cool, this Englishman, and I tried to be so also, but the perspiration would trickle into my eyes. The deal lay with him, and I may confess to you, my friends, that my hands shook so that I could hardly pick my cards from the rock. But when I raised them, what was the first thing that my eyes rested upon. It was the king, the king, the glorious king of trumps! My mouth was open to declare it when the words were frozen upon my lips by the appearance of my comrade.

He held his cards in his hand, but his jaw had fallen, and his eyes were staring over my shoulder with the most dreadful expression of consternation and surprise. I whisked round, and I was myself amazed at what I saw.

Three men were standing quite close to us—fifteen metres at the furthest. The middle one was of a good height, and yet not too tall—about the same height, in fact, that I am myself. He was clad in a dark uniform with a small cocked hat, and some sort of white plume upon the side. But I had little thought of his dress. It was his face, his gaunt cheeks, his beak-like nose, his masterful blue eyes, his thin, firm slit of a mouth which made one feel that this was a wonderful man, a man of a million. His brows were tied into a knot, and he cast such a glance at my poor Bart from under them that one by one the cards came fluttering down from his nerveless fingers. Of the two other men, one, who had a face as brown and hard as though it had been carved out of old oak, wore a bright red coat, while the other, a fine portly man with bushy sidewhiskers, was in a blue jacket with gold facings. Some little distance behind, three orderlies were holding as many horses, and an escort of lancers was waiting in the rear.

'Heh, Crauford, what the deuce is this?' asked the thin man.

'D'you hear, sir?' cried the man with the red coat. 'Lord Wellington wants to know what this means.'

My poor Bart broke into an account of all that had occurred, but that rock-face never softened for an instant.

'Pretty fine, 'pon my word, General Crauford,' he broke in. 'The discipline of this force must be maintained, sir. Report yourself at headquarters as a prisoner.'

It was dreadful to me to see the Bart mount his horse and ride off with hanging head. I could not endure it. I threw myself before this English General. I pleaded with him for my friend. I told him how I, Colonel Gerard, would witness what a dashing young officer he was. Ah, my eloquence might have melted the hardest heart; I brought tears to my own eyes, but none to his. My voice broke, and I could say no more.

'What weight do you put on your mules, sir, in the French service?' he asked. Yes, that was all this phlegmatic Englishman had to answer to these burning words of mine. That was his reply to what would have made a Frenchman weep upon my shoulder.

'What weight on a mule?' asked the man with the red coat.

'Two hundred and ten pounds,' said I.

'Then you load them deucedly badly,' said Lord Wellington. 'Remove the prisoner to the rear.'

His Lancers closed in upon me, and I—I was driven mad, as I thought that the game had been in my hands, and that I ought at that moment to be a free man. I held the cards up in front of the General.

'See, my lord!' I cried; 'I played for my freedom and I won, for, as you perceive, I hold the king.'

For the first time a slight smile softened his gaunt face.

'On the contrary,' said he, as he mounted his horse, 'it was I who won, for, as you perceive, my king holds you.'

THREE

How the King Held the Brigadier

Beginning 10 August 1810, as stated, and lasting for a
duration the reader may be amused to compute, but at
least a month's passage seems indicated.

Murat was undoubtedly an excellent cavalry officer, but he
had too much swagger, which spoils many a good soldier.
Lasalle, too, was a very dashing leader, but he ruined
himself with wine and folly. Now I, Etienne Gerard, was
always totally devoid of swagger, and at the same time I was
very abstemious, except, maybe, at the end of a campaign,
or when I met an old comrade-in-arms. For these reasons I
might, perhaps, had it not been for a certain diffidence, have
claimed to be the most valuable officer in my own branch of
the Service. It is true that I never rose to be more than a
chief of brigade, but then, as everyone knows, no one had a
chance of rising to the top unless he had the good fortune to
be with the Emperor in his early campaigns. Except Lasalle,
and Lobau, and Drouet, I can hardly remember any one of
the generals who had not already made his name before the
Egyptian business. Even I, with all my brilliant qualities,
could only attain the head of my brigade, and also the
special medal of honour, which I received from the Emperor
himself, and which I keep at home in a leathern pouch. But
though I never rose higher than this, my qualities were very
well known by those who had served with me, and also by
the English. After they had captured me in the way which
I described to you the other night, they kept a very good
guard over me at Oporto, and I promise you that they did
not give such a formidable opponent a chance of slipping
through their fingers. It was on the 10th of August that I
was escorted on board the transport which was to take us
to England, and behold me before the end of the month in
the great prison which had been built for us at Dartmoor!

51

'L'hôtel Français, et Pension,' we used to call it, for you understand that we were all brave men there, and that we did not lose our spirits because we were in adversity.

It was only those officers who refused to give their parole who were confined at Dartmoor, and most of the prisoners were seamen, or from the ranks. You ask me, perhaps, why it was that I did not give this parole, and so enjoy the same good treatment as most of my brother officers. Well, I had two reasons, and both of them were sufficiently strong.

In the first place, I had so much confidence in myself, that I was quite convinced that I could escape. In the second, my family, though of good repute, has never been wealthy, and I could not bring myself to take anything from the small income of my mother. On the other hand, it would never do for a man like me to be outshone by the bourgeois society of an English country town, or to be without the means of showing courtesies and attentions to those ladies whom I should attract. It was for these reasons that I preferred to be buried in the dreadful prison of Dartmoor. I wish now to tell you of my adventures in England, and of how far Milor Wellington's words were true when he said that his king would hold me.

And first of all I may say that if it were not that I have set off to tell you about what befell myself, I could keep you here until morning with my stories about Dartmoor itself, and about the singular things which occurred there. It was one of the very strangest places in the whole world, for there, in the middle of that great desolate waste, were herded together seven or eight thousand men—warriors you understand, men of experience and courage. Around there were a double wall and a ditch, and warders and soldiers, but, my faith! you could not coop men like that up like rabbits in a hutch! They would escape by twos and tens and twenties, and then the cannon would boom, and the search parties run, and we, who were left behind, would laugh and dance and shout 'Vive l'Empereur,' until the warders would turn their muskets upon us in their passion. And then we would have our little mutinies too, and up would come the infantry and the guns from Plymouth, and that would set us yelling 'Vive l'Empereur' once more, as though we wished them to hear us in Paris. We had lively moments at Dartmoor, and we contrived that those who were about us should be lively also.

You must know that the prisoners there had their own Courts of Justice, in which they tried their own cases, and inflicted their own punishments. Stealing and quarrelling were punished—but most of all treachery. When I came there first there was a man, Meunier, from Rheims, who had given information of some plot to escape. Well, that night, owing to some form or other which had to be gone through, they did not take him out from among the other prisoners, and though he wept and screamed, and grovelled upon the ground, they left him there amongst the comrades whom he had betrayed. That night there was a trial with a whispered accusation and a whispered defence, a gagged prisoner, and a judge whom none could see. In the morning, when they came for their man with papers for his release, there was not as much of him left as you could put upon your thumb nail. They were ingenious people, these prisoners, and they had their own way of managing.

We officers, however, lived in a separate wing, and a very singular group of people we were. They had left us our uniforms, so that there was hardly a corps which had served under Victor, or Massena, or Ney, which was not represented there, and some had been there from the time when Junot was beaten at Vimiera. We had chasseurs in their green tunics, and hussars, like myself, and blue-coated dragoons, and white-fronted lancers, and voltigeurs, and grenadiers, and men of the artillery and engineers. But the greater part were naval officers, for the English had had the better of us upon the seas. I could never understand this until I journeyed myself from Oporto to Plymouth, when I lay for seven days upon my back, and could not have stirred had I seen the eagle of the regiment carried off before my eyes. It was in perfidious weather like this that Nelson took advantage of us.

I had no sooner got into Dartmoor than I began to plan to get out again, and you can readily believe that with wits sharpened by twelve years of warfare, it was not very long before I saw my way.

You must know, in the first place, that I had a very great advantage in having some knowledge of the English language. I learned it during the months that I spent before Danzig, from Adjutant Obriant, of the Regiment Irlandais, who was sprung from the ancient kings of the country. I was quickly able to speak it with some facility, for I do not take long to master anything to which I set my mind. In three months I could not only express my meaning, but I could use the idioms of the people. It was Obriant who taught me to say 'Be jabers,' just as we might say 'Ma foi'; and also 'The curse of Crummle!' which means 'Ventre bleu!' Many a time I have seen the English smile with pleasure when they have heard me speak so much like one of themselves.

We officers were put two in a cell, which was very little to my taste, for my room-mate was a tall, silent man named Beaumont, of the Flying Artillery, who had been taken by the English cavalry at Astorga.

It is seldom I meet a man of whom I cannot make a friend, for my disposition and manners are—as you know them. But this fellow had never a smile for my jests, nor an ear for my sorrows, but would sit looking at me with his sullen eyes, until sometimes I thought that his two years of captivity had driven him crazy. Ah, how I longed that old Bouvet, or any of my comrades of the hussars was there, instead of this mummy of a man. But such as he was I had to make the best of him, and it was very evident that no escape could be made unless he were my partner in it, for what could I possibly do without his observing me? I hinted at it, therefore, and then by degrees I spoke more plainly, until it seemed to me that I had prevailed upon him to share my lot.

I tried the walls, and I tried the floor, and I tried the ceiling, but though I tapped and probed, they all appeared to be very thick and solid. The door was of iron, shutting with a spring lock, and provided with a small grating, through which a warder looked twice in every night. Within there were two beds, two stools, two washstands—nothing more. It was enough for my wants, for when had I had as much during those twelve years spent in camps? But how was I to get out? Night after night I thought of my five hundred hussars, and had dreadful nightmares, in which

I fancied that the whole regiment needed shoeing, or that my horses were all bloated with green fodder, or that they were foundered from bogland, or that six squadrons were clubbed in the presence of the Emperor. Then I would awake in a cold sweat, and set to work picking and tapping at the walls once more; for I knew very well that there is no difficulty which cannot be overcome by a ready brain and pair of cunning hands.

There was a single window in our cell, which was too small to admit a child. It was further defended by a thick iron bar in the centre. It was not a very promising point of escape, as you will allow, but I became more and more convinced that our efforts must be directed towards it. To make matters worse, it only led out into the exercise yard, which was surrounded by two high walls. Still, as I said to my sullen comrade, it is time to talk of the Vistula when you are over the Rhine. I got a small piece of iron, therefore, from the fittings of my bed, and I set to work to loosen the plaster at the top and the bottom of the bar. Three hours I would work, and then leap into my bed upon the sound of the warder's step. Then another three hours and then very often another yet, for I found that Beaumont was so slow and clumsy at it that it was on myself only that I could rely. I pictured to myself my Third of Hussars waiting just outside that window, with kettledrums and standards and leopard-skin schabraques all complete. Then I would work and work like a madman, until my iron was crusted with my own blood, as if with rust. And so, night by night, I loosened that stony plaster, and hid it away in the stuffing of my pillow, until the hour came when the iron shook; and then with one good wrench it came off in my hand, and my first step had been made towards freedom.

You will ask me what better off I was, since, as I have said, a child could not have fitted through the opening. I will tell you. I had gained two things—a tool and a weapon. With the one I might loosen the stone which flanked the window. With the other I might defend myself when I had scrambled through. So now I turned my attention to that stone, and I picked and picked with the sharpened end of my bar until I had worked out the mortar all round.

You understand, of course that during the day I replaced everything in its position, and that the warder was never permitted to see a speck upon the floor. At the end of three weeks I had separated the stone, and had the rapture of drawing it through, and seeing a hole left with ten stars shining through it, where there had been but four before. All was ready for us now, and I replaced the stone, smearing the edges of it round with a little fat and soot, so as to hide the cracks where the mortar should have been. In three nights the moon would be gone, and that seemed the best time for our attempt.

I had now no doubt at all about getting into the yard, but I had very considerable misgivings as to how I was to get out again. It would be too humiliating, after trying here, and trying there, to have to go back to my hole again in despair, or to be arrested by the guards outside, and thrown into those damp underground cells which are reserved for prisoners who are caught in escaping. I set to work, therefore, to plan what I should do. I have never, as you know, had the chance of showing what I could do as a general. Sometimes, after a glass or two of wine, I have found myself capable of thinking out surprising combinations, and have felt that if Napoleon had intrusted me with an army corps, things might have gone differently with him. But however that may be, there is no doubt that in the small stratagems of war, and in that quickness of invention which is so necessary for an officer of light cavalry, I could hold my own against anyone. It was now that I had need of it, and I felt sure that it would not fail me.

The inner wall which I had to scale was built of bricks, 12ft high, with a row of iron spikes, three inches apart, upon the top. The outer I had only caught a glimpse of once or twice, when the gate of the exercise yard was open. It appeared to be about the same height, and was also spiked at the top. The space between the walls was over twenty feet, and I had reason to believe that there were no sentries there, except at the gates. On the other hand, I know that there was a line of soldiers outside. Behold the little nut, my friends, which I had to open with no crackers, save these two hands.

One thing upon which I relied was the height of my comrade Beaumont. I have already said that he was a very tall man, six feet at least, and it seemed to me that if I could mount upon his shoulders, and get my hands upon the spikes, I could easily scale the wall. Could I pull my big companion up after me? That was the question, for when I set forth with a comrade, even though it be one for whom I bear no affection, nothing on earth would make me abandon him. If I climbed the wall and he could not follow me, I should be compelled to return to him. He did not seem to concern himself much about it, however, so I hoped that he had confidence in his own activity.

Then another very important matter was the choice of the sentry who should be on duty in front of my window at the time of our attempt. They were changed every two hours to insure their vigilance, but I, who watched them closely each night out of my window, knew that there was a great difference between them. There were some who were so keen that a rat could not cross the yard unseen, while others thought only of their own ease, and could sleep as soundly leaning upon a musket as if they were at home upon a feather bed. There was one especially, a fat, heavy man, who would retire into the shadow of the wall and doze so comfortably during his two hours, that I have dropped pieces of plaster from my window at his very feet, without his observing it. By good luck, this fellow's watch was due from twelve to two upon the night which we had fixed upon for our enterprise.

As the last day passed, I was so filled with nervous agitation that I could not control myself, but ran ceaselessly about my cell, like a mouse in a cage. Every moment I thought that the warder would detect the looseness of the bar, or that the sentry would observe the unmortared stone, which I could not conceal outside, as I did within. As for my companion, he sat brooding upon the end of his bed, looking at me in a sidelong fashion from time to time, and biting his nails like one who is deep in thought.

'Courage, my friend!' I cried, slapping him upon the shoulder. 'You will see your guns before another month be past.'

'That is very well,' said he. 'But whither will you fly when you get free?'

'To the coast,' I answered. 'All comes right for a brave man, and I shall make straight for my regiment.'

'You are more likely to make straight for the underground cells, or for the Portsmouth hulks,' said he.

'A soldier takes his chances,' I remarked. 'It is only the poltroon who reckons always upon the worst.'

I raised a flush in each of his sallow cheeks at that, and I was glad of it, for it was the first sign of spirit which I had ever observed in him. For a moment he put his hand out towards his water jug, as though he would have hurled it at me, but then he shrugged his shoulders and sat in silence once more, biting his nails, and scowling down at the floor. I could not but think, as I looked at him, that perhaps I was doing the Flying Artillery a very bad service by bringing him back to them.

I never in my life have known an evening pass as slowly as that one. Towards nightfall a wind sprang up, and as the darkness deepened it blew harder and harder, until a terrible gale was whistling over the moor. As I looked out of my window I could not catch a glimpse of a star, and the black clouds were flying low across the heavens. The rain was pouring down, and what with its hissing and splashing, and the howling and screaming of the wind, it was impossible for me to hear the steps of the sentinels. 'If I cannot hear them,' thought I, 'then it is unlikely that they can hear me'; and I waited with the utmost impatience until the time when the inspector should have come round for his nightly peep through our grating. Then having peered through the darkness, and seen nothing of the sentry, who was doubtless crouching in some corner out of the rain, I felt that the moment was come. I removed the bar, pulled out the stone, and motioned to my companion to pass through.

'After you, colonel,' said he.

'Will you not go first?' I asked.

'I had rather you showed me the way.'

'Come after me, then, but come silently, as you value your life.'

In the darkness I could hear the fellow's teeth chattering,

and I wondered whether a man ever had such a partner in such a desperate enterprise. I seized the bar, however, and mounting upon my stool, I thrust my head and shoulders into the hole. I had wriggled through as far as my waist, when my companion seized me suddenly by the knees, and yelled at the top of his voice: 'Help! Help! A prisoner is escaping!'

Ah, my friends, what did I not feel at that moment! Of course, I saw in an instant the game of this vile creature. Why should he risk his skin in climbing walls when he might be sure of a free pardon from the English for having prevented the escape of one so much more distinguished than himself? I had recognised him as a poltroon and a sneak, but I had not understood the depth of baseness to which he could descend. One who has spent his life among gentlemen and men of honour does not think of such things until they happen.

The blockhead did not seem to understand that he was lost more certainly than I. I writhed back in the darkness, and seizing him by the throat I struck him twice with my iron bar. At the first blow he yelped as a little cur does when you tread upon its paw. At the second, down he fell with a groan upon the floor. Then I seated myself upon my bed, and waited resignedly for whatever punishment my gaolers might inflict upon me.

But a minute passed and yet another, with no sound save the heavy snoring breathing of the senseless wretch upon the floor. Was it possible, then, that amid the fury of the storm his warning cries had passed unheeded? At first it was but a tiny hope, another minute and it was probable, another and it was certain. There was no sound in the corridor, none in the courtyard. I wiped the cold sweat from my brow, and asked myself what I should do next.

One thing seemed certain. The man on the floor must die. If I left him I could not tell how short a time it might be before he gave the alarm. I dare not strike a light, so I felt about in the darkness until my hand came upon something wet, which I knew to be his head. I raised my iron bar, but there was something, my friends, which prevented me from bringing it down. In the heat of fight I have slain many men—men of honour too, who had done me no injury.

Yet here was this wretch, a creature too foul to live, who had tried to work me so great a mischief, and yet I could not bring myself to crush his skull in. Such deeds are very well for a Spanish partida—or for that matter a sans-culotte of the Faubourg St Antoine—but not for a soldier and a gentleman like me.

However, the heavy breathing of the fellow made me hope that it might be a very long time before he recovered his senses. I gagged him therefore, and bound him with strips of blanket to the bed, so that in his weakened condition there was good reason to think that, in any case, he might not get free before the next visit of the warder. But now again I was faced with new difficulties, for you will remember that I had relied upon his height to help me over the walls. I could have sat down and shed tears of despair had not the thought of my mother and of the Emperor come to sustain me. 'Courage!' said I. 'If it were anyone but Etienne Gerard he would be in a bad fix now; that is a young man who is not so easily caught.'

I set to work therefore upon Beaumont's sheet as well as my own, and by tearing them into strips and then plaiting them together, I made a very excellent rope. This I tied securely to the centre of my iron bar, which was a little over a foot in length. Then I slipped out into the yard, where the rain was pouring and the wind screaming louder than ever. I kept in the shadow of the prison wall, but it was as black as the ace of spades, and I could not see my own hand in front of me. Unless I walked into the sentinel I felt that I had nothing to fear from him. When I had come under the wall I threw up my bar, and to my joy it stuck the very first time between the spikes at the top. I climbed up my rope, pulled it after me, and dropped down on the other side. Then I scaled the second wall, and was sitting astride among the spikes upon the top, when I saw something twinkle in the darkness beneath me. It was the bayonet of the sentinel below, and so close was it (the second wall being rather lower than the first) that I could easily, by leaning over, have unscrewed it from its socket. There he was, humming a tune to himself, and cuddling up against the wall to keep himself warm, little thinking that a desperate man within a few feet of him was within an ace of stabbing him to the heart with his own weapon. I was already bracing myself for the spring when the fellow, with an oath, shouldered his musket, and I heard his steps squelching through the mud as he resumed his beat. I slipped down my rope, and, leaving it hanging, I ran at the top of my speed across the moor.

Heavens, how I ran! The wind buffeted my face and buzzed in my nostrils. The rain pringled upon my skin and hissed past my ears. I stumbled into holes. I tripped over bushes. I fell among brambles. I was torn and breathless and bleeding. My tongue was like leather, my feet like lead, and my heart beating like a kettle-drum. Still I ran, and I ran, and I ran.

But I had not lost my head, my friends. Everything was done with a purpose. Our fugitives always made for the coast. I was determined to go inland, and the more so as I had told Beaumont the opposite. I would fly to the north, and they would seek me in the south. Perhaps you will ask me how I could tell which was which on such a night. I answer that it was by the wind. I had observed in the prison that it came from the north, and so, as long as I kept my face to it, I was going in the right direction.

Well, I was rushing along in this fashion when, suddenly, I saw two yellow lights shining out of the darkness in front of me. I paused for a moment, uncertain what I should do. I was still in my hussar uniform, you understand, and it seemed to me that the very first thing that I should aim at was to get some dress which should not betray me. If these lights came from a cottage, it was probable enough that I might find what I wanted there. I approached therefore, feeling very sorry that I had left my iron bar behind; for I was determined to fight to the death before I should be retaken.

But very soon I found that there was no cottage there. The lights were two lamps hung upon each side of a carriage, and by their glare I saw that a broad road lay in front of me. Crouching among the bushes, I observed that there were two horses to the equipage, that a small post-boy was standing at their heads, and that one of the wheels was lying in the road beside him. I can see them now, my friends: the steaming creatures, the stunted lad with his hands to their bits, and the big, black coach all shining with the rain, and balanced upon its three wheels. As I looked, the window was lowered, and a pretty little face under a bonnet peeped out from it.

'What shall I do?' the lady cried to the post-boy, in a voice of despair. 'Sir Charles is certainly lost, and I shall have to spend the night upon the moor.'

'Perhaps I can be of some assistance to madame,' said I, scrambling out from among the bushes into the glare of the lamps. A woman in distress is a sacred thing to me, and this one was beautiful. You must not forget that, although I was a colonel, I was only eight-and-twenty years of age.

My word, how she screamed, and how the post-boy stared! You will understand that after that long race in the darkness, with my shako broken in, my face smeared with dirt, and my uniform all stained and torn with brambles, I was not entirely the sort of gentleman whom one would choose to meet in the middle of a lonely moor. Still, after the first surprise, she soon understood that I was her very humble servant, and I could even read in her pretty eyes that my manner and bearing had not failed to produce an impression upon her.

'I am sorry to have startled you, madame,' said I. 'I chanced to overhear your remark, and I could not refrain from offering you my assistance.' I bowed as I spoke. You know my bow, and can realize what its effect was upon the lady.

'I am much indebted to you, sir,' said she. 'We have had a terrible journey since we left Tavistock. Finally, one of our wheels came off, and here we are helpless in the middle of the moor. My husband, Sir Charles, has gone on to get help, and I much fear that he must have lost his way.'

I was about to attempt some consolation, when I saw beside the lady a black travelling coat, faced with astrakhan, which her companion must have left behind him. It was exactly what I needed to conceal my uniform. It is true that I felt very much like a highway robber, but then, what would you have? Necessity has no law, and I was in an enemy's country.

'I presume, madame, that this is your husband's coat,' I remarked. 'You will, I am sure, forgive me, if I am compelled to—' I pulled it through the window as I spoke.

I could not bear to see the look of surprise and fear and disgust which came over her face.

'Oh, I have been mistaken in you!' she cried. 'You came to rob me, then, and not to help me. You have the bearing of a gentleman, and yet you steal my husband's coat.'

'Madame,' said I, 'I beg that you will not condemn me until you know everything. It is quite necessary that I should take this coat, but if you will have the goodness to tell me who it is who is fortunate enough to be your husband, I shall see that the coat is sent back to him.'

Her face softened a little, though she still tried to look severe. 'My husband,' she anwered, 'is Sir Charles Meredith, and he is travelling to Dartmoor Prison, upon important Government business. I only ask you, sir, to go upon your way, and to take nothing which belongs to him.'

'There is only one thing which belongs to him that I covet,' said I.

'And you have taken it from the carriage,' she cried.

'No,' I answered. 'It still remains there.'

She laughed in her frank English way.

'If, instead of paying me compliments, you were to return my husband's coat—' she began.

'Madame,' I answered, 'what you ask is quite impossible. If you will allow me to come into the carriage I will explain to you how necessary this coat is to me.'

Heavens knows into what foolishness I might have plunged myself had we not, at this instant, heard a faint hallo in the distance, which was answered by a shout from the little post-boy. In the rain and the darkness I saw a lantern some distance from us, but approaching rapidly.

'I am sorry, madame, that I am forced to leave you,' said I. 'You can assure your husband that I shall take every care of his coat.' Hurried as I was, I ventured to pause a moment to salute the lady's hand, which she snatched through the window with an admirable pretence of being offended at my presumption. Then, as the lantern was quite close to me, and the post-boy seemed inclined to interfere with my flight, I tucked my precious overcoat under my arm, and dashed off into the darkness.

And now I set myself to the task of putting as broad a stretch of moor between the prison and myself as the remaining hours of darkness would allow. Setting my face to the wind once more, I ran until I fell from exhaustion. Then, after five minutes of panting among the heather, I made another start, until again my knees gave way beneath me. I was young and hard, with muscles of steel, and a frame which had been toughened by twelve years of camp and field. Thus I was able to keep up this wild flight for another three hours, during which I still guided myself, you understand, by keeping the wind in my face. At the end of that time I calculated that I had put nearly twenty miles between the prison and myself. Day was about to break, so I crouched down among the heather upon the top of one of those small hills which abound in that country, with the intention of hiding myself until nightfall. It was no new thing for me to sleep in the wind and the rain, so, wrapping myself up in my thick warm cloak, I soon sank into a doze.

But it was not a refreshing slumber. I tossed and tumbled amid a series of vile dreams, in which everything seemed to go wrong with me. At last, I remember, I was charging an unshaken square of Hungarian Grenadiers, with a single squadron upon spent horses, just as I did at Elchingen. I stood in my stirrups to shout 'Vive l'Empereur!' and as I did so, there came the answering roar from my hussars, 'Vive l'Empereur!' I sprang from my rough bed, with the words still ringing in my ears, and then, as I rubbed my eyes, and wondered if I were mad, the same cry came again, five thousand voices in one long-drawn yell. I looked out from my screen of brambles, and saw in the clear light of morning the very last thing that I should have either expected or chosen.

It was Dartmoor Prison! There it stretched, grim and hideous, within a furlong of me. Had I run on for a few more minutes in the dark, I should have butted my shako against the wall. I was so taken aback at the sight, that I could scarcely realize what had happened. Then it all became clear to me, and I struck my head with my hands in my despair. The wind had veered from north to south during the night, and I, keeping my face always towards it, had run ten miles out, and ten miles in, winding up where I had started. When I thought of my hurry, my falls, my mad rushing and jumping, all ending in this, it seemed so absurd, that my grief changed suddenly to amusement, and I fell among the brambles, and laughed, and laughed, until my sides were sore. Then I rolled myself up in my cloak, and considered seriously what I should do.

One lesson which I have learned in my roaming life, my friends, is never to call anything a misfortune until you have seen the end of it. Is not every hour a fresh point of view? In this case I soon perceived that accident had done for me as much as the most profound cunning. My guards naturally commenced their search from the place where I had taken Sir Charles Meredith's coat, and from my hiding-place I could see them hurrying along the road to that point. Not one of them ever dreamed that I could have doubled back from there, and I lay quite undisturbed in the little bush-covered cup at the summit of my knoll. The prisoners had, of course, learned of my escape, and all day exultant yells, like that which had aroused me in the morning, resounded over the moor, bearing a welcome message of sympathy and companionship to my ears. How little did they dream that on the top of that very mound, which they could see from their windows, was lying the comrade whose escape they were celebrating. As for me—I could look down upon this herd of idle warriors, as they paced about the great exercise yard, or gathered in little groups, gesticulating joyfully over my success. Once I heard a howl of execration and I saw Beaumont, his head all covered with bandages, being led across the yard by two of the warders. I cannot tell you the pleasure which this sight gave me, for it proved that I had not killed him, and also that the others knew the true story of what had passed. They had all known me too well to think that I could have abandoned him.

All that long day I lay behind my screen of bushes, listening to the bells which struck the hours below.

My pockets were filled with bread which I had saved out

of my allowance, and on searching my borrowed overcoat I came upon a silver flask, full of excellent brandy and water, so that I was able to get through the day without hardship. The only other things in the pockets were a red silk handkerchief, a tortoise-shell snuff-box, and a blue envelope, with a red seal, addressed to the Governor of Dartmoor Prison. As to the first two, I determined to send them back when I should return the coat itself. The letter caused me more perplexity, for the Governor had always shown me every courtesy, and it offended my sense of honour that I should interfere with his correspondence. I had almost made up my mind to leave it under a stone upon the roadway within musket-shot of the gate. This would guide them in their search for me, however, and so, on the whole, I saw no better way than just to carry the letter with me in the hope that I might find some means of sending it back to him. Meanwhile I packed it safely away in my innermost pocket.

There was a warm sun to dry my clothes, and when night fell I was ready for my journey. I promise you that there were no mistakes this time. I took the stars for my guides, as every hussar should be taught to do, and I put eight good leagues between myself and the prison. My plan now was to obtain a complete suit of clothes from the first person whom I could waylay, and I should then find my way to the north coast, where there were many smugglers and fishermen who would be ready to earn the reward which was paid by the Emperor to those who brought escaping prisoners across the Channel. I had taken the panache from my shako so that it might escape notice, but even with my fine overcoat I feared that sooner or later my uniform would betray me. My first care must be to provide myself with a complete disguise.

When day broke, I saw a river upon my right and a small town upon my left—the blue smoke reeking up above the moor. I should have liked well to have entered it, because it would have interested me to see something of the customs of the English, which differ very much from those of other nations. Much as I should have wished, however, to have seen them eat their raw meat and sell their wives, it would have been dangerous until I had got rid of my uniform.

My cap, my moustache, and my speech would all help to betray me. I continued to travel towards the north therefore, looking about me continually, but never catching a glimpse of my pursuers.

About mid-day I came to where, in a secluded valley, there stood a single small cottage without any other building in sight. It was a neat little house, with a rustic porch and a small garden in front of it, with a swarm of cocks and hens. I lay down among the ferns and watched it, for it seemed to be exactly the kind of place where I might obtain what I wanted. My bread was finished, and I was exceedingly hungry after my long journey; I determined, therefore, to make a short reconnaissance, and then to march up to this cottage, summon it to surrender, and help myself to all that I needed. It could, at least, provide me with a chicken and with an omelette. My mouth watered at the thought.

As I lay there, wondering who could live in this lonely place, a brisk little fellow came out through the porch, accompanied by another older man, who carried two large clubs in his hands. These he handed to his young companion, who swung them up and down, and round and round, with extraordinary swiftness. The other, standing beside him, appeared to watch him with great attention, and occasionally to advise him. Finally he took a rope, and began skipping like a girl, the other still gravely observing him. As you may think, I was utterly puzzled as to what these people could be, and could only surmise that the one was a doctor, and the other a patient who had submitted himself to some singular method of treatment.

Well, as I lay watching and wondering, the older man brought out a greatcoat, and held it while the other put it on and buttoned it to his chin. The day was a warmish one, so that this proceeding amazed me even more than the other. 'At least,' thought I, 'it is evident that his exercise is over'; but, far from this being so, the man began to run, in spite of his heavy coat, and as it chanced, he came right over the moor in my direction. His companion had re-entered the house, so that this arrangement suited me admirably. I would take the small man's clothing, and hurry on to some village where I could buy provisions. The chickens were certainly tempting, but still there were at least two men in the house, so perhaps it would be wiser for me, since I had no arms, to keep away from it.

I lay quietly then among the ferns. Presently I heard the steps of the runner, and there he was quite close to me, with his huge coat, and the perspiration running down his face. He seemed to be a very solid man—but small—so small that I feared that his clothes might be of little use to me. When I jumped out upon him he stopped running, and looked at me in the greatest astonishment.

'Blow my dickey,' said he, 'give it a name, guv'nor! Is it a circus, or what?' That was how he talked, though I cannot pretend to tell you what he meant by it.

'You will excuse me, sir,' said I, 'but I am under the necessity of asking you to give me your clothes.'

'Give you what?' he cried.

'Your clothes.'

'Well, if this don't lick cock-fighting!' said he. 'What am I to give you my clothes for?'

'Because I need them.'

'And suppose I won't?'

'Be jabers,' said I, 'I shall have no choice but to take them.'

He stood with his hands in the pockets of his greatcoat, and a most amused smile upon his square-jawed, clean-shaven face.

'You'll take them, will you?' said he. 'You're a very leery cove, by the look of you, but I can tell you that you've got the wrong sow by the ear this time. I know who you are. You're a runaway Frenchy, from the prison yonder, as anyone could tell with half an eye. But you don't know who I am, else you wouldn't try such a plant as that. Why, man, I'm the Bristol Bustler, nine stone champion, and them's my training quarters down yonder.'

He stared at me as if this announcement of his would have crushed me to the earth, but I smiled at him in my turn, and looked him up and down, with a twirl of my moustache.

'You may be a very brave man, sir,' said I, 'but when I tell you that you are opposed to Colonel Etienne Gerard, of the Hussars of Conflans, you will see the necessity of giving up your clothes without further parley.'

'Look here, mounseer, drop it!' he cried; 'this'll end by your getting pepper.'

'Your clothes, sir, this instant!' I shouted, advancing fiercely upon him.

For answer he threw off his heavy greatcoat, and stood in a singular attitude, with one arm out, and the other across his chest, looking at me with a curious smile. For myself, I knew nothing of the methods of fighting which these people have, but on horse or on foot, with arms or without them, I am always ready to take my own part. You understand that a soldier cannot always choose his own methods, and that it is time to howl when you are living among wolves. I rushed at him, therefore, with a warlike shout, and kicked him with both my feet. At the same moment my heels flew into the air, I saw as many flashes as at Austerlitz, and the back of my head came down with a crash upon a stone. After that I can remember nothing more.

When I came to myself I was lying upon a truckle-bed, in a bare, half-furnished room. My head was ringing like a bell, and when I put up my hand, there was a lump like a walnut over one of my eyes. My nose was full of a pungent smell, and I soon found that a strip of paper soaked in vinegar was fastened across my brow. At the other end of the room this terrible little man was sitting with his knee bare, and his elderly companion was rubbing it with some liniment. The latter seemed to be in the worst of tempers, and he kept up a continual scolding, which the other listened to with a gloomy face.

'Never heard tell of such a thing in my life,' he was saying. 'In training for a month with all the weight of it on my shoulders, and then when I get you as fit as a trout, and within two days of fighting the likeliest man on the list, you let yourself into a by-battle with a foreigner.'

'There, there! Stow your gab!' said the other, sulkily. 'You're a very good trainer, Jim, but you'd be better with less jaw.'

'I should think it was time to jaw,' the elderly man answered. 'If this knee don't get well before Wednesday, they'll have it that you fought a cross, and a pretty job you'll have next time you look for a backer.'

'Fought a cross!' growled the other. 'I've won nineteen battles, and no man ever so much as dared to say the word "cross" in my hearin'. How the deuce was I to get out of it when the cove wanted the very clothes off my back?'

'Tut, man, you know that the beak and the guards were within a mile of you. You could have set them on to him as well then as now. You'd have got your clothes back again all right.'

'Well, strike me!' said the Bustler, 'I don't often break my trainin', but when it comes to givin' up my clothes to a Frenchy who couldn't hit a dint in a pat o' butter, why, it's more than I can swaller.'

'Pooh, man, what are the clothes worth? D'you know that Lord Rufton alone has five thousand pounds on you? When you jump the ropes on Wednesday, you'll carry every penny of fifty thousand into the ring. A pretty thing to turn up with a swollen knee and a story about a Frenchman!'

'I never thought he'd ha' kicked,' said the Bustler.

'I suppose you expected he'd fight Broughton's rules, and strict P.R.? Why, you silly, they don't know what fighting is in France.'

'My friends,' said I, sitting up on my bed, 'I do not understand very much of what you say, but when you speak like that it is foolishness. We know so much about fighting in France, that we have paid our little visit to nearly every capital in Europe, and very soon we are coming to London. But we fight like soldiers, you understand, and not like gamins in the gutter. You strike me on the head. I kick you on the knee. It is child's play. But if you will give me a sword, and take another one, I will show you how we fight over the water.'

They both stared at me in their solid, English way.

'Well, I'm glad you're not dead, mounseer,' said the elder one at last. 'There wasn't much sign of life in you when the Bustler and me carried you down. That head of yours ain't thick enough to stop the crook of the hardest hitter in Bristol.'

'He's a game cove, too, and he came for me like a

bantam,' said the other, still rubbing his knee. 'I got my old left-right in, and he went over as if he had been pole-axed. It wasn't my fault, mounseer. I told you you'd get pepper if you went on.'

'Well, it's something to say all your life, that you've been handled by the finest light-weight in England,' said the older man, looking at me with an expression of congratulation upon his face. 'You've had him at his best, too—in the pink of condition, and trained by Jim Hunter.'

'I am used to hard knocks,' said I, unbuttoning my tunic, and showing my two musket wounds. Then I bared my ankle also, and showed the place in my eye where the guerilla had stabbed me.

'He can take his gruel,' said the Bustler.

'What a glutton he'd have made for the middle-weights,' remarked the trainer; 'with six months' coaching he'd astonish the fancy. It's a pity he's got to go back to prison.'

I did not like that last remark at all. I buttoned up my coat and rose from the bed.

'I must ask you to let me continue my journey,' said I.

'There's no help for it, mounseer,' the trainer answered. 'It's a hard thing to send such a man as you back to such a place, but business is business, and there's a twenty pound reward. They were here this morning, looking for you, and I expect they'll be round again.'

His words turned my heart to lead.

'Surely, you would not betray me,' I cried. 'I will send you twice twenty pounds on the day that I set foot upon France. I swear it upon the honour of a French gentleman.'

But I only got head-shakes for a reply. I pleaded, I argued, I spoke of the English hospitality and the fellowship of brave men, but I might as well have been addressing the two great wooden clubs which stood balanced upon the floor in front of me. There was no sign of sympathy upon their bull-faces.

'Business is business, mounseer,' the old trainer repeated. 'Besides, how am I to put the Bustler into the ring on Wednesday if he's jugged by the beak for aidin' and abettin' a prisoner of war? I've got to look after the Bustler, and I take no risks.'

This, then, was the end of all my struggles and strivings. I was to be led back again like a poor silly sheep who has broken through the hurdles. They little knew me who could fancy that I should submit to such a fate. I had heard enough to tell me where the weak point of these two men was, and I showed, as I have often showed before, that Etienne Gerard is never so terrible as when all hope seems to have deserted him. With a single spring I seized one of the clubs and swung it over the head of the Bustler.

'Come what may,' I cried, '*you* shall be spoiled for Wednesday.'

The fellow growled out an oath, and would have sprung at me, but the other flung his arms round him and pinned him to the chair.

'Not if I know it, Bustler,' he screamed. 'None of your games while I am by. Get away out of this, Frenchy. We only want to see your back. Run away, run away, or he'll get loose!'

It was good advice, I thought, and I ran to the door, but as I came out into the open air my head swam round and I had to lean against the porch to save myself from falling. Consider all that I had been through, the anxiety of my escape, the long, useless flight in the storm, the day spent amid wet ferns, with only bread for food, the second journey by night, and now the injuries which I had received in attempting to deprive the little man of his clothes. Was it wonderful that even I should reach the limits of my endurance? I stood there in my heavy coat and my poor battered shako, my chin upon my chest, and my eyelids over my eyes. I had done my best, and I could do no more. It was the sound of horses' hoofs which made me at last raise my head, and there was the grey-moustached Governor of Dartmoor Prison not ten paces in front of me, with six mounted warders behind him.

'So, Colonel,' said he, with a bitter smile, 'we have found you once more.'

When a brave man has done his utmost, and has failed, he shows his breeding by the manner in which he accepts his defeat. For me, I took the letter which I had in my pocket, and stepping forward, I handed it with such grace of manner as I could summon to the Governor.

'It has been my misfortune, sir, to detain one of your letters,' said I.

He looked at me in amazement, and beckoned to the warders to arrest me. Then he broke the seal of the letter. I saw a curious expression come over his face as he read it.

'This must be the letter which Sir Charles Meredith lost,' said he.

'It was in the pocket of his coat.'

'You have carried it for two days?'

'Since the night before last.'

'And never looked at the contents?'

I showed him by my manner that he had committed an indiscretion in asking a question which one gentleman should not have put to another.

To my surprise he burst out into a roar of laughter.

'Colonel,' said he, wiping the tears from his eyes, 'you have really given both yourself and us a great deal of unnecessary trouble. Allow me to read the letter which you carried with you in your flight.'

And this was what I heard:—

'On receipt of this you are directed to release Colonel Etienne Gerard, of the 3rd Hussars, who has been exchanged against Colonel Mason, of the Horse Artillery, now in Verdun.'

And as he read it, he laughed again, and the warders laughed, and the two men from the cottage laughed, and then, as I heard this universal merriment, and thought of all my hopes and fears, and my struggles and dangers, what could a debonair soldier do but lean against the porch once more, and laugh as heartily as any of them? And of them all was it not I who had the best reason to laugh, since in front of me I could see my dear France, and my mother, and the Emperor, and my horsemen; while behind lay the gloomy prison, and the heavy hand of the English king?

FOUR

How the Brigadier Slew
the Brothers of Ajaccio

September or October 1807. The Ajaccio episode described
by Napoleon would probably have taken place in the
last three months of 1792, after Napoleon's return from
Paris where he had been appalled and endangered by
the September massacres. The Corsican patriot, Pasquale
Paoli, outlawed Napoleon in 1793 forcing him into flight
from the island. Paoli then declared Corsica independent
of France but was himself forced into exile, and died on
5 February 1807, an event which presumably prompted
the decision of the Brothers to settle accounts with the
most notorious of the dead leader's defectors.

When I told you some little time ago how it was that I won
the special medal for valour, I finished, as you will doubtless
remember, by repeating the saying of the Emperor that I
had the stoutest heart in all his armies. In making that
remark, Napoleon was showing the insight for which he
was so famous. He disfigured his sentence, however, by
adding something about the thickness of my head. We will
pass that over. It is ungenerous to dwell upon the weaker
moments of a great man. I will only say this, that when the
Emperor needed an agent he was always very ready to do
me the honour of recalling the name of Etienne Gerard,
though it occasionally escaped him when rewards were to
be distributed. Still, I was a colonel at twenty-eight, and the
chief of a brigade at thirty-one, so that I have no reason to
be dissatisfied with my career. Had the wars lasted another
two or three years I might have grasped my bâton, and the
man who had his hand upon that was only one stride from
a throne. Murat had changed his hussar's cap for a crown,
and another light cavalry man might have done as much.
However, all those dreams were driven away by Waterloo,
and, although I was not able to write my name upon history,

it is sufficiently well known by all who served with me in the great wars of the Empire.

What I want to tell you to-night is about the very singular affair which first started me upon my rapid upward course, and which had the effect of establishing a secret bond between the Emperor and myself. There is just one little word of warning which I must give you before I begin. When you hear me speak, you must always bear in mind that you are listening to one who has seen history from the inside. I am talking about what my ears have heard and my eyes have seen, so you must not try to confute me by quoting the opinions of some student or man of the pen, who has written a book of history or memoirs. There is much which is unknown by such people, and much which never will be known by the world. For my own part, I could tell you some very surprising things were it discreet to do so. The facts which I am about to relate to you to-night were kept secret by me during the Emperor's lifetime, because I gave him my promise that it should be so, but I do not think that there can be any harm now in my telling the remarkable part which I played.

You must know, then, that at the time of the Treaty of Tilsit I was a simple lieutenant in the 10th Hussars, without money or interest. It is true that my appearance and my gallantry were in my favour, and that I had already won a reputation as being one of the best swordsmen in the army; but among the host of brave men who surrounded the Emperor it needed more than this to insure a rapid career. I was confident, however, that my chance would come, though I never dreamed that it would take so remarkable a form.

When the Emperor returned to Paris, after the declaration of peace in the year 1807, he spent much of his time with the Empress and the Court at Fontainebleau. It was the time when he was at the pinnacle of his career. He had in three successive campaigns humbled Austria, crushed Prussia, and made the Russians very glad to get upon the right side of the Niemen. The old Bulldog over the Channel was still growling, but he could not get very far from his kennel. If we could have made a perpetual peace at that moment, France would have taken a higher place than any nation since the days of the Romans. So I have heard the wise folk say, though for my part I had other things to think of. All the girls were glad to see the army back after its long absence, and you may be sure that I had my share of any favours that were going. You may judge how far I was a favourite in those days when I say that even now, in my sixtieth year—but why should I dwell upon that which is already sufficiently well known?

Our regiment of hussars was quartered with the horse chasseurs of the guard at Fontainebleau. It is, as you know, but a little place, buried in the heart of the forest, and it was wonderful at this time to see it crowded with Grand Dukes and Electors and Princes, who thronged round Napoleon like puppies round their master, each hoping that some bone might be thrown to him. There was more German than French to be heard in the street, for those who had helped us in the late war had come to beg for a reward, and those who had opposed us had come to try and escape their punishment. And all the time our little man, with his pale face and his cold, grey eyes, was riding to the hunt every morning, silent and brooding, all of them following in his train, in the hope that some word would escape him. And then, when the humour seized him, he would throw a hundred square miles to that man, or tear as much off the other, round off one kingdom by a river, or cut off another by a chain of mountains. That was how he used to do business, this little artilleryman, whom we had raised so high with our sabres and our bayonets. He was very civil to us always, for he knew where his power came from. We knew also, and showed it by the way in which we carried ourselves. We were agreed, you understand, that he was the finest leader in the world, but we did not forget that he had the finest men to lead.

Well, one day I was seated in my quarters playing cards with young Morat, of the horse chasseurs, when the door opened and in walked Lasalle, who was our Colonel. You know what a fine, swaggering fellow he was, and the sky-blue uniform of the Tenth suited him to a marvel. My faith, we youngsters were so taken by him that we all swore and diced and drank and played the deuce whether

we liked it or no, just that we might resemble our Colonel!
We forgot that it was not because he drank or gambled that
the Emperor was going to make him the head of the light
cavalry, but because he had the surest eye for the nature
of a position or for the strength of a column, and the best
judgment as to when infantry could be broken, or whether
guns were exposed, of any man in the army. We were too
young to understand all that, however, so we waxed our
moustaches and clinked our spurs and let the ferrules of
our scabbards wear out by trailing them along the pavement
in the hope that we should all become Lasalles. When he
came clanking into my quarters, both Morat and I sprang
to our feet.

'My boy,' said he, clapping me on the shoulder, 'the
Emperor wants to see you at four o'clock.'

The room whirled round me at the words, and I had to
lean my hands upon the edge of the card-table.

'What?' I cried. 'The Emperor!'

'Precisely,' said he, smiling at my astonishment.

'But the Emperor does not know of my existence, Colonel,' I protested. 'Why should he send for me?'

'Well, that's just what puzzles me,' cried Lasalle, twirling
his moustache. 'If he wanted the help of a good sabre, why
should he descend to one of my lieutenants when he might
have found all that he needed at the head of the regiment?
However,' he added, clapping me upon the shoulder again
in his hearty fashion, 'every man has his chance. I have had
mine, otherwise I should not be Colonel of the Tenth. I must
not grudge you yours. Forwards, my boy, and may it be the
first step towards changing your busby for a cocked hat.'

It was but two o'clock, so he left me, promising to come
back and to accompany me to the palace. My faith, what a
time I passed, and how many conjectures did I make as to
what it was that the Emperor could want of me! I paced
up and down my little room in a fever of anticipation.
Sometimes I thought that perhaps he had heard of the
guns which we had taken at Austerlitz; but then there
were so many who had taken guns at Austerlitz, and two
years had passed since the battle. Or it might be that he
wished to reward me for my affair with the *aide-de-camp* of

the Russian Emperor. But then again a cold fit would seize me, and I would fancy that he had sent for me to reprimand me. There were a few duels which he might have taken in ill part, and there were one or two little jokes in Paris since the peace.

But, no! I considered the words of Lasalle. 'If he had need of a brave man,' said Lasalle.

It was obvious that my Colonel had some idea of what was in the wind. If he had not known that it was to my advantage, he would not have been so cruel as to congratulate me. My heart glowed with joy as this conviction grew upon me, and I sat down to write to my mother and to tell her that the Emperor was waiting, at that very moment, to have my opinion upon a matter of importance. It made me smile as I wrote it to think that, wonderful as it appeared to me, it would probably only confirm my mother in her opinion of the Emperor's good sense.

At half-past three I heard a sabre come clanking against every step of my wooden stair. It was Lasalle, and with him was a little gentleman, very neatly dressed in black with dapper ruffles and cuffs. We did not know many civilians, we of the army, but, my word, this was one whom we could not afford to ignore! I had only to glance at those twinkling eyes, the comical, upturned nose, and the straight, precise mouth, to know that I was in the presence of the one man in France whom even the Emperor had to consider.

'This is Monsieur Etienne Gerard, Monsieur de Talley-rand,' said Lasalle.

I saluted, and the statesman took me in from the top of my panache to the rowel of my spur, with a glance that played over me like a rapier point.

'Have you explained to the Lieutenant the circumstances under which he is summoned to the Emperor's presence?' he asked, in his dry, creaking voice.

They were such a contrast, these two men, that I could not help glancing from one to the other of them: the little, black, sly politician, and the big, sky-blue hussar, with one fist on his hip and the other on the hilt of his sabre. They both took their seats as I looked, Talleyrand without a sound, and Lasalle with a clash and jingle like a prancing charger.

'It's this way, youngster,' said he, in his brusque fashion;
'I was with the Emperor in his private cabinet this morning
when a note was brought in to him. He opened it, and as
he did so he gave such a start that it fluttered down on to
the floor. I handed it up to him again, but he was staring at
the wall in front of him as if he had seen a ghost. "Fratelli
dell' Ajaccio," he muttered; and then again, "Fratelli dell'
Ajaccio." I don't pretend to know more Italian than a man
can pick up in two campaigns, and I could make nothing
of this. It seemed to me that he had gone out of his mind;
and you would have said so also, Monsieur de Talleyrand,
if you had seen the look in his eyes. He read the note, and
then he sat for half an hour or more without moving.'

'And you?' asked Talleyrand.

'Why, I stood there not knowing what I ought to do.
Presently he seemed to come back to his senses.

'"I suppose, Lasalle," said he, "that you have some
gallant young officers in the Tenth?"'

'"They are all that, sire," I answered.

'"If you had to pick one who was to be depended upon for
action, but who would not think too much—you understand
me, Lasalle—which would you select?" he asked.

'I saw that he needed an agent who would not penetrate
too deeply into his plans.

'"I have one," said I, "who is all spurs and moustaches,
with never a thought beyond women and horses."

'"That is the man I want," said Napoleon. "Bring him
to my private cabinet at four o'clock."

'So, youngster, I came straight away to you at once, and
mind that you do credit to the 10th Hussars.'

I was by no means flattered by the reasons which had led
to my Colonel's choice, and I must have shown as much in
my face, for he roared with laughter and Talleyrand gave a
dry chuckle also.

'Just one word of advice before you go, Monsieur Gerard,'
said he: 'you are now coming into troubled waters, and
you might find a worse pilot than myself. We have none
of us any idea as to what this little affair means, and,
between ourselves, it is very important to us, who have the
destinies of France upon our shoulders, to keep ourselves in

touch with all that goes on. You understand me, Monsieur Gerard?'

I had not the least idea what he was driving at, but I bowed and tried to look as if it was clear to me.

'Act very guardedly, then, and say nothing to anybody,' said Talleyrand. 'Colonel de Lasalle and I will not show ourselves in public with you, but we will await you here, and we will give you our advice when you have told us what has passed between the Emperor and yourself. It is time that you started now, for the Emperor never forgives unpunctuality.'

Off I went on foot to the palace, which was only a hundred paces off. I made my way to the antechamber, where Duroc, with his grand new scarlet and gold coat, was fussing about among the crowd of people who were waiting. I heard him whisper to Monsieur de Caulaincourt that half of them were German Dukes who expected to be made Kings, and the other half German Dukes who expected to be made paupers. Duroc, when he heard my name, showed me straight in, and I found myself in the Emperor's presence.

I had, of course, seen him in camp a hundred times, but I had never been face to face with him before. I have no doubt that if you had met him without knowing in the least who he was, you would simply have said that he was a sallow little fellow with a good forehead and fairly well-turned calves. His tight white cashmere breeches and white stockings showed off his legs to advantage. But even a stranger must have been struck by the singular look of his eyes, which could harden into an expression which would frighten a grenadier. It is said that even Auguereau, who was a man who had never known what fear was, quailed before Napoleon's gaze, at a time, too, when the Emperor was but an unknown soldier. He looked mildly enough at me, however, and motioned me to remain by the door. De Meneval was writing to his dictation, looking up at him between each sentence with his spaniel eyes.

'That will do. You can go,' said the Emperor, abruptly. Then, when the secretary had left the room, he strode across with his hands behind his back, and he looked me up and down without a word. Though he was a small man himself, he was very fond of having fine-looking fellows about him, and so I think that my appearance gave him pleasure. For my own part, I raised one hand to the salute and held the other upon the hilt of my sabre, looking straight ahead of me, as a soldier should.

'Well, Monsieur Gerard,' said he, at last, tapping his forefinger upon one of the brandebourgs of gold braid upon the front of my pelisse, 'I am informed that you are a very deserving young officer. Your Colonel gives me an excellent account of you.'

I wished to make a brilliant reply, but I could think of nothing save Lasalle's phrase that I was all spurs and moustaches, so it ended in my saying nothing at all. The Emperor watched the struggle which must have shown itself upon my features, and when, finally, no answer came he did not appear to be displeased.

'I believe that you are the very man that I want,' said he. 'Brave and clever men surround me upon every side. But a brave man who—' He did not finish his sentence, and for my own part I could not understand what he was driving at. I contented myself with assuring him that he could count upon me to the death.

'You are, as I understand, a good swordsman?' said he.

'Tolerable, sire,' I answered.

'You were chosen by your regiment to fight the champion of the Hussars of Chambarant?' said he.

I was not sorry to find that he knew so much of my exploits.

'My comrades, sire, did me that honour,' said I.

'And for the sake of practice you insulted six fencing masters in the week before your duel?'

'I had the privilege of being out seven times in as many days, sire,' said I.

'And escaped without a scratch?'

'The fencing master of the 23rd Light Infantry touched me on the left elbow, sire.'

'Let us have no more child's play of the sort, monsieur,' he cried, turning suddenly to that cold rage of his which was so appalling. 'Do you imagine that I place veteran soldiers in these positions that you may practise quarte and tierce upon them? How am I to face Europe if my soldiers turn their points upon each other? Another word of your duelling, and I break you between these fingers.'

I saw his plump white hands flash before my eyes as he spoke, and his voice had turned to the most discordant hissing and growling. My word, my skin pringled all over as I listened to him, and I would gladly have changed my position for that of the first man in the steepest and narrowest breach that ever swallowed up a storming party. He turned to the table, drank off a cup of coffee, and then when he faced me again every trace of this storm had vanished, and he wore that singular smile which came from his lips but never from his eyes.

'I have need of your services, Monsieur Gerard,' said he. 'I may be safer with a good sword at my side, and there are reasons why yours should be the one which I select. But first of all I must bind you to secrecy. Whilst I live what passes between us to-day must be known to none but ourselves.'

I thought of Talleyrand and of Lasalle, but I promised.

'In the next place, I do not want your opinions or conjectures, and I wish you to do exactly what you are told.'

I bowed.

'It is your sword that I need, and not your brains. I will do the thinking. Is that clear to you?'

'Yes, sire.'

'You know the Chancellor's Grove, in the forest?'

I bowed.

'You know also the large double fir-tree where the hounds assembled on Tuesday?'

Had he known that I met a girl under it three times a week, he would not have asked me. I bowed once more without remark.

'Very good. You will meet me there at ten o'clock to-night.'

I had got past being surprised at anything which might happen. If he had asked me to take his place upon the Imperial throne I could only have nodded my busby.

'We shall then proceed into the wood together,' said the Emperor. 'You will be armed with a sword, but not with pistols. You must address no remark to me, and I shall say nothing to you. We will advance in silence. You understand?'

'I understand, sire.'

'After a time we shall see a man, or more probably two men, under a certain tree. We shall approach them together. If I signal to you to defend me, you will have your sword ready. If, on the other hand, I speak to these men, you will wait and see what happens. If you are called upon to draw, you must see that neither of them, in the event of there being two, escapes from us. I shall myself assist you.'

'But, sire,' I cried, 'I have no doubt that two would not be too many for my sword; but would it not be better that I should bring a comrade than that you should be forced to join in such a struggle?'

'Ta, ta, ta,' said he. 'I was a soldier before I was an Emperor. Do you think, then, that artillerymen have not swords as well as the hussars? But I ordered you not to argue with me. You will do exactly what I tell you. If swords are once out, neither of these men is to get away alive.'

'They shall not, sire,' said I.

'Very good. I have no more instructions for you. You can go.'

I turned to the door, and then an idea occurring to me I turned.

'I have been thinking, sire—' said I.

He sprang at me with the ferocity of a wild beast. I really thought he would have struck me.

'Thinking!' he cried. 'You, *you*! Do you imagine I chose you out because you could think? Let me hear of your doing such a thing again! You, the one man—but, there! You meet me at the fir-tree at ten o'clock.'

My faith, I was right glad to get out of the room. If I have a good horse under me, and a sword clanking against my stirrup-iron, I know where I am. And in all that relates to green fodder or dry, barley and oats and rye, and the handling of squadrons upon the march, there is no one who can teach me very much. But when I meet a Chamberlain and a Marshal of the Palace, and have to pick my words with an Emperor, and find that everybody hints instead of talking straight out, I feel like a troop-horse who has been

put in a lady's calèche. It is not my trade, all this mincing
and pretending. I have learned the manners of a gentleman,
but never those of a courtier. I was right glad then to get into
the fresh air again, and I ran away up to my quarters like a
schoolboy who has just escaped from the seminary master.

But as I opened the door, the very first thing that my eye
rested upon was a long pair of sky-blue legs with hussar
boots, and a short pair of black ones with knee-breeches
and buckles. They both sprang up together to greet me.

'Well, what news?' they cried, the two of them.

'None,' I answered.

'The Emperor refused to see you?

'No, I have seen him.'

'And what did he say?'

'Monsieur de Talleyrand,' I answered, 'I regret to say
that it is quite impossible for me to tell you anything about
it. I have promised the Emperor.'

'Pooh, pooh, my dear young man,' said he, sidling up to
me, as a cat does when it is about to rub itself against you.
'This is all among the friends, you understand, and goes no
further than these four walls. Besides, the Emperor never
meant to include me in this promise.'

'It is but a minute's walk to the palace, Monsieur de
Talleyrand,' I answered; 'if it would not be troubling you
too much to ask you to step up to it and bring back the
Emperor's written statement that he did not mean to include
you in this promise, I shall be happy to tell you every word
that passed.'

He showed his teeth at me then like the old fox that
he was.

'Monsieur Gerard appears to be a little puffed up,' said
he. 'He is too young to see things in their just proportion. As
he grows older he may understand that it is not always very
discreet for a subaltern of cavalry to give such very abrupt
refusals.'

I did not know what to say to this, but Lasalle came to
my aid in his downright fashion.

'The lad is quite right,' said he. 'If I had known that there
was a promise I should not have questioned him. You know
very well, Monsieur de Talleyrand, that if he had answered

you, you would have laughed in your sleeve and thought as much about him as I think of the bottle when the burgundy is gone. As for me, I promise you that the Tenth would have had no room for him, and that we should have lost our best swordsman if I had heard him give up the Emperor's secret.'

But the statesman became only the more bitter when he saw that I had the support of my Colonel.

'I have heard, Colonel de Lasalle,' said he, with an icy dignity, 'that your opinion is of great weight upon the subject of light cavalry. Should I have occasion to seek information about that branch of the army, I shall be very happy to apply to you. At present, however, the matter concerns diplomacy, and you will permit me to form my own views upon that question. As long as the welfare of France and the safety of the Emperor's person are largely committed to my care, I will use every means in my power to secure them, even if it should be against the Emperor's own temporary wishes. I have the honour, Colonel de Lasalle, to wish you a very good day!'

He shot a most unamiable glance in my direction, and, turning upon his heel, he walked with little, quick, noiseless steps out of the room.

I could see from Lasalle's face that he did not at all relish finding himself at enmity with the powerful Minister. He rapped out an oath or two, and then, catching up his sabre and his cap, he clattered away down the stairs. As I looked out of the window I saw the two of them, the big blue man and the little black one, going up the street together. Talleyrand was walking very rigidly, and Lasalle was waving his hands and talking, so I suppose that he was trying to make his peace.

The Emperor had told me not to think, and I endeavoured to obey him. I took up the cards from the table where Morat had left them, and I tried to work out a few combinations at écarté. But I could not remember which were trumps, and I threw them under the table in despair. Then I drew my sabre and practised giving point until I was weary, but it was all of no use at all. My mind *would* work, in spite of myself. At ten o'clock I was to meet the Emperor in the forest. Of all extraordinary combinations of events in the whole world, surely this was the last which would have occurred to me when I rose from my couch that morning. But the responsibility – the dreadful responsibility! It was all upon my shoulders. There was no one to halve it with me. It made me cold all over. Often as I have faced death upon the battlefield, I have never known what real fear was until that moment. But then I considered that after all I could but do my best like a brave and honourable gentleman, and above all obey the orders which I had received, to the very letter. And, if all went well, this would surely be the foundation of my fortunes. Thus, swaying between my fears and my hopes, I spent the long, long evening until it was time for me to keep my appointment.

I put on my military overcoat, as I did not know how much of the night I might have to spend in the woods, and I fastened my sword outside it. I pulled off my hussar boots also, and wore a pair of shoes and gaiters, that I might be lighter upon my feet. Then I stole out of my quarters and made for the forest, feeling very much easier in my mind, for I am always at my best when the time of thought has passed and the moment for action arrived.

I passed the barracks of the Chasseurs of the Guards, and the line of cafés all filled with uniforms. I caught a glimpse as I went by of the blue and gold of some of my comrades, amid the swarm of dark infantry coats and the light green of the Guides. There they sat, sipping their wine and smoking their cigars, little dreaming what their comrade had on hand. One of them, the chief of my squadron, caught sight of me in the lamplight, and came shouting after me into the street. I hurried on, however, pretending not to hear him, so he, with a curse at my deafness, went back at last to his wine bottle.

It is not very hard to get into the forest at Fontainebleau. The scattered trees steal their way into the very streets, like the tirailleurs in front of a column. I turned into a path, which led to the edge of the woods, and then I pushed rapidly forward towards the old fir-tree. It was a place which, as I have hinted, I had my own reasons for knowing well, and I could only thank the Fates that it was not one of the nights upon which Léonie would be waiting for me. The poor child would have died of terror at sight of the Emperor. He might have been too harsh with her – and worse still, he might have been too kind.

There was a half moon shining, and, as I came up to our trysting-place, I saw that I was not the first to arrive. The Emperor was pacing up and down, his hands behind him and his face sunk somewhat forward upon his breast. He wore a grey great-coat with a capote over his head. I had seen him in such a dress in our winter campaign in Poland, and it was said that he used it because the hood was such an excellent disguise. He was always fond, whether in the camp or in Paris, of walking round at night, and overhearing the talk in the cabarets or round the fires. His figure, however, and his way of carrying his head and his hands, were so well known that he was always recognised, and then the talkers would just say whatever they thought would please him best.

My first thought was that he would be angry with me for having kept him waiting, but as I approached him, we heard the big church clock of Fontainebleau clang out the hour of ten. It was evident, therefore, that it was he who was too soon, and not I too late. I remembered his order that I should make no remark, so contented myself with halting within four paces of him, clicking my spurs together, grounding my sabre, and saluting. He glanced at me, and then without a word he turned and walked slowly through the forest, I keeping always about the same distance behind him. Once or twice he seemed to me to look apprehensively to right and to left, as if he feared that someone was observing us. I looked also, but although I have the keenest sight, it was quite impossible to see anything except the ragged patches of moonshine between the great black shadows of the trees. My ears are as quick as my eyes, and once or twice I thought that I heard a twig crack; but you know how many sounds there are in a forest at night, and how difficult it is even to say what direction they come from.

We walked for rather more than a mile, and I knew exactly what our destination was, long before we got there. In the centre of one of the glades there is the shattered stump of what must at some time have been a most gigantic tree. It is called the Abbot's Beech, and there are so many ghostly stories about it, that I know many a brave soldier who would not care about mounting sentinel over it. However, I cared as little for such folly as the Emperor did, so we crossed the glade and made straight for the old broken trunk. As we approached, I saw that two men were waiting for us beneath it.

When I first caught sight of them they were standing rather behind it, as if they were not anxious to be seen, but as we came nearer they emerged from its shadow and walked forward to meet us. The Emperor glanced back at me, and slackened his pace a little, so that I came within arm's length of him. You may think that I had my hilt well to the front, and that I had a very good look at these two people who were approaching us. The one was tall, remarkably so, and of a very spare frame, while the other was rather below the usual height, and had a brisk, determined way of walking. They each wore black cloaks, which were slung right across their figures, and hung down upon one side, like the mantles of Murat's dragoons. They had flat black caps, like those which I have since seen in Spain, which threw their faces into darkness, though I could see the gleam of their eyes from beneath them. With the moon behind them and their long black shadows walking in front, they were such figures as one might expect to meet at night near the Abbot's Beech. I can remember that they had a stealthy way of moving, and that as they approached, the moonshine formed two white diamonds between their legs and the legs of their shadows.

The Emperor had paused, and these two strangers came to a stand also within a few paces of us. I had drawn up close to my companion's elbow, so that the four of us were facing each other without a word spoken. My eyes were particularly fixed upon the taller one, because he was slightly the nearer to me, and I became certain as I watched him that he was in the last state of nervousness. His lean figure was quivering all over, and I heard a quick, thin panting like that of a tired dog. Suddenly one of them gave a short, hissing signal. The tall man bent his back and his knees like a diver about to spring, but before he could move, I had jumped with drawn sabre in front of him. At the same instant the smaller man bounded past me, and buried a long poniard in the Emperor's heart.

My God! the horror of that moment! It is a marvel that I did not drop dead myself. As in a dream, I saw the grey coat whirl convulsively round, and caught a glimpse in the moonlight of three inches of red point which jutted out from between the shoulders. Then down he fell with a dead man's gasp upon the grass, and the assassin, leaving his weapon buried in his victim, threw up both his hands and shrieked with joy. But I—I drove my sword through his midriff with such frantic force, that the mere blow of the hilt against the end of his breast-bone sent him six paces before he fell, and left my reeking blade ready for the other. I sprang round upon him with such a lust for blood upon me as I had never felt, and never have felt, in all my days. As I turned, a dagger flashed before my eyes, and I felt the cold wind of it pass my neck and the villain's wrist jar upon my shoulder. I shortened my sword, but he winced away from me, and an instant afterwards was in full flight, bounding like a deer across the glade in the moonlight.

But he was not to escape me thus. I knew that the murderer's poniard had done its work. Young as I was, I had seen enough of war to know a mortal blow. I paused but for an instant to touch the cold hand.

'Sire! Sire!' I cried, in an agony; and then as no sound came back and nothing moved, save an ever-widening dark circle in the moonlight, I knew that all was indeed over. I sprang madly to my feet, threw off my great-coat, and ran at the top of my speed after the remaining assassin.

Ah, how I blessed the wisdom which had caused me to come in shoes and gaiters! And the happy thought which had thrown off my coat. He could not get rid of his mantle, this wretch, or else he was too frightened to think of it. So it was that I gained upon him from the beginning. He must have been out of his wits, for he never tried to bury himself in the darker parts of the woods, but he flew on from glade to glade, until he came to the heath-land which leads up to the great Fontainebleau quarry. There I had him in full sight, and knew that he could not escape me. He ran well, it is true—ran as a coward runs when his life is at stake. But I ran as Destiny runs when it gets behind a man's heels. Yard by yard I drew in upon him. He was rolling and staggering. I could hear the rasping and crackling of his breath. The great gulf of the quarry suddenly yawned in front of his path, and glancing at me over his shoulder, he gave a shriek of despair. The next instant he had vanished from my sight.

Vanished utterly, you understand. I rushed to the spot, and gazed down into the black abyss. Had he hurled himself over? I had almost made up my mind that he had done so, when a gentle sound rising and falling came out of the darkness beneath me. It was his breathing once more, and it showed me where he must be. He was hiding in the tool-house.

At the edge of the quarry and beneath the summit there is a small platform upon which stands a wooden hut for the use of the labourers. It was into this, then, that he had darted. Perhaps he had thought, the fool, that, in the darkness, I would not venture to follow him. He little knew Etienne Gerard. With a spring I was on the platform, with another I was through the doorway, and then, hearing him in the corner, I hurled myself down upon the top of him.

He fought like a wild cat, but he never had a chance with his shorter weapon. I think that I must have transfixed him with that first mad lunge, for, though he struck and struck, his blows had no power in them, and presently his dagger tinkled down upon the floor. When I was sure that he was dead, I rose up and passed out into the moonlight. I climbed up on to the heath again, and wandered across it as nearly out of my mind as a man could be. With the blood singing in my ears, and my naked sword still clutched in my hand, I walked aimlessly on until, looking round me, I found that I had come as far as the glade of the Abbot's Beech, and saw in the distance that gnarled stump which must ever be associated with the most terrible moment of my life. I sat down upon a fallen trunk with my sword across my knees and my head between my hands, and I tried to think about what had happened and what would happen in the future.

The Emperor had committed himself to my care. The

Emperor was dead. Those were the two thoughts which clanged in my head, until I had no room for any other ones. He had come with me and he was dead. I had done what he had ordered when living. I had revenged him when dead. But what of all that? The world would look upon me as responsible. They might even look upon me as the assassin. What could I prove? What witnesses had I? Might I not have been the accomplice of these wretches? Yes, yes, I was eternally dishonoured—the lowest, most despicable creature in all France. This then was the end of my fine military ambitions—of the hopes of my mother. I laughed bitterly at the thought. And what was I to do now? Was I to go into Fontainebleau, to wake up the palace, and to inform them that the great Emperor had been murdered within a pace of me? I could not do it – no, I could not do it! There was but one course for an honourable gentleman whom Fate had placed in so cruel a position. I would fall upon my dishonoured sword, and so share, since I could not avert, the Emperor's fate. I rose with my nerves strung to this last piteous deed, and as I did so, my eyes fell upon something which struck the breath from my lips. The Emperor was standing before me!

He was not more than ten yards off, with the moon shining straight upon his cold, pale face. He wore his grey overcoat, but the hood was turned back, and the front open, so that I could see the green coat of the Guides, and the white breeches. His hands were clasped behind his back, and his chin sunk forward upon his breast, in the way that was usual with him.

'Well,' said he in his hardest and most abrupt voice, 'what account do you give of yourself?'

I believe that, if he had stood in silence for another minute, my brain would have given way. But those sharp military accents were exactly what I needed to bring me to myself. Living or dead, here was the Emperor standing before me and asking me questions. I sprang to the salute.

'You have killed one, I see,' said he, jerking his head towards the beech.

'Yes, sire.'

'And the other escaped?'

'No, sire, I killed him also.'

'What!' he cried. 'Do I understand that you have killed them both?' He approached me as he spoke with a smile which set his teeth gleaming in the moonlight.

'One body lies there, sire,' I answered. 'The other is in the tool-house at the quarry.'

'Then the Brothers of Ajaccio are no more,' he cried, and after a pause, as if speaking to himself: 'The shadow has passed me for ever.' Then he bent forward and laid his hand upon my shoulder.

'You have done very well, my young friend,' said he. 'You have lived up to your reputation.'

He was flesh and blood, then, this Emperor. I could feel the little, plump palm that rested upon me. And yet I could not get over what I had seen with my own eyes, and so I stared at him in such bewilderment that he broke once more into one of his smiles.

'No, no, Monsieur Gerard,' said he, 'I am not a ghost, and you have not seen me killed. You will come here, and all will be clear to you.'

He turned as he spoke, and led the way towards the great beech stump.

The bodies were still lying upon the ground, and two men were standing beside them. As we approached I saw from the turbans that they were Roustem and Mustafa; the two Mameluke servants. The Emperor paused when he came to the grey figure upon the ground, and turning back the hood which shrouded the features, he showed a face which was very different from his own.

'Here lies a faithful servant who has given up his life for his master,' said he. 'Monsieur de Goudin resembles me in figure and in manner, as you must admit.'

What a delirium of joy came upon me when these few words made everything clear to me. He smiled again as he saw the delight which urged me to throw my arms round him and to embrace him, but he moved a step away, as if he had divined my impulse.

'You are unhurt?' he asked.

'I am unhurt, sire. But in another minute I should in my despair—'

'Tut, tut!' he interrupted. 'You did very well. He should himself have been more on his guard. I saw everything which passed.'

'You saw it, sire!'

'You did not hear me follow you through the wood, then? I hardly lost sight of you from the moment that you left your quarters until poor De Goudin fell. The counterfeit Emperor was in front of you and the real one behind. You will now escort me back to the palace.'

He whispered an order to his Mamelukes, who saluted in silence and remained where they were standing. For my part, I followed the Emperor with my pelisse bursting with pride. My word, I have always carried myself as a hussar should, but Lasalle himself never strutted and swung his dolman as I did that night! Who should clink his spurs and clatter his sabre if it were not I—I, Etienne Gerard – the confidant of the Emperor, the chosen swordsman of the light cavalry, the man who slew the would-be assassins of Napoleon? But he noticed my bearing and turned upon me like a blight.

'Is that the way to carry yourself on a secret mission?' he hissed, with that cold glare in his eyes. 'Is it thus that you will make your comrades believe that nothing remarkable has occurred? Have done with this nonsense, monsieur, or you will find yourself transferred to the sappers, where you would have harder work and duller plumage.'

That was the way with the Emperor. If ever he thought that anyone might have a claim upon him, he took the first opportunity to show him the gulf that lay between. I saluted and was silent, but I must confess to you that it hurt me after all that had passed between us. He led on to the palace, where we passed through the side door and up into his own cabinet. There were a couple of grenadiers at the staircase, and their eyes started out from under their fur caps, I promise you, when they saw a young lieutenant of hussars going up to the Emperor's room at midnight. I stood by the door, as I had done in the afternoon, while he flung himself down in an arm-chair, and remained silent so long that it seemed to me that he had forgotten all about me. I ventured at last upon a slight cough to remind him.

'Ah, Monsieur Gerard,' said he, 'you are very curious, no doubt, as to the meaning of all this?'

'I am quite content, sire, if it is your pleasure not to tell me,' I answered.

'Ta, ta, ta,' said he, impatiently. 'These are only words. The moment that you were outside that door you would begin making inquiries about what it means. In two days your brother officers would know about it, in three days it would be all over Fountainebleau, and it would be in Paris on the fourth. Now, if I tell you enough to appease your curiosity, there is some reasonable hope that you may be able to keep the matter to yourself.'

He did not understand me, this Emperor, and yet I could only bow and be silent.

'A few words will make it clear to you,' said he, speaking very swiftly and pacing up and down the room. 'They were Corsicans, these two men. I had known them in my youth. We had belonged to the same society—Brothers of Ajaccio, as we called ourselves. It was founded in the old Paoli days, you understand, and we had some strict rules of our own which were not infringed with impunity.'

A very grim look came over his face as he spoke, and it seemed to me that all that was French had gone out of him, and that it was the pure Corsican, the man of strong passions and of strange revenges, who stood before me. His memory had gone back to those early days of his, and for five minutes, wrapped in thought, he paced up and down the room with his quick little tiger steps. Then with an impatient wave of his hands he came back to his palace and to me.

'The rules of such a society,' he continued, 'are all very well for a private citizen. In the old days there was no more loyal brother than I. But circumstances change, and it would be neither for my welfare nor for that of France that I should now submit myself to them. They wanted to hold me to it, and so brought their fate upon their own heads. These were the two chiefs of the order, and they had come from Corsica to summon me to meet them at the spot which they named. I knew what such a summons meant. No man had ever returned from obeying one. On the other hand, if I did not go, I was sure that disaster would follow. I am a brother myself, you remember, and I know their ways.'

Again there came that hardening of his mouth and cold glitter of his eyes.

'You perceive my dilemma, Monsieur Gerard,' said he. 'How would you have acted yourself, under such circumstances?'

'Given the word to the 10th Hussars, sire,' I cried. 'Patrols could have swept the woods from end to end, and brought these two rascals to your feet.'

He smiled, but he shook his head.

'I had very excellent reasons why I did not wish them taken alive,' said he. 'You can understand that an assassin's tongue might be as dangerous a weapon as an assassin's dagger. I will not disguise from you that I wished to avoid scandal at all cost. That was why I ordered you to take no pistols with you. That also is why my Mamelukes will remove all traces of the affair, and nothing more will be heard about it. I thought of all possible plans, and I am convinced that I selected the best one. Had I sent more than one guard with De Goudin into the woods, then the brothers would not have appeared. They would not change their plans or miss their chance for the sake of a single man. It was Colonel Lasalle's accidental presence at the moment when I received the summons which led to my choosing one of his hussars for the mission. I selected you, Monsieur Gerard, because I wanted a man who could handle a sword, and who would not pry more deeply into the affair than I desired. I trust that, in this respect, you will justify my choice as well as you have done in your bravery and skill.'

'Sire,' I answered, 'you may rely upon it.'

'As long as I live,' said he, 'you never open your lips upon this subject.'

'I dismiss it entirely from my mind, sire. I will efface it from my recollection as if it had never been. I will promise you to go out of your cabinet at this moment exactly as I was when I entered it at four o'clock.'

'You cannot do that,' said the Emperor, smiling. 'You were a lieutenant at that time. You will permit me, Captain, to wish you a very good-night.'

FIVE

How the Brigadier Came
to the Castle of Gloom

February 1807, as stated. The Duroc of this exploit
should not be identified with the soldier-courtier Géraud
Duroc, who appears in other adventures and was Napoleon's steward and one of his closest friends; that Duroc
married the daughter of a Spanish financier and was
killed in May 1813 at Reichenbach (the German one, as
opposed to the Swiss waterfall which would account for
another illustrious character in Conan Doyle's writings).

You do very well, my friends, to treat me with some little rev-
erence, for in honouring me you are honouring both France
and yourselves. It is not merely an old, grey-moustached
officer whom you see eating his omelette or draining his
glass, but it is a piece of history, and of the most glorious
history which our own or any country has ever had. In me
you see one of the last of those wonderful men, the men
who were veterans when they were yet boys, who learned to
use a sword earlier than a razor, and who during a hundred
battles had never once let the enemy see the colour of their
knapsacks. For twenty years we were teaching Europe how
to fight, and even when they had learned their lesson it
was only the thermometer, and never the bayonet, which
could break the Grand Army down. Berlin, Naples, Vienna,
Madrid, Lisbon, Moscow—we stabled our horses in them
all. Yes, my friends, I say again that you do well to send
your children to me with flowers, for these ears have heard
the trumpet calls of France, and these eyes have seen her
standards in lands where they may never be seen again.

Even now, when I doze in my arm-chair, I can see
those great warriors stream before me—the green-jacketed
chasseurs, the giant cuirassiers, Poniatowsky's lancers, the
white-mantled dragoons, the nodding bearskins of the horse

grenadiers. And then there comes the thick, low rattle of the drums, and through wreaths of dust and smoke I see the line of high bonnets, the row of brown faces, the swing and toss of the long, red plumes amid the sloping lines of steel. And there rides Ney with his red head, and Lefebvre with his bulldog jaw, and Lannes with his Gascon swagger; and then amidst the gleam of brass and the flaunting feathers I catch a glimpse of *him*, the man with the pale smile, the rounded shoulders, and the far-off eyes. There is an end of my sleep, my friends, for up I spring from my chair, with a cracked voice calling and a silly hand outstretched, so that Madame Titaux has one more laugh at the old fellow who lives among the shadows.

Although I was a full Chief of the Brigade when the wars came to an end, and had every hope of soon being made a General of Division, it is still rather to my earlier days that I turn when I wish to talk of the glories and the trials of a soldier's life. For you will understand that when an officer has so many men and horses under him, he has his mind full of recruits and remounts, fodder and farriers, and quarters, so that even when he is not in the face of the enemy, life is a very serious matter for him. But when he is only a lieutenant or a captain, he has nothing heavier than his epaulettes upon his shoulders, so that he can clink his spurs and swing his dolman, drain his glass and kiss his girl, thinking of nothing save of enjoying a gallant life. That is the time when he is likely to have adventures, and it is most often to that time that I shall turn in the stories which I may have for you. So it will be to-night when I tell you of my visit to the Castle of Gloom; of the strange mission of Sub-Lieutenant Duroc, and of the horrible affair of the man who was once known as Jean Carabin, and afterwards as the Baron Straubenthal.

You must know, then, that in the February of 1807, immediately after the taking of Danzig, Major Legendre and I were commissioned to bring four hundred remounts from Prussia into Eastern Poland.

The hard weather, and especially the great battle at Eylau, had killed so many of the horses that there was some danger of our beautiful Tenth of Hussars becoming a battalion of light infantry. We knew, therefore, both the Major and I, that we should be very welcome at the front. We did not advance very rapidly, however, for the snow was deep, the roads detestable, and we had but twenty returning invalids to assist us. Besides, it is impossible, when you have a daily change of forage, and sometimes none at all, to move horses faster than a walk. I am aware that in the story-books the cavalry whirls past at the maddest of gallops; but for my own part, after twelve campaigns, I should be very satisfied to know that my brigade could always walk upon the march and trot in the presence of the enemy. This I say of the hussars and chausseurs, mark you, so that it is far more the case with cuirassiers or dragoons.

For myself I am fond of horses, and to have four hundred of them, of every age and shade and character, all under my own hands, was a very great pleasure to me. They were from Pomerania for the most part, though some were from Normandy and some from Alsace, and it amused us to notice that they differed in character as much as the people of those provinces. We observed also, what I have often proved since, that the nature of a horse can be told by his colour, from the coquettish light bay full of fancies and nerves, to the hardy chestnut, and from the docile roan to the pig-headed rusty-black. All this has nothing in the world to do with my story, but how is an officer of cavalry to get on with his tale when he finds four hundred horses waiting for him at the outset? It is my habit, you see, to talk of that which interests myself, and so I hope that I may interest you.

We crossed the Vistula opposite Marienwerder, and had got as far as Riesenberg, when Major Legendre came into my room in the post-house with an open paper in his hand.

'You are to leave me,' said he, with despair upon his face.

It was no very great grief to me to do that, for he was, if I may say so, hardly worthy to have such a subaltern. I saluted, however, in silence.

'It is an order from General Lasalle,' he continued; 'you are to proceed to Rossel instantly, and to report yourself at the headquarters of the regiment.'

No message could have pleased me better. I was already very well thought of by my superior officers, although I may say that none of them had quite done me justice. It was evident to me, therefore, that this sudden order meant that the regiment was about to see service once more, and that Lasalle understood how incomplete my squadron would be without me. It is true that it came at an inconvenient moment, for the keeper of the post-house had a daughter—one of those ivory-skinned, black haired Polish girls—whom I had hoped to have some further talk with. Still, it is not for the pawn to argue when the fingers of the player move him from the square; so down I went, saddled my big black charger, Rataplan, and set off instantly upon my lonely journey.

My word, it was a treat for those poor Poles and Jews, who have so little to brighten their dull lives, to see such a picture as that before their doors. The frosty morning air made Rataplan's great black limbs and the beautiful curves of his back and sides gleam and shimmer with every gambade. As for me, the rattle of hoofs upon a road, and the jingle of bridle chains which comes with every toss of a saucy head, would even now set my blood dancing though my veins. You may think, then, how I carried myself in my five-and-twentieth year—I, Etienne Gerard, the picked horseman and surest blade in the ten regiments of hussars. Blue was our colour in the Tenth— a sky-blue dolman and pelisse with a scarlet front—and it was said of us in the army that we could set a whole population running, the women towards us, and the men away. There were bright eyes in the Riesenberg windows that morning, which seemed to beg me to tarry; but what can a soldier do, save to kiss his hand and shake his bridle as he rides upon his way?

It was a bleak season to ride through the poorest and ugliest country in Europe, but there was a cloudless sky above, and a bright, cold sun, which shimmered on the huge snowfields. My breath reeked into the frosty air, and Rataplan sent up two feathers of steam from his nostrils, while the icicles drooped from the side-irons of his bit. I let him trot to warm his limbs, while for my own part I had too much to think of to give much heed to the cold. To north and south stretched the great plains, mottled over with dark clumps of fir and lighter patches of larch. A few cottages peeped out here and there, but it was only three months since the Grand Army had passed that way, and you know what that meant to a country. The Poles were our friends, it was true, but out of a hundred thousand men, only the Guard had waggons, and the rest had to live as best they might. It did not surprise me, therefore, to see no signs of cattle and no smoke from the silent houses. A weal had been left across the country where the great host had passed, and it was said that even the rats were starved wherever the Emperor had led his men.

By midday I had got as far as the village of Saalfeldt, but as I was on the direct road for Osterode, where the Emperor was wintering, and also for the main camp of the seven divisions of infantry, the highway was choked with carriages and carts. What with artillery caissons and waggons and couriers, and the ever-thickening stream of recruits and stragglers, it seemed to me that it would be a very long time before I should join my comrades. The plains, however, were five feet deep in snow, so there was nothing for it but to plod upon our way. It was with joy, therefore, that I found a second road which branched away from the other, trending through a fir-wood towards the north. There was a small auberge at the cross-roads, and a patrol of the Third Hussars of Conflans—the very regiment of which I was afterwards colonel—were mounting their horses at the door. On the steps stood their officer, a slight, pale young man, who looked more like a young priest from a seminary than a leader of the devil-may-care rascals before him.

'Good day, sir,' said he, seeing that I pulled up my horse.

'Good-day,' I answered. 'I am Lieutenant Etienne Gerard, of the Tenth.'

I could see by his face that he had heard of me. Everybody had heard of me since my duel with the six fencing-masters. My manner, however, served to put him at his ease with me.

'I am Sub-Lieutenant Duroc, of the Third,' said he.

'Newly joined?' I asked.

'Last week.'

I had thought as much, from his white face and from the

way in which he let his men lounge upon their horses. It was
not so long, however, since I had learned myself what it was
like when a schoolboy has to give orders to veteran troopers.
It made me blush, I remember, to shout abrupt commands
to men who had seen more battles than I had years, and it
would have come more natural for me to say, 'With your
permission, we shall now wheel into line,' or, 'If you think
it best, we shall trot.' I did not think the less of the lad,
therefore, when I observed that his men were somewhat out
of hand, but I gave them a glance which stiffened them in
their saddles.

'May I ask, monsieur, whether you are going by this
northern road?' I asked.

'My orders are to patrol it as far as Arensdorf,' said he.

'Then I will, with your permission, ride so far with
you,' said I. 'It is very clear that the longer way will be
the faster.'

So it proved, for this road led away from the army into a
country which was given over to Cossacks and marauders,
and it was as bare as the other was crowded. Duroc and I
rode in front, with our six troopers clattering in the rear.
He was a good boy, this Duroc, with his head full of the
nonsense that they teach at St Cyr, knowing more about
Alexander and Pompey than how to mix a horse's fodder
or care for a horse's feet. Still, he was, as I have said,
a good boy, unspoiled as yet by the camp. It pleased me
to hear him prattle away about his sister Marie and about
his mother in Amiens. Presently we found ourselves at the
village of Hayenau. Duroc rode up to the post-house and
asked to see the master.

'Can you tell me,' said he, 'whether the man who calls
himself the Baron Straubenthal lives in these parts?'

The postmaster shook his head, and we rode upon
our way.

I took no notice of this, but when, at the next village, my
comrade repeated the same question, with the same result, I
could not help asking who this Baron Straubenthal might be.

'He is a man,' said Duroc, with a sudden flush upon his
boyish face, 'to whom I have a very important message to
convey.'

Well, this was not satisfactory, but there was something in my companion's manner which told me that any further questioning would be distasteful to him. I said nothing more, therefore, but Duroc would still ask every peasant whom we met whether he could give him any news of the Baron Straubenthal.

For my own part I was endeavouring, as an officer of light cavalry should, to form an idea of the lay of the country, to note the course of the streams, and to mark the places where there should be fords. Every step was taking us farther from the camp round the flanks of which we were travelling. Far to the south a few plumes of grey smoke in the frosty air marked the position of some of our outposts. To the north, however, there was nothing between ourselves and the Russian winter quarters. Twice on the extreme horizon I caught a glimpse of the glitter of steel, and pointed it out to my companion. It was too distant for us to tell whence it came, but we had little doubt that it was from the lance-heads of marauding Cossacks.

The sun was just setting when we rode over a low hill and saw a small village upon our right, and on our left a high black castle, which jutted out from amongst the pine-woods. A farmer with his cart was approaching us— a matted-haired, downcast fellow, in a sheepskin jacket.

'What village is this?' asked Duroc.

'It is Arensdorf,' he answered, in his barbarous German dialect.

'Then here I am to stay the night,' said my young companion. Then, turning to the farmer, he asked his eternal question, 'Can you tell me where the Baron Straubenthal lives?'

'Why, it is he who owns the Castle of Gloom,' said the farmer, pointing to the dark turrets over the distant fir forest.

Duroc gave a shout like the sportsman who sees his game rising in front of him. The lad seemed to have gone off his head—his eyes shining, his face deathly white, and such a grim set about his mouth as made the farmer shrink away from him. I can see him now, leaning forward on his brown horse, with his eager gaze fixed upon the great black tower.

'Why do you call it the Castle of Gloom?' I asked.

'Well, it's the name it bears upon the countryside,' said the farmer. 'By all accounts there have been some black doings up yonder. It's not for nothing that the wickedest man in Poland has been living there these fourteen years past.'

'A Polish nobleman?' I asked.

'Nay, we breed no such men in Poland,' he answered.

'A Frenchman, then?' cried Duroc.

'They say that he came from France.'

'And with red hair?'

'As red as a fox.'

'Yes, yes, it is my man,' cried my companion, quivering all over in his excitement. 'It is the hand of Providence which has led me here. Who can say that there is not justice in this world? Come, Monsieur Gerard, for I must see the men safely quartered before I can attend to this private matter.'

He spurred on his horse, and ten minutes later we were at the door of the inn of Arensdorf, where his men were to find their quarters for the night.

Well, all this was no affair of mine, and I could not imagine what the meaning of it might be. Rossel was still far off, but I determined to ride on for a few hours and take my chance of some wayside barn in which I could find shelter for Rataplan and myself. I had mounted my horse, therefore, after tossing off a cup of wine, when young Duroc came running out of the door and laid his hand upon my knee.

'Monsieur Gerard,' he panted, 'I beg of you not to abandon me like this!'

'My good sir,' said I, 'if you would tell me what is the matter and what you would wish me to do, I should be better able to tell you if I could be of any assistance to you.'

'You can be of the very greatest,' he cried. 'Indeed, from all that I have heard of you, Monsieur Gerard, you are the one man whom I should wish to have by my side to-night.'

'You forget that I am riding to join my regiment.'

'You cannot, in any case, reach it to-night. To-morrow will bring you to Rossel. By staying with me you will confer the very greatest kindness upon me, and you will aid me in a matter which concerns my own honour and the honour of my family. I am compelled, however, to confess to you that some personal danger may possibly be involved.'

It was a crafty thing for him to say. Of course, I sprang from Rataplan's back and ordered the groom to lead him back into the stables.

'Come into the inn,' said I, 'and let me know exactly what it is that you wish me to do.'

He led the way into a sitting-room, and fastened the door lest we should be interrupted. He was a well-grown lad, and as he stood in the glare of the lamp, with the light beating upon his earnest face and upon his uniform of silver grey, which suited him to a marvel, I felt my heart warm towards him. Without going so far as to say that he carried himself as I had done at his age, there was at least similarity enough to make me feel in sympathy with him.

'I can explain it all in a few words,' said he. 'If I have not already satisfied your very natural curiosity, it is because the subject is so painful a one to me that I can hardly bring myself to allude to it. I cannot, however, ask for your assistance without explaining to you exactly how the matter lies.

'You must know, then, that my father was the well-known banker, Christophe Duroc, who was murdered by the people during the September massacres. As you are aware, the mob took possession of the prisons, chose three so-called judges to pass sentence upon the unhappy aristocrats, and then tore them to pieces when they were passed out into the street. My father had been a benefactor of the poor all his life. There were many to plead for him. He had the fever, too, and was carried in, half-dead, upon a blanket. Two of the judges were in favour of acquitting him; the third, a young Jacobin, whose huge body and brutal mind had made him a leader among these wretches, dragged him, with his own hands, from the litter, kicked him again and again with his heavy boots, and hurled him out of the door, where in an instant he was torn limb from limb under circumstances which are too horrible for me to describe. This, as you perceive, was murder, even under their own unlawful laws, for two of their own judges had pronounced in my father's favour.

'Well, when the days of order came back again, my elder brother began to make inquiries about this man. I was only a child then, but it was a family matter, and it was discussed in my presence. The fellow's name was Carabin. He was one of Sansterre's Guard, and a noted duellist. A foreign lady named the Baroness Straubenthal having been dragged before the Jacobins, he had gained her liberty for her on the promise that she with her money and estates should be his. He had married her, taken her name and title, and escaped out of France at the time of the fall of Robespierre. What had become of him we had no means of learning.

'You will think, doubtless, that it would be easy for us to find him, since we had both his name and his title. You must remember, however, that the Revolution left us without money, and that without money such a search is very difficult. Then came the Empire, and it became more difficult still, for, as you are aware, the Emperor considered that the 18th Brumaire brought all accounts to a settlement, and that on that day a veil had been drawn across the past. None the less, we kept our own family story and our own family plans.

'My brother joined the army, and passed with it through all Southern Europe, asking everywhere for the Baron Straubenthal. Last October he was killed at Jena, with his mission still unfulfilled. Then it became my turn, and I have the good fortune to hear of the very man of whom I am in search at one of the first Polish villages which I have to visit, and within a fortnight of joining my regiment. And then, to make the matter even better, I find myself in the company of one whose name is never mentioned throughout the army save in connection with some daring and generous deed.'

This was all very well, and I listened to it with the greatest interest, but I was none the clearer as to what young Duroc wished me to do.

'How can I be of service to you?' I asked.

'By coming up with me.'

'To the Castle?'

'Precisely.'

'When?'

'At once.'

'But what do you intend to do?'

'I shall know what to do. But I wish you to be with me, all the same.'

Well, it was never in my nature to refuse an adventure, and, besides, I had every sympathy with the lad's feelings. It is very well to forgive one's enemies, but one wishes to give them something to forgive also. I held out my hand to him, therefore.

'I must be on my way for Rossel tomorrow morning, but to-night I am yours,' said I.

We left our troopers in snug quarters, and, as it was but a mile to the Castle, we did not disturb our horses. To tell the truth, I hate to see a cavalry man walk, and I hold that just as he is the most gallant thing upon earth when he has his saddle-flaps between his knees, so he is the most clumsy when he has to loop up his sabre and his sabre-tasche in one hand and turn in his toes for fear of catching the rowels of his spurs. Still, Duroc and I were of the age when one can carry things off, and I dare swear that no woman at least would have quarrelled with the appearance of the two young hussars, one in blue and one in grey, who set out that night from the Arensdorf post-house. We both carried our swords, and for my own part I slipped a pistol from my holster into the inside of my pelisse, for it seemed to me that there might be some wild work before us.

The track which led to the Castle wound through pitch-black fir-wood, where we could see nothing save the ragged patch of stars above our head. Presently, however, it opened up, and there was the Castle right in front of us, about as far as a carbine would carry. It was a huge, uncouth place, and bore every mark of being exceedingly old, with turrets at every corner, and a square keep on the side which was nearest to us. In all its great shadow there was no sign of light save for a single window, and no sound came from it. To me there was something awful in its size and its silence, which corresponded so well with its sinister name. My companion pressed on eagerly, and I followed him along the ill-kept path which led to the gate.

There was no bell or knocker upon the great, iron-studded door, and it was only by pounding with the hilts of our sabres that we could attract attention. A thin, hawk-faced man, with a beard up to his temples, opened it at last. He carried a lantern in one hand, and in the other a chain which held an enormous black hound. His manner at the first moment was threatening, but the sight of our uniforms and of our faces turned it into one of sulky reserve.

'The Baron Straubenthal does not receive visitors at so late an hour,' said he, speaking in very excellent French.

'You can inform Baron Straubenthal that I have come eight hundred leagues to see him, and that I will not leave until I have done so,' said my companion. I could not have said it with a better voice and manner.

The fellow took a sidelong look at us, and tugged at his black beard in his perplexity.

'To tell the truth, gentlemen,' said he, 'the Baron has a cup or two of wine in him at this hour, and you would certainly find him a more entertaining companion if you were to come again in the morning.'

He had opened the door a little wider as he spoke, and I saw by the light of the lamp in the hall behind him that three other rough fellows were standing there, one of whom held another of these monstrous hounds. Duroc must have seen it also, but it made no difference to his resolution.

'Enough talk,' said he, pushing the man to one side. 'It is with your master that I have to deal.'

The fellows in the hall made way for him as he strode in among them, so great is the power of one man who knows what he wants over several who are not sure of themselves. My companion tapped one of them upon the shoulder with as much assurance as though he owned him.

'Show me to the Baron,' said he.

The man shrugged his shoulders, and answered something in Polish. The fellow with the beard, who had shut and barred the front door, appeared to be the only one among them who could speak French.

'Well, you shall have your way,' said he, with a sinister smile. 'You shall see the Baron. And perhaps, before you have finished, you will wish that you had taken my advice.'

We followed him down the hall, which was stone-flagged

and very spacious, with skins scattered upon the floor, and the heads of wild beasts upon the walls. At the farther end he threw open a door, and we entered.

It was a small room, scantily furnished, with the same marks of neglect and decay which met us at every turn. The walls were hung with discoloured tapestry, which had come loose at one corner, so as to expose the rough stonework behind. A second door, hung with a curtain, faced us upon the other side. Between lay a square table, strewn with dirty dishes and the sordid remains of a meal. Several bottles were scattered over it. At the head of it, and facing us, there sat a huge man, with a lion-like head, and great shock of orange-coloured hair. His beard was of the same glaring hue; matted and tangled and coarse as a horse's mane. I have seen some strange faces in my time, but never one more brutal than that, with its small, vicious, blue eyes, its white, crumpled cheeks, and the thick, hanging lip which protruded over his monstrous beard. His head swayed about on his shoulders, and he looked at us with the vague, dim gaze of a drunken man. Yet he was not so drunk but that our uniforms carried their message to him.

'Well, my brave boys,' he hiccoughed. 'What is the latest news from Paris, eh? You're going to free Poland, I hear, and have meantime all become slaves yourselves – slaves to a little aristocrat with his grey coat and his three-cornered hat. No more citizens either, I am told, and nothing but monsieur and madame. My faith, some more heads will have to roll into the sawdust basket some of these mornings.'

Duroc advanced in silence, and stood by the ruffian's side.

'Jean Carabin,' said he.

The Baron started, and the film of drunkenness seemed to be clearing from his eyes.

'Jean Carabin,' said Duroc, once more.

He sat up and grasped the arms of his chair.

'What do you mean be repeating that name, young man?' he asked.

'Jean Carabin, you are a man whom I have long wished to meet.'

'Supposing that I once had such a name, how can it

concern you, since you must have been a child when I bore it?'

'My name is Duroc.'

'Not the son of—?'

'The son of the man you murdered.'

The Baron tried to laugh, but there was terror in his eyes.

'We must let bygones be bygones, young man,' he cried. 'It was our life or theirs in those days: the aristocrats or the people. Your father was of the Gironde. He fell. I was of the mountain. Most of my comrades fell. It was all the fortune of war. We must forget all this and learn to know each other better, you and I.' He held out a red, twitching hand as he spoke.

'Enough,' said young Duroc. 'If I were to pass my sabre through you as you sit in that chair, I should do what is just and right. I dishonour my blade by crossing it with yours. And yet you are a Frenchman, and have even held a commission under the same flag as myself. Rise, then, and defend yourself!'

'Tut, tut!' cried the Baron. 'It is all very well for you young bloods—'

Duroc's patience could stand no more. He swung his open hand into the centre of the great orange beard. I saw a lip fringed with blood, and two glaring eyes above it.

'You shall die for that blow.'

'That is better,' said Duroc.

'My sabre!' cried the other; 'I will not keep you waiting, I promise you!' and he hurried from the room.

I have said that there was a second door covered with a curtain. Hardly had the Baron vanished when there ran from behind it a woman, young and beautiful. So swiftly and noiselessly did she move that she was between us in an instant, and it was only the shaking curtains which told us whence she had come.

'I have seen it all,' she cried. 'Oh, sir, you have carried yourself splendidly.' She stooped to my companion's hand, and kissed it again and again ere he could disengage it from her grasp.

'Nay, madame, why should you kiss my hand?' he cried.

'Because it is the hand which struck him on his vile, lying mouth. Because it may be the hand which will avenge my mother. I am his step-daughter. The woman whose heart he broke was my mother. I loathe him, I fear him. Ah, there is his step!' In an instant she had vanished as suddenly as she had come. A moment later, the Baron entered with a drawn sword in his hand, and the fellow who had admitted us at his heels.

'This is my secretary,' said he. 'He will be my friend in this affair. But we shall need more elbow-room than we can find here. Perhaps you will kindly come with me to a more spacious apartment.'

It was evidently impossible to fight in a chamber which was blocked by a great table. We followed him out, therefore, into the dimly-lit hall. At the farther end a light was shining through an open door.

'We shall find what we want in here,' said the man with the dark beard. It was large, empty room, with rows of barrels and cases round the walls. A strong lamp stood upon a shelf in the corner. The floor was level and true, so that no swordsman could ask for more. Duroc drew his sabre and sprang into it. The Baron stood back with a bow and motioned me to follow my companion. Hardly were my heels over the threshold when the heavy door crashed behind us and the key screamed in the lock. We were taken in a trap.

For a moment we could not realize it. Such incredible baseness was outside all our experiences. Then, as we understood how foolish we had been to trust for an instant a man with such a history, a flush of rage came over us, rage against his villainy and against our own stupidity. We rushed at the door together, beating it with our fists and kicking with our heavy boots. The sound of our blows and our execrations must have resounded through the Castle. We called to this villain, hurling at him every name which might pierce even into his hardened soul. But the door was enormous—such a door as one finds in mediæval castles—made of huge beams clamped together with iron. It was as easy to break as a square of the Old Guard. And our cries appeared to be of as little avail as our blows, for they only brought for answer the clattering echoes from the high roof above us. When you have done some soldiering, you soon learn to put up with what cannot be altered. It was I, then, who first recovered my calmness, and prevailed upon Duroc to join with me in examining the apartment which had become our dungeon.

There was only one window, which had no glass in it and was so narrow that one could not so much as get one's head through. It was high up, and Duroc had to stand upon a barrel in order to see from it.

'What can you see?' I asked.

'Fir-woods, and an avenue of snow between them,' said he. 'Ah!' he gave a cry of surprise.

I sprang upon the barrel beside him. There was, as he said, a long, clear strip of snow in front. A man was riding down it, flogging his horse and galloping like a madman. As we watched, he grew smaller and smaller, until he was swallowed up by the black shadows of the forest.

'What does that mean?' asked Duroc.

'No good for us,' said I. 'He may have gone for some brigands to cut our throats. Let us see if we cannot find a way out of this mouse-trap before the cat can arrive.'

The one piece of good fortune in our favour was that beautiful lamp. It was nearly full of oil, and would last us until morning. In the dark our situation would have been far more difficult. By its light we proceeded to examine the packages and cases which lined the walls. In some places there was only a single line of them, while in one corner they were piled nearly to the ceiling. It seemed that we were in the storehouse of the Castle, for there were a great number of cheeses, vegetables of various kinds, bins full of dried fruits, and a line of wine barrels. One of these had a spigot in it, and as I had eaten little during the day, I was glad of a cup of claret and some food. As to Duroc, he would take nothing, but paced up and down the room in a fever of impatience. 'I'll have him yet!' he cried, every now and then. 'The rascal shall not escape me!'

This was all very well, but it seemed to me, as I sat on a great round cheese eating my supper, that this youngster was thinking rather too much of his own family affairs and too little of the fine scrape into which he had got me. After all, his father had been dead fourteen years, and nothing could set that right; but here was Etienne Gerard, the most dashing lieutenant in the whole Grand Army, in imminent danger of being cut off at the very outset of his brilliant career. Who was ever to know the heights to which I might have risen if I were knocked on the head in this hole-and-corner business, which had nothing whatever to do with France or the Emperor? I could not help thinking what a fool I had been, when I had a fine war before me and everything which a man could desire, to go off upon a hare-brained expedition of this sort, as if it were not enough to have a quarter of a million Russians to fight against, without plunging into all sorts of private quarrels as well.

'That is all very well,' I said at last, as I heard Duroc muttering his threats. 'You may do what you like to him when you get the upper hand. At present the question rather is, what is *he* going to do to us?'

'Let him do his worst!' cried the boy. 'I owe a duty to my father.'

'That is mere foolishness,' said I. 'If you owe a duty to your father, I owe one to my mother, which is to get us out of this business safe and sound.'

My remark brought him to his senses.

'I have thought too much of myself!' he cried. 'Forgive me, Monsieur Gerard. Give me your advice as to what I should do.'

'Well,' said I, 'it is not for our health that they have shut us up here among the cheeses. They mean to make an end of us if they can. That is certain. They hope that no one knows that we have come here, and that none will trace us if we remain. Do your hussars know where you have gone to?'

'I said nothing.'

'Hum! It is clear that we cannot be starved here. They must come to us if they are to kill us. Behind a barricade of barrels we could hold our own against the five rascals whom we have seen. That is, probably, why they have sent that messenger for assistance.'

'We must get out before he returns.'

'Precisely, if we are to get out at all.'

'Could we not burn down this door?' he cried.

'Nothing could be easier,' said I. 'There are several casks of oil in the corner. My only objection is that we should ourselves be nicely toasted, like two little oyster pâtés.'

'Can you not suggest something?' he cried, in despair. 'Ah, what is that?'

There had been a low sound at our little window, and a shadow came between the stars and ourselves. A small, white hand was stretched into the lamplight. Something glittered between the fingers.

'Quick! Quick!' cried a woman's voice.

We were on the barrel in an instant.

'They have sent for the Cossacks. Your lives are at stake. Ah, I am lost! I am lost!'

There was the sound of rushing steps, a hoarse oath, a blow, and the stars were once more twinkling through the window. We stood helpless upon our barrel with our blood cold with horror. Half a minute afterwards we heard a smothered scream, ending in a choke. A great door slammed somewhere in the silent night.

'Those ruffians have seized her. They will kill her,' I cried.

Duroc sprang down with the inarticulate shouts of one whose reason had left him. He struck the door so frantically with his naked hands that he left a blotch of blood with every blow.

'Here is the key!' I shouted, picking one from the floor. 'She must have thrown it in at the instant that she was torn away.'

My companion snatched it from me with a shriek of joy. A moment later he dashed it down upon the boards. It was so small that it was lost in the enormous lock. Duroc sank upon one of the boxes with his head between his hands. He sobbed in his despair. I could have sobbed, too, when I thought of the woman and how helpless we were to save her.

But I am not easily baffled. After all, this key must have been sent to us for a purpose. The lady could not bring us that of the door, because this murderous step-father of hers would most certainly have it in his pocket. Yet this other must have a meaning, or why should she risk her life to place it in our hands? It would say little for our wits if we could not find out what that meaning might be.

I set to work moving all the cases out from the wall, and Duroc, gaining new hope from my courage, helped me with all his strength. It was no light task, for many of them were large and heavy. On we went, working like maniacs, slinging barrels, cheeses, and boxes pell-mell into the middle of the room. At last there only remained one huge barrel of vodki, which stood in the corner. With our united strength we rolled it out, and there was a little low wooden door in the wainscot behind it. The key fitted, and with a cry of delight we saw it swing open before us. With the lamp in my hand, I squeezed my way in, followed by my companion.

We were in the powder-magazine of the castle—a rough, walled cellar, with barrels all round it, and one with the top staved in in the centre. The powder from it lay in a black heap upon the floor. Beyond there was another door, but it was locked.

'We are no better off than before,' cried Duroc. 'We have no key.'

'We have a dozen,' I cried.

I pointed to the line of powder barrels.

'You would blow this door open?'

'Precisely.'

'But you would explode the magazine.'

It was true, but I was not at the end of my resources.

'We will blow open the store-room door,' I cried.

I ran back and seized a tin box which had been filled with candles. It was about the size of my shako—large enough to hold several pounds of powder. Duroc filled it while I cut off the end of a candle. When we had finished, it would have puzzled a colonel of engineers to make a better petard. I put three cheeses on the top of each other and placed it above them, so as to lean against the lock. Then we lit our candle-end and ran for shelter, shutting the door of the magazine behind us.

It is no joke, my friends, to lie among all those tons of powder, with the knowledge that if the flame of the explosion should penetrate through one thin door our blackened limbs would be shot higher than the Castle keep. Who could have believed that a half-inch of candle could take so long to burn? My ears were straining all the time for the thudding of the hoofs of the Cossacks who were coming to destroy us. I had almost made up my mind that the candle must have gone out when there was a smack like a bursting bomb, our door flew to bits, and pieces of cheese, with a shower of turnips, apples, and splinters of cases, were shot in among us. As we rushed out we had to stagger through an impenetrable smoke, with all sorts of débris beneath our feet, but there was a glimmering square where the dark door had been. The petard had done its work.

In fact, it had done more for us than we had even ventured to hope. It had shattered gaolers as well as gaol. The first thing that I saw as I came out into the hall was a man with a butcher's axe in his hand, lying flat upon his back, with a gaping wound across his forehead. The second was a huge dog, with two of its legs broken, twisting in agony upon the floor. As it raised itself up I saw the two broken ends flapping like flails. At the same instant I heard a cry, and there was Duroc, thrown against the wall, with the other hound's teeth in his throat. He pushed it off with his left hand, while again and again he passed his sabre through its body, but it was not until I blew out its brains with my pistol that the iron jaws relaxed, and the fierce, bloodshot eyes were glazed in death.

There was no time for us to pause. A woman's scream from in front—a scream of mortal terror—told us that even now we might be too late. There were two other men in the hall, but they cowered away from our drawn swords and furious faces. The blood was streaming from Duroc's neck and dyeing the grey fur of his pelisse. Such was the lad's fire, however, that he shot in front of me, and it was only over his shoulder that I caught a glimpse of the scene as we rushed into the chamber in which we had first seen the master of the Castle of Gloom.

The Baron was standing in the middle of the room, with his tangled mane bristling like an angry lion. He was, as I have said, a huge man, with enormous shoulders; and as he stood there, with his face flushed with rage and his sword advanced, I could not but think that, in spite of all his villanies, he had a proper figure for a grenadier. The lady lay cowering in a chair behind him. A weal across one of her white arms and a dog-whip upon the floor were enough to show that our escape had hardly been in time to save her from his brutality. He gave a howl like a wolf as we broke in, and was upon us in an instant, hacking and driving, with a curse at every blow.

I have already said that the room gave no space for swordsmanship. My young companion was in front of me in the narrow passage between the table and the wall, so that I could only look on without being able to aid him. The lad knew something of his weapon, and was as fierce and active as a wild cat, but in so narrow a space the weight and strength of the giant gave him the advantage. Besides, he was an admirable swordsman. His parade and riposte were as quick as lightening. Twice he touched Duroc upon the shoulder, and then, as the lad slipped up on a lunge, he whirled up his sword to finish him before he could recover his feet. I was quicker than he, however, and took the cut upon the pommel of my sabre.

'Excuse me,' said I, 'but you have still to deal with Etienne Gerard.'

He drew back and leaned against the tapestry-covered wall, breathing in little, hoarse gasps, for his foul living was against him.

'Take your breath,' said I. 'I will await your convenience.'

'You have no cause of quarrel against me,' he panted.

'I owe you some little attention,' said I, 'for having shut me up in your store-room. Besides, if all other were wanting, I see cause enough upon that lady's arm.'

'Have your way, then!' he snarled, and leaped at me like a madman. For a minute I saw only the blazing blue eyes, and the red glazed point which stabbed and stabbed, rasping off to right or to left, and yet ever back at my throat and my breast. I had never thought that such good sword-play was to be found at Paris in the days of the Revolution. I do not suppose that in all my little affairs I have met six men who had a better knowledge of their weapon. But he knew that I was his master. He read death in my eyes, and I could see that he read it. The flush died from his face. His breath came in shorter and in thicker gasps. Yet he fought on, even after the final thrust had come, and died still hacking and cursing, with foul cries upon his lips, and his blood clotting upon his orange beard. I who speak to you have seen so many battles, that my old memory can scarce contain their names, and yet of all the terrible sights which these eyes have rested upon, there is none which I care to think of less than of that orange beard with the crimson stain in the centre, from which I had drawn my sword point.

It was only afterwards that I had time to think of all this. His monstrous body had hardly crashed down upon the floor before the woman in the corner sprang to her feet, clapping her hands together and screaming out her delight. For my part I was disgusted to see a woman take such delight in a deed of blood, and I gave no thought as to the terrible wrongs which must have befallen her before she could so far forget the gentleness of her sex. It was on my tongue to tell her sharply to be silent, when a strange, choking smell took the breath from my nostrils, and a sudden, yellow glare brought out the figures upon the faded hangings.

'Duroc, Duroc!' I shouted, tugging at his shoulder. 'The Castle is on fire!'

The boy lay senseless upon the ground, exhausted by his wounds. I rushed out into the hall to see whence the danger came. It was our explosion which had set alight to the dry framework of the door. Inside the store-room some of the boxes were already blazing. I glanced in, and as I did so my blood was turned to water by the sight of the powder barrels beyond, and of the loose heap upon the floor. It might be seconds, it could not be more than minutes, before the flames would be at the edge of it. These eyes will be closed in death, my friends, before they cease to see those crawling lines of fire and the black heap beyond.

How little I can remember what followed. Vaguely I can recall how I rushed into the chamber of death, how I seized Duroc by one limp hand and dragged him down the hall, the woman keeping pace with me and pulling at the other arm. Out of the gateway we rushed, and on down the snow-covered path until we were on the fringe of the fir forest. It was at that moment that I heard a crash behind me, and, glancing round, saw a great spout of fire shoot up into the wintry sky. An instant later there seemed to come a second crash far louder than the first. I saw the fir trees and the stars whirling round me, and I fell unconscious across the body of my comrade.

It was some weeks before I came to myself in the post-house of Arensdorf, and longer still before I could be told all that had befallen me. It was Duroc, already able to go soldiering, who came to my bedside and gave me an account of it. He it was who told me how a piece of timber had struck me on the head and had laid me almost dead upon the ground. From him, too, I learned how the Polish girl had run to Arensdorf, how she had roused our hussars, and how she had only just brought them back in time to save us from the spears of the Cossacks who had been summoned from their bivouac by that same black-bearded secretary whom we had seen galloping so swiftly over the snow. As to the brave lady who had twice saved our lives, I could not learn very much about her at that moment from Duroc, but when I chanced to meet him in Paris two years later, after the campaign of Wagram, I was not very much surprised to find that I needed no introduction to his bride, and that by the queer turns of fortune he had himself, had he chosen to use it, that very name and title of the Baron Straubenthal, which showed him to be the owner of the blackened ruins of the Castle of Gloom.

SIX

How the Brigadier Took the Field
Against the Marshal Millefleurs

5 March 1811 was the date of Massena's retreat from
Santarem. He took Wellington's troops by surprise in
so doing, but had clearly not envisaged an encounter
between the garrulous Gerard and an English acquaintance. In the event, his oversight in not enjoining discretion on Gerard did not affect the outcome, for reasons
which become evident. An American publication of
this story in August 1895 was entitled 'The Countess'
Rescue'.

Massena was a thin, sour little fellow, and after his hunting
accident he had only one eye, but when it looked out from
under his cocked hat there was not much upon a field of battle
which escaped it. He could stand in front of a battalion, and
with a single sweep tell you if a buckle or a gaiter button were
out of place. Neither the officers nor the men were very fond
of him, for he was, as you know, a miser, and soldiers love
that their leaders should be free-handed. At the same time,
when it came to work they had a very high respect for him,
and they would rather fight under him than under anyone
except the Emperor himself, and Lannes, when he was alive.
After all, if he had a tight grasp upon his money-bags, there
was a day also, you must remember, when that same grip was
upon Zurich and Genoa. He clutched on to his positions as he
did to his strong box, and it took a very clever man to loosen
him from either.

When I received his summons I went gladly to his headquarters, for I was always a great favourite of his, and there
was no officer of whom he thought more highly. That was
the best of serving with those good old generals, that they
knew enough to be able to pick out a fine soldier when they
saw one. He was seated alone in his tent, with his chin upon

his hand, and his brow as wrinkled as if he had been asked for a subscription. He smiled, however, when he saw me before him.

'Good day, Colonel Gerard.'

'Good day, Marshal.'

'How is the Third of Hussars?'

'Seven hundred incomparable men upon seven hundred excellent horses.'

'And your wounds—are they healed?'

'My wounds never heal, Marshal,' I answered.

'And why?'

'Because I have always new ones.'

'General Rapp must look to his laurels,' said he, his face all breaking into wrinkles as he laughed. 'He has had twenty-one from the enemy's bullets, and as many from Larrey's knives and probes. Knowing that you were hurt, Colonel, I have spared you of late.'

'Which hurt me most of all.'

'Tut, tut! Since the English got behind these accursed lines of Torres Vedras, there has been little for us to do. You did not miss much during your imprisonment at Dartmoor. But now we are on the eve of action.'

'We advance?'

'No, retire.'

My face must have shown my dismay. What, retire before this sacred dog of a Wellington—he who had listened unmoved to my words, and had sent me to his land of fogs! I could have sobbed as I thought of it.

'What would you have?' cried Massena, impatiently. 'When one is in check, it is necessary to move the king.'

'Forwards,' I suggested.

He shook his grizzled head.

'The lines are not to be forced,' said he. 'I have already lost General St Croix and more men than I can replace. On the other hand, we have been here at Santarem for nearly six months. There is not a pound of flour nor a jug of wine on the country-side. We must retire.'

'There is flour and wine in Lisbon,' I persisted.

'Tut, you speak as if an army could charge in and charge out again like your regiment of hussars. If Soult were here with thirty thousand men—but he will not come. I sent for you, however, Colonel Gerard, to say that I have a very singular and important expedition which I intend to place under your direction.'

I pricked up my ears, as you can imagine. The Marshal unrolled a great map of the country and spread it upon the table. He flattened it out with his little, hairy hands.

'This is Santarem,' he said, pointing.

I nodded.

'And here, twenty-five miles to the east, is Almeixal, celebrated for its vintages and for its enormous Abbey.'

Again I nodded; I could not think what was coming.

'Have you heard of the Marshal Millefleurs?' asked Massena.

'I have served with all the Marshals,' said I, 'but there is none of that name.'

'It is but the nickname which the soldiers have given him,' said Massena. 'If you had not been away from us for some months, it would not be necessary for me to tell you about him. He is an Englishman, and a man of good breeding. It is on account of his manners that they have given him his title. I wish you to go to this polite Englishman at Almeixal.'

'Yes, Marshal.'

'And to hang him to the nearest tree.'

'Certainly, Marshal.'

I turned briskly upon my heels, but Massena recalled me before I could reach the opening of his tent.

'One moment, Colonel,' said he; 'you had best learn how matters stand before you start. You must know, then, that this Marshal Millefleurs, whose real name is Alexis Morgan, is a man of very great ingenuity and bravery. He was an officer in the English Guards, but having been broken for cheating at cards, he left the army. In some manner he gathered a number of English deserters round him and took to the mountains. French stragglers and Portuguese brigands joined him, and he found himself at the head of five hundred men. With these he took possession of the Abbey of Almeixal, sent the monks about their business, fortified the place, and gathered in the plunder of all the country round.'

'For which it is high time he was hanged,' said I, making once more for the door.

'One instant!' cried the Marshal, smiling at my impatience. 'The worst remains behind. Only last week the Dowager Countess of La Ronda, the richest woman in Spain, was taken by these ruffians in the passes as she was journeying from King Joseph's Court to visit her grandson. She is now a prisoner in the Abbey, and is only protected by her—'

'Grandmotherhood,' I suggested.

'Her power of paying a ransom,' said Massena. 'You have three missions, then: to rescue this unfortunate lady; to punish this villain; and, if possible, to break up this nest of brigands. It will be a proof of the confidence which I have in you when I say that I can only spare you half a squadron with which to accomplish all this.'

My word, I could hardly believe my ears! I thought that I should have had my regiment at the least.

'I would give you more,' said he, 'but I commence my retreat to-day, and Wellington is so strong in horse that every trooper becomes of importance. I cannot spare you another man. You will see what you can do, and you will report yourself to me at Abrantes not later than to-morrow night.'

It was very complimentary that he should rate my powers so high, but it was also a little embarrassing. I was to rescue an old lady, to hang an Englishman, and to break up a band of five hundred assassins—all with fifty men. But after all, the fifty men were Hussars of Conflans, and they had an Etienne Gerard to lead them. As I came out into the warm Portuguese sunshine my confidence had returned to me, and I had already begun to wonder whether the medal which I had so often deserved might not be waiting for me at Almeixal.

You may be sure that I did not take my fifty men at haphazard. They were all old soldiers of the German wars, some of them with three stripes, and most of them with two. Oudet and Papilette, two of the best sub-officers in the regiment, were at their head. When I had them formed up in fours, all in silver grey and upon chestnut horses, with their leopard skin shabracks and their little red panaches, my heart beat high at the sight. I could not look at their weather-stained faces, with the great moustaches which bristled over their chin-straps, without feeling a glow of confidence, and, between ourselves, I have no doubt that was exactly how they felt when they saw their young Colonel on his great black war-horse riding at their head.

Well, when we got free of the camp and over the Tagus, I threw out my advance and my flankers, keeping my own place at the head of the main body. Looking back from the hills above Santarem, we could see the dark lines of Massena's army, with the flash and twinkle of the sabres and bayonets as he moved his regiments into position for their retreat. To the south lay the scattered red patches of the English outposts, and behind the grey smoke-cloud which rose from Wellington's camp—thick, oily smoke, which seemed to our poor starving fellows to bear with it the rich smell of seething camp-kettles. Away to the west lay a curve of blue sea flecked with the white sails of the English ships.

You will understand that as we were riding to the east, our road lay away from both armies. Our own marauders, however, and the scouting parties of the English, covered the country, and it was necessary with my small troop that I should take every precaution. During the whole day we rode over desolate hill-sides, the lower portions covered by the budding vines, but the upper turning from green to grey, and jagged along the skyline like the back of a starved horse. Mountain streams crossed our path, running west to the Tagus, and once we came to a deep strong river, which might have checked us had I not found the ford by observing where houses had been built opposite each other upon either bank. Between them, as every scout should know, you will find your ford. There was none to give us information, for neither man nor beast, nor any living thing except great clouds of crows, was to be seen during our journey.

The sun was beginning to sink when we came to a valley clear in the centre, but shrouded by huge oak trees upon either side. We could not be more than a few miles from Almeixal, so it seemed to me to be best to keep among the groves, for the spring had been an early one and the leaves were already thick enough to conceal us. We were riding

then in open order among the great trunks, when one of my
flankers came galloping up.

'There are English across the valley, Colonel,' he cried, as
he saluted.

'Cavalry or infantry?'

'Dragoons, Colonel,' said he; 'I saw the gleam of their
helmets, and heard the neigh of a horse.'

Halting my men, I hastened to the edge of the wood. There
could be no doubt about it. A party of English cavalry was
travelling in a line with us, and in the same direction I caught
a glimpse of their red coats and of their flashing arms glowing
and twinkling among the tree-trunks. Once, as they passed
through a small clearing, I could see their whole force, and
I judged that they were of about the same strength as my
own—a half squadron at the most.

You who have heard some of my little adventures will give
me credit for being quick in my decisions, and prompt in
carrying them out. But here I must confess that I was in two
minds. On the one hand there was the chance of a fine cavalry
skirmish with the English. On the other hand, there was my
mission at the Abbey of Almeixal, which seemed already to
be so much above my power. If I were to lose any of my
men, it was certain that I should be unable to carry out my
orders. I was sitting my horse, with my chin in my gauntlet,
looking across at the rippling gleams of light from the further
wood, when suddenly one of these red-coated Englishmen
rode out from the cover, pointing at me and breaking into a
shrill whoop and halloa as if I had been a fox. Three others
joined him, and one who was a bugler sounded a call which
brought the whole of them into the open. They were, as I
had thought, a half squadron, and they formed a double line
with a front of twenty-five, their officer—the one who had
whooped at me—at their head.

For my own part, I had instantly brought my own troopers
into the same formation, so that there we were, hussars and
dragoons, with only two hundred yards of grassy sward
between us. They carried themselves well, those red-coated
troopers, with their silver helmets, their high white plumes,
and their long, gleaming swords; while, on the other hand,
I am sure that they would acknowledge that they had never

looked upon finer light horsemen than the fifty hussars of Conflans who were facing them. They were heavier, it is true, and they may have seemed the smarter, for Wellington used to make them burnish their metal work, which was not usual among us. On the other hand, it is well known that the English tunics were too tight for the sword-arm, which gave our men an advantage. As to bravery, foolish, inexperienced people of every nation always think that their own soldiers are braver than any others. There is no nation in the world which does not entertain this idea. But when one has seen as much as I have done, one understands that there is no very marked difference, and that although nations differ very much in discipline, they are all equally brave—except that the French have rather more courage than the rest.

Well, the cork was drawn and the glasses ready, when suddenly the English officer raised his sword to me as if in a challenge, and cantered his horse across the grassland. My word, there is no finer sight upon earth than that of a gallant man upon a gallant steed! I could have halted there just to watch him as he came with such careless grace, his sabre down by his horse's shoulder, his head thrown back, his white plume tossing—youth and strength and courage, with the violet evening sky above and the oak trees behind. But it was not for me to stand and stare. Etienne Gerard may have his faults, but, my faith, he was never accused of being backward in taking his own part. The old horse, Rataplan, knew me so well that he had started off before ever I gave the first shake to the bridle.

There are two things in this world that I am very slow to forget, the face of a pretty woman, and the legs of a fine horse. Well, as we drew together, I kept on saying, 'Where have I seen those great roan shoulders? Where have I seen that dainty fetlock?' Then suddenly I remembered, and as I looked up at the reckless eyes and the challenging smile, whom should I recognise but the man who had saved me from the brigands and played me for my freedom—he whose correct title was Milor the Hon. Sir Russell Bart!

'Bart!' I shouted.

He had his arm raised for a cut, and three parts of his body open to my point, for he did not know very much about the use of the sword. As I brought my hilt to the salute he dropped his hand and stared at me.

'Halloa!' said he. 'It's Gerard!' You would have thought by his manner that I had met him by appointment. For my own part I would have embraced him had he but come an inch of the way to meet me.

'I thought we were in for some sport,' said he. 'I never dreamed that it was you.'

I found this tone of disappointment somewhat irritating. Instead of being glad at having met a friend, he was sorry at having missed an enemy.

'I should have been happy to join in your sport, my dear Bart,' said I. 'But I really cannot turn my sword upon a man who saved my life.'

'Tut, never mind about that.'

'No, it is impossible. I should never forgive myself.'

'You make too much of a trifle.'

'My mother's one desire is to embrace you. If ever you should be in Gascony—'

'Lord Wellington is coming there with 60,000 men.'

'Then one of them will have a chance of surviving,' said I, laughing. 'In the meantime, put your sword in your sheath!'

Our horses were standing head to tail, and the Bart. put out his hand and patted me on the thigh.

'You're a good chap, Gerard,' said he. 'I only wish you had been born on the right side of the Channel.'

'I was,' said I.

'Poor fellow!' he cried, with such an earnestness of pity that he set me laughing again. 'But look here, Gerard,' he continued, 'this is all very well, but it is not business, you know. I don't know what Massena would say to it, but our Chief would jump out of his riding-boots if he saw us. We weren't sent out here for a picnic—either of us.'

'What would you have?'

'Well, we had a little argument about our hussars and dragoons, if you remember. I've got fifty of the Sixteenth all chewing their carbine bullets behind me. You've got as many fine-looking boys over yonder, who seem to be fidgeting in their saddles. If you and I took the right flanks we should not spoil each other's beauty—though a little blood-letting is a friendly thing in this climate.'

There seemed to me to be a good deal of sense in what he said. For the moment Mr Alexis Morgan and the Countess of La Ronda and the Abbey of Almeixal went right out of my head, and I could only think of the fine level turf and of the beautiful skirmish which we might have.

'Very good, Bart,' said I. 'We have seen the front of your dragoons. We shall now have a look at their backs.'

'Any betting?' he asked.

'The stake,' said I, 'is nothing less than the honour of the Hussars of Conflans.'

'Well, come on!' he answered. 'If we break you, well and good—if you break us, it will be all the better for Marshal Millefleurs.'

When he said that I could only stare at him in astonishment.

'Why for Marshal Millefleurs?' I asked.

'It is the name of a rascal who lives out this way. My dragoons have been sent by Lord Wellington to see him safely hanged.'

'Name of a name!' I cried. 'Why, my hussars have been sent by Massena for that very object.'

We burst out laughing at that, and sheathed our swords. There was a whirr of steel from behind us as our troopers followed our example.

'We are allies,' he cried.

'For a day.'

'We must join forces.'

'There is no doubt of it.'

And so, instead of fighting, we wheeled our half squadrons round and moved in two little columns down the valley, the shakos and the helmets turned inwards, and the men looking their neighbours up and down, like old fighting dogs with tattered ears who have learned to respect each other's teeth. The most were on the broad grin, but there were some on either side who looked black and challenging, especially the English sergeant and my own sub-officer Papilette. They were men of habit, you see, who could not change all their ways of thinking in a moment. Besides, Papilette had lost his only brother at Busaco. As for the Bart and me, we rode together at the head and chatted about all that had occurred to us since that famous game of écarté of which I have told you. For my own part, I spoke to him of my adventures in England. They are a very singular people, these English. Although he knew that I had been engaged in twelve campaigns, yet I am sure that the Bart thought more highly of me because I had had an affair with the Bristol Bustler. He told me, too, that the Colonel who presided over his court-martial for playing cards with a prisoner, acquitted him of neglect of duty, but nearly broke him because he thought that he had not cleared his trumps before leading his suit. Yes, indeed, they are a singular people.

At the end of the valley the road curved over some rising ground before winding down into another wider valley beyond. We called a halt when we came to the top; for there, right in front of us, at the distance of about three miles, was a scattered, grey town, with a single enormous building upon the flank of the mountain which overlooked it. We could not doubt that we were at last in sight of the Abbey that held the gang of rascals whom we had come to disperse. It was only now, I think, that we fully understood what a task lay in front of us, for the place was a veritable fortress, and it was evident that cavalry should never have been sent out upon such an errand.

'That's got nothing to do with us,' said the Bart; 'Wellington and Massena can settle that between them.'

'Courage!' I answered. 'Piré took Leipzig with fifty hussars.'

'Had they been dragoons,' said the Bart, laughing, 'he would have had Berlin. But you are senior officer: give us a lead, and we'll see who will be the first to flinch.'

'Well,' said I, 'whatever we do must be done at once, for my orders are to be on my way to Abrantes by to-morrow night. But we must have some information first, and here is someone who should be able to give it to us.'

There was a square, whitewashed house standing by the roadside, which appeared, from the bush hanging over the door, to be one of those wayside tabernas which are provided for the muleteers. A lantern was hung in the porch, and by its light we saw two men, the one in the brown habit of a Capuchin monk, and the other girt with an apron, which showed him to be the landlord. They were conversing together so earnestly that we were upon them before they were aware of us. The innkeeper turned to fly, but one of the Englishmen seized him by the hair, and held him tight.

'For mercy's sake, spare me,' he yelled. 'My house has been gutted by the French and harried by the English, and my feet have been burned by the brigands. I swear by the Virgin that I have neither money nor food in my inn, and the good Father Abbot, who is starving upon my doorstep, will be witness to it.'

'Indeed, sir,' said the Capuchin, in excellent French, 'what this worthy man says is very true. He is one of the many victims to these cruel wars, although his loss is but a feather-weight compared to mine. Let him go,' he added, in English, to the trooper, 'he is too weak to fly, even if he desired to.'

In the light of the lantern I saw that this monk was a magnificent man, dark and bearded, with the eyes of a hawk, and so tall that his cowl came up to Rataplan's ears. He wore the look of one who had been through much suffering, but he carried himself like a king, and we could form some opinion of his learning when we each heard him talk our own language as fluently as if he were born to it.

'You have nothing to fear,' said I, to the trembling innkeeper. 'As to you, father, you are, if I am not mistaken, the very man who can give us the information which we require.'

'All that I have is at your service, my son. But,' he added with a wan smile, 'my Lenten fare is always somewhat meagre, and this year it has been such that I must ask you for a crust of bread if I am to have the strength to answer your questions.'

We bore two days' rations in our haversacks, so that he soon had the little he had asked for. It was dreadful to see the wolfish way in which he seized the piece of dried goat's flesh which I was able to offer him.

'Time presses, and we must come to the point,' said I. 'We want your advice as to the weak points of yonder Abbey, and concerning the habits of the rascals who infest it.'

He cried out something which I took to be Latin, with his hands clasped and his eyes upturned. 'The prayer of the just availeth much,' said he, 'and yet I had not dared to hope that mine would have been so speedily answered. In me you see the unfortunate Abbot of Almeixal, who has been cast out by this rabble of three armies with their heretical leader. Oh! to think of what I have lost!' his voice broke, and the tears hung upon his lashes.

'Cheer up, sir,' said the Bart. 'I'll lay nine to four that we have you back again by to-morrow night.'

'It is not of my own welfare that I think,' said he, 'nor even of that of my poor, scattered flock. But it is of the holy relics which are left in the sacrilegious hands of these robbers.'

'It's even betting whether they would ever bother their heads about them,' said the Bart 'But show us the way inside the gates, and we'll soon clear the place out for you.'

In a few short words the good Abbot gave us the very points that we wished to know. But all that he said only made our task more formidable. The walls of the Abbey were forty feet high. The lower windows were barricaded, and the whole building loopholed for musketry fire. The gang preserved military discipline, and their sentries were too numerous for us to hope to take them by surprise. It was more than ever evident that a battalion of grenadiers and a couple of breaching pieces were what was needed. I raised my eyebrows, and the Bart began to whistle.

'We must have a shot at it, come what may,' said he.

The men had already dismounted, and, having watered their horses, were eating their suppers. For my own part I went into the sitting-room of the inn with the Abbot and the Bart, that we might talk about our plans.

I had a little cognac in my *sauve vie*, and I divided it among us—just enough to wet our moustaches.

'It is unlikely,' said I, 'that those rascals know anything about our coming. I have seen no signs of scouts along the road. My own plan is that we should conceal ourselves in some neighbouring wood, and then, when they open their gates, charge down upon them and take them by surprise.'

The Bart was of opinion that this was the best that we could do, but, when we came to talk it over, the Abbot made us see that there were difficulties in the way.

'Save on the side of the town there is no place within a mile of the Abbey where you could shelter man or horse,' said he. 'As to the townsfolk, they are not to be trusted. I fear, my son, that your excellent plan would have little chance of success in the face of the vigilant guard which these men keep.'

'I see no other way,' answered I. 'Hussars of Conflans are not so plentiful that I can afford to run half a squadron of them against a forty foot wall with five hundred infantry behind it.'

'I am a man of peace,' said the Abbot, 'and yet I may, perhaps, give a word of counsel. I know these villains and their ways. Who should do so better, seeing that I have stayed for a month in this lonely spot, looking down in weariness of heart at the Abbey which was my own? I will tell you now what I should myself do if I were in your place.'

'Pray tell us, father,' we cried, both together.

'You must know that bodies of deserters, both French and English, are continually coming in to them, carrying their weapons with them. Now, what is there to prevent you and your men from pretending to be such a body, and so making your way into the Abbey?'

I was amazed at the simplicity of the thing, and I embraced the good Abbot. The Bart, however, had some objections to offer.

'That is all very well,' said he, 'but if these fellows are as sharp as you say, it is not very likely that they are going to let a hundred armed strangers into their crib. From all I have heard of Mr Morgan, or Marshal Millefleurs, or whatever the rascal's name is, I give him credit for more sense than that.'

'Well, then,' I cried, 'let us send fifty in, and let them at daybreak throw open the gates to the other fifty, who will be waiting outside.'

We discussed the question at great length and with much foresight and discretion. If it had been Massena and Wellington instead of two young officers of light cavalry, we could not have weighed it all with more judgement. At last we agreed, the Bart and I, that one of us should indeed go with fifty men under pretence of being deserters, and that in the early morning he should gain command of the gate and admit the others. The Abbot, it is true, was still of opinion that it was dangerous to divide our force, but finding that we were both of the same mind, he shrugged his shoulders and gave in.

'There is only one thing that I would ask,' said he. 'If you lay hands upon Marshal Millefleurs—this dog of a brigand—what will you do with him?'

'Hang him,' I answered.

'It is too easy a death,' cried the Capuchin, with a vindictive glow in his dark eyes. 'Had I my way with him—but, oh, what thoughts are these for a servant of God to harbour!' He clapped his hands to his forehead like one who is half demented by his troubles, and rushed out of the room.

There was an important point which we had still to settle, and that was whether the French or the English party should have the honour of entering the Abbey first. My faith, it was asking a great deal of Etienne Gerard that he should give place to any man at such a time! But the poor Bart pleaded so hard, urging the few poor skirmishes which he had seen against my four-and-seventy engagements, that at last I consented that he should go. We had just clasped hands over the matter when there broke out such a shouting and cursing and yelling from the front of the inn, that out we rushed with our drawn sabres in our hands, convinced that the brigands were upon us.

You may imagine our feelings when, by the light of the lantern which hung from the porch, we saw a score of our hussars and dragoons all mixed in one wild heap, red coats and blue, helmets and busbies, pomelling each other to their hearts' content. We flung ourselves upon them, imploring, threatening, tugging at a lace collar, or at a spurred heel, until, at last, we had dragged them all apart. There they stood, flushed and bleeding, glaring at each other, and all panting together like a line of troop horses after a ten-mile chase. It was only with our drawn swords that we could keep them from each other's throats. The poor Capuchin stood in the porch in his long brown habit, wringing his hands and calling upon all the saints for mercy.

He was indeed, as I found upon inquiry, the innocent cause of all the turmoil, for, not understanding how soldiers look upon such things, he had made some remark to the English sergeant that it was a pity that his squadron was not as good as the French. The words were not out of his mouth before a dragoon knocked down the nearest hussar, and then, in a moment, they all flew at each other like tigers. We would trust them no more after that, but the Bart moved his men to the front of the inn, and I mine to the back, the English all scowling and silent, and our fellows shaking their fists and chattering, each after the fashion of their own people.

Well, as our plans were made, we thought it best to carry them out at once, lest some fresh cause of quarrel should break out between our followers. The Bart and his men rode off, therefore, he having first torn the lace from his sleeves, and the gorget and sash from his uniform, so that he might pass as a simple trooper. He explained to his men what it was that was expected of them, and though they did not raise a cry or wave their weapons as mine might have done, there was an expression upon their stolid and clean-shaven faces which filled me with confidence. Their tunics were left unbuttoned, their scabbards and helmets stained with dirt, and their harness badly fastened, so that they might look the part of deserters, without order or discipline. At six o'clock next morning they were to gain command of the main gate of the Abbey, while at that same hour my hussars were to gallop up to it from outside. The Bart and I pledged our words to it before he trotted off with his detachment. My sergeant, Papilette, with two troopers, followed the English at a distance, and returned in half an hour to say that, after some parley, and the flashing of lanterns upon them from the grille, they had been admitted into the Abbey.

So far, then, all had gone well. It was a cloudy night with a sprinkling of rain, which was in our favour, as there was the less chance of our presence being discovered. My vedettes I placed two hundred yards in every direction, to guard against a surprise, and also to prevent any peasant who might stumble upon us from carrying the news to the Abbey. Oudin and Papilette were to take turns of duty, while the others with their horses had snug quarters in a great wooden granary. Having walked round and seen that all was as it should be, I flung myself upon the bed which the innkeeper had set apart for me, and fell into a dreamless sleep.

No doubt you have heard my name mentioned as being the beau-ideal of a soldier, and that not only by friends and admirers like our fellow-townsfolk, but also by old officers of the great wars who have shared the fortunes of those famous campaigns with me. Truth and modesty compel me to say, however, that this is not so. There are some gifts which I lack—very few, no doubt—but, still, amid the vast armies of the Emperor there may have been some who were free from those blemishes which stood between me and perfection. Of bravery I say nothing. Those who have seen me in the field are best fitted to speak about that. I have often heard the soldiers discussing round the camp-fires as to who was the bravest man in the Grand Army. Some said Murat, and some said Lasalle, and some Ney; but for my own part, when they asked me, I merely shrugged my shoulders and smiled. It would have seemed mere conceit if I had answered that there was no man braver than Brigadier Gerard. At the same time, facts are facts, and a man knows best what his own feelings are. But there are other gifts besides bravery which are necessary for a soldier, and one of them is that he should be a light sleeper. Now, from my boyhood onwards, I have been hard to wake, and it was this which brought me to ruin upon that night.

It may have been about two o'clock in the morning that I was suddenly conscious of a feeling of suffocation. I tried to call out, but there was something which prevented me from uttering a sound. I struggled to rise, but I could only flounder like a hamstrung horse. I was strapped at the ankles, strapped at the knees, and strapped again at the wrists. Only my eyes were free to move, and there at the foot of my couch, by the light of a Portuguese lamp, whom should I see but the Abbot and the innkeeper!

The latter's heavy, white face had appeared to me when I looked upon it the evening before to express nothing but stupidity and terror. Now, on the contrary, every feature bespoke brutality and ferocity. Never have I seen a more dreadful-looking villain. In his hand he held a long, dull-coloured knife. The Abbot, on the other hand, was as polished and dignified as ever. His Capuchin gown had been thrown open, however, and I saw beneath it a black-frogged coat, such as I have seen among the English officers. As our eyes met he leaned over the wooden end of the bed and laughed silently until it creaked again.

'You will, I am sure, excuse my mirth, my dear Colonel Gerard,' said he. 'The fact is, that the expression upon your face when you grasped the situation was just a little funny. I have no doubt that you are an excellent soldier, but I hardly think that you are fit to measure wits with the Marshal Millefleurs, as your fellows have been good enough to call me. You appear to have given me credit for singularly little intelligence, which argues, if I may be allowed to say so, a want of acuteness upon your own part. Indeed, with the single exception of my thick-headed compatriot, the British dragoon, I have never met anyone who was less competent to carry out such a mission.'

You can imagine how I felt and how I looked, as I listened to this insolent harangue, which was all delivered in that flowery and condescending manner which had gained this rascal his nickname. I could say nothing, but they must have read my threat in my eyes, for the fellow who had played the part of the innkeeper whispered something to his companion.

'No, no, my dear Chenier, he will be infinitely more valuable alive,' said he. 'By the way, Colonel, it is just as well that you are a sound sleeper, for my friend here, who is a little rough in his ways, would certainly have cut your throat if you had raised any alarm. I should recommend you to keep in his good graces, for Sergeant Chenier, late of the 7th Imperial Light Infantry, is a much more dangerous person than Captain Alexis Morgan, of His Majesty's foot-guards.'

Chenier grinned and shook his knife at me, while I tried to look the loathing which I felt at the thought that a soldier of the Emperor could fall so low.

'It may amuse you to know,' said the Marshal, in that soft, suave voice of his, 'that both your expeditions were watched from the time that you left your respective camps. I think that you will allow that Chenier and I played our parts with some subtlety. We had made every arrangement for your reception at the Abbey, though we had hoped to receive the whole squadron instead of half. When the gates are secured behind them, our visitors find themselves in a very charming little mediæval quadrangle, with no possible exit, commanded by musketry fire from a hundred windows. They may choose to be shot down; or they may choose to surrender. Between ourselves, I have not the slightest doubt that they have been wise enough to do the latter. But since you are naturally interested in the matter, we thought that you would care to come with us and to see for yourself. I think I can promise you that you will find your titled friend waiting for you at the Abbey with a face as long as your own.'

The two villains began whispering together, debating, as far as I could hear, which was the best way of avoiding my vedettes.

'I will make sure that it is all clear upon the other side of the barn,' said the Marshal at last. 'You will stay here, my good Chenier, and if the prisoner gives any trouble you will know what to do.'

So we were left together, this murderous renegade and I—he sitting at the end of the bed, sharpening his knife upon his boot in the light of the single smoky little oil-lamp. As to me, I only wonder now as I look back upon it, that I did not go mad with vexation and self-reproach as I lay helplessly upon the couch, unable to utter a word or move a finger, with the knowledge that my fifty gallant lads were so close to me, and yet with no means of letting them know the straits to which I was reduced. It was no new thing for me to be a prisoner; but to be taken by these renegades, and to be led into their Abbey in the midst of their jeers, befooled and outwitted by their insolent leaders—that was indeed more than I could endure. The knife of the butcher beside me would cut less deeply than that.

I twitched softly at my wrists, and then at my ankles, but whichever of the two had secured me was no bungler at his work. I could not move either of them an inch. Then I tried to work the handkerchief down over my mouth, but the ruffian beside me raised his knife with such a threatening snarl that I had to desist. I was lying still looking at his bull neck, and wondering whether it would ever be my good fortune to fit it for a cravat, when I heard returning steps coming down the inn passage and up the stair. What word would the villain bring back? If he found it impossible to kidnap me, he would probably murder me where I lay. For my own part, I was indifferent which it might be, and I looked at the doorway with the contempt and defiance which I longed to put into words. But you can imagine my feelings, my dear friends, when, instead of the tall figure and dark, sneering face of the Capuchin, my eyes fell upon the grey pelisse and huge moustaches of my good little sub-officer, Papilette!

The French soldier of those days had seen too much to be ever taken by surprise. His eyes had hardly rested upon my bound figure and the sinister face beside me before he had seen how the matter lay.

'Sacred name of a dog!' he growled, and out flashed his great sabre. Chenier sprang forward at him with his knife, and then, thinking better of it, he darted back and stabbed frantically at my heart. For my own part, I had hurled myself off the bed on the side opposite him, and the blade grazed my side before ripping its way through blanket and sheet. An instant later I heard the thud of a heavy fall, and then almost simultaneously a second object struck the floor—something lighter but harder, which rolled under the bed. I will not horrify you with details, my friends. Suffice it that Papilette was one of the strongest swordsmen in the regiment, and that his sabre was heavy and sharp. It left a red blotch upon my wrists and my ankles, as it cut the thongs which bound me.

When I had thrown off my gag, the first use which I made of my lips was to kiss the sergeant's scarred cheeks. The next was to ask him if all was well with the command. Yes, they had had no alarms. Oudin had just relieved him, and he had come to report. Had he seen the Abbot? No, he had seen nothing of him. Then we must form a cordon and prevent his escape. I was hurrying out to give the orders, when I heard a slow and measured step enter the door below, and come creaking up the stairs.

Papilette understood it all in an instant. 'You are not to kill him,' I whispered, and thrust him into the shadow on one side of the door; I crouched on the other. Up he came, up and up, and every footfall seemed to be upon my heart. The brown skirt of his gown was not over the threshold before we were both on him, like two wolves on a buck. Down we crashed, the three of us, he fighting like a tiger, and with such amazing strength that he might have broken away from the two of us. Thrice he got to his feet, and thrice we had him over again, until Papilette made him feel that there was a point to his sabre. He had sense enough then to know that the game was up, and to lie still while I lashed him with the very cords which had been around my own limbs.

'There has been a fresh deal, my fine fellow,' said I, 'and you will find that I have some of the trumps in *my* hand this time.'

'Luck always comes to the aid of a fool,' he answered. 'Perhaps it is as well, otherwise the world would fall too completely into the power of the astute. So, you have killed Chenier, I see. He was an insubordinate dog, and always smelt abominably of garlic. Might I trouble you to lay me upon the bed? The floor of these Portuguese tabernas is hardly a fitting couch for anyone who has prejudices in favour of cleanliness.'

I could not but admire the coolness of the man, and the way in which he preserved the same insolent air of condescension in spite of this sudden turning of the tables. I dispatched Papilette to summon a guard, whilst I stood over our prisoner with my drawn sword, never taking my eyes off him for an instant, for I must confess that I had conceived a great respect for his audacity and resource.

'I trust,' said he, 'that your men will treat me in a becoming manner.'

'You will get your deserts—you may depend upon that.'

'I ask nothing more. You may not be aware of my exalted birth, but I am so placed that I cannot name my father without treason, nor my mother without a scandal. I cannot *claim* Royal honours, but these things are so much more graceful when they are conceded without a claim. The thongs are cutting my skin. Might I beg you to loosen them?'

'You do not give me credit for much intelligence,' I remarked, repeating his own words.

'*Touché*,' he cried, like a pinked fencer. 'But here come your men, so it matters little whether you loosen them or not.'

I ordered the gown to be stripped from him and placed him under a strong guard. Then, as morning was already breaking, I had to consider what my next step was to be. The poor Bart. and his Englishmen had fallen victims to the deep scheme which might, had we adopted all the crafty suggestions of our adviser, have ended in the capture of the whole instead of the half of our force. I must extricate them if it were still possible. Then there was the old lady, the Countess of La Ronda, to be thought of. As to the Abbey, since its garrison was on the alert it was hopeless to think of capturing that. All turned now upon the value which they placed upon their leader. The game depended upon my playing that one card. I will tell you how boldly and how skilfully I played it.

It was hardly light before my bugler blew the assembly, and out we trotted on to the plain. My prisoner was placed on horseback in the very centre of the troops. It chanced that there was a large tree just out of musket-shot from the main gate of the Abbey, and under this we halted. Had they opened the great doors in order to attack us, I should have charged home on them; but, as I had expected, they stood upon the defensive, lining the long wall and pouring down a torrent of hootings and taunts and derisive laughter upon us. A few fired their muskets, but finding that we were out of reach they soon ceased to waste their powder. It was the strangest sight to see that mixture of uniforms, French, English, and Portuguese, cavalry, infantry and artillery, all wagging their heads and shaking their fists at us.

My word, their hubbub soon died away when we opened our ranks, and showed whom we had got in the midst of us! There was silence for a few seconds, and then such a howl of rage and grief! I could see some of them dancing like madmen upon the wall. He must have been a singular person, this prisoner of ours, to have gained the affection of such a gang.

I had brought a rope from the inn, and we slung it over the lower bough of the tree.

'You will permit me, monsieur, to undo your collar,' said Papilette, with mock politeness.

'If your hands are perfectly clean,' answered our prisoner, and set the whole half-squadron laughing.

There was another yell from the wall, followed by a profound hush as the noose was tightened round Marshal Millefleurs' neck. Then came a shriek from a bugle, the Abbey gates flew open, and three men rushed out waving white cloths in their hands. Ah, how my heart bounded with joy at the sight of them. And yet I would not advance an inch to meet them, so that all the eagerness might seem to be upon their side. I allowed my trumpeter, however, to wave a handkerchief in reply, upon which the three envoys came running towards us. The Marshal, still pinioned, and with the rope round his neck, sat his horse with a half smile, as one who is slightly bored and yet strives out of courtesy not to show it. If I were in such a situation I could not wish to carry myself better, and surely I can say no more than that.

They were a singular trio, these ambassadors. The one was a Portuguese caçadore in his dark uniform, the second a French chasseur in the lightest green, and the third a big English artilleryman in blue and gold. They saluted, all three, and the Frenchman did the talking.

'We have thirty-seven English dragoons in our hands,' said he. 'We give you our most solemn oath that they shall all hang from the Abbey wall within five minutes of the death of our Marshal.'

'Thirty-seven!' I cried. 'You have fifty-one.'

'Fourteen were cut down before they could be secured.'

'And the officer?'

'He would not surrender his sword save with his life. It was not our fault. We would have saved him if we could.'

Alas for my poor Bart! I had met him but twice, and yet he was a man very much after my heart. I have always had a regard for the English for the sake of that one friend. A braver man and a worse swordsman I have never met.

I did not, as you may think, take these rascals' word for anything. Papilette was dispatched with one of them, and returned to say that it was too true. I had now to think of the living.

'You will release the thirty-seven dragoons if I free your leader?'

'We will give you ten of them.'

'Up with him!' I cried.

'Twenty,' shouted the chasseur.

'No more words,' said I. 'Pull on the rope!'

'All of them,' cried the envoy, as the cord tightened round the Marshal's neck.

'With horses and arms?'

They could see that I was not a man to jest with.

'All complete,' said the chasseur, sulkily.

'And the Countess of La Ronda as well?' said I.

But here I met with firmer opposition. No threats of mine could induce them to give up the Countess. We tightened the cord. We moved the horse. We did all but leave the Marshal suspended. If once I broke his neck the dragoons were dead men. It was as precious to me as to them.

'Allow me to remark,' said the Marshal, blandly, 'that you are exposing me to a risk of quinsy. Do you not think, since there is a difference of opinion upon this point, that it would be an excellent idea to consult the lady herself? We would neither of us, I am sure, wish to over-ride her own inclinations.'

Nothing could be more satisfactory. You can imagine how quickly I grasped at so simple a solution. In ten minutes she was before us, a most stately dame, with her grey curls peeping out from under her mantilla. Her face was as yellow as though it reflected the countless doubloons of her treasury.

'This gentleman,' said the Marshal, 'is exceedingly anxious to convey you to a place where you will never see us more. It is for you to decide whether you would wish to go with him, or whether you prefer to remain with me.'

She was at his horse's side in an instant. 'My own Alexis,' she cried, 'nothing can ever part us.'

He looked at me with a sneer upon his handsome face.

'By the way, you made a small slip of the tongue, my dear Colonel,' said he. 'Except by courtesy, no such person exists as the Dowager Countess of La Ronda. The lady whom I have the honour to present to you is my very dear wife, Mrs Alexis Morgan—or shall I say Madame la Marèchale Millefleurs?'

It was at this moment that I came to the conclusion that I was dealing with the cleverest, and also the most unscrupulous, man whom I had ever met. As I looked upon this unfortunate old woman my soul was filled with wonder and disgust. As for her, her eyes were raised to his face with such a look as a young recruit might give to the Emperor.

'So be it,' said I, at last; 'give me the dragoons and let me go.'

They were brought out with their horses and weapons, and the rope was taken from the Marshal's neck.

'Good-bye, my dear Colonel,' said he. 'I am afraid that you will have rather a lame account to give of your mission, when you find your way back to Massena, though, from all I hear, he will probably be too busy to think of you. I am free to confess that you have extricated yourself from your difficulties with greater ability than I had given you credit for. I presume that there is nothing which I can do for you before you go?'

'There is one thing.'

'And that is?'

'To give fitting burial to this young officer and his men.'

'I pledge my word to it.'

'And there is one other.'

'Name it.'

'To give me five minutes in the open with a sword in your hand and a horse between your legs.'

'Tut, tut!' said he. 'I should either have to cut short your promising career, or else to bid adieu to my own bonny bride. It is unreasonable to ask such a request of a man in the first joys of matrimony.'

I gathered my horsemen together and wheeled them into column.

'Au revoir,' I cried, shaking my sword at him. 'The next time you may not escape so easily.'

'Au revoir,' he answered. 'When you are weary of the Emperor, you will always find a commission waiting for you in the service of the Marshal Millefleurs.'

SEVEN

How the Brigadier was Tempted by the Devil

6 April 1814, or on one of the next two or three days.
Marmont's defection to the Allies became generally
known on 6 April, and Napoleon secretly abdicated
on that day but still retained the hopes he outlined
at the end of this exploit. Gerard would not of course
have known that on 4 April Ney, Macdonald and—as a
reluctant accomplice—Berthier had forced Napoleon to
offer abdication to the Czar Alexander I of Russia with
proviso of entail on his son, terms swept aside when
Marmont's treachery became known. When Napoleon
returned from Elba, Berthier, unable to face the conflict
of loyalties between his devotion to his old master and
his desire to stay at peace, committed suicide.

The spring is at hand, my friends. I can see the little green
spearheads breaking out once more upon the chestnut trees,
and the café tables have all been moved into the sunshine. It
is more pleasant to sit there, and yet I do not wish to tell my
little stories to the whole town. You have heard my doings as
a lieutenant, as a squadron officer, as a colonel, as the chief
of a brigade. But now I suddenly become something higher
and more important. I become history.

If you have read of those closing years of the life of the
Emperor which were spent in the Island of St Helena, you
will remember that, again and again, he implored permission
to send out one single letter which should be unopened by
those who held him. Many times he made this request, and
even went so far as to promise that he would provide for
his own wants and cease to be an expense to the British
Government if it were granted to him. But his guardians
knew that he was a terrible man, this pale, fat gentleman in
the straw hat, and they dared not grant him what he asked.
Many have wondered who it was to whom he could have had
anything so secret to say. Some have supposed that it was to

his wife, and some that it was to his father-in-law; some that it was to the Emperor Alexander, and some to Marshal Soult. What will you think of me, my friends, when I tell you it was to me—to me, the Brigadier Gerard—that the Emperor wished to write! Yes, humble as you see me, with only my 100 francs a month of half-pay between me and hunger, it is none the less true that I was always in the Emperor's mind, and that he would have given his left hand for five minutes' talk with me. I will tell you to-night how this came about.

It was after the Battle of Fére-Champenoise, where the conscripts in their blouses and their sabots made such a fine stand, that we, the more long-headed of us, began to understand that it was all over with us. Our reserve ammunition had been taken in the battle, and we were left with silent guns and empty caissons. Our cavalry, too, was in a deplorable condition, and my own brigade had been destroyed in the great charge at Craonne. Then came the news that the enemy had taken Paris, that the citizens had mounted the white cockade; and finally, most terrible of all, that Marmont and his corps had gone over to the Bourbons. We looked at each other and asked how many more of our generals were going to turn against us. Already there were Jourdan, Marmont, Murat, Bernadotte, and Jomini—though nobody minded much about Jomini, for his pen was always sharper than his sword. We had been ready to fight Europe, but it looked now as though we were to fight Europe and half of France as well.

We had come to Fontainebleau by a long, forced march, and there we were assembled, the poor remnants of us, the corps of Ney, the corps of my cousin Gerard, and the corps of Macdonald: twenty-five thousand in all, with seven thousand of the guard. But we had our prestige, which was worth fifty thousand, and our Emperor, who was worth fifty thousand more. He was always among us, serene, smiling, confident, taking his snuff and playing with his little riding-whip. Never in the days of his greatest victories have I admired him as much as I did during the Campaign of France.

One evening I was with a few of my officers drinking a glass of wine of Suresnes. I mention that it was wine of

Suresnes just to show you that times were not very good with us. Suddenly I was disturbed by a message from Berthier that he wished to see me. When I speak of my old comrades-in-arms, I will, with your permission, leave out all the fine foreign titles which they had picked up during the wars. They are excellent for a Court, but you never heard them in the camp, for we could not afford to do away with our Ney, our Rapp, or our Soult—names which were as stirring to our ears as the blare of our trumpets blowing the reveille. It was Berthier, then, who sent to say that he wished to see me.

He had a suite of rooms at the end of the gallery of Francis the First, not very far from those of the Emperor. In the ante-chamber were waiting two men whom I knew well: Colonel Despienne, of the 57th of the line, and Captian Tremeau, of the Voltigeurs. They were both old soldiers—Tremeau had carried a musket in Egypt— and they were also both famous in the army for their courage and their skill with weapons. Tremeau had become a little stiff in the wrist, but Despienne was capable at his best of making me exert myself. He was a tiny fellow, about three inches short of the proper height for a man—he was exactly three inches shorter than myself—but both with the sabre and with the small-sword he had several times almost held his own against me when we used to exhibit at Verron's Hall of Arms in the Palais Royal. You may think that it made us sniff something in the wind when we found three such men called together into one room. You cannot see the lettuce and the dressing without suspecting a salad.

'Name of a pipe!' said Tremeau, in his barrack-room fashion. 'Are we then expecting three champions of the Bourbons?'

To all of us the idea appeared not improbable. Certainly in the whole army we were the very three who might have been chosen to meet them.

'The Prince of Neufchâtel desires to speak with the Brigadier Gerard,' said a footman, appearing at the door.

In I went, leaving my two companions consumed with impatience behind me. It was a small room, but very gorgeously furnished. Berthier was seated opposite to me at a little table, with a pen in his hand and a note-book open before him. He was looking weary and slovenly – very different from that Berthier who used to give the fashion to the army, and who had so often set us poorer officers tearing our hair by trimming his pelisse with fur, one campaign, and with grey astrakhan the next. On his clean-shaven, comely face there was an expression of trouble, and he looked at me as I entered his chamber in a way which had in it something furtive and displeasing.

'Chief of Brigade Gerard!' said he.

'At your service, your Highness!' I answered.

'I must ask you, before I go further, to promise me, upon your honour as a gentleman and a soldier, that what is about to pass between us shall never be mentioned to any third person.'

My word, this was a fine beginning! I had no choice but to give the promise required.

'You must know, then, that it is all over with the Emperor,' said he, looking down at the table and speaking very slowly, as if he had a hard task in getting out the words. 'Jourdan at Rouen and Marmont at Paris have both mounted the white cockade, and it is rumoured that Talleyrand has talked Ney into doing the same. It is evident that further resistance is useless, and that it can only bring misery upon our country. I wish to ask you, therefore, whether you are prepared to join me in laying hands upon the Emperor's person, and bringing the war to a conclusion by delivering him over to the allies.'

I assure you that when I heard this infamous proposition put forward by the man who had been the earliest friend of the Emperor, and who had received greater favours from him than any of his followers, I could only stand and stare at him in amazement. For his part he tapped his pen-handle against his teeth, and looked at me with a slanting head.

'Well?' he asked.

'I am a little deaf upon one side,' said I, coldly. 'There are some things which I cannot hear. I beg that you will permit me to return to my duties.'

'Nay, but you must not be headstrong,' said he, rising up and laying his hand upon my shoulder. 'You are aware that the Senate has declared against Napoleon, and that the Emperor Alexander refuses to treat with him.'

'Sir,' I cried, with passion, 'I would have you know that I do not care the dregs of a wine-glass for the Senate or for the Emperor Alexander either.'

'Then for what do you care?'

'For my own honour and for the service of my glorious master, the Emperor Napoleon.'

'That is all very well,' said Berthier, peevishly, shrugging his shoulders. 'Facts are facts, and as men of the world, we must look them in the face. Are we to stand against the will of the nation? Are we to have civil war on the top of all our misfortunes? And, besides, we are thinning away. Every hour comes the news of fresh desertions. We have still time to make our peace, and, indeed, to earn the highest reward, by giving up the Emperor.'

I shook so with passion that my sabre clattered against my thigh.

'Sir,' I cried, 'I never thought to have seen the day when a Marshal of France would have so far degraded himself as to put forward such a proposal. I leave you to your own conscience; but as for me, until I have the Emperor's own order, there shall always be the sword of Etienne Gerard between his enemies and himself.'

I was so moved by my own words and by the fine position which I had taken up, that my voice broke, and I could hardly refrain from tears. I should have liked the whole army to have seen me as I stood with my head so proudly erect and my hand upon my heart proclaiming my devotion to the Emperor in his adversity. It was one of the supreme moments of my life.

'Very good,' said Berthier, ringing a bell for the lackey. 'You will show the Chief of Brigade Gerard into the salon.'

The footman led me into an inner room, where he desired me to be seated. For my own part, my only desire was to get away, and I could not understand why they should wish to detain me. When one has had no change of uniform during a whole winter's campaign, one does not feel at home in a palace.

I had been there about a quarter of an hour when the

footman opened the door again, and in came Colonel
Despienne. Good heavens, what a sight he was! His face
was as white as a guardsman's gaiters, his eyes projecting,
the veins swollen upon his forehead, and every hair of his
moustache bristling like those of an angry cat. He was too
angry to speak, and could only shake his hands at the ceiling
and make a gurgling in his throat. 'Parricide! Viper!' those
were the words that I could catch as he stamped up and
down the room.

Of course it was evident to me that he had been subjected
to the same infamous proposals as I had, and that he had
received them in the same spirit. His lips were sealed to
me, as mine were to him, by the promise which we had
taken, but I contented myself with muttering 'Atrocious!
Unspeakable!'—so that he might know that I was in
agreement with him.

Well, we were still there, he striding furiously up and
down, and I seated in the corner, when suddenly a most
extraordinary uproar broke out in the room which we had
just quitted. There was a snarling, worrying growl, like that
of a fierce dog which has got his grip. Then came a crash
and a voice calling for help. In we rushed, the two of us,
and, my faith, we were none too soon.

Old Tremeau and Berthier were rolling together upon the
floor, with the table upon the top of them. The Captain had
one of his great, skinny, yellow hands upon the Marshal's
throat, and already his face was lead-coloured, and his eyes
were starting from their sockets. As to Tremeau, he was
beside himself, with foam upon the corners of his lips, and
such a frantic expression upon him that I am convinced, had
we not loosened his iron grip, finger by finger, that it would
never have relaxed while the Marshal lived. His nails were
white with the power of his grasp.

'I have been tempted by the devil!' he cried, as he staggered to his feet. 'Yes, I have been tempted by the devil!'

As to Berthier, he could only lean against the wall, and
pant for a couple of minutes, putting his hands up to his
throat and rolling his head about. Then, with an angry
gesture, he turned to the heavy blue curtain which hung
behind his chair.

'There, sire!' he cried, furiously, 'I told you exactly what would come of it.'

The curtain was torn to one side and the Emperor stepped out into the room. We sprang to the salute, we three old soldiers, but it was all like a scene in a dream to us, and our eyes were as far out as Berthier's had been. Napoleon was dressed in his green coated chasseur uniform, and he held his little silver-headed switch in his hand. He looked at us each in turn, with a smile upon his face—that frightful smile in which neither eyes nor brow joined—and each in turn had, I believe, a pringling on his skin, for that was the effect which the Emperor's gaze had upon most of us. Then he walked across to Berthier and put his hand upon his shoulder.

'You must not quarrel with blows, my dear Prince,' said he; 'they are your title to nobility.' He spoke in that soft, caressing manner which he could assume. There was no one who could make the French tongue sound so pretty as the Emperor, and no one who could make it more harsh and terrible.

'I believe he would have killed me,' cried Berthier, still rolling his head about.

'Tut, tut! I should have come to your help had these officers not heard your cries. But I trust that you are not really hurt!' He spoke with earnestness, for he was in truth very fond of Berthier—more so than of any man, unless it were of poor Duroc.

Berthier laughed, though not with a very good grace.

'It is new for me to receive my injuries from French hands,' said he.

'And yet it was in the cause of France,' returned the Emperor. Then, turning to us, he took old Tremeau by the ear. 'Ah, old grumbler,' said he, 'you were one of my Egyptian grenadiers, were you not, and had your musket of honour at Marengo. I remember you very well, my good friend. So the old fires are not yet extinguished! They still burn up when you think that your Emperor is wronged. And you, Colonel Despienne, you would not even listen to the tempter. And you, Gerard, your faithful sword is ever to be between me and my enemies. Well, well, I have had some traitors about me, but now at last we are beginning to see who are the true men.'

You can fancy, my friends, the thrill of joy which it gave us when the greatest man in the whole world spoke to us in this fashion. Tremeau shook until I thought he would have fallen, and the tears ran down his gigantic moustache. If you had not seen it, you could never believe the influence which the Emperor had upon those coarse-grained, savage old veterans.

'Well, my faithful friends,' said he, 'if you will follow me into this room, I will explain to you the meaning of this little farce which we have been acting. I beg, Berthier, that you will remain in this chamber, and so make sure that no one interrupts us.'

It was new for us to be doing business, with a Marshal of France as sentry at the door. However, we followed the Emperor as we were ordered, and he led us into the recess of the window, gathering us around him and sinking his voice as he addressed us.

'I have picked you out of the whole army,' said he, 'as being not only the most formidable but also the most faithful of my soldiers. I was convinced that you were all three men who would never waver in your fidelity to me. If I have ventured to put that fidelity to the proof, and to watch you whilst attempts were at my orders made upon your honour, it was only because, in the days when I have found the blackest treason amongst my own flesh and blood, it is necessary that I should be doubly circumspect. Suffice it that I am well convinced now that I can rely upon your valour.'

'To the death, sire!' cried Tremeau, and we both repeated it after him.

Napoleon drew us all yet a little closer to him, and sank his voice still lower.

'What I say to you now I have said to no one—not to my wife or my brothers; only to you. It is all up with us, my friends. We have come to our last rally. The game is finished, and we must make provision accordingly.'

My heart seemed to have changed to a nine-pounder ball as I listened to him. We had hoped against hope, but now when he, the man who was always serene and who always had reserves—when he, in that quiet, impassive voice of his, said that everything was over, we realized that the clouds had shut for ever, and the last gleam gone. Tremeau snarled and gripped at his sabre, Despienne ground his teeth, and for my own part I threw out my chest and clicked my heels to show the Emperor that there were some spirits which could rise to adversity.

'My papers and my fortune must be secured,' whispered the Emperor. 'The whole course of the future may depend upon my having them safe. They are our base for the next attempt—for I am sure that these poor Bourbons would find that my footstool is too large to make a throne for them. Where am I to keep these precious things? My belongings will be searched—so will the houses of my supporters. They must be secured and concealed by men whom I can trust with that which is more precious to me than my life. Out of the whole of France, you are those whom I have chosen for this sacred trust.

'In the first place, I will tell you what these papers are. You shall not say that I have made you blind agents in the matter. They are the official proof of my divorce from Josephine, of my legal marriage to Marie Louise, and of the birth of my son and heir, the King of Rome. If we cannot prove each of these, the future claim of my family to the throne of France falls to the ground. Then there are securities to the value of forty millions of francs—an immense sum, my friends, but of no more value than this riding switch when compared to the other papers of which I have spoken. I tell you these things that you may realize the enormous importance of the task which I am committing to your care. Listen, now, while I inform you where you are to get these papers, and what you are to do with them.

'They were handed over to my trusty friend, the Countess Walewski, at Paris, this morning. At five o'clock she starts for Fontainebleau in her blue berline. She should reach here between half-past nine and ten. The papers will be concealed in the berline, in a hiding-place which none know but herself. She has been warned that her carriage will be stopped outside the town by three mounted officers, and she will hand the packet over to your care. You are the younger man, Gerard, but you are of the senior grade. I confide to your care this amethyst ring, which you will show the lady as a token of your mission, and which you will leave with her as a receipt for her papers.

'Having received the packet, you will ride with it into the forest as far as the ruined dove-house—the Colombier. It is possible that I may meet you there—but if it seems to me to be dangerous, I will send my body-servant, Mustapha, whose directions you may take as being mine. There is no roof to the Colombier, and to-night will be a full moon. At the right of the entrance you will find three spades leaning against the wall. With these you will dig a hole three feet deep in the north-eastern corner—that is, in the corner to the left of the door, and nearest to Fontainebleau. Having buried the papers, you will replace the soil with great care, and you will then report to me at the palace.'

These were the Emperor's directions, but given with an accuracy and minuteness of detail such as no one but himself could put into an order. When he had finished, he made us swear to keep his secret as long as he lived, and as long as the papers should remain buried. Again and again he made us swear it before he dismissed us from his presence.

Colonel Despienne had quarters at the 'Sign of the Pheasant,' and it was there that we supped together. We were all three men who had been trained to take the strangest turns of fortune as part of our daily life and business, yet we were all flushed and moved by the extra-ordinary interview which we had had, and by the thought of the great adventure which lay before us. For my own part, it had been my fate three several times to take my orders from the lips of the Emperor himself, but neither the incident of the Ajaccio murderers nor the famous ride which I made to Paris appeared to offer such opportunities as this new and most intimate commission.

'If things go right with the Emperor,' said Despienne, 'we shall all live to be marshals yet.'

We drank with him to our future cocked hats and our bâtons.

It was agreed between us that we should make our way

separately to our rendezvous, which was to be the first milestone upon the Paris road. In this way we should avoid the gossip which might get about if three men who were so well known were to be seen riding out together. My little Violette had cast a shoe that morning, and the farrier was at work upon her when I returned, so that my comrades were already there when I arrived at the trysting-place. I had taken with me not only my sabre, but also my new pair of English rifled pistols, with a mallet for knocking in the charges. They had cost me a hundred and fifty francs at Trouvel's, in the Rue de Rivoli, but they would carry far further and straighter than the others. It was with one of them that I had saved old Bouvet's life at Leipzig.

The night was cloudless, and there was a brilliant moon behind us, so that we always had three black horsemen riding down the white road in front of us. The country is so thickly wooded, however, that we could not see very far. The great palace clock had already struck ten, but there was no sign of the Countess. We began to fear that something might have prevented her from starting.

And then suddenly we heard her in the distance. Very faint at first were the birr of wheels and the tat-tat-tat of the horses' feet. Then they grew louder and clearer and louder yet, until a pair of yellow lanterns swung round the curve, and in their light we saw the two big brown horses tearing along with the high, blue carriage at the back of them. The postillion pulled them up panting and foaming within a few yards of us. In a moment we were at the window and had raised our hands in a salute to the beautiful pale face which looked out at us.

'We are the three officers of the Emperor, madame,' said I, in a low voice leaning my face down to the open window. 'You have already been warned that we should wait upon you.'

The countess had a very beautiful, cream-tinted complexion of a sort which I particularly admire, but she grew whiter and whiter as she looked at me. Harsh lines deepened upon her face until she seemed, even as I looked at her, to turn from youth into age.

'It is evident to me,' she said, 'that you are three impostors.'

If she had struck me across the face with her delicate hand she could not have startled me more. It was not her words only, but the bitterness with which she hissed them out.

'Indeed, madame,' said I. 'You do us less than justice. These are the Colonel Despienne and Captain Tremeau. For myself, my name is Brigadier Gerard, and I have only to mention it to assure anyone who has heard of me that—'

'Oh, you villains!' she interrupted. 'You think that because I am only a woman I am very easily to be hood-winked! You miserable impostors!'

I looked at Despienne, who had turned white with anger, and at Tremeau, who was tugging at his moustache.

'Madame,' said I, coldly, 'when the Emperor did us the honour to intrust us with this mission, he gave me this amethyst ring as a token. I had not thought that three hon-ourable gentlemen would have needed such corroboration, but I can only confute your unworthy suspicions by placing it in your hands.'

She held it up in the light of the carriage lamp, and the most dreadful expression of grief and of horror contorted her face.

'It is his!' she screamed, and then, 'Oh, my God, what have I done? What have I done?'

I felt that something terrible had befallen. 'Quick, mad-ame, quick!' I cried. 'Give us the papers!'

'I have already given them.'

'Given them! To whom?'

'To three officers.'

'When?'

'Within the half-hour.'

'Where are they?'

'God help me, I do not know. They stopped the berline, and I handed them over to them without hesitation, thinking that they had come from the Emperor.'

It was a thunder-clap. But those are the moments when I am at my finest.

'You remain here,' said I, to my comrades. 'If three horsemen pass you, stop them at any hazard. The lady will describe them to you. I will be with you presently.' One shake of the bridle, and I was flying into Fontainbleau as only Violette could have carried me. At the palace I flung myself off, rushed up the stairs, brushed aside the lackeys who would have stopped me, and pushed my way into the Emperor's own cabinet. He and Macdonald were busy with pencil and compasses over a chart. He looked up with an angry frown at my sudden entry, but his face changed colour when he saw that it was I.

'You can leave us, Marshal,' said he, and then, the instant that the door was closed: 'What news about the papers?'

'They are gone,' said I, and in a few curt words I told him what had happened. His face was calm, but I saw the compasses quiver in his hand.

'You must recover them, Gerard!' he cried. 'The destinies of my dynasty are at stake. Not a moment is to be lost! To horse, sir, to horse!'

'Who are they, sire?'

'I cannot tell. I am surrounded with treason. But they will take them to Paris. To whom should they carry them but to the villain Talleyrand? Yes, yes, they are on the Paris road, and may yet be overtaken. With the three best mounts in my stables and—'

I did not wait to hear the end of the sentence. I was already clattering down the stair. I am sure that five minutes had not passed before I was galloping Violette out of the town with the bridle of one of the Emperor's own Arab chargers in either hand. They wished me to take three, but I should have never dared to look my Violette in the face again. I feel that the spectacle must have been superb when I dashed up to my comrades and pulled the horses on to their haunches in the moonlight.

'No one has passed?'

'No one.'

'Then they are on the Paris road. Quick! Up and after them!'

They did not take long, those good soldiers. In a flash they were upon the Emperor's horses, and their own left masterless by the roadside. Then away we went upon our long chase, I in the centre, Despienne upon my right, and Tremeau a little behind, for he was the heavier man. Heavens, how we galloped! The twelve flying hoofs roared and roared along the hard, smooth road. Poplars and moon, black bars and silver streaks, for mile after mile our course lay along the same chequered track, with our shadows in front and our dust behind. We could hear the rasping of bolts and the creaking of shutters from the cottages as we thundered past them, but we were only three dark blurs upon the road by the time that the folk could look after us. It was just striking midnight as we raced into Corbail; but an ostler with a bucket in each hand was throwing his black shadow across the golden fan which was cast from the open door of the inn.

'Three riders!' I gasped. 'Have they passed?'

'I have just been watering their horses,' said he. 'I should think they—'

'On, on, my friends!' and away we flew, striking fire from the cobblestones of the little town. A gendarme tried to stop us, but his voice was drowned by our rattle and clatter. The houses slid past, and we were out on the country road again, with a clear twenty miles between ourselves and Paris. How could they escape us, with the finest horses in France behind them? Not one of the three had turned a hair, but Violette was always a head and shoulders to the front. She was going within herself, too, and I knew by the spring of her that I had only to let her stretch herself, and the Emperor's horses would see the colour of her tail.

'There they are!' cried Despienne.

'We have them!' growled Tremeau.

'On, comrades, on!' I shouted, once more.

A long stretch of white road lay before us in the moonlight. Far away down it we could see three cavaliers, lying low upon their horses' necks. Every instant they grew larger and clearer as we gained upon them. I could see quite plainly that the two upon either side were wrapped in mantles and rode upon chestnut horses, whilst the man between them was dressed in a chasseur uniform and mounted upon a grey. They were keeping abreast, but it was easy enough to see from the way in which he gathered his legs for each spring that the centre horse was far the fresher of the three.

And the rider appeared to be the leader of the party, for we continually saw the glint of his face in the moonshine as he looked back to measure the distance between us. At first it was only a glimmer, then it was cut across with a moustache, and at last when we began to feel their dust in our throats I could give a name to my man.

'Halt, Colonel de Montluc!' I shouted. 'Halt, in the Emperor's name!'

I had known him for years as a daring officer and an unprincipled rascal. Indeed there was a score between us, for he had shot my friend, Treville, at Warsaw, pulling his trigger, as some said, a good second before the drop of the handkerchief.

Well, the words were hardly out of my mouth when his two comrades wheeled round and fired their pistols at us. I heard Despienne give a terrible cry, and at the same instant both Tremeau and I let drive at the same man. He fell forward with his hands swinging on each side of his horse's neck. His comrade spurred on to Tremeau, sabre in hand, and I heard the crash which comes when a strong cut is met by a stronger parry. For my own part I never turned my head, but I touched Violette with the spur for the first time and flew after the leader. That he should leave his comrades and fly was proof enough that I should leave mine and follow.

He had gained a couple of hundred paces, but the good little mare set that right before we could have passed two milestones. It was in vain that he spurred and thrashed like a gunner driver on a soft road. His hat flew off with his exertions, and his bald head gleamed in the moonshine. But do what he might, he still heard the rattle of the hoofs growing louder and louder behind him. I could not have been twenty yards from him, and the shadow head was touching the shadow haunch, when he turned with a curse in his saddle and emptied both his pistols, one after the other, into Violette.

I have been wounded myself so often that I have to stop and think before I can tell you the exact number of times. I have been hit by musket balls, by pistol bullets, and by bursting shell, besides being pierced by bayonet, lance, sabre, and finally by a bradawl, which was the most painful of any. Yet out of all these injuries I have never known the same deadly sickness as came over me when I felt the poor, silent, patient creature, which I had come to love more than anything in the world except my mother and the Emperor, reel and stagger beneath me. I pulled my second pistol from my holster and fired point-blank between the fellow's broad shoulders. He slashed his horse across the flank with his whip, and for a moment I thought that I had missed him. But then on the green of his chasseur jacket I saw an ever-widening black smudge, and he began to sway in his saddle, very slightly at first, but more and more with every bound, until at last over he went, with his foot caught in the stirrup and his shoulders thud-thud-thudding along the road, until the drag was too much for the tired horse, and I closed my hand upon the foam-spattered bridle-chain. As I pulled him up it eased the stirrup leather, and the spurred heel clinked loudly as it fell.

'Your papers!' I cried, springing from my saddle. 'This instant!'

But even as I said it, the huddle of the green body and the fantastic sprawl of the limbs in the moonlight told me clearly enough that it was all over with him. My bullet had passed through his heart, and it was only his own iron will which had held him so long in the saddle. He had lived hard, this Montluc, and I will do him justice to say that he died hard also.

But it was the papers—always the papers—of which I thought. I opened his tunic and I felt in his shirt. Then I searched his holsters and his sabre-tasche. Finally I dragged off his boots, and undid his horse's girth so as to hunt under the saddle. There was not a nook or crevice which I did not ransack. It was useless. They were not upon him.

When this stunning blow came upon me I could have sat down by the roadside and wept. Fate seemed to be fighting against me, and that is an enemy from whom even a gallant hussar might not be ashamed to flinch. I stood with my arm over the neck of my poor wounded Violette, and I tried to think it all out, that I might act in the wisest way. I was aware that the Emperor had no great respect for my wits, and I longed to show him that he had done me an injustice. Montluc had not the papers. And yet Montluc had sacrificed his companions in order to make his escape. I could make nothing of that. On the other hand, it was clear that, if he had not got them, one or other of his comrades had. One of them was certainly dead. The other I had left fighting with Tremeau, and if he escaped from the old swordsman he had still to pass me. Clearly, my work lay behind me.

I hammered fresh charges into my pistols after I had turned this over in my head. Then I put them back in the holsters, and I examined my little mare, she jerking her head and cocking her ears the while, as if to tell me that an old soldier like herself did not make a fuss about a scratch of two. The first shot had merely grazed her off shoulder, leaving a skin-mark, as if she had brushed a wall. The second was more serious. It had passed through the muscle of her neck, but already it had ceased to bleed. I reflected that if she weakened I could mount Montluc's grey, and meanwhile I led him along beside us, for he was a fine horse, worth fifteen hundred francs at the least, and it seemed to me that no one had a better right to him than I.

Well, I was all impatience now to get back to the others, and I had just given Violette her head, when suddenly I saw something glimmering in a field by the roadside. It was the brasswork upon the chasseur hat which had flown from Montluc's head; and at the sight of it a thought made me jump in the saddle. How could the hat have flown off? With its weight, would it not have simply dropped? And here it lay, fifteen paces from the roadway! Of course, he must have thrown it off when he had made sure that I would overtake him. And if he threw it off—I did not stop to reason any more, but sprang from the mare with my heart beating the *pas-de-charge*. Yes, it was all right this time. There, in the crown of the hat was stuffed a roll of papers in a parchment wrapper bound round with yellow ribbon. I pulled it out with the one hand, and holding the hat in the other, I danced for joy in the moonlight. The Emperor would see that he had not made a mistake when he put his affairs into the charge of Etienne Gerard.

I had a safe pocket on the inside of my tunic just over my heart, where I kept a few little things which were dear to me, and into this I thrust my precious roll. Then I sprang upon Violette, and was pushing forward to see what had become of Tremeau, when I saw a horseman riding across the field in the distance. At the same instant I heard the sound of hoofs approaching me, and there in the moonlight was the Emperor upon his white charger, dressed in his grey overcoat and his three-cornered hat, just as I had seen him so often upon the field of battle.

'Well!' he cried, in the sharp, sergeant-major way of his. 'Where are my papers?'

I spurred forward and presented them without a word. He broke the ribbon and ran his eyes rapidly over them. Then, as we sat our horses head to tail, he threw his left arm across me with his hand upon my shoulder. Yes, my friends, simple as you see me, I have been embraced by my great master.

'Gerard,' he cried, 'you are a marvel!'

I did not wish to contradict him, and it brought a flush of joy upon my cheeks to know that he had done me justice at last.

'Where is the thief, Gerard?' he asked.

'Dead, sire.'

'You killed him?'

'He wounded my horse, sire, and would have escaped had I not shot him.'

'Did you recognise him?'

'De Montluc is his name, sire—a Colonel of Chasseurs.'

'Tut,' said the Emperor. 'We have got the poor pawn, but the hand which plays the game is still out of our reach.' He sat in silent thought for a little, with his chin sunk upon his chest. 'Ah, Talleyrand, Talleyrand,' I heard him mutter. 'If I had been in your place and you in mine, you would have crushed a viper when you held it under your heel. For five years I have known you for what you are, and yet I have let you live to sting me. Never mind, my brave,' he continued, turning to me, 'there will come a day of reckoning for everybody, and when it arrives, I promise you that my friends will be remembered as well as my enemies.'

'Sire,' said I, for I had had time for thought as well as he, 'if your plans about these papers have been carried to the ears of your enemies, I trust that you do not think that it was owing to any indiscretion upon the part of myself or of my comrades.'

'It would be hardly reasonable for me to do so,' he answered, 'seeing that this plot was hatched in Paris, and that you only had your orders a few hours ago.'

'Then how— ?'

'Enough,' he cried sternly. 'You take an undue advantage of your position.'

That was always the way with the Emperor. He would chat with you as with a friend and a brother, and then when he had wiled you into forgetting the gulf which lay between you, he would suddenly, with a word or with a look, remind you that it was as impassable as ever. When I have fondled my old hound until he has been encouraged to paw my knees, and I have then thrust him down again, it has made me think of the Emperor and his ways.

He reined his horse round, and I followed him in silence and with a heavy heart. But when he spoke again his words were enough to drive all thought of myself out of my mind.

'I could not sleep until I knew how you had fared,' said he. 'I have paid a price for my papers. There are not so many of my old soldiers left that I can afford to lose two in one night.'

When he said 'two' it turned me cold.

'Colonel Despienne was shot, sire,' I stammered.

'And Captain Tremeau cut down. Had I been a few minutes earlier I might have saved him. The other escaped across the fields.'

I remembered that I had seen a horseman a moment before I had met the Emperor. He had taken to the fields to avoid me, but if I had known, and Violette been unwounded, the old soldier would not have gone unavenged. I was thinking sadly of his sword-play, and wondering whether it was his stiffening wrist which had been fatal to him, when Napoleon spoke again.

'Yes, Brigadier,' said he, 'you are now the only man who will know where these papers are concealed.'

It must have been imagination, my friends, but for an instant I may confess that it seemed to me that there was a tone in the Emperor's voice which was not altogether one of sorrow. But the dark thought had hardly time to form itself in my mind before he let me see that I was doing him an injustice.

'Yes, I have paid a price for my papers,' he said, and I heard them crackle as he put his hand up to his bosom. 'No man has ever had more faithful servants—no man since the beginning of the world.'

As he spoke we came upon the scene of the struggle. Colonel Despienne and the man whom we had shot lay together some distance down the road, while their horses grazed contentedly beneath the poplars. Captain Tremeau lay in front of us upon his back, with his arms and legs stretched out, and his sabre broken short off in his hand. His tunic was open, and a huge blood-clot hung like a dark handkerchief out of a slit in his white shirt. I could see the gleam of his clenched teeth from under his immense moustache.

The Emperor sprang from his horse and bent down over the dead man.

'He was with me since Rivoli,' said he, sadly. 'He was one of my old grumblers in Egypt.'

And the voice brought the man back from the dead. I saw his eyelids shiver. He twitched his arm, and moved the sword-hilt a few inches. He was trying to raise it in a salute. Then the mouth opened, and the hilt tinkled down on to the ground.

'May we all die as gallantly,' said the Emperor, as he rose, and from my heart I added 'Amen.'

There was a farm within fifty yards of where we were standing, and the farmer, roused from his sleep by the clatter of hoofs and the cracking of pistols, had rushed out to the roadside. We saw him now, dumb with fear and astonishment, staring open-eyed at the Emperor. It was to him that we committed the care of the four dead men and of the horses also. For my own part, I thought it best to leave Violette with him and to take De Montluc's grey with me, for he could not refuse to give me back my own mare, whilst there might be difficulties about the other. Besides, my little friend's wound had to be considered, and we had a long return ride before us.

The Emperor did not at first talk much upon the way. Perhaps the deaths of Despienne and Tremeau still weighed heavily upon his spirits. He was always a reserved man, and in those times, when every hour brought him the news of some success of his enemies or defection of his friends, one could not expect him to be a merry companion. Nevertheless, when I reflected that he was carrying in his bosom those papers which he valued so highly, and which only a few hours ago appeared to be for ever lost, and when I further thought that it was I, Etienne Gerard, who had placed them there, I felt that I had deserved some little consideration. The same idea may have occurred to him, for when we had at last left the Paris high road, and had entered the forest, he began of his own accord to tell me that which I should have most liked to have asked him.

'As to the papers,' said he, 'I have already told you that there is no one now, except you and me, who knows where they are to be concealed. My Mameluke carried the spades to the pigeon-house, but I have told him nothing. Our plans, however, for bringing the packet from Paris have been formed since Monday. There were three in the secret, a woman and two men. The woman I would trust with my life; which of the two men has betrayed us I do not know, but I think that I may promise to find out.'

We were riding in the shadow of the trees at the time, and I could hear him slapping his riding-whip against his boot, and taking pinch after pinch of snuff, as was his way when he was excited.

'You wonder, no doubt,' said he, after a pause, 'why these rascals did not stop the carriage at Paris instead of at the entrance to Fontainebleau.'

In truth, the objection had not occurred to me, but I did not wish to appear to have less wits than he gave me credit for, so I answered that it was indeed surprising.

'Had they done so they would have made a public scandal, and run a chance of missing their end. Short of taking the berline to pieces, they could not have discovered the hiding-place. He planned it well—he could always plan well—and he chose his agents well also. But mine were the better.'

It is not for me to repeat to you, my friends, all that was said to me by the Emperor as we walked our horses amid the black shadows and through the moon-silvered glades of the great forest. Every word of it is impressed upon my memory, and before I pass away it is likely that I will place it all upon paper, so that others may read it in the days to come. He spoke freely of his past, and something also of his future; of the devotion of Macdonald, of the treason of Marmont, of the little King of Rome, concerning whom he talked with as much tenderness as any bourgeois father of a single child; and, finally, of his father-in-law, the Emperor of Austria, who would, he thought, stand between his enemies and himself. For myself, I dared not say a word, remembering how I had already brought a rebuke upon myself; but I rode by his side, hardly able to believe that this was indeed the great Emperor, the man whose glance sent a thrill through me, who was now pouring out his thoughts to me in short, eager sentences, the words rattling and racing like the hoofs of a galloping squadron. It is possible that, after the word-splittings and diplomacy of a Court, it was a relief to him to speak his mind to a plain soldier like myself.

In this way the Emperor and I—even after years it sends a flush of pride into my cheeks to be able to put those words together—the Emperor and I walked our horses through the Forest of Fontainebleau, until we came at last to the Colombier. The three spades were propped against the wall upon the right-hand side of the ruined door, and at the sight of them the tears sprang to my eyes as I thought of the hands for which they were intended. The Emperor seized one and I another.

'Quick!' said he. 'The dawn will be upon us before we get back to the palace.'

We dug the hole, and placing the papers in one of my pistol holsters to screen them from the damp, we laid them at the bottom and covered them up. We then carefully removed all marks of the ground having been disturbed, and we placed a large stone upon the top. I dare say that since the Emperor was a young gunner, and helped to train his pieces against Toulon, he had not worked so hard with his hands. He was mopping his forehead with his silk handkerchief long before we had come to the end of our task.

The first grey cold light of morning was stealing through the tree trunks when we came out together from the old pigeon-house. The Emperor laid his hand upon my shoulder as I stood ready to help him to mount.

'We have left the papers there,' said he, solemnly, 'and I desire that you shall leave all thought of them there also. Let the recollection of them pass entirely from your mind, to be revived only when you receive a direct order under my own hand and seal. From this time onwards you forget all that has passed.'

'I forget it, sire,' said I.

We rode together to the edge of town, where he desired that I should separate from him. I had saluted, and was turning my horse, when he called me back.

'It is easy to mistake the points of the compass in the forest,' said he. 'Would you not say that it was in the north-eastern corner that we buried them?'

'Buried what, sire?'

'The papers, of course,' he cried, impatiently.

'What papers, sire?'

'Name of a name! Why, the papers that you have recovered for me.'

'I am really at a loss to know what your Majesty is talking about.'

He flushed with anger for a moment, and then he burst out laughing.

'Very good, Brigadier!' he cried. 'I begin to believe that you are as good a diplomatist as you are a soldier, and I cannot say more than that.'

So that was my strange adventure in which I found myself the friend and confident agent of the Emperor. When he returned from Elba he refrained from digging up the papers until his position should be secure, and they still remained in the corner of the old pigeon-house after his exile to St Helena. It was at this time that he was desirous of getting them into the hands of his own supporters, and for that purpose he wrote me, as I afterwards learned, three letters, all of which were intercepted by his guardians. Finally, he offered to support himself and his own establishment—which he might very easily have done out of the gigantic sum which belonged to him—if they would only pass one of his letters unopened. This request was refused, and so, up to his death in '21, the papers still remained where I have told you. How they came to be dug up by Count Bertrand and myself, and who eventually obtained them, is a story which I would tell you, were it not that the end has not yet come.

Some day you will hear of those papers and you will see how, after he has been so long in his grave, that great man can still set Europe shaking. When that day comes, you will think of Etienne Gerard, and you will tell your children that you have heard the story from the lips of the man who was the only one living of all who took part in that strange history—the man who was tempted by Marshal Berthier, who led that wild pursuit upon the Paris road, who was honoured by the embrace of the Emperor, and who rode with him by moonlight in the Forest of Fontainebleau. The buds are bursting and the birds are calling, my friends. You may find better things to do in the sunlight than listening to the stories of an old, broken soldier. And yet you may well treasure what I say, for the buds will have burst and the birds sung in many seasons before France will see such another ruler as he whose servants we were proud to be.

EIGHT

How the Brigadier Played for a Kingdom

First days of March, 1813. Prussia had concluded a
Convention with Russia secretly agreeing to alliance
against Napoleon in late February, but only declared
its intentions openly on 13 March, until which time
its quiescence was still a possibility. The twenty-two
year-old poet Karl Theodor Körner was at this time
journeying from Vienna to Leipzig, in the reverse
direction from Gerard, evangelising by song. He was
killed fighting the French on 26 August 1813. His father
is said to have been Schiller's closest friend.

It has sometimes struck me that some of you, when you
have heard me tell these little adventures of mine, may
have gone away with the impression that I was conceited.
There could not be a greater mistake than this, for I have
always observed that really fine soldiers are free from this
failing. It is true that I have had to depict myself sometimes
as brave, sometimes as full of resource, always as interesting;
but, then, it really was so, and I had to take the facts as I
found them. It would be an unworthy affectation if I were
to pretend that my career has been anything but a fine one.
The incident which I will tell you to-night, however, is one
which you will understand that only a modest man would
describe. After all, when one has attained such a position
as mine, one can afford to speak of what an ordinary man
might be tempted to conceal.

You must know, then, that after the Russian campaign the
remains of our poor army were quartered along the western
bank of the Elbe, where they might thaw their frozen blood
and try, with the help of the good German beer, to put a little
between their skin and their bones. There were some things
which we could not hope to regain, for I daresay that three
large commissariat fourgons would not have sufficed to carry
the fingers and the toes which the army had shed during that

retreat. Still, lean and crippled as we were, we had much to be thankful for when we thought of our poor comrades whom we had left behind, and of the snowfields—the horrible, horrible snowfields. To this day, my friends, I do not care to see red and white together. Even my red cap thrown down upon my white counterpane has given me dreams in which I have seen those monstrous plains, the reeling, tortured army, and the crimson smears which glared upon the snow behind them. You will coax no story out of me about that business, for the thought of it is enough to turn my wine to vinegar and my tobacco to straw.

Of the half-million who crossed the Elbe in the autumn of the year '12, about forty thousand infantry were left in the spring of '13. But they were terrible men, these forty thousand: men of iron, eaters of horses, and sleepers in the snow; filled, too, with rage and bitterness against the Russians. They would hold the Elbe until the great army of conscripts, which the Emperor was raising in France, should be ready to help them to cross it once more.

But the cavalry was in a deplorable condition. My own hussars were at Borna, and when I paraded them first, I burst into tears at the sight of them. My fine men and my beautiful horses—it broke my heart to see the state to which they were reduced. 'But, courage,' I thought, 'they have lost much, but their Colonel is still left to them.' I set to work, therefore, to repair their disasters, and had already constructed two good squadrons, when an order came that all colonels of cavalry should repair instantly to the depots of the regiments in France to organize the recruits and the remounts for the coming campaign.

You will think, doubtless, that I was overjoyed at this chance of visiting home once more. I will not deny that it was a pleasure to me to know that I should see my mother again, and there were a few girls who would be very glad at the news; but there were others in the army who had a stronger claim. I would have given my place to any who had wives and children whom they might not see again. However, there is no arguing when the blue paper with the little red seal arrives, so within an hour I was off upon my great ride from the Elbe to the Vosges. At last, I was to have a period of quiet. War lay behind my mare's tail and peace in front of her nostrils. So I thought, as the sound of the bugles died in the distance, and the long, white road curled away in front of me through plain and forest and mountain, with France somewhere beyond the blue haze which lay upon the horizon.

It is interesting, but it is also fatiguing, to ride in the rear of an army. In the harvest time our soldiers could do without supplies, for they had been trained to pluck the grain in the fields as they passed, and to grind it for themselves in their bivouacs. It was at that time of year, therefore, that those swift marches were performed which were the wonder and the despair of Europe. But now the starving men had to be made robust once more, and I was forced to draw into the ditch continually as the Coburg sheep and the Bavarian bullocks came streaming past with waggon loads of Berlin beer and good French cognac. Sometimes, too, I would hear the dry rattle of the drums and the shrill whistle of the fifes, and long columns of our good little infantry men would swing past me with the white dust lying thick upon their blue tunics. These were old soldiers drawn from the garrisons of our German fortresses, for it was not until May that the new conscripts began to arrive from France.

Well, I was rather tired of this eternal stopping and dodging, so that I was not sorry when I came to Altenburg to find that the road divided, and that I could take the southern and quieter branch. There were few wayfarers between there and Greiz, and the road wound through groves of oaks and beeches, which shot their branches across the path. You will think it strange that a Colonel of hussars should again and again pull up his horse in order to admire the beauty of the feathery branches and the little, green, new-budded leaves, but if you had spent six months among the fir trees of Russia you would be able to understand me.

There was something, however, which pleased me very much less than the beauty of the forests, and that was the words and looks of the folk who lived in the woodland villages. We had always been excellent friends with the Germans, and during the last six years they had never seemed to bear us any malice for having made a little free with their country. We had shown kindnesses to the men and received them from the women, so that good, comfortable Germany was a second home to all of us. But now there was something which I could not understand in the behaviour of the people. The travellers made no answer to my salute; the foresters turned their heads away to avoid seeing me; and in the villages the folk would gather into knots in the roadway and would scowl at me as I passed. Even women would do this, and it was something new for me in those days to see anything but a smile in a woman's eyes when they were turned upon me.

It was in the hamlet of Schmolin, just ten miles out of Altenburg, that the thing became most marked. I had stopped at the little inn there just to damp my moustache and to wash the dust out of poor Violette's throat. It was my way to give some little compliment, or possibly a kiss, to the maid who served me; but this one would have neither the one nor the other, but darted a glance at me like a bayonet-thrust. Then when I raised my glass to the folk who drank their beer by the door they turned their backs on me, save only one fellow, who cried, 'Here's a toast for you, boys! Here's to the letter T!' At that they all emptied their beer mugs and laughed; but it was not a laugh that had good-fellowship in it.

I was turning this over in my head and wondering what their boorish conduct could mean, when I saw, as I rode from the village, a great T new carved upon a tree. I had already seen more than one in my morning's ride, but I had given no thought to them until the words of the beer-drinker gave them an importance. It chanced that a respectable-looking person was riding past me at the moment, so I turned to him for information.

'Can you tell me, sir,' said I, 'what this letter T is?'

He looked at it and then at me in the most singular fashion. 'Young man,' said he, 'it is not the letter N.' Then before I could ask further he clapped his spurs into his horse's ribs and rode, stomach to earth, upon his way.

At first his words had no particular significance in my mind, but as I trotted onwards Violette chanced to half turn her dainty head, and my eyes were caught by the gleam of the brazen N's at the end of the bridle-chain. It was the Emperor's mark. And those T's meant something which was opposite to it. Things had been happening in Germany, then, during our absence, and the giant sleeper had begun to stir. I thought of the mutinous faces that I had seen, and I felt that if I could only have looked into the hearts of these people I might have had some strange news to bring into France with me. It made me the more eager to get my remounts, and to see ten strong squadrons behind my kettledrums once more.

While these thoughts were passing through my head I had been alternately walking and trotting, as a man should who has a long journey before and a willing horse beneath him. The woods were very open at this point, and beside the road there lay a great heap of fagots. As I passed there came a sharp sound from among them, and, glancing round, I saw a face looking out at me—a hot, red face, like that of a man who is beside himself with excitement and anxiety. A second glance told me that it was the very person with whom I had talked an hour before in the village.

'Come nearer!' he hissed. 'Nearer still! Now dismount and pretend to be mending the stirrup leather. Spies may be watching us, and it means death to me if I am seen helping you.'

'Death!' I whispered. 'From whom?'

'From the Tugendbund. From Lutzow's night-riders. You Frenchmen are living on a powder-magazine, and the match has been struck which will fire it.'

'But this is all strange to me,' said I, still fumbling at the leathers of my horse. 'What is this Tugendbund?'

'It is the secret society which has planned the great rising which is to drive you out of Germany, just as you have been driven out of Russia.'

'And these T's stand for it?'

'They are the signal. I should have told you all this in the village, but I dared not be seen speaking to you. I galloped through the woods to cut you off, and concealed both my horse and myself.'

'I am very much indebted to you,' said I, 'and the more

so as you are the only German that I have met to-day from whom I have had common civility.'

'All that I possess I have gained through contracting for the French armies,' said he. 'Your Emperor has been a good friend to me. But I beg that you will ride on now, for we have talked long enough. Beware only of Lutzow's night-riders!'

'Banditti?' I asked.

'All that is best in Germany,' said he. 'But for God's sake ride forwards, for I have risked my life and exposed my good name in order to carry you this warning.'

Well, if I had been heavy with thought before, you can think how I felt after my strange talk with the man among the fagots. What came home to me even more than his words was his shivering, broken voice, his twitching face, and his eyes glancing swiftly to right and left, and opening in horror whenever a branch cracked upon a tree. It was clear that he was in the last extremity of terror, and it is possible that after I had left him I heard a distant gunshot and a shouting from somewhere behind me. It may have been some sportsman halloaing to his dogs, but I never again heard or saw the man who had given me my warning.

I kept a good look-out after this, riding swiftly where the country was open, and slowly where there might be an ambuscade. It was serious for me, since 500 good miles of German soil lay in front of me; but somehow I did not take it very much to heart, for the Germans had always seemed to me to be a kindly, gentle people, whose hands closed more readily round a pipe-stem than a swordhilt—not out of want of valour, you understand, but because they are genial, open souls, who would rather be on good terms with all men. I did not know then that beneath that homely surface there lurks a devilry as fierce as, and far more persistent than, that of the Castilian or the Italian.

And it was not long before I had shown to me that there was something far more serious abroad than rough words and hard looks. I had come to a spot where the road runs upwards through a wild tract of heathland and vanishes into an oak wood. I may have been half-way up the hill when, looking forward, I saw something gleaming under the shadow of the tree-trunks, and a man came out with a coat which was so slashed and spangled with gold that he blazed like a fire in the sunlight. He appeared to be very drunk, for he reeled and staggered as he came towards me. One of his hands was held up to his ear and clutched a great red handkerchief, which was fixed to his neck.

I had reined up the mare and was looking at him with some disgust, for it seemed strange to me that one who wore so gorgeous a uniform should show himself in such a state in broad daylight. For his part, he looked hard in my direction and came slowly onwards, stopping from time to time and swaying about as he gazed at me. Suddenly, as I again advanced, he screamed out his thanks to Christ, and, lurching forwards, he fell with a crash upon the dusty road. His hands flew forward with the fall, and I saw that what I had taken for a red cloth was a monstrous wound, which had left a great gap in his neck, from which a dark blood-clot hung, like an epaulette upon his shoulder.

'My God!' I cried, as I sprang to his aid. 'And I thought you were drunk!'

'Not drunk, but dying,' said he. 'But thank Heaven that I have seen a French officer while I have still strength to speak.'

I laid him among the heather and poured some brandy down his throat. All round us was the vast countryside, green and peaceful, with nothing living in sight save only the mutilated man beside me.

'Who has done this?' I asked, 'and what are you? You are French, and yet the uniform is strange to me.'

'It is that of the Emperor's new guard of honour. I am the Marquis of Château St Arnaud, and I am the ninth of my blood who has died in the service of France. I have been pursued and wounded by the night-riders of Lutzow, but I hid among the brushwood yonder, and waited in the hope that a Frenchman might pass. I could not be sure at first if you were friend or foe, but I felt that death was very near, and that I must take the chance.'

'Keep your heart up, comrade,' said I; 'I have seen a man with a worse wound who has lived to boast of it.'

'No, no,' he whispered; 'I am going fast.' He laid his

hand upon mine as he spoke, and I saw that his fingernails were already blue. 'But I have papers here in my tunic which you must carry at once to the Prince of Saxe-Felstein, at his Castle of Hof. He is still true to us, but the Princess is our deadly enemy. She is striving to make him declare against us. If he does so, it will determine all those who are wavering, for the King of Prussia is his uncle and the King of Bavaria his cousin. These papers will hold him to us if they can only reach him before he takes the last step. Place them in his hands to-night, and, perhaps, you will have saved all Germany for the Emperor. Had my horse not been shot, I might, wounded as I am—' he choked, and the cold hand tightened into a grip which left mine as bloodless as itself. Then, with a groan, his head jerked back, and it was all over with him.

Here was a fine start for my journey home. I was left with a commission of which I knew little, which would lead me to delay the pressing needs of my hussars, and which at the same time was of such importance that it was impossible for me to avoid it. I opened the Marquis's tunic, the brilliance of which had been devised by the Emperor in order to attract those young aristocrats from whom he hoped to raise these new regiments of his Guard. It was a small packet of papers which I drew out, tied up with silk, and addressed to the Prince of Saxe-Felstein. In the corner, in a sprawling, untidy hand, which I knew to be the Emperor's own, was written: 'Pressing and most important.' It was an order to me, those four words—an order as clear as if it had come straight from the firm lips with the cold grey eyes looking into mine. My troopers might wait for their horses, the dead Marquis might lie where I had laid him amongst the heather, but if the mare and her rider had a breath left in them the papers should reach the Prince that night.

I should not have feared to ride by the road through the wood, for I have learned in Spain that the safest time to pass through a guerilla country is after an outrage, and that the moment of danger is when all is peaceful. When I came to look upon my map, however, I saw that Hof lay further to the south of me, and that I might reach it more directly by keeping to the moors. Off I set, therefore, and had not gone fifty yards before two carbine shots rang out of the brushwood and a bullet hummed past me like a bee. It was clear that the night-riders were bolder in their ways than the brigands of Spain, and that my mission would have ended where it had begun if I had kept to the road.

It was a mad ride, that—a ride with a loose rein, girth-deep in heather and in gorse, plunging through bushes, flying down hillsides, with my neck at the mercy of my dear little Violette. But she—she never slipped, she never faltered, as swift and as surefooted as if she knew that her rider carried the fate of all Germany beneath the buttons of his pelisse. And I—I had long borne the name of being the best horseman in the six brigades of light cavalry, but I never rode as I rode then. My friend the Bart has told me of how they hunt the fox in England, but the swiftest fox would have been captured by me that day. The wild pigeons which flew overhead did not take a straighter course than Violette and I below. As an officer, I have always been ready to sacrifice myself for my men, though the Emperor would not have thanked me for it, for he had many men, but only one—well, cavalry leaders of the first class are rare.

But here I had an object which was indeed worth a sacrifice, and I thought no more of my life than of the clods of earth that flew from my darling's heels.

We struck the road once more as the light was failing, and galloped into the little village of Lobenstein. But we had hardly got upon the cobble-stones when off came one of the mare's shoes, and I had to lead her to the village smithy. His fire was low, and his day's work done, so that it would be an hour at the least before I could hope to push on to Hof. Cursing at the delay, I strode into the village inn and ordered a cold chicken and some wine to be served for my dinner. It was but a few more miles to Hof, and I had every hope that I might deliver my papers to the Prince on that very night, and be on my way for France next morning with despatches for the Emperor in my bosom. I will tell you now what befell me in the inn of Lobenstein.

The chicken had been served and the wine drawn, and I had turned upon both as a man may who has ridden such a ride, when I was aware of a murmur and a scuffling in the hall outside my door. At first I thought that it was some brawl between peasants in their cups, and I left them to settle their own affairs. But of a sudden there broke from among the low, sullen growl of the voices such a sound as would send Etienne Gerard leaping from his death-bed. It was the whimpering cry of a woman in pain. Down clattered my knife and my fork, and in an instant I was in the thick of the crowd which had gathered outside my door.

The heavy-cheeked landlord was there and his flaxen-haired wife, the two men from the stables, a chambermaid, and two or three villagers. All of them, women and men, were flushed and angry, while there in the centre of them, with pale cheeks and terror in her eyes, stood the loveliest woman that ever a soldier would wish to look upon. With her queenly head thrown back, and a touch of defiance mingled with her fear, she looked as she gazed round her like a creature of a different race from the vile, coarse-featured crew who surrounded her. I had not taken two steps from my door before she sprang to meet me, her hand resting upon my arm and her blue eyes sparkling with joy and triumph.

'A French soldier and a gentleman!' she cried. 'Now at last I am safe.'

'Yes, madam, you are safe,' said I, and I could not resist taking her hand in mine in order that I might reassure her. 'You have only to command me,' I added, kissing the hand as a sign that I meant what I was saying.

'I am Polish,' she cried; 'the Countess Palotta is my name. They abuse me because I love the French. I do not know what they might have done to me had Heaven not sent you to my help.'

I kissed her hand again lest she should doubt my intentions. Then I turned upon the crew with such an expression as I know how to assume. In an instant the hall was empty.

'Countess,' said I, 'you are now under my protection. You are faint, and a glass of wine is necessary to restore you.' I offered her my arm and escorted her into my room, where she sat by my side at the table and took the refreshment which I offered her.

How she blossomed out in my presence, this woman, like

a flower before the sun! She lit up the room with her beauty. She must have read my admiration in my eyes, and it seemed to me that I also could see something of the sort in her own. Ah! my friends, I was no ordinary-looking man when I was in my thirtieth year. In the whole light cavalry it would have been hard to find a finer pair of whiskers. Murat's may have been a shade longer, but the best judges are agreed that Murat's were a shade too long. And then I had a manner. Some women are to be approached in one way and some in another, just as a siege is an affair of fascines and gabions in hard weather and of trenches in soft. But the man who can mix daring with timidity, who can be outrageous with an air of humility and presumptuous with a tone of deference, that is the man whom mothers have to fear. For myself, I felt that I was the guardian of this lonely lady, and knowing what a dangerous man I had to deal with, I kept strict watch upon myself. Still, even a guardian has his privileges, and I did not neglect them.

But her talk was as charming as her face. In a few words she explained that she was travelling to Poland, and that her brother who had been her escort had fallen ill upon the way. She had more than once met with ill-treatment from the country folk because she could not conceal her good-will towards the French. Then turning from her own affairs she questioned me about the army, and so came round to myself and my own exploits. They were familiar to her, she said, for she knew several of Poniatowski's officers, and they had spoken of my doings. Yet she would be glad to hear them from my own lips. Never have I had so delightful a conversation. Most women make the mistake of talking rather too much about their own affairs, but this one listened to my tales just as you are listening now, ever asking for more and more and more. The hours slipped rapidly by, and it was with horror that I heard the village clock strike eleven, and so learned that for four hours I had forgotten the Emperor's business.

'Pardon me, my dear lady,' I cried, springing to my feet, 'but I must on instantly to Hof.'

She rose also, and looked at me with a pale, reproachful face. 'And me?' she said. 'What is to become of me?'

'It is the Emperor's affair. I have already stayed far too long. My duty calls me, and I must go.'

'You must go? And I must be abandoned alone to these savages? Oh, why did I ever meet you? Why did you ever teach me to rely upon your strength?' Her eyes glazed over, and in an instant she was sobbing upon my bosom.

Here was a trying moment for a guardian! Here was a time when he had to keep a watch upon a forward young officer. But I was equal to it. I smoothed her rich brown hair and whispered such consolations as I could think of in her ear, with one arm round her, it is true, but that was to hold her lest she should faint. She turned her tear-stained face to mine. 'Water,' she whispered. 'For God's sake, water!'

I saw that in another moment she would be senseless. I laid the drooping head upon the sofa, and then rushed furiously from the room, hunting from chamber to chamber for a carafe. It was some minutes before I could get one and hurry back with it. You can imagine my feelings to find the room empty and the lady gone.

Not only was she gone, but her cap and silver-mounted riding switch which had lain upon the table were gone also. I rushed out and roared for the landlord. He knew nothing of the matter, had never seen the woman before, and did not care if he never saw her again. Had the peasants at the door seen anyone ride away? No, they had seen nobody. I searched here and searched there, until at last I chanced to find myself in front of a mirror, where I stood with my eyes staring and my jaw as far dropped as the chin-strap of my shako would allow.

Four buttons of my pelisse were open, and it did not need me to put my hand up to know that my precious papers were gone. Oh! the depth of cunning that lurks in a woman's heart. She had robbed me, this creature, robbed me as she clung to my breast. Even while I smoothed her hair and whispered kind words into her ear, her hands had been at work beneath my dolman. And here I was, at the very last step of my journey, without the power of carrying out this mission which had already deprived one good man of his life, and was likely to rob another one of his credit. What would the Emperor say when he heard that I had lost his

despatches? Would the army believe it of Etienne Gerard?
And when they heard that a woman's hand had coaxed them
from me, what laughter there would be at mess-table and
at camp-fire! I could have rolled upon the ground in my
despair.

But one thing was certain—all this affair of the fracas in
the hall and the persecution of the so-called Countess was a
piece of acting from the beginning. This villainous innkeeper
must be in the plot. From him I might learn who she was
and where my papers had gone. I snatched my sabre from
the table and rushed out in search of him. But the scoundrel
had guessed what I would do, and had made his preparations
for me. It was in the corner of the yard that I found him, a
blunderbuss in his hands and a mastiff held upon a leash by
his son. The two stable-hands, with pitchforks, stood upon
either side, and the wife held a great lantern behind him,
so as to guide his aim.

'Ride away, sir, ride away!' he cried, with a crackling
voice. 'Your horse is ready, and no one will meddle with
you if you go your way; but if you come against us, you
are alone against three brave men.'

I had only the dog to fear, for the two forks and the
blunderbuss were shaking about like branches in a wind.
Still, I considered that, though I might force an answer
with my sword-point at the throat of this fat rascal, still I
should have no means of knowing whether that answer was
the truth. It would be a struggle, then, with much to lose
and nothing certain to gain. I looked them up and down,
therefore, in a way that set their foolish weapons shaking
worse than ever, and then, throwing myself upon my mare, I
galloped away with the shrill laughter of the landlady jarring
upon my ears.

I had already formed my resolution. Although I had lost
my papers, I could make a very good guess as to what
their contents would be, and this I would say from my
own lips to the Prince of Saxe-Felstein, as though the
Emperor had commissioned me to convey it in that way.
It was a bold stroke and a dangerous one, but if I went
too far I could afterwards be disavowed. It was that or
nothing, and when all Germany hung on the balance the

game should not be lost if the nerve of one man could save it.

It was midnight when I rode into Hof, but every window was blazing, which was enough in itself, in that sleepy country, to tell the ferment of excitement in which the people were. There was hooting and jeering as I rode through the crowded streets, and once a stone sang past my head, but I kept upon my way, neither slowing nor quickening my pace, until I came to the palace. It was lit from base to battlement, and the dark shadows, coming and going against the yellow glare, spoke of the turmoil within. For my part, I handed my mare to a groom at the gate, and striding in I demanded, in such a voice as an ambassador should have, to see the Prince instantly, upon business which would brook no delay.

The hall was dark, but I was conscious as I entered of a buzz of innumerable voices, which hushed into silence as I loudly proclaimed my mission. Some great meeting was being held then—a meeting which, as my instincts told me, was to decide this very question of war and peace. It was possible that I might still be in time to turn the scale for the Emperor and for France. As to the major-domo, he looked blackly at me, and showing me into a small ante-chamber he left me. A minute later he returned to say that the Prince could not be disturbed at present, but that the Princess would take my message.

The Princess! What use was there in giving it to her? Had I not been warned that she was German in heart and soul, and that it was she who was turning her husband and her State against us?

'It is the Prince that I must see,' said I.

'Nay, it is the Princess,' said a voice at the door, and a woman swept into the chamber. 'Von Rosen, you had best stay with us. Now, sir, what is it that you have to say to either Prince or Princess of Saxe-Felstein?'

At the first sound of the voice I had sprung to my feet. At the first glance I had thrilled with anger. Not twice in a lifetime does one meet that noble figure, that queenly head, those eyes as blue as the Garonne, and as chilling as her winter waters.

'Time presses, sir!' she cried, with an impatient tap of her foot. 'What have you to say to me?'

'What have I to say to you?' I cried. 'What can I say, save that you have taught me never to trust a woman more? You have ruined and dishonoured me for ever.'

She looked with arched brows at her attendant.

'Is this the raving of fever, or does it come from some less innocent cause?' said she. 'Perhaps a little blood-letting—'

'Ah, you can act!' I cried. 'You have shown me that already.'

'Do you mean that we have met before?'

'I mean that you have robbed me within the last two hours.'

'This is past all bearing,' she cried, with an admirable affectation of anger. 'You claim, as I understand, to be an ambassador, but there are limits to the privileges which such an office brings with it.'

'You brazen it admirably,' said I. 'Your Highness will not make a fool of me twice in one night.' I sprang forward and, stooping down, caught up the hem of her dress. 'You would have done well to change it after you had ridden so far and so fast,' said I.

It was like the dawn upon a snow-peak to see her ivory cheeks flush suddenly to crimson.

'Insolent!' she cried. 'Call for the foresters and have him thrust from the palace!'

'I will see the Prince first.'

'You will never see the Prince. Ah! Hold him, Von Rosen, hold him!'

She had forgotten the man with whom she had to deal—was it likely that I would wait until they could bring their rascals? She had shown me her cards too soon. Her game was to stand between me and her husband. Mine was to speak face to face with him at any cost. One spring took me out of the chamber. In another I had crossed the hall. An instant later I had burst into the great room from which the murmur of the meeting had come. At the far end I saw a figure upon a high chair under a daïs. Beneath him was a line of high dignitaries, and then on every side I saw vaguely the heads of a vast assembly. Into the centre of the room I strode, my sabre clanking, my shako under my arm.

'I am the messenger of the Emperor,' I shouted. 'I bear his message to his Highness the Prince of Saxe-Felstein.'

The man beneath the daïs raised his head, and I saw that his face was thin and wan, and that his back was bowed as though some huge burden was balanced between his shoulders.

'Your name, sir?' he asked.

'Colonel Etienne Gerard, of the Third Hussars.'

Every face in the gathering was turned upon me, and I heard the rustle of the innumerable necks and saw countless eyes without meeting one friendly one amongst them. The woman had swept past me, and was whispering, with many shakes of her head and dartings of her hands, into the Prince's ear. For my own part I threw out my chest and curled my moustache, glancing round in my own debonair fashion at the assembly. They were men, all of them, professors from the college, a sprinkling of their students, soldiers, gentlemen, artisans, all very silent and serious. In one corner there sat a group of men in black, with riding-coats drawn over their shoulders. They leaned their heads to each other, whispering under their breath, and with every movement I caught the clank of their sabres or the clink of their spurs.

'The Emperor's private letter to me informs me that it is the Marquis Château St Arnaud who is bearing his despatches,' said the Prince.

'The Marquis has been foully murdered,' I answered, and a buzz rose up from the people as I spoke. Many heads were turned, I noticed, towards the dark men in the cloaks.

'Where are your papers?' asked the Prince.

'I have none.'

A fierce clamour rose instantly around me. 'He is a spy! He plays a part!' they cried. 'Hang him!' roared a deep voice from the corner, and a dozen others took up the shout. For my part, I drew out my handker-chief and flicked the dust from the fur of my pelisse. The Prince held out his thin hands, and the tumult died away.

'Where, then, are your credentials, and what is your message?'

'My uniform is my credential, and my message is for your private ear.'

He passed his hand over his forehead with the gesture of a weak man who is at his wits' end what to do. The Princess stood beside him with her hand upon his throne, and again whispered in his ear.

'We are here in council together, some of my trusty subjects and myself,' said he. 'I have no secrets from them, and whatever message the Emperor may send to me at such a time concerns their interests no less than mine.'

There was a hum of applause at this, and every eye was turned once more upon me. My faith, it was an awkward position in which I found myself, for it is one thing to address eight hundred hussars, and another to speak to such an audience on such a subject. But I fixed my eyes upon the Prince, and tried to say just what I should have said if we had been alone, shouting it out, too, as though I had my regiment on parade.

'You have often expressed friendship for the Emperor,' I cried. 'It is now at last that this friendship is about to be tried. If you will stand firm, he will reward you as only he can reward. It is an easy thing for him to turn a Prince into a King and a province into a power. His eyes are fixed upon you, and though you can do little to harm him, you can ruin yourself. At this moment he is crossing the Rhine with two hundred thousand men. Every fortress in the country is in his hands. He will be upon you in a week, and if you have played him false, God help both you and your people. You think that he is weakened because a few of us got the chilblains last winter. Look there!' I cried, pointing to a great star which blazed through the window. 'That is the Emperor's star. When it wanes, he will wane — but not before.'

You would have been proud of me, my friends, if you could have seen and heard me, for I clashed my sabre as I spoke, and swung my dolman as though my regiment was picketed outside in the courtyard. They listened to me in silence, but the back of the Prince bowed more and more as though the burden which weighed upon it was greater than his strength. He looked round with haggard eyes.

'We have heard a Frenchman speak for France,' said he. 'Let us have a German speak for Germany.'

The folk glanced at each other, and whispered to their neighbours. My speech, as I think, had its effect, and no man wished to be the first to commit himself in the eyes of the Emperor. The Princess looked round her with blazing eyes, and her clear voice broke the silence.

'Is a woman to give this Frenchman his answer?' she cried. 'Is it possible, then, that among the night-riders of Lutzow there is none who can use his tongue as well as his sabre?'

Over went a table with a crash, and a young man had bounded upon one of the chairs. He had the face of one inspired—pale, eager, with wild hawk eyes, and tangled hair. His sword hung straight from his side, and his riding-boots were brown with mire.

'It is Korner!' the people cried. 'It is young Korner, the poet! Ah, he will sing, he will sing.'

And he sang! It was soft, at first, and dreamy, telling of old Germany, the mother of nations, of the rich, warm plains, and the grey cities, and the fame of dead heroes. But then verse after verse rang like a trumpet-call. It was of the Germany of now, the Germany which had been taken unawares and overthrown, but which was up again, and snapping the bonds upon her giant limbs. What was life that one should covet it? What was glorious death that one should shun it? The mother, the great mother, was calling. Her sigh was in the night wind. She was crying to her own children for help. Would they come? Would they come? Would they come?

Ah, that terrible song, the spirit face and the ringing voice! Where were I, and France, and the Emperor? They did not shout, these people, they howled. They were up on the chairs and the tables. They were raving, sobbing, the tears running down their faces. Korner had sprung from the chair, and his comrades were round him with their sabres in the air. A flush had come into the pale face of the Prince, and he rose from his throne.

'Colonel Gerard,' said he, 'you have heard the answer which you are to carry to your Emperor. The die is cast, my children. Your Prince and you must stand or fall together.'

He bowed to show that all was over, and the people with a shout made for the door to carry the tidings into the town. For my own part, I had done all that a brave man might, and so I was not sorry to be carried out amid the stream. Why should I linger in the palace? I had had my answer and must carry it, such as it was. I wished neither to see Hof nor its people again until I entered it at the head of a vanguard. I turned from the throng, then, and walked silently and sadly in the direction in which they had led the mare.

It was dark down there by the stables, and I was peering round for the ostler, when suddenly my two arms were seized from behind. There were hands at my wrists and at my throat, and I felt the cold muzzle of a pistol under my ear.

'Keep your lips closed, you French dog,' whispered a fierce voice. 'We have him, captain.'

'Have you the bridle?'

'Here it is.'

'Sling it over his head.'

I felt the cold coil of leather tighten round my neck. An ostler with a stable lantern had come out and was gazing upon the scene. In its dim light I saw stern faces breaking everywhere through the gloom, with the black caps and dark cloaks of the night-riders.

'What would you do with him, captain?' cried a voice.

'Hang him at the Palace Gate.'

'An ambassador?'

'An ambassador without papers.'

'But the Prince?'

'Tut, man, do you not see that the Prince will then be committed to our side? He will be beyond all hope of forgiveness. At present he may swing round to-morrow as he has done before. He may eat his words, but a dead hussar is more than he can explain.'

'No, no, Von Strelitz, we cannot do it,' said another voice.

'Can we not? I shall show you that!' and there came a

jerk on the bridle which nearly pulled me to the ground. At the same instant a sword flashed and the leather was cut through within two inches of my neck.

'By Heaven, Korner, this is rank mutiny,' cried the captain. 'You may hang yourself before you are through with it.'

'I have drawn my sword as a soldier and not as a brigand,' said the young poet. 'Blood may dim its blade, but never dishonour. Comrades, will you stand by and see this French gentleman mishandled?'

A dozen sabres flew from their sheaths, and it was evident that my friends and my foes were about equally balanced. But the angry voices and the gleam of steel had brought the folk running from all parts.

'The Princess!' they cried. 'The Princess is coming!'

And even as they spoke I saw her in front of us, her sweet face framed in the darkness. I had cause to hate her, for she had cheated and befooled me, and yet it thrilled me then and thrills me now to think that my arms have embraced her, and that I have felt the scent of her hair in my nostrils. I know not whether she lies under her German earth, or whether she still lingers, a grey-haired woman in her Castle of Hof, but she lives ever, young and lovely, in the heart and the memory of Etienne Gerard.

'For shame!' she cried, sweeping up to me, and tearing with her own hands the noose from my neck. 'You are fighting in God's own quarrel, and yet you would begin with such a devil's deed as this. This man is mine, and he who touches a hair of his head will answer for it to me.'

They were glad enough to slink off into the darkness before those scornful eyes. Then she turned once more to me.

'You can follow me, Colonel Gerard,' she said. 'I have a word that I would speak to you.'

I walked behind her to the chamber into which I had originally been shown. She closed the door, and then looked at me with the archest twinkle in her eyes.

'Is it not confiding of me to trust myself with you?' said she. 'You will remember that it is the Princess of Saxe-Felstein and not the poor Countess Palotta of Poland.'

'Be the name what it might,' I answered, 'I helped a lady whom I believed to be in distress, and I have been robbed of my papers and almost of my honour as a reward.'

'Colonel Gerard,' said she, 'we have been playing a game, you and I, and the stake was a heavy one. You have shown by delivering a message which was never given to you that you would stand at nothing in the cause of your country. My heart is German as yours is French, and I also would go all lengths, even to deceit and to theft, if at this crisis I can help my suffering fatherland. You see how frank I am.'

'You tell me nothing that I have not seen.'

'But now that the game is played and won, why should we bear malice? I will say this, that if ever I were in such a plight as that which I pretended in the inn of Lobenstein, I should never wish to meet a more gallant protector or a truer-hearted gentleman than Colonel Etienne Gerard. I had never thought that I could feel for a Frenchman as I felt for you when I slipped the papers from your breast.'

'But you took them, none the less.'

'They were necessary to me and to Germany. I knew the arguments which they contained and the effect which they would have upon the Prince. If they had reached him all would have been lost.'

'Why should your Highness descend to such expedients when a score of these brigands, who wished to hang me at your castle gate, would have done the work as well?'

'They are not brigands, but the best blood of Germany,' she cried, hotly. 'If you have been roughly used you will remember the indignities to which every German has been subjected, from the Queen of Prussia downwards. As to why I did not have you waylaid upon the road, I may say that I had parties out on all sides, and that I was waiting at Lobenstein to hear of their success. When instead of their news you yourself arrived I was in despair, for there was only the one weak woman betwixt you and my husband. You see the straits to which I was driven before I used the weapon of my sex.'

'I confess that you have conquered me, your Highness, and it only remains for me to leave you in possession of the field.'

'But you will take your papers with you.' She held them out to me as she spoke. 'The Prince has crossed the Rubicon now, and nothing can bring him back. You can return these to the Emperor and tell him that we refused to receive them. No one can accuse you then of having lost your despatches. Good-bye, Colonel Gerard, and the best I can wish you is that when you reach France you may remain there. In a year's time there will be no place for a Frenchman upon this side of the Rhine.'

And thus it was that I played the Princess of Saxe-Felstein with all Germany for a stake, and lost my game to her. I had much to think of as I walked my poor, tired Violette along the highway which leads westward from Hof. But amid all the thoughts there came back to me always the proud, beautiful face of the German woman, and the voice of the soldier-poet as he sang from the chair. And I understood then that there was something terrible in this strong, patient Germany—this mother root of nations—and I saw that such a land, so old and so beloved, never could be conquered. And as I rode I saw that the dawn was breaking, and that the great star at which I had pointed through the palace window was dim and pale in the western sky.

Lyn Webster Wilde is a film-maker a[...]ter who has made a special study of myth. She has a deg[...]sh from Cambridge University and has written five b[...]ction and non-fiction. She now lives in Wales and is p[...]ature film.

A Brief History of the Amazons

WOMEN WARRIORS IN MYTH AND HISTORY

LYN WEBSTER WILDE

ROBINSON

ROBINSON

First published in Great Britain in 1999 as *On the Trail of the Women Warriors*
by Constable and Co. Ltd

This paperback edition published in 2016 by Robinson

A CIP catalogue record for this book
is available from the British Library.

ISBN: 978-1-47213-677-0

Typeset by Hewer Text UK Ltd, Edinburgh
Printed and bound in Great Britain by CPI Group (UK) Ltd, Croydon CR0 4YY

Papers used by Robinson are from well-managed forests and other responsible sources

MIX
Paper from
responsible sources
FSC® C104740

Robinson
An imprint of
Little, Brown Book Group
Carmelite House
50 Victoria Embankment
London EC4Y 0DZ

An Hachette UK Company
www.hachette.co.uk

www.littlebrown.co.uk

To Colin, who married the enemy

Contents

List of Illustrations

....

Acknowledgements

....

Firstly, deepest thanks to Natasha Ward for coming with me to the Ukraine and Moldova as both friend and intrepreter. Without her sunny charm and linguistic brilliance many doors would never have opened. In Ukraine Yura, Lida and Alyosha Serov, Anna Danielnova Shandur, Vira Nanivska and Valery Ivanov offered the warmest hospitality, whilst Dr Vitaly Zubar of the Archaeological Institute took us under his wing and introduced us to the right people, including Dr Elena Fialko, Lyubov Klotchko, Professor Vetschislav Mursin and Ekaterina Bunyatin. Their fascinating and painstaking work deserves a much bigger audience than it has had so far. Those two modern-day warrior women Dr Jeannine Davis-Kimball and Professor Renate Rolle were generous with their time and insights. Frank and Nina Andrashko were patient and helpful in the face of my dogged attempts to contact Professor Rolle. Dr Mark Tkachuk looked after us in Moldova, whilst Mustafa Akkaya, the Director of Samsun Museum, showed me the sights and finds of the Black Sea coastal area with justifiable pride and enthusiasm. In Konya Mustafa Elma and Mehmet Turan made it possible for me to see the private, non-commercial face of dervish whirling.

Back in Britain I want to thank: 'Morocco' for the dancing and first-hand information about the Tuareg; Robin Waterfield for his patient help with the Greek sources and permission to quote from his excellent translation of Herodotus; Diane Stein for introducing me to the hidden world of the Hittites and Hurrians; Professor Oliver Gurney for his detailed responses to my questions about the throne-goddess; Jill Hart for her translations from the Hittite; Professor Mary Boyce for the example of her academic rigour and Jenny Lewis for permission to quote her poem 'The Amazon' in full.

Sincere gratitude is also due to the many friends who have inspired me, challenged me or fed me useful tidbits: Diane Binnington, Pomme Clayton, Cindy Davies, Lyn Hartman, Cherry Gilchrist, Nick Heath, Dr Sarah Shaw, Andrew O'Connell, Jane Oldfield, Chris Spencer, Jackie Spreckley, and the generous spirits of the Amazons Existed Internet Club including 'Artemis', 'Myrina' and Katherine Griffis.

Lastly I am very grateful to my parents, Jan and Drew Webster, for helping me out financially while I wrote the book, and to my husband, Colin, for being supportive to me while suffering excruciating back pain himself.

Time Chart

		CRETE AND GREECE		AMAZONS (*in myth*)
NEOLITHIC AGE	5000 BC			
	3000 BC			
BRONZE AGE	2000 BC		2000 BC	**Time of African Amazons**
	1600 BC	Snake Goddesses Cretan civilisation peaks **Heroic Age**	1600 BC	**Time of the Amazons**
	1250 – 1200 BC	Time of Hercules Trojan War	1256 BC	Amazons attack Athens Penthesilea dies at Troy
		Dorians invade **Dark Ages**		Last Amazons flee to Scythia
	750 BC			Amazons in Homer
IRON AGE		Black Sea Colonies set up **Archaic Greek Age**	600 BC	Amazons appear in art and literature
	500 BC			
		Classical Greek Age	425 BC	Herodotus, Lysias, Hippocrates mention Amazons
	330 BC			
		Hellenistic Greek Age		

STEPPES		ANATOLIA	MESOPOTAMIA
		6800 – 5700 BC	Çatal Hüyük the 'lady with leopards'
3500 BC	Cucuteni idols made near Kiev		Inanna worshipped in Sumeria/Akkad
2650 BC		2500 BC	Hattians at Alaca Hüyük
2000 BC		2000 BC	Ishtar worshipped at Babylon
	Nomads roam Steppes	1900 BC	Assyrian trade routes to Zalpa Hittite Empire
	Earliest woman warrior grave in Georgia	1200 BC	Hittite Empire falls
			Neo-Hittite Empire Kukuba worshipped
	Cimmerians attack Anatolia	750 BC	Shawushka worshipped at Nineveh
600 BC			Phrygian Empire Cybele worshipped
	Graves of Scythian and Sauromatian women warriors	556 BC	Artemis temple built at Ephesus
300 BC	Graves of Sarmatian fighting women		

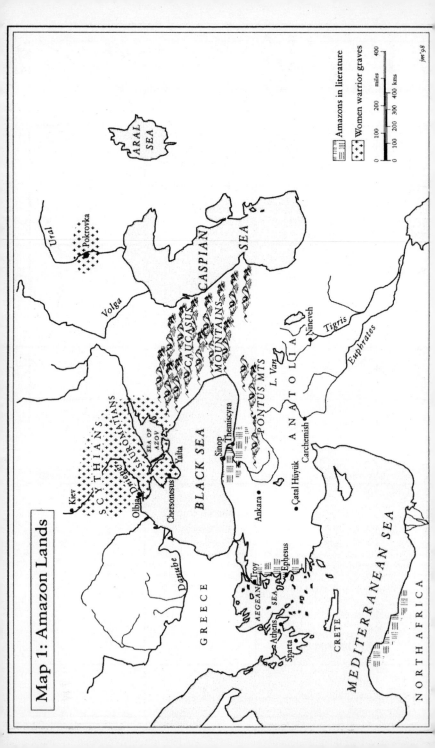

Map 1: Amazon Lands

Amazons in literature

Women warrior graves

jm '98

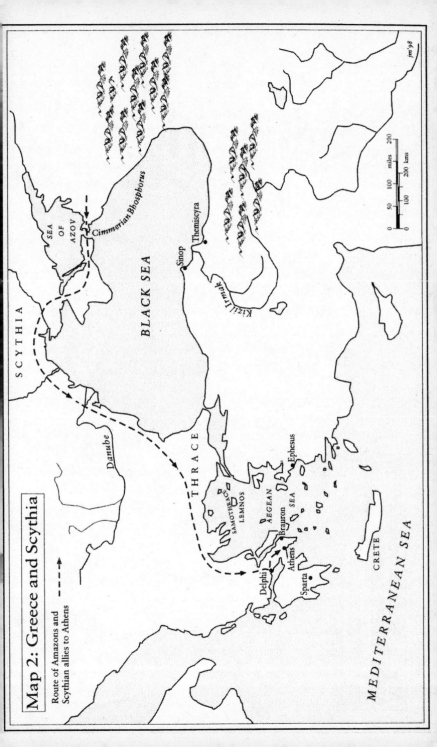

Map 2: Greece and Scythia

Route of Amazons and
Scythian allies to Athens   ■ ■ ■ ▶

jm '98

SCYTHIA

SEA
OF
AZOV

Cimmerian Bhosphorus

BLACK SEA

Sinop

Themiscyra

Kizil Irmak

Danube

THRACE

SAMOTHRACE
LEMNOS

AEGEAN
SEA

Ephesus

Delphi

Brauron

Athens

Sparta

CRETE

MEDITERRANEAN SEA

200
100   miles
100   200 kms
50
0   0

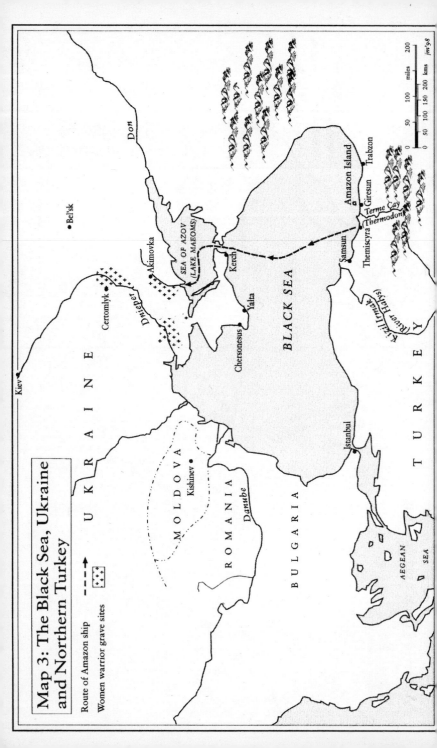

Map 3: The Black Sea, Ukraine and Northern Turkey

Route of Amazon ship ▪▪▪▶

Women warrior grave sites ✠✠✠

jm'98

200

100   miles

50   100   150   200 kms

0   50   100

UKRAINE

Kiev •

Certomlyk •

Bel'sk •

Dnieper

Akimovka •

Don

SEA OF AZOV
(LAKE MAEOMS)

Kerch •

Chersonesus •

Yalta •

BLACK SEA

Samsun •

Amazon Island

Trabzon •

Giresun •

Terme Cay

Themiscyra Thermodon

Kizilirmak
(River Halys)

TURKEY

Istanbul •

MOLDOVA

Kishinev •

Danube

ROMANIA

BULGARIA

AEGEAN
SEA

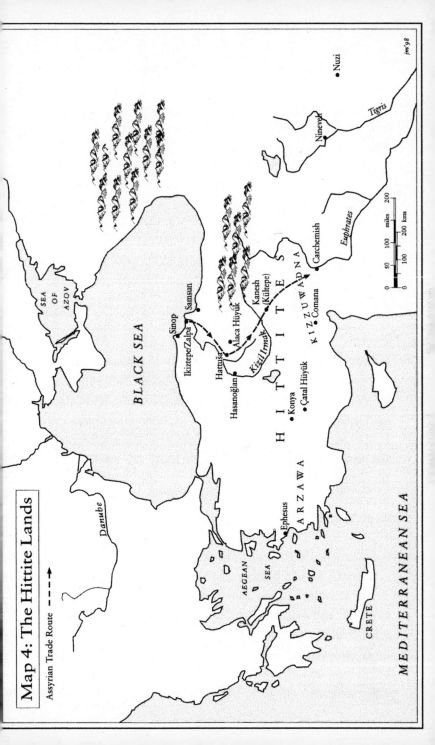

Map 4: The Hittite Lands

Assyrian Trade Route --- →

jm '98

BLACK SEA

SEA OF AZOV

Danube

AEGEAN SEA

CRETE

MEDITERRANEAN SEA

Ephesus

ARZAWA

Konya
Çatal Hüyük

Hasanoğlan

Hattuša

Ikiztepe/Zalpa
Sinop

Samsun

Alaca Hüyük

Kanesh (Kültepe)

Kızıl Irmak

H I T T I T E S

K I Z Z U W A D N A

Comana

Carchemish

Euphrates

Nineveh

Tigris

Nuzi

0   50   100   150   200
0   100   200 kms
         miles

Introduction: Who Were the Amazons?

....

I came across the Amazons for the first time while producing a comedy programme for the BBC called *Revolting Women*. Every week we had a serial, 'Bogwomen', about a matriarchal tribe who lived without men in the bogs outside Manchester. The inspiration for this humorous tribe, the writer explained, was the mythical race of Amazons, who, I soon found out, were far from the peace-loving characters in our serial: they were violent resisters of masculine rule, they fought ruthlessly, they killed or mutilated their male offspring, and they had promiscuous, anonymous sex in order to get pregnant. They were as beautiful as they were cruel.

This was the beginning of my fascination with the Amazons. I quickly discovered that they had little to do with the River Amazon in South America, but belonged to the fringe of the Classical Greek world, to western Asia and the steppes around the Black Sea. The true Amazons fought in the pages of Homer and Herodotus in the Bronze and Iron Ages, whilst the South American connection comes from much later travellers' tales of armed bands of women who were called 'Amazons' after their Greek forebears. But who the Amazons really were, once you got beyond the references in myth, history and legend, was where the real mystery began for me.

I read what I could about them and eventually became possessed by a desire to discover if they really had existed or not. This was not easy – I was unwittingly stepping into a labyrinth that would not spew me out until I had followed the clues it offered right to the bitter end. This quest has taken me through the dustiest depths of libraries, into the brilliant but cluttered minds of academics, through the realms of feminism both inspirational and ideological, into the world of sorcerers, psychologists and magicians; and finally into the deepest recesses of my own sense of gender identity. I have found out astonishing things, not just about the Amazons, but also about how the human mind works, how it jumps to conclusions and often sees only what it wants to see, not what really is (if, that is, there *is* indeed anything that *really* is). I have also had to struggle with my own tendency to be carried away by the broad dazzling sweep of things and ignore the telling detail, for in this story the detail is very important.

The very idea of the Amazons, of ruthless women warriors who live apart from men, excites people at a deep level. It brings out the sex-warrior in some women: they would like to do violent things to the men they feel have hurt and abused them; it acts as an erotic goad to many men – they love the thought of being dominated by a beautiful springy-limbed maiden, or of subduing her after a fair fight. Others of both sexes feel very disturbed by the idea of women engaging in battle, rejecting their 'natural' tenderness in favour of ruthlessness and mastery. Feminists have a sense of ownership about the Amazons and want to idealise them, though that is difficult! Jungians find their female violence a disturbing aberration in the ordered world of archetypes; classicists and archaeologists are warily interested in them – or else make exaggerated claims, as do some of the Amazon enthusiasts with sites on the Internet who have made their minds up *a priori* that these wonderful women definitely did exist just as the myths say. And for many goddess-worshipping women, the Amazons are part of a heritage they would not relinquish at any price.

When you are talking about the Amazons, objectivity is very hard to find; and yet while conducting this investigation it was no use my trying to stay safely on the academic high-ground. Every 'fact' or 'suggestion' about the Amazons has reverberations and implications for our understanding of what women and men are, and what they can be, if we remove our ideas of what they *should* be. Nowadays we talk freely in our new jargon about 'empowerment', but can we *really* imagine what kind of 'power' a middle-aged priestess at Çatal Hüyük in Central Anatolia would have had, just from looking at her 8,000-year-old sculpted portrait with skulls and leopards in a museum showcase? And how did a young Scythian woman warrior feel about the need to learn to fight, to use a bow and arrow, a spear? Did she delight in the exercise of her aggression, or yearn to be at home with her mother, or her husband and children? How did a Mesopotamian man or woman view the power of the beautiful and terrifying war-goddess Ishtar, with her wings and weapons and lions too? What made the male followers of the Phrygian Cybele willing to castrate themselves in order to serve as her priests?

We cannot ignore these questions if we want to understand who the Amazons were and how the myths about them were made and moulded. They were mentioned for the very first time in Homer, who called them 'women the equal of men'. In the sixth century BC Aeschylus wrote about 'those famous Amazons, who live without men and feed on flesh', saying they were 'virgins fearless in battle'. A century later Hellanicus described them as 'golden-shielded, silver-sworded, man-loving, male-child-slaughtering Amazons'. Thereafter, the fascinating variations begin.

The Amazons were principally renowned for two attributes: that they fought, bravely and ruthlessly, and that they lived without men, only seeking out masculine society once a year in order to conceive. In some versions they gave any male children back to their fathers; in others, they mutilated or killed them. Some authors reported that they seared off one breast in childhood, so as to be able to pull back their bows unimpeded or so that the energy went into their bow-pulling arm. The Athenians classified them, along with Persians and Centaurs, as barbarous enemies who were always eventually defeated by the home team. They have always been depicted as slim, well-muscled and attractive, whether with pert breasts and well-turned thighs on sixth-century BC black-figure vases, or in push-up corsets and skimpy tunics in *Xena, Warrior Princess* on television.

3

When I first began my research into the Amazons I presumed that they were real and had existed. I knew little about ancient history or about the Classical Greeks; I was happy to swallow the large claims of feminist writers like Marija Gimbutas or Merlin Stone that there had been matriarchal societies in the Neolithic and Bronze Ages and that the Amazons may have been remnants of these. Under the entry 'Amazons', fat feminist encyclopaedias would list all sorts of impressive fighting women from Valkyries to Celtic goddesses, and confidently quote from sources that proved on close examination to be somewhat unreliable. It was swampy ground indeed. Then, as the early and rather naïve feminist enthusiasms were laid aside, a new consensus grew up: the Amazons did *not* exist. Official. Many erudite articles were written, most by feminist classicists, pointing out that the Amazons were a kind of compensatory mechanism for the Greek patriarchs – they subjugated their own women so thoroughly that their guilty consciences created a myth to show the dreadful things that would happen if women threw off the yoke. Or it was a classic 'reversal' myth, asking the question 'What would happen if men didn't rule the roost?' The answer was always 'bad things'. Backed up as it was by many fine minds, this consensus was rather awe-inspiring, but I was not convinced.

I had an image in my mind that would not go away – it was of two women, tough, stringy young women on horseback in an expanse of swampy grassland. Limitless horizons, a sense of freedom and power. The women are not fighting, they are just chatting, enjoying the stillness and freshness of dawn while their horses crop the long grass. I could smell the wild thyme, sense their desire to linger, not to get on with what they had to do. And yet I knew that these were Amazons, women who could ride and fight and, if necessary, kill. Whether they lived apart from men, the image did not say.

I knew it was just an image but it had power over me. It said to me: 'Go and *see*! Don't accept the consensus view.' It seemed to me that these academics were in love with their own neat reasoning and none of them had left their desks, libraries and computers to go and actually *look for* the Amazons. I had a hunch that they were wrong, and I was not willing to give up this hunch just because the very idea made the academics laugh. But where was I to start?

Like every researcher I started by 'making a few phone calls'. It was not encouraging: one jovial male archaeologist told me that the Amazons were almost certainly 'Hittites in kilts', whom the Greeks had mistaken at a distance for women; one distinguished Jungian scholar said rather crossly that the Amazons were 'an aberration' in which she was not in the least interested. I studiously followed up the references in the fat feminist volumes only to find them leading to the works of American ideologues who were more interested in proving points than discovering the truth, or that they quoted as 'fact' the marvellous poetic ramblings and speculations from Robert Graves's *White Goddess* or *Greek Myths*.

As I searched I began to feel that the tales of the Amazons were the beginning of a very long thread that seemed to lead right to the heart of the mystery of the differences between male and female energy – not towards tedious debates about gender roles, but something much more suggestive and challenging. For instance, when I came across references to the power of Hittite 'magic-women' or priestesses I had to ask myself, 'What *kind* of power are we talking about here?' We live in a Christian culture where women still have few public spiritual roles (they are now allowed to be priests, but certainly not priestesses who embody female sexual power). How can we know about that kind of power? I mentioned earlier the famous goddess/priestess figurine from Çatal Hüyük – she is the lady with leopards who has the sagging breasts and belly of an older woman who has borne many children. In Konya, 50 kilometres from Çatal Hüyük, I saw what seemed to be her 'twin', a live twentieth-century peasant woman less than 5 feet tall, with great pendulous breasts and an enormous half-moon stomach. She emanated a raw animal power that we women of Western Europe have almost entirely lost. I felt like a skimpy wraith in comparison with her.

In the same vein, the archaeologist Jeannine Davis-Kimball, excavator of women warrior graves in South Russia, told me of an encounter with a nomadic horsewoman in Mongolia:

> . . . a wonderful young Mongol woman rode over. She sat 'tall in the saddle', was well built, and wore her hair pulled back to reveal a strong face. She had the confidence and at the same time the ease that one ascribes to our western cowboys. I was with Victoria Veit, a Mongolian specialist from Munich, and the Mongol woman rode up to Victoria and me, stopped her horse, and then, as if we were old friends, posed for photos with us. Soon I was quite amused because a young man (sort of flopping at the edges) rode up to see what was going on. He never had the élan that the woman did. I can well imagine that she took care of many situations quite nicely.

So what you will find in this book is not simply a quest, or an exploration of the sources of the Amazon myth, but the story of an encounter with lost forms of female power. I aim to look that power squarely in the face and not to romanticise, glamorise or demonise it. I am telling the story from the point of view of a woman of the very late second millennium AD, who wanted to find that power again and *know* what it was – although not, I might stress, to be possessed by it or by the spirit of the ruthless warrior Amazons of the Dark Ages. I am not a classicist, Hittitologist, archaeologist, anthropologist, historian or scientist, but I have struggled to master the relevant findings in all these fields and feel that this book could only be written by a generalist like myself. Any of the above specialists would be hard put not to become ensnared by the complexities of their fields, for if they dared to step outside their speciality or take a risk, they would be jumped on and denounced by their fellow academics. Fortunately, I have no academic reputation to build or protect.

However, I do not want to write the kind of book that ends up by connecting everything with everything else – or tells of an investigation that ends up proving exactly the point that the author wanted to prove to start with. Neither am I aiming to catalogue every woman warrior who ever picked up a sword or bow in any culture, however picturesque such women can be (Jessica Amanda Salmondson has already done the job in her *Encyclopedia of Amazons*). Instead, this book confines itself in the main to a consideration of the Amazons of Greek mythology, examines various possibilities as to what the source of their images and their myth may have been – and also suggests some new ones.

It is not possible to plunge straight into the heart of the matter. Because there is very little objectivity in this field, with everyone wanting to prove a point or a theory of some sort, unless you are well prepared for the journey you risk falling in love with the first siren who sings within earshot, the first theory that sounds plausible. This was my own experience at any rate. Therefore chapter one will try to lay out the essence of the Amazon myth. It will attempt to give a bird's eye view of the Greek society in which they sprang up, which told their story, painted their image and admired their beauty and strength, in order to place them into their context and then lay out all the possible directions one might take in trying to find out where they came from. In chapter two the search begins in earnest and takes us to the Ukrainian steppe and the Black Sea to examine the extraordinary finds of the remains of women warriors in Iron Age graves. Chapter three explores the enigmatic figure of Artemis, the Amazons' goddess; chapter four examines the dark Medusa-face of the goddess and some of the female-dominated religious cults of the ancient Greek world. Chapter five returns to the Turkish coast of the Black Sea to search for traces of the Amazon city, Themiscyra, in order to attempt to solve the mystery of the Hittite 'throne-goddesses' and find out about the power of the 'magic-women'. In chapter six we travel further back in time to meet Ishtar of Babylon and the leopard-lady of Çatal Hüyük and examine what the Edwardian writers called 'the oriental idea of sex confusion'. Chapter seven follows the trail of the African Amazons right up to the matriarchal customs of the present-day Tuareg, while chapter eight asks who the last Amazons were, and whether they have any true descendants today.

When I started out on this investigation I genuinely thought that the graves of the Scythian women warriors in Russia and the Ukraine would provide some kind of definitive answer to the question: who were the Amazons? What they in fact did was make me realise that there was not just one answer: that the truth of how the myth was built and elaborated was infinitely more complex.

My search has led me in unpredictable directions and to unexpected conclusions, but there are a couple of words that I will have to use which I should explain now in order to avoid confusion. The first is 'matripotestal', which means 'mother-powered', and I use it sometimes rather than 'matriarchal' to describe societies where the Great Mother Goddess is the central religious power, but that may not be 'matriarchal' societies in which women hold actual political power. The second is *shakti*, which is a Hindu word used to describe the female partner of a god and the power that she embodies. It evokes a sense of this power that is at once erotic, inexhaustible, captivating, terrifying, sensual, annihilating – the divine female in action. This power, however, does not belong to the goddess – it arises between herself and the god; it is an *active* power, and you can see it very clearly in the figurines of the snake-goddesses of Crete, or the dancing Parvati statues in your local Indian restaurant. It is *not* the fecund, sleepy, peaceful earth-mother energy beloved of sentimental goddess-worshippers. It is the bright, burning, vital power of the archetypal feminine, whether expressed in divine or human form. I have found it an indispensable word while writing this book because, whatever else you say about Amazons, you have to admit they are full of *shakti*. But they withhold the *shakti* from men, which cannot of course, in the long run, be a positive thing for civilisation. Therefore they must be destroyed. But before they ride off into the long night of the losers of history, let us find out exactly who they were.

CHAPTER ONE

Essence of Amazon

·················

In Britain, until recently, if you wanted to relax on a Saturday night you could switch on the television and treat yourself to an hour of *Hercules* followed by an hour of *Xena, Warrior Princess*. Both programmes presented swashbuckling tales set in a mythical Greek dark age in which evil battled with good and good eventually won. The two heroes, Hercules and Xena, with their magical strength and dry, self-deprecating humour, seemed to exist in the same realm, to fight on the same side – the side of the good. But in fact, in the world of Greek myth, the Amazons and Hercules were sworn and bitter enemies. So how could Amazonian Xena and Hercules both be fighting on the side of right?

The 'golden-shielded, silver-sworded, man-loving, male-child-slaughtering Amazons' were worthy opponents of the great hero, Hercules. For the ninth of his Twelve Labours he was required to go on a mission against them, to steal the girdle of Hippolyta, their queen. Because they were daughters of Ares, the god of war, the Amazons' queen was entitled to wear Ares' golden girdle. This girdle, a kind of snake made of fabric, leather or metal, is a symbol for sexual power, channelled and kept within civilised bounds. In Greek marriage ceremonies, when the bridegroom loosed the bride's girdle it signified the end of her free maidenhood and the opening of her body to her husband and to pregnancy. If you look at the little Minoan snake-goddess (see illustration) you will see how two of the three snakes she wears actually form the girdle that goes round her hips and covers her womb. She is a graphic illustration of what a 'girdle' can actually signify. For the Amazons, that band of women warriors who lived without men, it was also a symbol of their self-sufficient *shakti*-power. The loss of their queen's girdle would mean the end of their independent existence.

In Diodorus of Sicily's version of the story,[1] Hercules sails to Themiscyra, the Amazon capital on the Black Sea coast, and demands the girdle from Hippolyta. She refuses, and there follows a bloody battle in which all her champions are slain one by one. They all have beautiful names: Aella, which means 'whirlwind', Philippis, Prothoe, Eriboia, Celaeno, Eurybia, Phoebe, Deianera, Asteria, Marpe, Tecmessa and Alcippe, who had vowed to remain a virgin all her life, and died keeping her vow. Only after Hercules had slaughtered nearly all of these brave warriors and more or less exterminated the race of Amazons did Melanippe, their commander, admit defeat. The story tells how Hercules let Melanippe go 'in exchange for her girdle'; in other words, he raped her, knowing that this would be a worse humiliation than death, and he gave Antiope, who was a princess, to Theseus, in thanks for his support.

Meanwhile Theseus, the Athenian hero who had accompanied Hercules on the trip, had returned to Athens with Antiope, and made her his slave – meaning, of course, his concubine. Perhaps, outside the heat of battle, he was not such an uncivilised man, because it seems that Antiope grew fond of him. But the remaining Amazons did not know this and banded together with Scythian allies from the other side of the Black Sea, and set off to attack Athens and rescue Antiope. They came by way of the Cimmerian Bosphorus, through Thrace to Attica, and pitched their camp on a hill outside Athens (see Map 2). In the battle that ensued, Antiope, who by now had a son with Theseus called Hippolyte, fought on the Athenian side. She died fighting bravely against her own sisters while the Amazons were routed, the remnants of their army returning to Scythia with their allies.

In another, later, version[2] Hippolyta comes aboard Hercules' ship when it first arrives in the harbour at Themiscyra, falls in love with him, and offers him the girdle as a gift. All could have been well, but the goddess Hera, Hercules' mother, goes around the city spreading the rumour that these Greek pirates are planning to abduct Hippolyta, and so the Amazons mount their horses and attack Hercules' ship. At this point he kills Hippolyta and strips her of her girdle and battle-axe, which he presents to Queen Omphale (something of an Amazon herself), who puts it amongst the sacred regalia of the Lydian kings.

Whichever version you opt for, this story marks a decisive shift in the psyche of Western man: he ceases to be the mother's *son*, and becomes instead her *master*. He literally steals the girdle that embodies sexual power, the *shakti*, from the Great Mother – who has hitherto been seen as the source of all things, the ultimate power in the universe. Masculinity was only a small thing in relation to her encompassing femaleness. Camille Paglia writes: 'Masculinity flows from the Great Mother as an aspect of herself and is recalled and cancelled by her at will. Her son is a servant of her cult. There is no going beyond her. Motherhood blankets existence.'[3]

This is not a situation that a hero can tolerate. Hercules embodies the spirit of the patriarchal Dorians who arrived in Greece around 1200 BC, took power, and gradually shaped the old goddess-worshipping cultures into a new form. Hercules is the Dorians' mythical representative, an agent of change, the man who performs the necessary acts to transform a society still held fast in the grip of the earth mysteries. Masculine man begins to control and subdue feminine nature and the society that results from this transformation is Classical Greece, which produced Socrates, democracy, tragedy and rationalism, and whose spirit still informs our own civilisation.

The Amazons are the key to a forgotten country way back in time before this decisive step was taken in favour of our sort of civilisation. I do not believe that this step was automatically a bad thing: it was probably a necessary thing, and it cannot be undone. The time in which the idea of Amazons was created and perpetuated was the period running up to and including Classical Greece, 700–400 BC, and it was a borderland time between two realities, one ancient and one modern; one mysterious and almost unknowable, the other familiar. To know about the nature of the Amazons it is necessary to plunge back into that unknown world, bearing in mind that we have to avoid the strong temptation to project our own longings and fantasies into it.

THE NAME AND THE MYTH

As an introduction to the spirit of the Amazons, it is instructive to consider all the different meanings that have been given for their name. The commonest explanation is that the word is Greek and means 'without breasts, breastless', perhaps referring to the reported Amazon custom of searing off a breast in childhood in order to be able to draw the bow-string back unimpeded, or to divert all their strength into the right shoulder and arm which would be used in wielding weapons. Of course they may have appeared breastless because they bound up and flattened one of their breasts with a wide leather or linen strap so that it would not get in the way, as contemporary female archers sometimes do, or because they were simply very well-exercised bow-women whose shoulder and back muscles had developed so as to minimise their breasts.

The second most common explanation of the word 'Amazon' is that it is Armenian and means 'moon-women'. This leads into a whole world of possibilities as to their origin as priestesses of various moon-goddesses. Donald Sobol[4] thinks the name could refer to the Indian goddess Uma and gives *Uma-Soona*='children of Uma'. Amastris (an early Black Sea settlement) then becomes 'Uma's women' (*Stri*=woman). Another derivation for Amazon could be Phoenician *am*='mother', and *azon* or *adon*, 'lord', giving 'mother-lord'. He suggests Amazons could be women of Ephesus who 'gave up reaping for war', giving *amao*='reap' and *zonai*='wearing girdles'. An epithet that Herodotus attaches to them is *Oiorpata*, meaning 'man-killers', and Aeschylus calls them 'man-hating' and 'manless'.

Nothing about the Amazons may be taken too definitely or literally: the myths are not simple or clear and the travellers' tales may or may not be true – there is no way of knowing. For instance, there are other versions and variations of the Hercules/Hippolyta/Theseus/Antiope myth recounted above: many writers from Homer's time to ours have added theirs, each changing details and adding elements. Robert Graves's virtuoso performance in *The Greek Myths* has been enormously influential, but whereas he wrote it in a speculative, tricksterish spirit, perhaps already in thrall to the 'White Goddess', a whole generation of literal-minded feminists have repeated some of his wilder ideas as if they were gospel truth.

There are two questions we have to ask before we can begin to search intelligently for the source of the Amazon myth; first, what kind of society created, embellished and relished the Amazon image? And second, exactly *when* and *where* were the 'real' Amazons supposed to have lived?

AMAZONS AND THE ATHENIAN SPIRIT

Greece between 700 and 400 BC was a society in the throes of exciting and turbulent change and the Athenians were the instigators of it. But it was also a period in which women gradually lost the relative freedom and status they possessed in the Heroic Age (1600–1100 BC), as portrayed by Homer and the other writers of epics, and were turned into a servile underclass, along with the slaves with whom they shared much of their lives.

A girl would normally be married at the age of fourteen to a man of about thirty whose previous sexual experience would have been either with slaves or prostitutes, or with other men. The bride, however, had to be a virgin. This system may have evolved because of the low proportion of females in the population, probably as a result of the custom of 'exposing' girl babies (letting them die) in favour of male offspring. A young widow could serve as a wife in a series of marriages until she reached menopause or died in childbirth. One study of skeletal remains found the average adult longevity in Classical Greece to be forty-five for males and thirty-six for females, which implies that a significant proportion of women did die in childbirth, since in a modern developed society women on average live three years longer than men. A typical Athenian woman might bear five or six children in the course of her life.[5]

The Athenian girl remained in someone's protection throughout her life, whether he be a father, husband, son or a male relative. However, her dowry was to remain intact throughout her lifetime – it could be used for her support, but her guardian could not dispose of it. Divorce was easy to get, with no stigma; all a man had to do was send his wife away from the house. A woman seeking divorce, however, had to get a male relative to intercede and bring the case before the archon (magistrate). Only three cases are known of in the classical period where divorce proceeded from the wife's side. Children were the property of the father and remained in the father's house when a marriage was dissolved through death, and probably also in the case of divorce.

Boys had extensive mental and physical education but girls, because they married young, missed out except for the domestic arts. The age differential made husbands paternal, and indeed the wife had the status of a minor vis-à-vis her husband under Athenian law. The sexes lived separately – women and slaves upstairs, men downstairs. Free women were usually secluded so that they would not be seen by men who were not close relatives. Distance between husbands and wives could therefore be great: Socrates, for instance, dismissed his wife, the mother of his children, from his deathbed. Men had a public life in beautiful and spacious public buildings where they could go to exercise, discuss politics and philosophy and consort with their lovers, while women stayed in dark, often squalid and unsanitary homes with children and slaves for company. Women of all social classes worked mainly indoors or near the house in order to guard it, and better-off women sent slaves out to do errands and go to the market, missing out on the freedom that at least poorer women had to go out to fetch water, wash clothes, borrow utensils. Women could not buy or sell land, and there were not many respectable trades open to them. Male guardians managed their property.

Respectable women probably did not attend the theatre – which must have been one of the great pleasures of Greek life – although *hetairai* did. *Hetairai* were 'companions to men', who could be, at the top end of the social scale, educated and beautiful courtesans. The most famous woman in fifth-century Athens was Aspasia, the companion of Pericles, the Tyrant of Athens. She started life as a *hetaira* and ended it as a madam, but was widely respected: Socrates visited her and brought along pupils. Pericles cherished Aspasia and would kiss her on leaving and returning home. Clearly it was an unconventional relationship and Aspasia must have been a very strong-minded and independent woman.

Female slaves were freely available to their masters and their masters' friends for sex. Men could have a concubine on much the same basis as a wife. Homosexual love, usually between an older man and a young boy, was considered normal – and indeed even superior to love between a man and a woman. Under Solon's law, the guardian of a woman caught *in flagrante* had the right to sell her into slavery. The penalty for rape was monetary but the wronged husband did have the legal right to kill his wife's seducer. Intercourse three times a month was deemed sufficient for women. Since most men were likely to be either having homosexual encounters or sleeping with slaves, we can guess that the sexual experience of most women was somewhat unsatisfactory. Unsurprisingly, masturbation occurred and was acknowledged – some vase paintings depict phallic instruments being used by women for self-stimulation, and it is also mentioned in Aristophanes' play, *Lysistrata*.

Looking back on a society where the aristocratic women had almost no freedom and the high-class courtesans were the only category of women who were able to meet and talk to men on equal terms, it would be possible to argue, as Mandy Merch does, that the Amazons were simply a creation of the newly powerful patriarchs: 'The Amazons are introduced into myth not as an independent force but as the vanquished opponents of heroes credited with the establishment and protection of the Athenian state – its founding fathers, so to speak. Patriotism reinforces patriarchalism.'

Merch notes that life for Athenian women was 'short, arduous and secluded', and that 'the resulting tension between the Athenian state and its female members found its way into artistic expression, particularly in the tragedies which show women rebelling ... the Amazon myth can be interpreted as an expression of this unease'. She claims that 'the Amazon myth resolved this tension by representing such a rebellion as already concluded in deserved defeat'.[6] Merch puts it well, and it is easy to be convinced by her arguments, but the fact that the Athenians were fascinated by the idea and image of the Amazons, that they picked it up and embellished it in art and story, does not mean that there were no 'real' prototype Amazons – nor that there were no roads to freedom at all for Athenian and other Greek women.

THE SECRET FREEDOMS OF WOMEN

There was one area in which the suppressed and secluded class of women – and also slaves and some foreigners – were allowed to function as equals with men: the Eleusinian mysteries. Each year in the autumn, the nine-day-long ceremony was held in which, in the Classical Age, any sincere person could come and be initiated into the mysteries of Demeter, as long as they spoke Greek and had not sullied their hands with human blood. At the heart of the mystery was the relationship between the earth-goddess Demeter and her maiden daughter Persephone, or Kore. Kore is picking flowers in a meadow when she is abducted by Hades, the lord of the Underworld. Demeter mourns her loss violently and seeks her throughout the universe, withdrawing her benevolence from the natural world so that everything withers and fails. The myth tells how they are eventually reunited in great joy and fertility is restored to the world. In the course of the ceremony there was also a sacred marriage in which a sacred child is conceived: these mysteries were a legacy of old pre-Dorian, earth-based rites, possibly originating in Crete, in which the female as earth-goddess was paramount. Sophocles wrote 'thrice blessed are those among men who, after beholding these rites, go down to Hades. Only for them is there life; all the rest will suffer misery.'

Nobody knows exactly what happened at the climax of the rites – and indeed without the long slow preparations that were designed to alter the state of consciousness it would probably mean little to us if we did – but the important matter for us is that the Eleusinian mysteries were not only open to women, but preserved the essence of the old matripotestal religion at the heart of increasingly patriarchal Greece for nearly 2,000 years, from their inauguration in about 1350 BC until they ended three centuries after the birth of Christ.

Slightly earlier in the year was the three-day festival of Thesmophoria, a very ancient and mysterious rite in which piglets were sacrificed. It was only for women. Only free women of unblemished character were allowed to participate. They had to be chaste for three days in preparation, but were required to indulge in foul language and obscenities as part of the rite. Wealthy husbands were obliged to bear the cost of the festival.

On an even more earthy level there were the rites of Dionysus, the god who was brought up as a girl and whose main followers were always women. In the late 500 AD there are vase paintings of fierce and brutal Dionysiac rituals where maenads (female followers of the god Dionysus) inflamed with wine or other substances would tear animals apart with their bare hands.

Then there were the oracles, the most famous perhaps those at Delphi and Dodona. In earlier times these sites were probably sacred simply to the goddess whose priestess-prophets would commune with her and give oracles. Delphi was named after the female serpent Delphyne, who used to live in the chasm there with her mate, the Python. The god Apollo killed the Python and made the Delphic priestess work in his service. She would sit on a tripod, breathe fumes from a crack in the earth, go into a trance and make her utterances, which would then be interpreted by a priest. The oracle of Zeus at Dodona was thought to have been brought from Egypt by a kidnapped priestess. The ancient priestesses of the shrine went barefoot, never washed their feet, and slept on the bare ground (all symbolic ways to keep in touch with Mother Earth). They listened for the words of Zeus in the rustlings of the leaves and the clinking of brass vessels hanging from the branches of the oak tree sacred to the god. In later times, they too were joined by priests as the Dorian incomers made sure their father gods 'married' the local mother-goddesses.

Although they secluded and circumscribed their women, the Greeks must have been strongly aware of their power, whether sexual and earthy as in the Dionysian rites, or prophetic as in the oracles, or comforting and transcendent as in the Eleusinian earth-goddess, Demeter. Indeed, Athens *belonged* to Athene, the great warrior-goddess, and Artemis, the virgin huntress, was worshipped under her different names all over the Greek world. She was of course the Amazons' main goddess, and it was said that they had founded her temple in Ephesus. Therefore in the religious and spiritual sphere the feminine was still powerful.

Thus in Athens in the sixth and fifth centuries BC we have a society in which democracy is evolving, art and philosophy flowering, women are utterly suppressed, and misogyny is rife – and yet in which there is a strong subliminal recognition of feminine power as expressed in religious rites. This provides an interesting contrast to our own society in which women are regarded as equals but have only recently acquired any public religious role, as women priests. To find out where the Amazons stand in relation to this we need to consider the spiritual aspects of their myth. Apollonius Rhodius, who wrote about Jason and the Argonauts in the third century BC, associates the Amazons with the worship of Ares:

> Then all together they [Jason and his men] went to the temple of Ares to offer sacrifice of sheep and in haste they stood round the altar, which was outside the roofless temple, an altar built of pebbles, within which a black stone stood fixed, a sacred thing, to which of yore the Amazons all used to pray. Nor was it lawful for them, when they came from the opposite coast, to burn on this altar offerings of sheep and oxen, but they used to slay horses which they kept in great herds.[7]

There is a hint here of a religious role for the Amazons that I will explore in detail later, but for now notice only the black stone, normally associated with the great goddess Cybele from Phrygia, in western Anatolia, and the horse-sacrifice that links them with the horse-people of the steppes. The association of Amazons with horses is there in many of their names: Hippolyta – 'of the stampeding horse'; Melanippe – 'black mare'; Alcippe – 'powerful mare'.

THE STRONG WOMEN OF SPARTA

In Athens and most of the civilised Greek city-states women were treated primarily as breeders, but Sparta was very different. Even though Spartans were supposed to be Dorians – that is, of Hercules' patriarchal line – and though they honed the notion of warriorship to a sharp and lethal edge, women were actually much freer there than in Athens. This was partly because they were valued as 'mothers of warriors' and therefore needed to be nourished and exercised as well as the boys. Spartan women married later, at around eighteen, which meant they were physically more mature when they had their first child, and much less likely to suffer complications. Xenophon praised the Spartans for nourishing girls as well as boys, for it was unusual amongst the Greeks to do so.

Spartan boys from the mid-sixth century BC onwards were subjected to a rigorous regime, designed to turn them into tough warriors; they were taken away from their parents at seven and lived in age-cohorts, eating, training and sleeping in dormitories. They stayed in these men-only societies until they were thirty. But the girls exercised too, possibly in the nude as the boys did – and certainly wearing the *peplos* (outer robes) with slit skirts which left the thighs bare and allowed freedom of movement. Housework and clothes-making were left to the inferior classes – citizen women occupied themselves with gym, music, the management of house and child-rearing. And, of course, with sex!

In certain circumstances adultery was not frowned upon – the state wasn't too bothered who the father of a child was as long as he was a Spartan citizen, and since Spartan men were often away for long periods on campaigns, it was accepted that their wives would conceive children with other men. The pool of warriors, depleted by war, had to be renewed somehow. Spartan women were famous for their outspokenness – there is an anthology of their witticisms attributed to Plutarch.

Spartan marriage custom harked back to a time when a bride really did have to be captured or kidnapped – but now it was ritualised into a mock-capture for which the girl wore boys' clothes and had her hair shorn. Whether this was to make it easier for the man, practised as he would be in homosexuality, to make the switch to heterosexual intercourse, or whether it was intended as a rite of passage for the girls, to mark the end of their inviolate maidenhood and the beginning of a new phase in which like a shorn sheep they would be sacrificed for the perpetuation of the species, we do not know. Or was it done so that fierce Artemis, protector of the young and innocent, should not know that one of her own was being taken?

Spartan women were well-nourished and well-muscled. They had a fair degree of sexual freedom (erotic relationships between girls and older women were encouraged) and were allowed to speak their minds. When they visited Athens they must have appeared quintessentially Amazonian in their appearance and behaviour. You can just imagine a farther telling off his hoyden daughter: 'Stop behaving like a Spartan hussy!'

Therefore, Classical Athens was not like contemporary Tehran, where all women are currently obliged to obey the patriarchal rule: *hetairai* and Spartans, priestesses and ordinary women at festivals were allowed a wide latitude of behaviour. A citizen might not allow his wife any of these freedoms, but he would see them practised in the marketplace.

The Spartans were descendants of the Dorian warriors, the 'Heraclids', of whom the hero Hercules was an embodiment, while the Athenians were Ionians, inheritors of the Mycenaean tradition, a more civilised and cultured strand with the cunning Theseus as their favourite hero. The Spartans hung on to the dour ideals of the past and were ultra-conservative, whilst Athens was experimenting with the tools of democracy. There was tension between them throughout the Classical period, resulting in several bloody wars late in the fifth century. But then, as the Greek city-states flourished and sent out immigrants to Italy, Sicily and the Black Sea shore, a new empire was burgeoning in the east – the Persian Empire, under Darius. The Persians were seen as barbarians, smooth-faced trouser-wearers in funny hats who threatened the basis of Greek civilisation. A bitter war was fought towards the beginning of the fifth century, which the Greeks finally won (against the odds) at the famous battles of Marathon and Salamis.[8] Some commentators feel that the story of Theseus' battle against the Amazons at Athens was invented to deal with the emotions aroused by the Persian wars – the Persians seemed like effeminate men, the Amazons were like masculine women; they both dared to challenge the Greeks on their own ground; and they both reeked of a different way of life that the Athenian Greeks must have found both fascinating and repellent.

AMAZONS IN ART

Indeed the great wave of enthusiasm for depicting Amazons in art, either on vases or in friezes, happened after the Battle of Marathon in 490 BC. Aeschylus refers to their occupation of the 'rock of Ares' at Athens in 458 BC in his play *The Eumenides*. John Boardman suggests a 'late invention' for the whole story to combine the invasions and victories of 490 BC and 480 BC in a single myth-historical parable.[9] The only objection to this is: why did the Greeks not simply celebrate their victory over the barbarians in their form as Persians? Why did they need to be transmuted into Amazons? Clearly something else was going on, and I hope in the course of this book to make clear what it might have been.

The Amazons appear on vases and other decorative objects from the late seventh century onwards. In the earliest example (a votive shield) the Hero, probably Hercules, towers over the Amazon, with massive thighs and upraised sword, grabbing her by the crest of her helmet, while she puts up a puny arm to restrain him. There is no doubt that she is about to die. But the cheerful crudity of the painting stops the scene from being poignant, to the modern eye at least. Hercules has something that could be a girdle slung round his neck, which means that the scene could be from the Battle of Themiscyra where Hercules stole the girdle of the Amazon queen. Or, if this is not a girdle, it is probably Achilles and Penthesilea fighting at Troy. Penthesilea was the bold Amazon queen who came to Troy to fight against the Greeks and perished at Achilles' hand. When he lifted her helmet to see her dead face, he fell in love with her.

By the sixth century BC, as the craze for Amazon scenes grows, we see Hercules in combat with Amazons on lots of vases – he usually wears his lionskin (won when he killed the ferocious Nemean lion by strangling it, and then flaying the pelt to wear as armour) and looks very male and well-muscled. Sometimes his own head emerges from the lion's jaws so that he appears as half man and half wild beast. The conventions of the times dictated that male skin was painted black and female skin white, so his Amazon, sometimes called Andromache, looks pale and vulnerable next to him. She is often depicted as if realising, too late, the folly of taking on such a man-beast; she is trying to step back and escape. In the earlier works the Amazons usually wear a short tunic and a crested helmet, but later, in the fifth century, more and more Amazons were depicted in 'orien-tal' clothes: tight spotted or striped trousers and a long-sleeved top, a pointed cap and earrings. The favourite theme was man versus woman in single combat and certainly in some cases there is a strong erotic element – Hercules springs forward and Andromache yields by falling to her knees. Yet the figure of the plucky Amazon has to command respect, game to fight on as she is in the face of the super-naturally gifted warrior Hercules.

Male potency is sometimes stressed even more, with one or more of the fighters in a group painted nude (in one case, Hercules' penis seems to be erect, as men's penises often are when they are aroused to battle-fervour), and, in the later works particularly, the Amazons are lissom and pretty, showing off strapping thighs and occasionally naked breasts.

Some of the images are very vivid and powerful: a Greek and an Amazon face each other mounted on leggy horses, and as they fight we see another Amazon dying entangled under the horse's hooves; a Greek warrior in his black animal-skin carries off a dead Amazon draped round his shoulders like a white hind, and in one refreshingly naturalistic scene an Amazon in a very long pointed cap and dark close-fitting top and trousers warily approaches a frightened horse with a long pole, as if training it. In some cases the scenes evoke excitement and brutal sexuality; in others there is a refined dancer-like poignancy; in still others, particularly the later ones, the Amazons are jauntily decorative, even a little narcissistic, as they check their bows clad in chequerboard suits or wield their axes and spears rather self-consciously. On one late vase, there is a determined-looking beefy girl in short black tunic who pulls back a sling while showing her noble profile and who conveys a real sense of muscle and athletic power.

Clearly these Amazon images are not accurate depictions of real Amazons. They reflect the mood and the fantasies of their time, just as Xena or Lara Croft or Tank Girl do in our own period. And yet there may be clues about real Amazons embedded in some of the images: in one piece now in the Louvre, an Amazon with a negroid turn of feature approaches an altar on her knees. She is wearing a long tunic and an animal-skin tied round her middle; on her head is a scarf with a diadem set in it. Quiver and bow are hung up behind her and a palm tree is shown behind the altar. Dietrich von Bothmer[10] thinks that she is taking refuge in the sacred sanctuary of Artemis at Ephesus, but she may be an African Amazon from Libya, such as Diodorus described in the first century BC. Other cups show Egyptian archers, attendants of Memnon, on the same vases as Amazons and palm trees. In one red-figure cup an Amazon carries a spear with a sickle attached; this is a weapon that Herodotus associated with the Carians and Lycians, the peoples with matrilineal customs from the Aegean coast of Turkey, which has many Amazonian connections.

Amazons were often included in battle scenes on friezes of temples, sometimes alongside other 'mythical' enemies of the Greeks such as Centaurs. The Bassae Frieze from the Temple of Apollo at Bassae in Arcadia was carved in marble between 420 and 400 BC. Buxom, round-limbed women in graceful robes engage virile men in helmets in a battle that has the flowing quality of a dream. The women's faces are the open innocent faces of girl students, surprised by the conflict they find themselves in; the men look noble and affronted, as if they would rather be elsewhere. The women's tunics fall open to reveal outstanding breasts; the naked bodies of the male warriors are beautifully arranged to show their well-proportioned limbs. Arms are flung up to frame and circle a bonny face, skirts to fly open and show a well-turned thigh. The Bassae Frieze is more erotic than martial. However, it is not misogynistic: the women are big, bold and brave, the equal of the men. Their bodies are powerful, healthy and real-looking, not distorted as women's bodies often are in later art by the whims of body-fascism. Oh yes, the Greeks knew that women were a force to be reckoned with: deep down they must have known their patriarchal idyll could not last for ever: that the big barbarian Amazon women would come banging on their gates one day soon!

THE TIME OF THE AMAZONS

The true 'time of the Amazons' was back in the Bronze Age, although some of the authors who mention them seem to think they continued in existence right up to, and even beyond, Christian times. But the central myths about the Amazons point to the Bronze Age and so provide us with the most useful clues or keys. The story of the theft of Hippolyta's girdle by Hercules, the rape of Antiope by Theseus, and the Amazons' fruitless mission to take revenge on Athens and win back their power, make up a beacon clearly marking the end of an era, an era in which there were still some groups of women hanging on to the old sort of power. When was that era? Where were these women? What was that power? These are the questions I was asking myself as I set out on my journey of exploration. But first I had to make a close study of the basic texts.

The very first literary reference to the Amazons is in Homer, who was writing around 750 BC about events that are thought to have happened around 1200 BC, just before the fall of Mycenae and the decay of Crete. In between these two dates fall the Dark Ages about which, still, very little is known. The speaker here is the Trojan king, Priam: 'Once before now I travelled to Phrygia where the vines grow, and there I saw a host of Phrygian men with their quick horses ... which were camped along the bank of Sangarios. I too was numbered among them as their ally on the day *when the Amazons came, women the equal of men*. But even they were not as numerous as these bright-eyed Achaians.'[11]

We cannot deduce a great deal from this apart from the fact that the Amazons were associated with the area that became Phrygia (the west and central part of today's Turkey), in particular with the River Sangarios which was in the coastal strip that faces the Aegean Sea and Greece. The Amazons were known as 'women the equal of men', and this epithet is repeated later in the epic: 'Bellerophontes ... he slaughtered the Amazons, women the equal of men.' Note that Bellerophontes has first killed the Chimaera, a monster, which places the Amazons firmly in the category of unnatural and undesirable creatures who have to be destroyed for the good of all.

There is no mention in Homer of Penthesilea, the Amazon queen, and her cohorts being present at Troy, but later Greek writers refer to a lost epic called *Aethiopis* in which she comes to Troy and takes on Achilles, the Greek hero, in single combat. She fights bravely but is finally speared by Achilles, who, when he takes off her helmet, sees her lovely face and falls in love with her. There may be few Amazons in Homer but, as Sarah Pomeroy points out, there are many powerful women in Bronze Age epics – Helen, Andromache, Clytemnestra, Hecuba, Penelope, Arete, to name a few, and the epics give a generally positive picture of the life and status of women in the Heroic Age. They were expected to be modest, but were not secluded. Andromache and Helen walk freely through the streets of Troy, albeit always escorted, and wives, notably Helen, Arete and Penelope, may remain within the public rooms in the presence of male guests without scandal.

Sarah Pomeroy points out that 'a comparison between Archaic and Classical Athens gives the impression that women were forced into obscurity in the latter period . . . the curbing of aristocrats by the democracy of the 5th century entailed the repression of all women but leaned especially heavily on the aristocrats'. It is hard to accept that democracy actually took freedom away from women, but the misogyny that appears frequently in Classical Greek literature supports Pomeroy's case.

There are also traces in Bronze Age sagas of matrilocal patterns of marriage: a roving warrior would marry a princess and settle down in her kingdom, so that he could inherit her father's kingdom. In the marriages of Hippodamia, Atalanta and Jocasta we find the principle of matrilineal succession illustrated, meaning that the right to kingship comes through the female line so that a man becomes king by marrying a queen. (In Britain today we do not allow this: Prince Philip does not share sovereignty with his wife, the Queen.) Menelaus' and Helen's marriage was matrilineal *and* matrilocal: Menelaus is king by virtue of his position as Helen's husband, and therefore he might lose the throne if he loses her. The Trojan war was of course triggered by Menelaus' efforts to get Helen back from Paris.

Hesiod, who was writing a little later than Homer, is the first to link Hercules with the Amazons: 'the mighty Hercules, when he was journeying in quest of the horses of proud Laomedon – horses of the fleetest of foot that the Asian land nourished – destroyed in battle the tribe of the dauntless Amazons and drove them forth from all that land'.[12] King Laomedon was the guardian of the straits that led into the Black Sea, and this quote refers to the time between the Argonauts' voyage to get the Golden Fleece and the Trojan war. The Amazons here are once again linked with horses, with the land of Asia, and placed in a period just before the Trojan war.

The Amazons emerge into literature and art around 700 BC, in what is called the Archaic Age in Greece, and were popular throughout the Classical and Hellenistic periods (500 BC up to the birth of

Christ). Greeks writing about them usually placed them back in what we would call the later Bronze Age, or Hittite times (between 1900 and 1200 BC), but the various prototypes for the Amazons may have come from sources further back in time, and from cultures further north and east, so the time chart on p. xiv could be an essential aid to orientation as we travel backwards and forwards through the centuries on the track of the women warriors.

THE AMAZON HOMELANDS

With the Amazons, 'where?' is not nearly so easy to answer as 'when?' I discovered early on that there were several different areas associated with the warrior women, none of them in mainland Greece itself. One area was the Aegean coast of Turkey along with the islands close to it such as Crete and Samothrace; the other area was between the Pontus mountains and the Black Sea in Turkey, and the third area stretches from the Caucasus mountains east of the Black Sea way up into the steppes of the Ukraine and Russia. Diodorus also claimed that there had been an earlier race of Amazons in Libya. Because the geography of the Amazons can become rather complex, I would recommend the occasional glance at Map 1 on p. xvi, which shows these 'Amazon' areas.

The earliest references point to the Aegean coast of Turkey as the Amazon homeland, and Pliny said that the famous goddess-city of Ephesus, which lies halfway up this coast, had been founded by the Amazons. The Great Mother Goddess had her temple here. She was called Artemis, but this was not the gamine huntress Artemis with whom the Amazons are normally associated, but a goddess closer to Cybele who was worshipped in orgiastic rites in which flutes and drums were sounded and cymbals clashed.

On this coast in the Bronze Age there were native non-Greek people called Lydians, Carians and Lycians, some of whom were said to have matrilineal customs, and the Lydians had a queen, Omphale, who appears in mythology as the woman who buys Hercules as a slave (in a surprising reversal of his usual victorious battles against matriarchy) and actually makes him live and behave like a woman for a period of time. What could this odd episode point to? It reminded me of a story in the Hindu *Mahabharata* in which Arjuna has to live as a maidservant for a year. And, as I searched, I was to find the idea of gender swapping, or what Florence Bennett in 1912 calls 'the oriental idea of sex confusion', coming up again and again in relation to the Amazons.

THE SNAKE-GODDESS SPEAKS

I was not expecting to make any connections between Crete and the Amazons. One distinguished person who had written a book about Crete was very firm when I spoke to her: there were no traces of warrior women there at all! She sounded faintly irritated that I had even asked. But one day I was wandering in the dim cramped vaults of the London Library, in the lowest level, 'Topography', where the lack of oxygen on a hot day has often made me feel very peculiar. As I paused to gulp air, I happened to spot the six large and venerable volumes of Arthur Evans's *Palace of Minos*, written after he had excavated Knossos in the earliest years of this century. I expected to smile at the quaint ideas of this romantic Edwardian, but I was quickly enchanted by Evans's copious and detailed illustrations and disarmingly enthusiastic writing style. He loved the palace of Knossos and was able to evoke its magic as no one else has done since. As I reluctantly closed volume four, my eye caught an extraordinary illustration he had used as a frontispiece (see illustration). Evans had entitled it 'Our Lady of Sports', and it showed a lithe athletic young woman, arms raised, full breasts pushed forwards by a golden corslet, a strange masculine codpiece covering her loins. It was a beautiful but disturbing image. I made a note of it in my black notebook and closed the volume. Only months later did I begin to see what its relevance to the enigma of the Amazons might be.

There were other reasons that Crete was to prove important in thinking about Amazons: at the peak of the Minoan high-palatial civilisation the famous 'snake-goddesses' were made (you can see very good copies in the Ashmolean Museum in Oxford). These little figurines are erotic in a sharp, dynamic way, the breasts emphasised by being pushed up and out, the waist cinched and the lap or genital area covered with a decorative apron. They wear long bell-shaped tiered dresses and tall hats, sometimes with an animal sitting upon them. Some of the figures hold up a writhing snake in each hand, giving the impression that they are controlling a wild, galvanising energy. The figures seemed to say to me: 'I, as a priestess, embody the power of the goddess, I can show it to you and I can feel it – and I can control it. But beware of approaching it profanely because it is dangerous to the unwary.'

This tense, electric power and sexuality is well embodied in the symbolism of snakes, and I noticed that the Amazons were also frequently connected with snakes – the African branch wore the skins of giant snakes as armour and one of the all-female tribes they fought were the 'Gorgons', whose queen was Medusa, whose snakey locks and monstrous face turned men to stone if they looked upon her. She was literally a 'man-killer'. In a sixth-century relief from Corfu[13] you can see a Gorgon with two entwined snakes on her belly, wearing a short skirt which barely hides her genitals. It seems as if the snakes are really a disguise for the genitals that she conceals. George Thomson[14] mentions a 'well-known women's rite – in Greece especially associated with Demeter – of exposing the genitals by drawing up the skirt', the act that the old nurse Baubo performs to cheer Demeter up when she is seeking Persephone. The suggestion behind all this seemed to be that there was a power residing in the female vagina and uterus that was so terrifying it could kill you. Herodotus called the Amazons *Oiorpata*, man-killers. I began to wonder if this deadly epithet had as much to do with their sexuality as their martial ruthlessness.

Then I began to realise that there is an Amazon feature that is usually underplayed in favour of their fighting skills – that is, their promiscuous sexual practices. According to several sources, they had no husbands, but went out once a year and mated at random with men from a neighbouring tribe. This would be considered wildly aberrant behaviour in Classical Athens where monogamous marriage was the custom. But there was still a dim memory of another way of life, embodied in a tradition that says that Kekrops, the first king of Athens, invented matrimony and that before this time there had been no marriage, and intercourse was promiscuous with the results that sons did not know their fathers or fathers their sons. Children were named after their mothers. This sounded like the kind of matrilineal society that might breed Amazons: I began to feel that where I found archaic customs relating to sex I should be on the alert for the scent of the warrior women.

THE CITY OF THE AMAZONS

Themiscyra, the fabled city of the Amazons, was said to lie on the River Thermodon near the Black Sea in 'Pontus'. Many different sources mention it as their homeland and the modern consensus is that it must have been (if it existed) somewhere between Sinop and Giresun on the southern coast of the Black Sea in Turkey. One source actually mentions *three* Amazon cities in this area, but I discovered that so far no one had come up with convincing, or even suggestive, evidence that any of them, or Themiscyra, ever existed. One enthusiastic website was sure that the fortress of Dundartepe near Samsun was Themiscyra, but seemed to base this conviction simply on the happenstance that it was big, it was in the right place, and it was suitably dilapidated and picturesque.

I decided I would have to go to the Turkish Black Sea and look for myself. The books said it was a mysterious and inaccessible region, walled in by the Pontus mountains, naturally cut off from the rest of the land mass of which it is part, and yet connected via mountain valleys to the plains and mountains of the north and the east from where, in the Bronze Age, many waves of peoples and influence may have come. There were various intriguing sites in the region – Ikiztepe, which was a Bronze Age settlement; Palaeolithic, Phrygian and Hellenistic forts; the massive fortress of Akalan, which is probably Hittite, and the old Greek colonies of Amisos and Sinop. Did any of them have the right to be considered as Themiscyra, the city of the Amazons? I would do my best to find out.

BUT WHAT DOES THE SPHINX SAY?

But regardless of whether the Amazons were linked with the Black Sea coast in Turkey or Ephesus and the Aegean coast, if I travelled back further in time I kept bumping up against the powerful, enigmatic race of the Hittites. There is a Hittite sphinx in the Archaeological Museum in Istanbul who embodies a particular sort of brutish, cunning power, which used to seem to me quintessentially Hittite. But as I got to know the Hittites better, I realised they were not what they seemed. They were a patriarchal Indo-European people who arrived in Anatolia at the beginning of the second millennium BC, but as they mingled with the native Hattians and Luvians – and later with the Hurrians from the east – they evolved a mythology and a religious system in which the old female power, although challenged, was to some degree honoured. I discovered that there are fascinating old documents that bear witness to the extraordinary power of the sorceresses and priestesses of the early period of the Hittite empire. Could these 'magic-women' perhaps be the key to a city ruled or dominated by women? At the rock shrine of Yazilikaya near Ankara there is a peculiar figure marching amongst the lines of gods and goddesses, kings and queens – it is neither male nor female, but both. It is half-veiled and winged and now thought to be Shawushka,[15] the Hurrian/Hittite goddess of love and war. Did she/

he or some god/dess like her have war-like priestesses who could have been the prototype for the Amazons? Certainly some of the Victorians who explored the archaeology of the area thought so.[16]

As for the earliest forerunner of Cybele, the lion-goddess, she entered history in the sixth millennium BC in the figure of a fat 'mother-goddess' giving birth between her lions or leopards, which was found in a grain bin in Çatal Hüyük, one of the earliest 'towns' in the world, in the middle of the Anatolian plain. This small sculpture with her fat thighs and her blind eyes is so expressive and naturalistically moulded that it feels impossible that the civilisation that produced it should be alien to us. The vigour of the modelling is such that you expect the little figure to spring up and come towards you. What was the secret, the special genius, of Çatal Hüyük, and did it have any connection with my Amazons? Was it the beginning of the thread that would wind itself through the millennia and end up weaving the haunting image of the women warriors?

AMAZONS AND BARBARIANS

From the eighth century BC onwards, the expansive Greeks were beginning to found colonies around the Black Sea – for instance, Amisos, in what is now Samsun in Turkey, Phanagoria in the Taman peninsula (now Russian), and Chersonesus and Olbia in the Ukraine, which means that if there were any woman warriors amongst the barbarians they colonised, they would certainly be noticed. I knew that graves of women with weapons had been found in the Ukraine and in Russia, but was having great difficulty in getting hold of the archaeologists concerned. With one exception (Jeannine Davis-Kimball), either they spoke Russian or they were not eager to talk to me. So I decided simply to get a visa and go there, hoping that in the flesh I could persuade them to help me. In fact, what I learned from these women archaeologists exceeded my wildest expectations and opened up great vistas of human history and prehistory, of which, I have to admit, I was completely ignorant when I started out. The wealth of material in Russia and the Ukraine, which we encounter in the next chapter, is only, I suspect, the tip of an iceberg that will be swimming into our view in the next millennium. Its implications have not yet begun to seep into our collective consciousness. When they do, the first part of the Amazon message will have been delivered to our age.

CHAPTER TWO

The Secret of the Steppes

·················

Through my porthole I could see the full moon shining above the Black Sea, making a track of dancing light that rippled towards me like a white snake. Low on the horizon, red Mars skulked. The sea was as smooth and dark as an obsidian mirror. It was a night fitting to start a journey in search of the women who called themselves daughters of Ares (the Greek name for Mars) and who served the moon-goddess Artemis/Cybele with their sickle-shaped shields – the Amazons.

We had managed to get the last two places on a Russian cargo-boat sailing from Istanbul in Turkey to Yalta in the newly free Ukraine, our route as close as we could get to that followed by the Amazons who had survived the battle of Themiscyra. They were wretched captives in a Greek ship, destined for slavery – or worse. This was the low point in their history: after glorious centuries of independence, conquest and the founding of cities, they had been humiliated and routed by the archetypal patriarchal hero, Hercules. Maybe a few remnants had escaped to fight at Troy, but Penthesilea – their beautiful, brave queen – was due to die there, pierced by Achilles' spear.

From such moments one of the most potent myths of our civilisation was born. But what kind of 'truth' lay behind those moments? Upon what kind of reality was the myth built? In the Ukraine I was hoping at last to meet the women archaeologists whose work was proving that women very like the Amazons really did exist – and to see the bones, the armour and the weapons of some of those women warriors. Natasha, my friend and interpreter, was making, in reverse, a trip her mother had made back in 1945 when she fled her native Ukraine to go to Istanbul. Natasha's Russian mother had

Tartar blood in her and Natasha might well carry in her the genes of the nomadic women warriors who rode the steppes over 2,000 years ago.

The night before we stood on the deck drinking beer and watching the boat being crammed to the gunnels with goods bought to resell in the markets of Yalta and Odessa. We saw children's bikes, babies' buggies, electrical goods, boxes of grapes, all swinging in on the crane. The traders are mainly women: Natasha had to share a cabin with good-natured Galya and all her gear: there was barely room to wriggle to her bunk between all the boxes. My room-mate, a Britt Ekland look-alike, whom we called Blondinka, was selling another kind of ware. She did not sleep in the cabin either night, presumably having business elsewhere. She had a heavy, catarrhal listlessness that would have seemed tragic were not her eyes so dead. In fact, there was a layer of resigned sadness behind the eyes of all the women on board whether they were dealing in children's toys or sex. The bazaar at Istanbul is full of 'Natashas', which is what they call the Ukrainian and Russian women who come to sell themselves for dollars. There is plenty of custom for them in Muslim Istanbul, but plenty of contempt too.

Woken in the middle of the night to show our passports as the boat sailed out of the Bosphorus, we watched the mosques and minarets of Istanbul slip by in the moon-glare. Once into the Black Sea we felt as if we were on our way. In the confusing web of tales about the Amazons, the Black Sea is a central motif: their city Themiscyra was said to be on the Turkish coast near modern Samsun, their sacred island just off the shore of modern Giresun; Aeschylus places them, albeit somewhat vaguely (his geography being poor), in the Caucasus mountains to the east of the Black Sea. But the most significant account that mentions the Black Sea must be that given by Herodotus, the 'father of history', writing in the middle of the fifth century BC when Classical Greece was just past its most glorious period.

THE LAST AMAZONS

He explains that the Greeks and Amazons had been at war and that the Greeks finally subdued the savage women and sailed away in three ships with them, presumably taking them into slavery. In the middle of the Black Sea the Amazons rose up and overcame their captors, but unfortunately did not know anything about sailing a boat and so, after days of drifting at the mercy of the wind and waves, they were washed up on the shores of the Sea of Azov. They came across a herd of horses, which they promptly tamed and mounted, and set about pillaging the local Scythians.

The Scythians fought back and were astonished to find, when they examined the corpses of the Amazons they had slain, that their enemies were women. They decided not to try to kill the survivors but to woo them instead, thinking that they would make good strong children. So a group of young Scythian men went off and camped near the women, being careful to be on good behaviour so that eventually the women realised they meant no harm. I'll let Herodotus continue the story from here:

In the middle of every day the Amazons used to split up into ones or twos and go some way apart from one another in order to relieve themselves. When the Scythians noticed this, they did the same thing. One of them approached one of the women who was all alone and the Amazon did not repulse him, but let him have intercourse with her. She could not speak to him because they did not understand each other, but she used gestures to tell him to return the next day to the same place and to bring someone else with him; she made it clear to him that there should be two of them, and that she would bring another woman with her too. The young man returned to his camp and told the others the news. He kept the appointment the next day, taking someone else along too, and found another Amazon there as well, waiting for them. When the other young men found out, they joined in and tamed the remaining Amazons.

After that the two sides joined forces and lived together, forming couples consisting of a Scythian and the Amazon with whom he first had sex.[1]

The Amazons were willing to settle down with the men, but not as Scythian women. They wanted to keep up their old ways: 'we haven't learnt women's work. We shoot arrows, wield javelins, ride horses – things which your women never have anything to do with'. So the newly formed couples crossed the River Tanais and travelled east for three days and then north for another three, before settling down to begin the Sauromatian nation, whose womenfolk always hung on to the custom of hunting on horseback and going to war. Herodotus ends: 'One of their marriage customs is that no young woman may marry until she has killed a male enemy. Inability to fulfil this condition means that some of them do not marry until they are old.'

There has been much debate about whether Herodotus was principally a storyteller or a historian, but there is something about the human detail of this story that makes it stick in the mind, true or not. Herodotus makes the Amazons the ancestors of Sauromatian warrior women who were still living and fighting at the time he wrote, the fifth century BC, and I had come to the Ukraine to find out what kind of concrete evidence there was for these warrior women's existence.

As we grew closer to Yalta harbour on the morning of the second day we could see high white cliffs and people buzzing around on jet-skis beneath them. From such cliffs the cruel priestesses of Artemis Tauropolos flung the sacrificed bodies of shipwrecked sailors who came their way, and some people think that the Amazons are a memory of such a blood-stained band of women (see chapter four).

The Crimean coast is beautiful, lush and sad – in the gardens children play unnaturally quietly and people are subdued: they have no money and the future looks grim. That night we sat on a terrace high above Alupka, a faded seaside town near Yalta full of enormous empty sanatoria, staring down once again at the giant moon hanging over the Black Sea. The terrace and ramshackle 'holiday huts' around it belonged to 'Babushka', Natasha's mother-in-law. We slept in high, damp, lumpy beds, washed in the yard, and ate cucumber and tomato salad from a basin. Babushka was proud of her kingdom: her life had been very hard, but her third and last husband, a Jewish survivor of Auschwitz, had left her the huts and she let them out for 2 hriyvnas (65p) a night to impoverished city-dwellers needing a seaside break. Babushka's hero was Alexander the Great, the secret of whose success, she claimed, was that he fed his army on *kapusta*, cabbage. Cabbage would cure anything, she said. She had overheard a man on a bus saying so, and it had proved true in her own experience.

Alexander the Great had an interesting encounter with an Amazon, according to Diodorus and others. She was a warrior-queen called Thalestris and came to visit him with 200 soldiers while he was encamped in the wilderness, offering to sleep with him in order to beget a super-hero girl-child. They spent thirteen days (half a menstrual/moon cycle) together, hunting lions and making love, but sadly Thalestris died soon afterwards, and the marvellous child was never born. The real Thalestris may have been a nomadic warrior-princess in Bactria offered to Alexander by her father in about 329 BC.

The next day we hired a car and driver and set off down the coast. The driver was Hussein, a Tartar who had lately returned to Crimea from Samarkand to which his family had been exiled by Stalin in 1944, along with two and a half million other Tartars. Was it better here? 'It's *home*, he said pointedly, proudly showing us the new Tartar settlements springing up along the coast, houses half-built where the money has run out, with an occasional minaret promising that a mosque too was under construction.

We arrived at Chersonesus on the outskirts of Sevastopol in the late afternoon while a hot bright sun still beat down on the bleached columns and archways of what was once a fine Greek colony. Here in the four centuries up to the birth of Christ, cultured Greeks and barbarian Scythians had mingled in civilised intercourse, as they did at many other cities around the Black Sea. I was hoping there might be some evidence of women warriors here, perhaps a vase depicting them strolling in the streets in truculent bands, looking for handsome Greeks to sire their girl-children. At the archaeological site we were directed to a wooden house that perched above the ruins and looked down on to a beach full of sunbathers and swimmers who were disregarding the wonders of the ancient city. But when we knocked at the door, it was to be met with a groan. Vitaly Zubar, the site director, was in bed with flu.

He rose, sweating pitifully, in his swimming trunks, to pour us glasses of bitter-sweet Crimean wine, light up the first of many cigarettes, and sigh as he told us about the sorry state of archaeology in the Ukraine. There were hardly any digs going on at the moment because there was no money – he himself had not been paid for three months. There was no evidence of Amazons at Chersonesus, he said – no record of lithe-limbed women warriors strolling the streets. I realised I had been very naïve to think there might be. But there had been stuff found in the steppe, he said vaguely – yes, he would try to arrange for us to speak to the necessary people. Yes, he supposed he would take us on and look after us. He sighed heavily again as he announced this, lighting yet another cigarette and coughing profusely. Vitaly's world, like that of most Ukrainians in the summer of 1997, was a gloomy and apparently hopeless one. But being, as we found out later, the kindest of men, he felt he had no choice but to help us.

Several classical sources point to the Sauromatian women as the direct descendants of the Amazons, including Pseudo-Hippocrates writing in the late fifth century BC: 'Amazon women dislocate the joints of their male children at birth . . . some at knees, some at hips . . . to make them lame . . . so that the male race might not conspire against the female race.'[2] He repeats some of Herodotus' details and embellishes:

> And in Europe there is a Scythian race, dwelling round Lake Maeotis, which differs from the other races. Their name is Sauromatae. Their women, so long as they are virgins, ride, shoot, throw the javelin while mounted, and fight with their enemies. They do not lay aside their virginity until they have killed three of their enemies, and they do not marry before they have performed the traditional sacred rites. A woman who takes to herself a husband no longer rides, unless she is compelled to do so by a general expedition. They have no right breast; for while they are yet babies their mothers make red-hot a bronze instrument constructed for this very purpose and apply it to the right breast and cauterise it, so that its growth is arrested, and all its strength and bulk are diverted to the right shoulder and right arm.[3]

Then there is a mysterious and rather late writer called Justin who probably lived in the third century AD and was an abridger of a Roman called Trogus Pompeius. His version is different because he suggests that the original Amazons came *from* Scythia *to* the southern coast of the Black Sea, not the other way around. It happened like this: they fled from Scythia with their husbands under the leadership of two royal youths and settled near the River Thermodon. The husbands were all killed in skirmishes with the locals and the women set up as an independent colony. They were aggressive towards their neighbours and only made contact with men to sire children. Male children they put to death, girls they brought up to hunt and fight, searing off their right breasts in infancy so that they could shoot a bow better. They had two queens, Marpesia and Lampedo, who between them managed to conquer a large swathe of both Europe and Asia, before Marpesia and her army were destroyed and Hercules turned up to demand the girdle of one of them.

Regardless of whether the war-like women of the Scythians and Sauromatians were Amazon prototypes or their descendants, I needed to know what evidence there was of their existence. Renate Rolle was the key to that, and I knew that she was digging somewhere in the Ukraine.

SCYTHIANS AND AMAZONS: THE EVIDENCE

Renate Rolle knows more about the Scythians than almost anyone else alive, and it was in her book *The World of the Scythians* that I first came across accounts of graves of Iron Age women buried with their weapons. But Renate Rolle is a modest and elusive person and was not eager to meet me. I had spent months trying to contact her, mainly via Nina, the patient, English-speaking wife of her assistant, Frank Andrashko. I had phoned, faxed, written letters – both in English and painful German – and, in spite of Nina's efforts on my behalf, been met with a polite brush-off. The problem was that Professor Rolle spoke no English and my A level German was not good enough for proper conversation – and certainly not good enough for me to reveal my probity and sincerity. As Nina explained, Professor Rolle had had bad experiences with journalists who had taken up large chunks of her time without payment or acknowledgement. I did not blame her for her suspicions, but it was very frustrating.

However, Vitaly told us where she was – out in the middle of the steppes east of Kiev, excavating the great Scythian settlement at Bel'sk with Professor Murzin. This was miles from anywhere, even the train station at Poltava, and certainly unreachable by telephone (deliberately so, I guessed). We decided to go by car. 'You English ladies are so decisive,' grumbled Vitaly, lighting another cigarette and surreptitiously checking his pulse.

We arrived in the vicinity of Bel'sk (see Map 3) after days of torrential rain and could not find the site; the countryside was dark-dreary, flood-bound and threatening. None of the few drenched people we came across had any idea where the excavation or the professors were. Exasperated, our driver, Tolya, launched off along a pitted mud-track and soon we were stuck fast. A hundred yards away two gentlemen stood under an umbrella next to an equally stuck jeep. Asking them for help, Tolya found that the larger of them was Professor Vetchislav Murzin himself and that the shiny jeep belonged to Renate Rolle.

Round the corner we found Professor Renate Rolle herself, sitting under a canopy in front of her tent making notes with rain dripping all around her. She was very surprised to see us, but Natasha's charm, expressed in fluent Russian, is almost impossible to resist. Within five minutes we were drinking vodka and being shown a Scythian sword. Renate Rolle turned out to be round-faced, shy and serious with good humour soon breaking through. Her husband Willi, cheered up by the arrival of two eccentric English ladies in the rain, provided the jokes. At the very least, we were a distraction on a wet day when no digging was possible.

Bel'sk is an enigmatic place. It may even be the biggest inhabited earthwork ever discovered, covering 4,000 hectares and containing three separate villages. It was a kilometre across and had been surrounded in the Iron Age by walls 9 metres high, white wooden walls nearly 34 kilometres in circumference. Professors Rolle and Murzin confessed that they just do not know what it was *for!*

It flourished in the seventh century BC and had a mixed population – half Greeks and half Scythians. Within it is a huge cemetery, containing thousands of small *kurgans* (grave mounds). It seems as if all the inhabitants were warriors – the graves are full of shields, swords and coats of mail. Unfortunately the skeletons are in such a poor condition that it is impossible to know the sex of the warriors. However, a workshop has been found there which manufactured drinking cups out of human skulls – a custom described by Herodotus. Bel'sk was probably some kind of a fortress, which fits in well with the ferocious reputation that the Scythians have carried throughout history.

The Scythians were an Indo-Iranian people who arrived in the eighth century BC in the steppes that sweep down to the Black Sea and settled to a pastoralist life that exalted warrior skills and strengths, and in which horses played a central part. Some continued a nomadic life, herding horses and sheep and migrating to good pastures according to season, while others became more settled, grew grain and manufactured tools, weapons and ornaments, decorated in a vigorous curvilinear style which often shows the animals turning their heads back on themselves to bite or defend. Herodotus has a great time describing the customs of the bloodthirsty Scythians:

> The way a Scythian skins a head is as follows: he makes a circular cut around the head at the level of the ears and then he picks it up and shakes the scalp off the skull: next he scrapes the skin with a cow's rib, and then, having kneaded the skin with his hands, he has a kind of rag, which he proudly fastens to the bridle of the horse he is riding ... another common practice is to skin the right arms of their dead opponents, fingernails and all, and make covers for their quivers out of them.[4]

The Greeks and the Scythians seem like polar opposites: the Greek spirit emerging from its chthonic Dionysiac past into a lucid Apollonian period that was to bring extraordinary advances in philosophy, democracy and culture; the Scythians fierce, primitive, vagabondish, smokers of hemp, crackshot bowmen and riders. But in spite of (or perhaps because of) this, the colonising Greeks and the wandering Scythians who met up in the steppe lands of the Ukraine got on well, lived together in the Black Sea colonies, traded, influenced each other's art, and no doubt intermarried furiously. Herodotus records a myth that says that Hercules came to Scythia and, while searching for his lost horse, met a snake-woman (her top half human, snake from the buttocks down) who promised to return his horse if he copulated with her. He obliged: he got his horses back and she got three sons, one of which grew up to use his father's bow and girdle and become the progenitor of the Scythian race. Patriarchal hero meets mother-goddess again.

We stood in the middle of a field full of Scythian shards and bones with Professor Rolle, while the rain poured down on us, each encased in a pastel-coloured plastic mac provided by Professor Murzin. The Amazons still seemed far away. But they were nearer than we knew: Renate turned out to be one of those incorruptible, unstoppably persistent and honest people who discover amazing things and then are slow to take credit for them. Finally, we persuaded her to tell her story.

When she was a student back in 1965, she began to notice that, in some of the graves she was digging, the gender of the dead person was not at all obvious because the goods buried with them were both classically female things like spindles and mirrors *and* classically male instruments like knives, swords or arrows. Most previous generations of archaeologists had found a way of explaining such graves that did not involve the idea that women might be buried with weapons – in fact, they tended to presume that any burial with weapons would be that of a man. There were notable exceptions, such as the Russian Grakov, who thought they might indicate a woman-dominated society that could be the last remnant of a matriarchy, and also the amateur archaeologist Count Bobrinsky (see below), but Renate Rolle, being a woman and a very objective archaeologist herself, was keen to explore all options.

She actually started way back in the past, re-examining a grave found by Bobrinsky in the late nineteenth century. It was excavated in 1884 at Cholodni Yar on the left bank of the River Tiasmin. In this grave there were two skeletons: the main burial was of a woman, but at her feet lay the body of a young man of about eighteen years old. It was a fairly rich grave and the main goods were grouped around the female. On her ears had been large silver earrings; round her neck, a chain made from bones and glass beads; on her arm, a bronze brace-let. Next to her lay a bronze mirror, a clay loom-weight and iron plates upon which food gifts had once been placed. To her left at the head end lay two iron spear points, and underneath them was a smooth square plate that had been used as a whetstone; further down they found the remains of a brightly painted quiver made of leather and wood, forty-seven bronze three-flighted arrowheads, and two iron knives. Next to the head were two so-called 'sling-stones', although no one can be sure they were used as weapons. The young man's skeleton, on the other hand, had only two small bronze bells near it, plus an iron arm-ring and some little bits of jewellery.

What we seem to have here is the grave of a woman warrior of some social standing whose young male servant was killed to accom-pany her on her death journey. The woman had many of the classic female accoutrements – weaving and spinning tools are almost never found in male graves – but she also possessed a bow, knives and spears.

When I first heard Renate's description of this grave, I felt a chill run down my backbone: here we had traces of a world radically differ-ent from the Greek world, in which a woman might fight *and* be considered important enough to merit a sacrificed servant to look after her in the next world. In another grave from the sixth century BC Renate told of an 'Amazon' buried with a gold-studded cap who had both a servant and a horse buried with her, both probably ritually killed to accompany her. She seemed to have died from a blow, the trace of which remained over her right brow.

The oldest 'Amazon' grave documented by Renate is one found in ancient Colchis (now Georgia), which dates from the end of the second millennium BC. The woman had been buried in the sitting position on a pebble-lined floor with a short sword resting on her knees. An iron dagger had been placed on two small stones in front of her and a lance-point was lying next to her, under which was found the lower jawbone of a horse, suggesting maybe that the rest of the horse had been eaten at the funeral celebrations. Two bracelets, five rings made of bronze, an awl 10 centimetres long, some pearls and two earthenware vessels were also found. Studies by bone specialists show her to have been about 4 feet 8 inches tall, and between thirty and forty years old. On the left side of her skull was the trace of a serious wound – 28 millimetres long and 7 millimetres wide – the edges of which had started to heal at the time of her death. She had lived for some time after being wounded and the wound was thought to be the result of a blow from a spearpoint or stone.

An arrowhead found embedded in the skull of another young woman buried nearby probably accounted for her early death. In yet another grave, lions' claws were found lying next to the right hand of another woman warrior, the first archaeological evidence that corresponded to the images on the vases of Amazons dressed in lions' skins.

Renate began to dig herself. In the early 1980s she was working at Certomylik, in the lower reaches of the Dnieper, a very rich source of Scythian graves, many of them unmolested by robbers. In six of the fifty-three graves they found women with weapons:

Two hadn't been touched, one was a young woman with weapons, a bow and some arrowheads, and this little child lying on her arm. The two fingers of her right hand which would have had heavy use from pulling a bow showed clear signs of wear and tear. It was very moving. So you see these women warriors did have children, and they may have led perfectly normal married lives together with their families and husbands. They only fought when they had to, to defend their settlement, or if there was some particularly ferocious fighting going on. They used the bow – it's a good weapon for a woman because you don't need brute strength to use it, all you need is to be fast and flexible. We know they rode horses. Defensive weapons tend to be heavy, but even so we've found mail-shirts and armour in women's graves, so we know they used them. And some skeletons show signs of being wounded in battle.

It was important to Renate that the women warriors whose graves she dug up were ordinary, man-loving (as against man-killing), child-rearing women, not muscle-bound man-haters. She points out that women's physique suits them particularly well to horse-riding, and specifically distance-riding. Men who spend a great deal of time in the saddle can become impotent, because of the heat and friction on their testicles, whereas women have no such problem. The bow suits women well too: it requires less muscle strength to use than some other weapons, but it does demand calm, concentration, good coordination of hand and eye, and a precise sense of distance and timing. These are all skills that could be acquired through rigorous daily training in childhood. At one site Renate had found a girl of between ten and twelve years old buried with chain-mail armour, which suggests that she was already trained and considered ready to fight. She says that Scythian body armour was very elastic and practical and that certainly women and girls could have worn it without discomfort.

Renate imagined that the women warriors she found would have been slim and strong like today's all-round sportswomen. Certainly, to shoot arrows from horseback you would need to be very flexible and yet steady in the saddle. However, women are at a disadvantage when it comes to using a lance or a javelin. The angular adjustment of women's arm-bones makes the strength-transfer less effective than in men, which is why many women find over-arm bowling difficult. Penthesilea, who engaged in single combat with Achilles at Troy, put herself at a disadvantage by using a spear, and was run through by Achilles' own spear before long. Therefore the canny woman warrior would fight from a distance, either on horseback or from a vantage point where arrows could reach the enemy.

In most of the graves that Renate looked at the weapons were bows, arrows and knives. Armour and *heavy* weapons, such as lances, sling-stones and swords, were only found in about 20 per cent of the women warriors' graves, such as one on the northern Black Sea coast in which a young woman was buried with bronze and silver jewellery, bow and arrows, four lances and an iron-studded battle-girdle. These are the kind of weapons that someone like Penthesilea, who was planning to fight in close combat, would have had. The girdle, designed to protect the stomach and loins, would be the mark of a serious fighter, although in the case of Hippolyta there's ambiguity – are we talking about a warrior's loin-protection or a woman's girdle? We could perhaps imagine that, whilst most women fought from a distance if they could, there would be a select band of particularly strong and well-trained fighters who were able to fight hand-to-hand where necessary. Certainly this makes sense: if you look at any average class of girls at school there will be up to a fifth who are clearly bigger and stronger than the rest, whilst in a class of boys there will be an equivalent percentage who are smaller and weedier than the others. In a playground fight, the weaker boys would be no match for the big girls.

The Russian Vera Kovalevskaya points out that when their men were away fighting or hunting, nomadic women would have to be able to defend themselves, their animals and pasture-grounds competently. During the time that the Scythians advanced into Asia and achieved near-hegemony in the Near East, there was a period of twenty-eight years when the men would have been away on campaigns for long periods. During this time the women would not only have had to defend themselves, but also to reproduce, and this could well be the origin of the idea that Amazons mated once a year with their neighbours. If not, they probably got themselves impreg-nated by slaves.

Renate planned to stay at Bel'sk until October, sleeping in a tent, unobtainable by telephone, in the company of a few other Scythian-crazy folk, cooking on a fire outside, and scrabbling in the wet ground for clues as to why so many nomadic people had built a fortress and settled there. She obviously felt at home in the bleak steppe with a pet pig and goat and a few chickens for company. The pig was supposed to be eaten at some point, but I suspect Renate would never allow it. She is a warrior all right, and has had to fight the worst of East European bureaucracy to do her work, but I just felt that her ruthlessness was not the pig-slaughtering kind.

AMAZONS WITHOUT HORSES

One very surprising fact that comes out of Renate Rolle's work is that only in three out of fifteen sites where women warriors were found was there a horse buried. Male warriors were often buried with a horse or horse-related items. This is rather disturbing to our image of the archetypal Amazon on horseback. But, of course, if we follow Herodotus, we are dealing not with Amazons but with their descendants, the Sauromatian women. The Sauromatians are a wave of people who appeared in the eastern part of the Scythian territory in the sixth or fifth century BC. According to Hippocrates, these women only fought until they had won their spurs by killing three enemies in battle, then: 'a woman who takes to herself a husband no longer rides, unless she is compelled to do so by a general expedition.'[5]

For information about Sauromatian graves, Vitaly put us in touch with Ukrainian archaeologist Dr Elena Fialko who had been digging in the more eastern 'Sauromatian' parts of the Ukraine, above the sea of Azov near the Molochnaya and Dnieper rivers. The graves date from the fifth century BC and the first half of the fourth century BC. This is exactly the area into which Herodotus' Amazons are supposed to have migrated after they teamed up with the Scythian men.[6]

Unfortunately Elena was away while we were in Kiev and we had to communicate with her on our return by letter and telephone. Natasha would ring her and put the questions we had in our minds after reading her paper, recording the conversation on her answerphone. She would then ring me and play back the cassette, interpreting as she went. I would make notes, think of other questions, and she would ring Elena back – and so on!

Elena told us that it was the odd combination of the beautiful little bits and pieces along with weaponry that made the women whose graves she was digging up seem so individual and real. There were no big, exquisitely painted vases or anything especially valuable, just little knick-knacks mass-produced in the Greek style like lacquer bowls and jugs – the kind of thing that Greeks themselves would throw away without thinking. But for these Scythian women they were exotic and special, so they were buried with them, along with their spearheads, arrowheads and quivers. Over 2,000 years later the same little ornaments entranced Elena too:

> I was so elated, because when I was young growing up in Siberia and then Kiev, I had studied the classical world a lot . . . to take into my hands something made by the Greeks was wonderful. As soon as I saw them I wanted to pick them up and handle them . . . and I felt so proud, as a woman, to see how these women were given the full dignities of a warrior's burial – head to the west, lying on the back in a square pit burial with one side hollowed out. There was a warrior caste, and they were a part of it.

In one oval burial chamber near the village of Akimovka (see Map 3), Elena found a woman of between twenty-two and twenty-five years of age lying on her back with her head to the north. Under her head and her left side were scattered 575 colourful glass beads. She had gold and silver rings on her hands and a golden loop-shaped earring lay nearby; sixty golden studs/rosettes, forty-six golden buttons and twenty-eight other golden decorative studs depicting a deer, a woman's head and a Medusa head were lying close to her body. She also had a black lacquer vessel of Greek style, some lead loom weights and, finally, nine arrowheads and two fragmented knife blades. This well-off young woman must have looked wonderful in all her golden finery. Perhaps she would have only felt inclined to use her bow and arrows and her knife if necessity truly demanded it. Perhaps she was not a full member of the 'warrior caste'.

Close by, a twenty-five-year-old was buried with a bronze bracelet round her right wrist and a bronze mirror and a black lacquer bowl by her left hand, a metal spear and a javelin nearby, and two pretzel-shaped golden earrings (which may suggest she was a married woman, see later in this chapter). There was also a metal knife, a lead loom weight and three bronze arrowheads, plus in the corner a stone probably used for heating water. The spear and javelin suggest she was a more serious warrior.

In a third case in the village a woman was buried lying on her back with her legs half bent so that her left leg was leaning out at the hip with the knee not far from the elbow while the left heel was by the pelvis. It is a position that suggests either sexual intercourse or riding! That she was a warrior is suggested by the nine bronze arrowheads found with twenty glass 'eye' beads and three limestone pendants.

The women did not all come from the same social class: some are in deep main burials, with rich goods; some are shallow 'afterthought' burials with modest grave goods, but in this particular area there were an unusual number of women-warrior burials. The goods fall into two categories – typical female belongings like jewellery, mirrors, spindles and distaffs, and weapons such as arrowheads (usually bronze), spearheads, javelins (rare), fasteners for spearhead covers (sometimes some coarse fabric remains, suggesting that the spears were put into the graves in a fabric wrapping) and sling-stones. It is the *combination* of these two categories of goods that makes them stand out from other women's graves.

However, Elena noticed a conspicuous absence of the kind of weapons you would expect Herodotus' *Oiorpata* or man-killers to have – there were no *defensive* weapons like shields, no armour (except for studded belts found in three graves), and the only close-fighting weapons found were three swords – all bent, thus suggesting ritual use. Only one woman, in the forest steppe, was buried with a horse. None of the women was buried with the wooden cup inset with gold that you would find in many male warriors' graves. It is hard not to think that the women were regarded as slightly second-class warriors compared with the men.

Most of the burials were single burials, but in four cases the women were buried with tiny babies (perhaps having died in childbirth), one had two babies, and with servants.[7] The age breakdown is interesting:

Age group	Percentage
16–20	22%
25–35	47%
35–55	20%
60ish	11%

This suggests that women *could* serve as warriors from the age of sixteen to sixty, although a high proportion of women died in their late twenties and early thirties – in many cases probably from childbirth-related problems. In fifty cases, bronze mirrors, which would have been good reflectors when burnished, were found in the women's graves, and in some cases stone dishes with the remains of colouring materials. The stone dishes may have been used to grind cosmetic substances, which is in keeping with what Herodotus wrote about Scythian women: 'Their women take a rough stone and grind cedar incense, add water and cover their bodies and faces. It makes them smell good. Next day they take off the layer and are clean and shiny underneath.'

The mirrors and make-up suggest that these were ordinary young women who liked to look beautiful. Elena does not think that they were Herodotus' 'man-killers'. They were lightly armed and were not buried with any horse-accoutrements. She argues:

> In the steppe zone there are eighty female burials – only one has part of a horse's bridle. In the forest steppe there are twenty burials – in only one is a horse buried with an Amazon and one contains parts of a bridle. In men's graves bridles are very much part of grave goods. So we're unlikely to be helped out by Renate Rolle's ideas that, although women are less strong, they could be more lithe and flexible on horseback. Especially since Herodotus, talking about male Scythians, stresses how fast and flexible they are. But classical authors all say Scythians and Amazons learnt to ride and shoot arrows from earliest childhood – so there is a lack of correlation between the written sources and archaeological materials.

Elena's theory is that these were middle-class Scythian women doing military service when the tribe required it from them. So far, no Amazons have been found in very rich aristocratic graves. If the men were often away on forays, or moving their horses, sheep or cattle around, maybe it was essential for the women to be able to defend their settlements against aggressors. Elena continues:

> One point could explain the lack of horses and bridles in burials: Hippocrates said that, when they married, Sauromatian women stopped riding on horseback unless an emergency arose when all hands had to fight. In peacetime women had normal women's lives. But why then do all these graves contain weapons? Remember Herodotus said they could only marry after they'd killed three enemies and those who hadn't remained virgins until death. But in the Scythian graves 10

per cent of the women with weapons are at least sixty, so we have to assume they're not married – but they are also without bridles and therefore without horses.

It does not quite add up, although it seems to me quite natural to bury women with weapons if they have fought at *any* stage in their life, even if not recently, as a recognition of the part they played in defending the tribe, and in case they might need to protect themselves in the next world. As for the older women, perhaps these were not lifetime spinster-warriors, but tough older women who returned to fighting after their children had grown up. The absence of horses suggests that warriorship was seen as a very part-time activity for women, whereas for men it would constitute a large part of their identity.

And yet the archaeologists I spoke to in the Ukraine told me that 25 per cent of the Scythian graves with weapons that have been found are of women, which suggests that 25 per cent of all Scythian warriors were women. If this is true then this was a society with very different ideas about gender roles to our own. In fact, there is other evidence that this was the case – both Herodotus and Hippocrates talk about a caste of men called Enarees. Herodotus calls them 'women-men' and says they were soothsayers who used the bark of the lime tree to prophesy as they plaited and unplaited it between their fingers. They claimed to have learnt this method of divination from Aphrodite, which must be a Greek label for a Scythian goddess – perhaps Tabithi, who was their mother-goddess. He explains that in previous times the Scythians robbed a temple of Aphrodite and were punished by the goddess for their transgression by being inflicted with the 'women's disease', by which he presumably means menstruation. In many cultures men imitate menstruation by cutting their genitals to draw blood, thus magically 'stealing' women's mysterious power.

Hippocrates takes the story further:

> Moreover, the great majority among the Scythians become impotent, do women's work, live like women and converse accordingly. Such men they call Enarees . . . Scythians are the most impotent of men . . . because they always wear trousers and spend most of their time on their horses, so that they do not handle the parts but owing to cold and fatigue forget about sexual virility before any impulse is felt.[8]

What we have here seems to be men stealing female power by disguising themselves as women. The people who received the oracles at Delphi were normally women, because women were thought to have the capacity to *receive*. In order to acquire this power, maybe the Enarees were willing to lose their masculinity. Shamans of many cultures cross-dress in order to make their spirit flights, perhaps needing to generate energy within themselves by creating a male–female polarity, or to jolt themselves out of their habitual mode of consciousness by radically changing their identity. There is also a teaching in many spiritual traditions (Hinduism and Christianity particularly) that claims that if sexual energy is not spent in the normal way it can be saved and refined for other uses.

Therefore in Scythian and Sauromatian societies it would seem that you could be born a girl and become a brave warrior, or be born a boy and spend your life as a shaman and seer, too weak to be asked to fight. Maybe such flexibility was essential for the nomadic or semi-nomadic way of life.

Jeannine Davis-Kimball hit the news in 1997 when she announced that she had found graves of women warriors near the town of Pokrovka (see Map 1) close to the Russian border with Kazakhstan, a thousand miles further east of the Ukrainian finds. This was an intriguing development: it would mean that fighting women were a much more widespread phenomenon than had hitherto been realised. I had come across her work a year earlier while searching the Internet for Amazon information and we had talked via e-mail and telephone. She had finished digging at Pokrovka, but Jeannine told me that while we were in the Ukraine she would be in the new republic of Moldova (just west of the Ukraine and north of Romania), digging with a mixed bunch of Americans and Moldovans. Blithely I said we would go and meet her there.

This was no simple matter. You had to have a visa to enter Moldova, but, there being no Moldovan Embassy in Britain, you could not obtain the visa by personal visit. One Internet site said visas could be purchased at the airport in Kishinev on arrival, but a helpful friend-of-a-friend who knew the territory said he doubted that very much, and strongly advised us to get one in advance. This, though, meant sending our passports to Brussels. There was not enough time, and anyway Natasha was working abroad with her passport. We had no option but to take the risk.

Thus it was we found ourselves in Yalta about to buy tickets on Crimea Air to fly to Kishinev, being told by the unsmiling Soviet-era saleswoman that she could by no means guarantee that we would even be allowed on to the plane without visas. I looked at Natasha: she combines intense good will towards the world with bottomless ingenuity and guile. That very morning she had resolved an infuriating situation in which we seemed doomed to wait hours to renew our residence visas by barging into the principal bureaucrat's office and lecturing her angrily on the fact that the Ukraine was now supposed to be a free and friendly society and should therefore be welcoming foreigners like us and not making our lives a misery. I thought we would be thrown out or arrested. In fact, the woman sighed deeply and whisked us to the front of the queue. Surely Natasha would not be thwarted by mere border controls at Kishinev . . .

In the event we were intercepted when we landed in the Moldovan capital by a calm girl who spoke impeccable English and begged us to go and have coffee while she rang the Archaeological Institute on our behalf. Within an hour, a hundred dollars lighter for our instant visas, we were sitting in a room full of old bones chatting to Jeannine.

If you think you cannot be a mother and a warrior at the same time, you should meet Jeannine Davis-Kimball. This handsome and canny American woman, now in her sixties, had six children and worked for years as a nurse before she even thought of training as an archaeologist. Once she had qualified, in her late thirties, she chose the most difficult task possible for an archaeologist at that time – excavating in the central Asian republics of the Soviet Union. The steely persistence required to get past bureaucracy, venality and just plain anti-female obstructiveness might have made her into a self-serving cynic, but her toughness was tempered by a motherly kind-ness which had her rising at four in the morning for several days running to take the young Americans she had been working with to the airport to make sure they did not get 'ripped off' on their way home.

The graves that caused Jeannine's name to be splashed all over the world's press were found in large *kurgans* in the Russian flatlands north-east of the Ukraine (see Pokrovka on Map I), which are a continuation of the steppes that stretch from the Black Sea right across as far as China. Today most of the steppes are farmland, but in ancient times they would have been covered by long feathery grasses, scattered with sage, cornflower and other strong-scented wild flowers and grasses, making walking fragrant but laborious. This is why horseback was the way to travel: it would only take three months to ride from the edge of the Chinese steppes to the Black Sea. These were graves of Sauromatians, a nomadic people close to the Scythians in culture and habits, who arrived in these steppes from 600 BC onwards, and were replaced around 400 BC by the confusingly simi-lar-sounding Sarmatians.

Jeannine recalled vividly the day they found the first woman warrior: 'It was a very hot day, and this was the last burial, we were tired and ready to finish but we had to clean the skeleton. We had already found arrowheads, a quiver and a dagger, and then last of all we sexed the skeleton. It was definitely female.' With good materials, Jeannine explained, it is relatively easy to ascertain the gender of a skeleton by looking at the pelvis and the skull. The pelvis of a female has a wider notch and a different configuration, to facilitate child-bearing. And, except in children before puberty and in very old people, the male skull is bumpier, with a stronger brow-ridge and more pronounced mandible. A good physical anthropologist can get it right 90 per cent of the time.

Jeannine and her team also noted the unusual fact that, at Pokrovka, in general the women were buried with a wider variety and larger quantity of artefacts than the men, suggesting that they held high status within the community. They broke the female burials down into three main categories; the largest group (twenty-eight graves) were what we might call ordinary female burials where the grave goods were spindle whorls, bits of broken mirror (Jeannine says they would have been deliberately broken), stone and glass beads; the second group (five), whom she calls 'priestesses', had goods such as clay or stone altars, bone spoons, and intact bronze mirrors, whilst the third group (seven), 'warriors', also included iron swords or daggers, bronze arrowheads and whetstones for sharpening the weapons.

One thirteen- or fourteen-year-old girl had bowed leg bones, suggesting a life spent on horseback. She had dozens of arrowheads in a quiver made of wood and leather, a dagger and another bronze arrowhead in a leather pouch around her neck, perhaps worn as a protective amulet. A great boar's tusk lay at her feet. In another woman's body a bent arrowhead was found, suggesting that she had been killed in battle.

The 'best priestess' they found was a woman in her sixties. It seems that if you could survive the childbearing years (when you risked dying while giving birth, and then nutritional depletion while breast-feeding), you had a good chance of living on into your sixties.

But the male graves at Pokrovka were even more intriguing because whilst the majority were of warriors with iron swords and daggers, four seemed to belong to a different, lower class and were buried with a small child on their arm and almost no grave goods. One had a six-year-old child lying beside his leg. Jeannine is mystified by these burials. Were they servants who had looked after these children? Were they related to the children in some way? It is impossible to know but, once again, at the very least it reveals a society where gender roles were fluid.

Jeannine associates the mirror with healing. In the central Asian region of Tuva, even today she has seen shamans passing a mirror over the body of a sick person in order to detect subtle traces of the illness. If the ordinary women were buried with broken mirrors, suggesting that they would no longer have a reflection, maybe the priestess-women were thought to continue reflecting – that is, exerting power from beyond the grave. The mirror certainly is a primary female grave good, found in burials of women all over the world at all times. Even at Çatal Hüyük in the seventh millennium BC, women were buried with mirrors made out of lumps of polished volcanic obsidian. Seeing them in the Ankara Museum I experienced a very strong impulse to reach out, pick one up, and look at my face in it. I suspect this impulse must be universal, and surely stronger in women than in men.

The mirror moves us from a sense of 'us' to sense of 'I'; it makes us self-conscious. It tells us how we compare with others – am I more beautiful than you? Without a mirror, how would I know? Certainly I might have seen myself reflected in still water, but only on the horizontal plane which distorts the true likeness. A mirror held vertically reflects a face accurately, on the same plane. What would the effect be on someone of seeing their own face for the first time? It could be utterly terrifying and disorientating. Therefore in a society where there are not many mirrors, she who wields a mirror has a particular kind of power. Remember also that Medusa, the Gorgon queen, could only be viewed safely in a mirror, not directly.

For a nomadic people the little portable altar would be an extremely important object. It is a miniature sacred space; it is a threshold, a doorstep, a gateway between worlds. Things can be offered or burnt on it – that is, shifted from our world to the next. When someone dies you can still occasionally sense their presence, therefore it is natural to think that they must be existing in another world. When you burn something or offer something on an altar you are sending it to the other world. The altar is part of the house, even if it is a movable house, and therefore it is not surprising that the women had charge of it. These may not have been formal priestesses, but simply responsible women who could be trusted with something valuable and knew how to perform the rites properly.

The spoon may have been used to give substances that loosened the reins of perception, hallucinogens perhaps, or hemp (which we know the Scythians used). The shells showed traces of a white powder that might have been cosmetic, though it too could have been psychotropic.

From three women, three archaeologists, I now had clear and undeniable evidence that there were women warriors living in the steppe regions north of the Black Sea during Classical Greek times. Some 25 per cent of Scythian and Sauromatian warrior graves found in the Ukraine were of women. But were these women Amazons or something rather different? My next step was to find out.

It rained all the time we were in Kiev – hard, serious, drenching rain. Our feet squelched in our sandals, and our umbrella blew inside out one gloomy afternoon as we hurried from the metro to visit Vitaly in his office in a tall ramshackle block. The building was empty except for the concierge, as we marched up the stairs in the dark and entered a room full of melancholy rainy light. The Institute of Archaeology was in the process of moving, along with all its finds, so Vitaly worked on, unpaid, in this crepuscular between-worlds zone. Old-fashioned black telephones with silver dials sat on the desks and the rain hammered the dirty windows in a spiteful sort of way.

He had invited his colleague, Ekaterina Bunyatin, a Scythian specialist, to talk to us. She smoked fervently and anxiously throughout our conversation, as if we were the KGB, not two grateful British women humbly wishing to pick her brains. She looked very tired – a family illness was the explanation offered, but I guessed it was living in the Ukraine in 1997 that was taking its toll. We knew that, unless you had a small business on the side, or a helpful relative, or a country dacha, life could be as grim and penurious as in Dickens's England.

She loved the Scythians. They represented freedom and power to her. Sitting in that dingy rain-darkened room she transported us out into Iron Age Scythia:

> The important thing is to think in terms of the endless steppe, the covered wagons, the horsemen, people always arriving and setting off . . . these pastoralists were a very aggressive, very mobile people, always ready to fight . . . you find Scythian stuff in Chinese burials, China was constantly threatened by nomads, Toynbee called them the fellow-travellers of civilisation.
>
> But where did the Scythians come from? The Cimmerians who inhabited the steppes before them, from the fifth millennium until the end of the second, had no animal art. This animal-style art suddenly appeared. But where from? People say: 'the depths of Asia', but which Asia? The art has more relation with Thracian art!

Penthesilea was a Thracian, I remembered. Ekaterina felt sure that the Scythian women were equal to the men: 'The women's burials are so similar to the men's! I don't get any feeling from the burials that the attitude to women was different.'

Because the Institute was in the process of moving, it was difficult to see any of the grave goods. They were packed away in boxes; it would take all day to find anything at all, said Vitaly gloomily. But in the dim light we finally tracked down one hopeful tray. I had expected some kind of emotional reaction when I saw these things, but in truth they were not initially an impressive sight. The bronze mirror was dull and would not reflect our faces, though Vitaly assured us that, when polished, it would give an excellent reflection. The two golden earrings were beautiful, in a style that is still copied in every ethnic shop, and I itched to put them on, but dared not ask. The spearheads and knife blades were so rusty that it was impossible to imagine them as shiny and sharp, hanging on a warrior-girl's belt. But the arrowheads were still perfect, each a tiny, razor-edged death-dealing dart, waiting to be reunited with its shaft and sent zinging through the air. Could they not simply have used the bows and arrows for hunting, I wondered? Elena Fialko had said no: the presence of sling-stones and long and short spears in nearly half the graves suggested that these women were definitely fighters as well as hunters.

Lyubov Klotchko, whom we met next, in the Treasury Museum, agreed; for her, the freedom of the Scythian women was astonishing – perhaps because Ukrainian women seem to get the worst of both worlds: they have to work and they still get landed with most of the domestic tasks and childcare. Lyubov is a specialist in costume and had studied 300 burials of Scythian women. She reckoned that to be an 'Amazon' was part of these women's social role, and she had noticed something really extraordinary: 23 per cent of the Scythian women were buried with only one earring. As this 23 per cent of women were either very old, or very young, or they were women with weapons, Lyubov suspected that the single earring signified that its wearer was not actively engaged in bearing or bringing up children. The old women had borne their children long ago, the young ones were virgins, as also perhaps were the warriors, unless they were simply childless by choice or accident. Very few women warriors had two earrings – when they did, Lyubov thought this might mean that they did have children but could fight if necessary. It is curious that gay and lesbian people have picked up on this custom – of signifying sexual difference with one earring – more than two millennia later.

Lyubov had reconstructed the probable clothing of a Scythian woman warrior, from fragments found in graves (see illustration). The leather cap would be held in place by a wooden ring; the bracelets were of coiled snakes, reminiscent of the Greek symbolism for female power or *shakti*; the trousers, practical for riding, would be made of wool or linen or hessian. For Sarmatian women who came a little later, she had less evidence, although there is one intriguing first-century BC grave – of a Sarmatian priestess buried with a beautiful mirror with a little Buddha-like figure making up its handle, and she was wearing trousers under her dress. The costume that Lyubov has put together for the Scythian Amazons is not far at all from that illustrated on the Greek vases, which suggests that some of these scenes may have come from real life.

However, there was an added complication: some scholars,[9] noting the gender fluidity of Scythian and Sarmatian society, suggest that some of the bodies in these 'woman warrior' graves may not be women after all. Could they not be the men/women Enarees about whom Herodotus wrote? Whether castrated or hormonally modified by horse-riding or drugs, what would these men's skulls or pelvises look like? Could they be confused with women's? Or did they belong to an ambiguous third sex?

There is a cemetery at Golyamo Delchevo in north-east Bulgaria where archaeologists noticed there were three different 'packages' of grave goods: male, female, and 'asexual' (or 'non-gendered'), and some scholars are now arguing for the presence, in European prehistory, of a 'third, ambiguous, possibly liminal gender'.[10] Actual hermaphrodism is rare (one or two births in every thousand), but we all know people who don't fit either gender easily – assertive, slim-hipped girls, or gentle, rounded men – who may have a hormonal bias towards the opposite sex.

It could be that some of the women warriors' graves in the steppes are not in fact the graves of women but persons of 'a third, ambiguous and possibly liminal gender', in which case Amazons could as easily be beardless men as beefy women. Until DNA testing for gender of skeletal remains becomes possible and reliable in every case, we cannot know for sure.

But the gender-reversal game works both ways. Jeannine Davis-Kimball has studied nomadic societies right across Europe and Asia, from Western Russia to the Tien Shan in China, and she has paid particular attention to the grave goods of the 'Issyk Gold Man' who was found by a farmer near Almaty in Kazakhstan in 1969. In a sarcophagus made of large fir logs a skeleton was unearthed along with 4,000 golden ornaments including a torc decorated with snow leopards, scabbards for a dagger and a sword, a whip-handle and, most beautiful of all, an unusual and striking headdress from which flared upwards two pairs of feathers, flames or wings and four arrows to a height of 63 centimetres – which is really very tall. Jeannine noted that the sides of the headdress were decorated with 'gold-foil depictions of mountains, birds, snow-leopards with twisted torsos, winged tigers and mountain goats . . . and a small gold ram was set on its point'. Other objects found with the body included a bronze mirror and flat wooden dishes and beaters for koumiss (fermented mare's milk). The body was presumed to have been that of a young Saka chieftain (the Sakas were nomads closely related to the Scythians), but Jeannine has put forward the daring theory that it might be that of a woman.

She points out that very similar grave goods were found on the Ukok Plateau in the Altai mountains by Russian archaeologist Natalya Polosmak, in the grave of a high-status *woman* who may have been a priestess. She also had a bronze mirror, a koumiss-beater and a high headdress, and the style of tattoos on her body was close to that of the decorations on the Issyk man's gold finery. Natalya Polosmak had been able to study the tattoos because the princess's body had been preserved in ice for over 2,000 years, so that some of her skin was intact. Professor Orazak Ismagulov from the Kazak Institute of Archaeology, who has examined the Saka skeleton, admitted to Jeannine that it was of a very small person and *could* be that of a woman. There were three earrings with beads in the tomb which suggests the kind of jewellery not normally associated with men. Jeannine felt that the bones, spoon and mirror found in the grave related it to the 'priestess' graves she had excavated in Pokrovka. Finally she points out that some of the female mummies found in Xinjiang in the Taklimakan desert wore high conical hats.

Whether Jeannine is right or not, whether the gold person of Issyk is a woman warrior-priestess or a male chieftain, the point has been made that we cannot *assume* the skeleton to be male. The Greeks may have created a society in which gender roles were laid down and rigidly adhered to, but the nomad Scythians and Sauromatians across the water and to the east were much more pragmatic. If a man wanted to be a seer, he put on women's clothes and cut himself so that he bled like a woman, in order to steal her power. If a woman was strong and swift, or if the tribe was under pressure from enemies, then she would grab her bow and arrow, spear or javelin and sling-stones and join the fray.

But it was becoming clear that, although the graves of women with weapons found in the Ukraine and Russia definitely belonged to fighters who could use bow and arrow and other weapons if necessary, these warriors did not necessarily fight on horseback – indeed, according to Elena Fialko, they almost never did. Except in a few cases, neither did they use swords or other kinds of close-contact weaponry, and probably for that reason little armour has been found in the graves and not a single helmet. So far, these women's graves have always been found alongside those of men, proving that they did not belong to an all-female society. Greek colonists might well have come across such women, either skirmishing with their menfolk in war-bands or swaggering down the streets of Greek outpost towns on the Black Sea coast, such as Panticapaeum (now Kerch) or Chersonesus (near Sevastopol), and they would have looked strikingly different, in their trousers and leather caps, from the women at home. Living in a society where survival depended on adaptability, they would be physically strong and capable of exercising authority. Maybe they offer half an explanation for the Amazons, but I do not think they are the full story. They were free and independent as nomadic women have to be, but they were not exactly the 'golden-shielded, silver-sworded, man-loving, male-child-slaughtering Amazons' whom Hellanicus wrote about.

To track down the other elements in the Amazons we have to look elsewhere, to go back in time to the age they were supposed to have lived in, the Bronze Age, and the place they were supposed to inhabit, the fabled city of Themiscyra. And to get there we must go via the tangled threads of the women-only mystery traditions of Greece, and the goddess whom the Amazons worshipped, Artemis.

CHAPTER THREE

Artemis, Bright and Dark

If the Sauromatian women fighters were not the true Amazons, then who *were* the Amazons? 'There is no evidence that the Amazons, as described in Greek literature, ever existed. No Greek writer claims ever to have met an Amazon,' wrote classicist Sue Blundell with blunt finality.[1] I knew that *theoretically* she was right – the tales of the Amazons are always told at second hand, or reported as something that happened a long time ago, in the Heroic Age of the Trojan war and Hercules' labours. But I could not accept her sensible view as the last word on the subject. I felt we were viewing the separatist fighting women too much through modern eyes, unprepared to accept that back in the Greek Dark Ages, there may have been gender anomalies that had magical or religious purposes, and which we cannot imagine now.

I decided to search for the different elements of the Amazon myth – the separatism, the sexual promiscuity, the fighting and man-killing, the athleticism – in the hope that these might point to the source of the archetype. The Amazons are frequently referred to as followers or worshippers of Artemis, so here was a definite clue. The trouble was that Artemis was not one clear archetype – she had at least two and possibly more different forms in different places in Greece and Asia Minor. There was the tomboyish huntress Artemis with whom we are quite familiar, with her bow and arrow and her wild animals. Then there was the Great Mother Artemis, an earlier and more primitive form of her, much closer to Cybele, who was worshipped at the great temple of Artemis at Ephesus with ecstatic rites. The complication was that the Amazons were connected with *both* versions of Artemis. Maybe here was an important clue to the Amazons' origins: under the layer of tomboy aggression there could be a deeper layer that connected them with the orgiastic customs associated with the older form of the goddess.

It seemed that this next phase of my search would be less geographical and more psychological. I had to learn to cut through the predilection of my own time and culture for the tomboy Artemis and try to get to her deeper layers which might well stir up uncomfortable resonances to do with castration and human sacrifice – in short, reveal the unacceptable face of the Amazons. Maybe I would have to give up my own idealisation – the innocent image of the two young women on horseback.

THE TOMBOY ARTEMIS

I stand in the museum in Istanbul and stare at her. She does not look back at me. She lounges against a pillar, her face dispassionate and coldly beautiful. Her hair is negligently pulled back on to the nape of her neck, her chiton, tied under the taut, firm breasts, falls in easy folds to her knees allowing the outline of her powerful thighs to show through. On her upper arms a snake bracelet is wound, symbol of her coiled power. Her feet are long and heavily sandalled, her arms strong – but not too well-muscled; she is a boy-girl, a man-woman, and her body is inviting. But who would dare touch it? It belongs to her and you can sense that she does not intend to allow anyone access to its mysteries.

This statue of Artemis came from the island of Lesbos, one of the cities that the Amazons are supposed to have founded. Here is the cool lesbian look we see on singer kd lang as she swaggers on stage, the sexiness accentuated by the piquant mixture of boy and girl, and by the aura of virginity, of *noli me tangere*, that surrounds her. Here is the luscious but deadly power of Xena, Warrior Princess in her push-up battle-bra, and it always seems to go along with a sardonic little smile saying 'I know you find me attractive, but I have other fish to fry.' Television sit-com star Ellen and her partner are good examples of the genre – gamine, strong yet vulnerable, cool but not hostile towards men, with a glint of narcissism flashing behind the eyes.

Artemis as archetype was much enjoyed in Classical Greece and is tremendously popular in our own society. The gamine boy-girl look is one most adolescent girls aspire to – Sporty Spice of the Spice Girls hits the note bang on. It captures the normally all-too-brief period when girls are neither children nor women, when they are *maidens*, with all the spark, spunkiness and integrity of the virgin state. Artemis embodies this quality perfectly: she is normally presented as out hunting with her band of maidens, living a virginal life apart from men.

The most famous myth about Artemis concerns Actaeon, the young man who violated her maiden privacy by watching her bathing in a stream and whom, in punishment, she turned into a stag so that his own hounds tore him to pieces. In another tale, one of Artemis' nymphs, Callisto, is seduced by Zeus and becomes pregnant. Because Artemis demands total chastity from her followers she turns Callisto into a bear, and would have had her hunted to death, had Zeus not come to her aid and taken her up into the stars, where her image can be seen even today.

Artemis is wild and untamed herself, partaking of the ruthless nature of wild animals and the natural world. She can be appealed to by women in childbirth because animals give birth without much pain or trouble. But she absolutely and categorically refuses to fulfil the female roles herself: she will never become a wife or a mother. Indeed her virginity exists on her own terms: it does not necessarily signify that she is sexually inactive. She will never be owned, controlled or married, but she may take a lover if she wishes. She belongs to no man; she is chaste on her own terms, not those of men.

She has a bright and a dark side, the bright side relating to virginity, purity, rites of passage for girls and protection of the young and weak, and her relationship with her bright brother, Apollo; the dark side links up with Cybele and the old goddesses and leads off into the shamanic underworld of orgies, tearing to pieces, and human sacrifice. Her human sisters, the Amazons, share this duality, and by investigating it closely I hoped I might get nearer to the origins of the Amazons themselves.

THE BRIGHT SIDE OF ARTEMIS

The Amazons' virginity was of the 'belonging to no man' sort. They took sexual partners once a year, in order to beget children, perhaps also to get pleasure, but never committed themselves to one man. Most Greek girls would have no experience of an adult virgin state at all, since they were married just after puberty and thereafter kept in a married state by a society to whom a spinster or an independent woman were completely alien – unless she were a prostitute. Short- or long-term virginity might be required of a priestess, however, though she would be likely to be either young or past childbearing so that there was no unusual sacrifice of sexuality involved.

Virginity was more usually seen as a stage to be passed through on the way to maturity, but an important stage that certainly might be marked by rites of passage for girls as well as boys. Pausanias says that at Athens a girl had to be consecrated to Artemis at Brauron or Munichia before marriage. The initiation ceremonies they experienced sound very odd to us now and may well not have made complete sense to the Athenians of the fifth century BC because they are thought to be very ancient indeed, dating back to a time when shamanic dances and rituals brought man and animal much closer, and for a little girl to become a 'little bear' was not so hard.

The shrine of Artemis at Brauron in Attica (see Map 2) is set in a beautiful spot, close to a natural harbour and, in the Iron Age, near dense woods and springs, and yet, as Vincent Scully has pointed out, it possesses a strange double aspect: looking to the south from near the temple the landscape is harsh and jagged, to the north it is soft and calm, so that the place acts like a mirror for the two sides of woman's experience: beauty and harmony on the one hand, and on the other, contact with the violent primitive forces of the earth, particularly at the time of childbirth when the female's body is literally split open by forces that she cannot control.

Aged between five and ten, well before puberty struck, the little girls would come to Brauron for their initiation. They would change into short crocus-yellow tunics, supposed to look like bearskins, and make their way, pretending to be she-bears (*arktoi*) walking on their hind legs, through the idyllic countryside to the temple, which, Scully says, was a 'kind of megaron (shrine-room) crammed into the savage opening of the rocks'. When they came out of the 'den-like place' with its altar for burnt offerings, they moved between rocks that 'seemed to grind down upon the megaron in their cleft'.[2] In other words, the little shrine jammed into the rocks would have seemed like the interior of a female body and the exit from it like a narrow birth canal. The little girls would be 'reborn' in the initiation rite as women, ready to suffer what women must. And in a sense the girls were sacrifices themselves – on the altar of marriage and motherhood.

And yet we know they also danced for Artemis, learned about spinning, ran races and slept together in a dormitory, so we can imagine that many Athenian matrons remembered their time spent at Brauron, away from parents and brothers, dancing and playing with girls their own age, as an idyll. But they were actually being symbolically divested of their childish wildness (their bear-nature) and tamed and domesticated ready to serve in adult female life. If that sounds depressing to us, it might actually indicate a much profounder understanding of the sacrifice that motherhood demands of women than we have today where many people think of it as a 'right'. And, of course, in Classical Greece many young women would have died either in childbirth or of the complications of it. The period of seclusion at Brauron would give girls at least a brief taste of a different sort of life, before the need of the human race to perpetuate itself imposed itself on them. For some girls it might be a holy and religious experience. For others, the wild gigglers at the back of the class, it would be an opportunity for fun and excitement. The hope of their parents would be that girls who had been 'offered' to Artemis as children would be protected by her when it came to bearing children themselves. It would mark the death of their childish selves and the birth of the grown-up Athenian women destined for a life of seclusion and self-sacrifice.

The initiation into adulthood would be one of the first experiences an Athenian Greek girl would have of the religious function of women. This is not something we know a lot about nowadays, at least not consciously, because most of the people reading this book will have been brought up in a Christian, Muslim or Jewish society where men largely control the priesthood. But the year in Athens was marked by religious festivals, several of them for women only, and others with important roles for women to play. The Thesmophoria and the Haloa were the two most important women's mystery rites. On these occasions consciousness of women's sexual and generative powers was raised and celebrated. There would be both periods of quiet solemnity and fasting and periods of bawdy, life-affirming drinking and feasting, both considered appropriate to a religious festival. The power of women apart from men was apparent here, and this is why these festivals are so crucial in our search for the sources of the Amazon myth.

THE WOMEN'S MYSTERIES

The Thesmophoria were festivals in honour of Demeter, the goddess of grain and fertility. For women they offered a chance to be away from home for days at a time, without husband or children;

one version of the festival, in Syracuse, lasted ten days. Children, virgins and men were excluded: this was a rite open only to mature, sexually experienced women. Husbands were obliged to meet the costs.

The festival begins as the crowd of women make their way up the hill to the Thesmophorion, carrying food, cult equipment, and pigs for the sacrifice. There is a tinge of apprehension in the air and it is getting dark because the sacrifice takes place at night. At the top there is a deep pit, 'the chasm of Demeter and Kore', into which the women fling the squealing piglets while other women, called the 'Bailers', descend into it to collect up the remains of last year's sacrifice. The 'Bailers' have avoided intercourse for three days in order to be in a state of purity. They take care to make a noise while they are in the underground pit, so as to scare away the snakes that are supposed to live down there. They bring what they gather up and lay it on an altar: all the women present take some and will mix it with the seed they sow to bring a good harvest. One eye-witness mentions at this point that 'unspeakable sacred things are made of dough and carried up, models of snakes and male membra; they also take pine branches'.[3]

The pit or chasm represents the Underworld where death, dissolution, conception and rebirth occur, and this part of the rite is about the rape of Persephone, when she was snatched by Hades into the earth, and her mother, Demeter, had to go and search for her.

On the second day of the Athenian version of the festival the women sit on the ground on a bed of willow branches, which are supposed to have an anti-aphrodisiac effect, and fast. They are mourning the loss of Persephone.

On the third day, they make sacrifices and enjoy a great feast with meat to celebrate the goddess of beautiful birth, the Kalligeneia. They indulge in bawdy conversations, split into groups, and insult one another. Cakes made in the shape of phalluses are handled, and one source says the women worship a model of the female pudenda.

The exemplar for this behaviour is Baubo, who in the original Demeter myth is the old nurse who makes the mourning Demeter laugh by lifting her skirts and exposing her genitals. It is done as a joke on this occasion, but it probably refers back to very ancient rites that were deadly serious and to do with a moment of epiphany when the priestess showed forth the power of the goddess by showing her vulva. Anthropologist turned sorcerer Carlos Castaneda tells of the moment in his training when one of his women teachers exposes herself to him and makes him stare at her private parts for some time.[4] For him it was clearly a terrifying experience, not a sexually arousing one.

The women eat pomegranate pips whose red juice is associated with death, menstruation and birth. But although there is much ribaldry at the Thesmophoria, it is sacred ribaldry and all the women present must be sexually abstinent for the duration of the festival. Gruesome stories are told about what happens to men who dare to spy on the women while they celebrate: King Battos was castrated; Aristomenes of Messenia was overpowered by women with carving knives and taken captive. Herodotus says that the Thesmophoria was brought to Greece from Egypt by the Danaids,[5] which is one of the many connections with Egypt that we will come across on the trail of the Amazons.

Later in the wintertime, as part of the Haloa festival, women meet again at Eleusis for a secret nocturnal festival where they once again engage in bawdy conversation in the company of phalluses made of wood or dough.

Walter Burkert remarks that 'at the core of the festival there remains the dissolution of the family, the separation of the sexes, and the constitution of a society of women; once a year at least the women demonstrate their independence, their responsibility, their importance for the fertility of the community and the land'.[6]

An important ingredient of the Amazon myth, 'women living together apart from men', may have its origin in male curiosity about women's religious rites, and even a jealousy of the enjoyment and satisfaction that women got out of them. Men sense that, when women get together without allowing petty-minded resentments to intrude, a kind of power arises in which men cannot participate. It is what would now be called a 'witchy' sort of power which seems to work in an uncanny and unstraightforward sort of way. Our Christian society demonised that sort of power and thereby deprived women of a prime mode of spiritual functioning. But in Archaic and Classical Greece women were still hanging on to it; they were not peripheral in the religious world. They were in fact *central* to the Eleusinian mysteries, based on the theme of Demeter and her daughter Persephone, whose reunion was presented as a central symbolic event for both sexes. And Diodorus of Sicily believed that the Eleusinian mysteries came from Crete. And if we go back to Bronze Age Crete we will find that women had not merely an equal role in religious practice, but probably a central one. Not only did women hold religious power, but an Amazonian athleticism was encouraged in them that is directly in line with the tomboy eroticism of the bright side of Artemis. At the heart of this culture were the bull-games, in which both young men and young women participated.

THE BULL-LEAPERS OF CRETE, CIRCA 1600 BC

It is late afternoon and the air has begun to cool. In the dusty arena in front of the Bull Temple, men with basins are sprinkling water to damp the earth ready for the games. The audience is assembling, keeping their excitement in check, their voices down, so as not to get a telling-off from the marshals – or worse, from the aged priestesses whose eagle-eyes will supervise the ceremony.

In the cool of the outer chambers of the temple the young ones are preparing, oiling their bodies, doing stretching exercises, adjusting each other's hair so that it won't escape and get into their eyes at a critical moment when they vault the bulls. In the corner a boy and girl, aged about fourteen, practise leaping, somersaulting, falling and catching.

As the sun sets, the head-priest sounds the horn and the four boys of the four quarters begin to whirl their bull-roarers. The air is full of the whirring, groaning, keening noise. The audience falls silent and the big wooden gate creaks open. There is a long pause, as the bull-roarers' noise fades out and then the bull erupts into the arena. The people gasp: he is big and angry and his nostrils are snorting hot steam.

The first leaper is a tall slim boy with an azure head-band holding his long curly hair from his brow. His partner is a sturdy brown girl with strong shoulders and small breasts set widely apart. They are both naked except for a little codpiece apron over the loins. Their friends cheer madly as the boy darts around the bull, waiting for his chance, and the girl clutches her lily-goad, crouching ready to go.

And then, in the twinkling of an eye, the moment is there: the girl has distracted the bull by waving her goad, and the boy has launched himself forward, over the bull's back, and he's landed on the wet earth, the girl already there to steady him before they both turn and scamper out, both of them turning triumphant cartwheels as they go. Their friends and family scream and weep with joy.

Things do not always go so well. In the course of the evening, one boy is gored in the neck as he trips after his vault and has to be hauled out by the marshals whilst his partner distracts the bull with her goad. A girl-leaper (there is no bar to girls leaping, though only the strongest do) tries the impossible (which someone always does every once in a while): to grip the bull's horns and leap over its back lengthways. She gets her angle between the horns slightly wrong, is tossed by the maddened bull, and has her back broken. If she had succeeded she would have been fêted as an incarnation of the goddess for a year. You can expect two or three deaths in the first few days of the bull-games, but the audience does not mind too much – it is considered a fitting and glorious way to die.

At the end of the holy month of bull-games the champions are chosen, a boy and a girl, and on the night of the consecration they are taken first for their ritual bath and robing, and then to the gate of the labyrinth. Night is falling as they arrive, and they know what they must do: the high-priestess gives the girl her *clew*, a ball of golden thread in a ceramic pot, and she in turn pulls out the end of it to give to the boy, who fastens it to his belt and enters the labyrinth. His task is to feel his way in the pitch dark to the central chamber, confront what is there, and then return. Many of the boy-champions do not return, having perished in the dark entrails of the earth. In fact, there is nothing in the central chamber. What you have to face is your own fear, but the boys do not know that. For them there is always a monstrous minotaur to be faced in the dread dark of the labyrinth.

The above account of life in Knossos circa 1600 BC is not necessarily true of course, although it is based on evidence from the finds at Knossos and is, I hope, as likely as anyone else's version of what the Cretan religion was about. In *The Myth of the Goddess*, a fascinating and well-researched book, Jules Cashford and Ann Baring tell us that Crete from 2000 BC to 1200 BC was a civilised goddess-worshipping culture where beauty was both created and cherished and the people lived in harmony with nature. There was no warrior-cult and the vast majority of human figurines found at Knossos, where the labyrinth may have been, were of women, many either priestesses or goddesses with naked breasts, snakes wound round their arms and tall head-dresses. The book's account of life in Minoan Crete is vivid, but it sanitises and idealises too much. The authors leave out the extraordinary *erotic* power of the statuettes, the fact that the goddess's breasts are bared – not to suckle babies, but to show that they are engorged with the *shakti*-power. In the most well known of the little figurines, three snakes are entwined around the body of the goddess:

one has its tail in her left hand and travels round across her shoulders and behind her head to finish with its head in her right palm. The other two form a knot in her lap and then, making a kind of girdle on the way, climb upwards so that the head of one appears at the top of her high headdress and the other coils his tail around her right ear. The pulsating energy embodied in this figure is not soft or maternal – it is the kind of power you can sense in the Indian dancing Parvati figures. That the cinched waists and pushed-out breasts remind us of the pneumatic figures of cartoon wild women or cyberspace heroine Lara Croft is not accidental, because this is our contemporary way of embodying the same kind of quality. The genius of Crete was not just that they knew how to arouse and embody this fundamental female power, but they knew how to *use* it too, in the religious sense, so that it did not lead either to decadence and corruption or fuel war and aggressions. It may not have been a matriarchal culture, women may not have had much public power, but, in religious terms, the role of the female was very well understood.

The sacred bull-games, whatever the details were really like, must have been an enormously exciting occasion, combining danger, physical beauty, skill, cruelty, eroticism and religious experience. Apart from the thrill of watching the girls and boys pit themselves against the bull, by the end of the games a great surge of sexual energy would have been built up. The smell of human sweat and bulls' excrement, of blood and earth, the polarity of man and beast, the sudden moments of danger either overcome or yielded to, the flesh pierced by horn, the beauty of the oiled young bodies . . . this was the energy that the Cretans knew how to channel via the games, the initiatory ordeal of the labyrinth and the sacred marriage. Its spin-offs were the lovely buildings with their murals of leaping dolphins, beautiful youths of both sexes and lily flowers; their delicate yet vigorous ceramic figurines.

In relation to our Amazon quest, the important point is that girls were trained to be bull-leapers along with the boys. There are murals that show girls performing in the bull-ring to prove it – although they are more usually shown as catchers and assistants than leapers. The lean, light, flexible body required was admired in both girls and boys, men and women. Perhaps the most stunning example is the figurine that Arthur Evans, the excavator of Knossos, called 'Our Lady of Sports'.[7] She stands, very slim and lithe, with her arms upraised in a gesture that could either be that of epiphany or of waiting to catch a bull-leaper, perhaps deliberately both. She wears a corslet that compresses her waist and seems to push up her breasts which are prominent and firm, and is attached at the waist to a metal codpiece, an item of clothing quite definitely associated with the male and the protection of the male member. This gives the figure a weird hermaphroditic quality that Evans has an interesting way of explaining. He believes that the girls who were to take part in the bull-leaping sports had to undergo some sort of ritual sex transformation, perhaps because the sport was originally an all-male event. The putting on of the stylised codpiece may have been part of this, intended to imbue them with all the strength they would need to survive the dangerous sport. The juxtaposition of female beauty and sexuality with male power is a classic Amazon trait, which we will come across again and again in this investigation.

If we return to contemplate the many figurines of the goddess or her priestess with naked breasts it becomes clear that breasts in Crete were not considered primarily as being there to suckle children, but as an adornment and a badge of strength. The breasts of the snake-goddesses or priestesses are thrust forward, engorged with power, the nipples erect, signifying arousal. You will see the same sort of breasts on Indian statues of Parvati and the other *shaktis* – they are embodying the power of the god, his presence; they *are* the power of the god, his presence. There is no room for trivial gender-sniping here; the point is that it is quite impossible to say to which sex the power belongs. In fact, it belongs to neither, only to the divine source of both. Our contemporary Christian (or post-Christian) society sees it differently: the *shakti*-serpent is a dangerous force that needs to be chained or conquered. It cannot be destroyed, however, because it is the power that keeps the world in existence.

The Amazons' power is in their breasts. In spite of the stories about them, having one breast seared off in childhood, they are always shown in art with two breasts, which are usually firm and prominent. The breasts signify both sexuality and strength, giving the same kind of message as Evans's 'Our Lady of Sports'. The young women bull-leapers of Crete have a similar body shape, with much less developed breasts, which you would expect in athletic adoles-cents, but otherwise they confirm the same archetype – Artemis in action, which is why Crete being one of the sources of the Amazon image should not be discounted. Certainly there was much trade and coming and going across the sea between Crete and Anatolia, Egypt and Greece from the middle of the third millennium onwards, if not earlier. Many of the sites connected with the Amazons have strong links with Crete, particularly Ephesus.

After 1200 when the Dorians invaded Crete, the brilliant culture there began to decline, but there are still flashes and glimpses of the old power – in works like the little goddess on horseback who dates from this post-palatial period (see illustration). Or *is* she a goddess? Could she in fact be an Amazon?

ARTEMIS OF EPHESUS

'Great is Diana of the Ephesians!' These were the defiant words chanted by the citizens of Ephesus as they streamed into the great theatre of Ephesus to riot against the new religion of Christianity. In particular the silversmith, Demetrius, who made model silver shrines for Diana, was angry that his business was failing because of this man Paul who preached that 'they be no gods which can be made with hands'.[8] Diana is the Roman name for Artemis, the goddess of the Amazons, and the Ephesians must have been doing good business from the people who came to pay her homage from all over the ancient world. It was an ugly moment for Paul and the other Christian apostles, but the astute town clerk managed to pacify the crowd and they escaped without harm.

The riots were in vain: the new religion would sweep the Western world and sweep away the last vestiges of the worship of the goddess at Ephesus. It is said that St John brought Mary, the mother of Jesus, here after the crucifixion and today there is a little church sacred to her in Ephesus that has become a place of pilgrimage, cleverly catching all the emotion that would have gone to the Great Goddess in the old days. By Christian times, the cult of Diana/Artemis had become decadent but, in its heyday, Ephesus was something very different, one of the great sacred cities to emerge from the Dark Ages and bear witness to a sophisticated temple-culture that must have brought both comfort and inspiration to many.

The first Ionian Greek settlers arrived there in the eighth century BC. Pindar claims that the Amazons founded the sanctuary of Artemis at Ephesus on their way to wage war on the Athenians, Pausanias denies it, whilst Tacitus compromises by saying that the Amazons started the tradition of using the temple as a sanctuary. The earliest mentions of Amazons in literature (in Homer and Hesiod) connect them with this area and there are many other places on the Aegean coast of Turkey that are said to have been founded by the Amazons – Smyrma (Izmir), Cyme, Myrina on Lemnos, Priene, Pitane, the island of Samothrace, and the town of Mytilene on Lesbos. There is definitely a scent of Amazons hanging round the whole coastline. Herodotus wrote:

> The Lycians were originally from Crete . . . their way of life is a
> mixture of Cretan and Carian. One custom which is peculiar to
> them, and like nothing to be found anywhere else in the world,
> is that they take their names from their mothers rather than

from their fathers. Suppose someone asks his neighbour who he is: he will describe himself in terms of this mother's ancestry – that is, he will list all the mothers on his mother's side. Also, if a female citizen and a male slave live together, her children are considered legitimate, whereas if a male citizen – even one of the highest rank – marries a woman from another country or a concubine, his children have no rights of citizenship.[9]

This is interesting in relation to Amazonian sexual practices, indicating a pre-patriarchal attitude to sex reminiscent of the customs of the Tuareg people in North Africa (see chapter six).

Mina Zografou[10] is convinced that Ephesus and the surrounding area constitutes the Amazon homeland. But she points out that the original Amazons may not have been an all-female group and that 'Amazon' could have been an ethnic term. She argues that the ethnic Amazons are likely to have been one of the remnants of a pre-Indo-European people from Crete or the Aegean, who lasted at least until the Mycenaean Greeks immigrated into the area. Hercules and Bellerophon can then be seen as ethnic-cleansing (my term) heroes who come down from Greece to rid the kingdoms of Lycia and Troy of undesirable elements in the form of Amazons and other peoples of older stock and different ethnic origin. Sadly, we know too well from our own times how virulent ethnic hatred can be, and this argument is quite persuasive.

Florence Bennett[11], writing in 1912, also comes out in support of the Aegean coastline of Turkey (ancient Mysia, Caria and Lydia) as the Amazon homeland, claiming that in this area the figure or head of an Amazon was in vogue as a coin-type, something that is rarely found elsewhere. The Amazons then could have been either men or women of those native populations who still held to the old matripotestal ways, of which Ephesus was a sacred centre. The priestesses of Artemis' temple could have provided some of the colour and detail for the travellers' tales that found their way back to Athens.

THE TEMPLE OF ARTEMIS

If the great temple of Artemis built around 550 BC were still standing, we might well have some direct evidence of what the priestesses who served it were like, but unfortunately it was burnt down in 356 BC by a crazy egotist who wanted his name to live for ever (which is precisely why I am *not* naming him!). However, excavations early this century revealed nearly 3,000 objects, many of them votive gifts of ivory or precious metal, and scraps of sculptural relief.

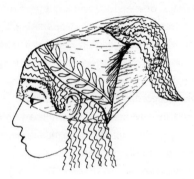

The woman in this relief wears a pointed cap with a hole in the crown through which a pony-tail was drawn. W.R. Lethaby points out that such pony-tails have been found in Minoan works, strengthening once again the link with Crete, and that this pointed cap was a common characteristic of Amazon dress on vases, suggesting that this person was perhaps an Amazon.[12]

Within the temple precincts was a statue of the goddess. Pliny said it was very ancient and Vitruvius stated that it was made of cedar wood. The Book of Acts in the Bible talks of it having fallen from heaven, and we know that a copy set up by Xenophon was covered in gold plate. Lethaby believes it was a 'tall rude figure standing between two animals' placed in what was probably a sanctuary open to the sky, and this sounds like the most accurate description to me.

When the temple was rebuilt by the people of Ephesus in 334 BC, it became one of the wonders of the world. It was served by a caste of eunuch priests called *essenes* (meaning king bees) and a chief priest called *megabyxos*. There were also virgin priestesses working there, but women were actually forbidden to enter the sanctuary, which shows how far the cult of Artemis had been taken over by the priests by this time. The famous statue of Artemis, with the myriad pendulous breasts hanging from its chest, dominated the shrine. Some people claim that the 'breasts' are not breasts but bulls' testicles, eggs or fruits such as dates, or even the testicles of men who had castrated themselves in honour of Artemis, but I suspect the ambiguity is intentional – they are all these things, as befits a Mother Goddess to whom men sacrifice their manhood.

And yet even in the third century BC, once the temple's glory had faded, there lingered, as Robert Graves has pointed out, 'a tradition of armed priestesses . . . at Ephesus and other cities in Asia Minor'. He is referring to Callimachus' poem 'Hymn to Artemis' in which he mentions 'combat dances performed by the Amazons', the implications of which are discussed fully in chapter five. For me, this was the single most important clue connecting the Amazons of Greek legend with the priestesses of the Great Mother Artemis at Ephesus.

If we were able to travel back to the time of the *old* temple when a priestess (not a priest) held sway, what would we find? Piecing together evidence from Crete and elsewhere, it might have been something like this:

> . . . he was not himself that day really anyway, what with the heat and the strange pungent oriental smells and the dense crowds of people who had come for the festival. It was all so alien, so different from civilised Athens even during the Panathenaia. He felt elated, light on his feet, excited, as if something wonderful was going to happen. How fortunate

they had landed here to get provisions and trade some of their perishables just at the time of the great festival of Artemis.

And now they had wormed their way through to the front of the crowd in the courtyard of the temple, past young men with smooth chins and long oiled hair tied up in top-knots who smelled of girls' perfume and flashed eyes ringed with kohl at them, and sweating matrons with toddlers squealing in their arms, come to be blessed by the goddess.

It started quite quietly with little girls doing a circle dance in short yellow tunics, their voices piping out in praise of Artemis, every so often one of them getting a step wrong and peeking up at the terrace above the temple steps to check if the priestess in charge had seen. There was a crane dance by boys which someone said was an ancient custom from Crete in the days when the goddess lived in the laby-rinth and a boy would be sent in to kill a monster for her every year.

Then there was jingling and ringing of metal and hordes of armed women swarmed out into the square, shrieking shrilly like wild birds in terror. They were dressed just like men in plumed helmets and short tunics with shields, swords and axes in their hands. They made a circle and began their war-dance, all stepping and whirling in strict time so that their heads moved together and their crests bobbed from side to side. He was mesmerised, he could not believe that the warriors he saw really were women, and yet as they chanted and shrieked he could tell from their voices that they were. As they moved, stamping heavily on the ground, stirring up the dust and banging their shields like Corybantes, he felt the excitement rising higher and higher in his chest. Some of the girls were really good-looking, with fine dark eyes, neat ankles, and pert breasts that would pop out from behind their shields when they lunged. Their fierceness was utterly astonishing to him, but arousing too.

'Are they warriors or priestesses?' he asked his friend. 'Both, I suppose,' came the reply. Suddenly there was a wail like that of a lost soul from Hades and into the arena burst a crowd of long-haired men in loin-cloths all carrying either drums or cymbals and, whilst the warrior women backed off to widen the circle, they sprang into its centre and beat out a ragged, compelling rhythm. The crowd began to stamp and move in time with them, so he guessed that something amazing would happen soon. He craned his neck to see, but nothing had changed up in the temple. The presiding priestesses stood as sternly as before, bow in one hand and torch held aloft in the other.

The dervishes drummed, their brothers clashed their cymbals and wailed, the women leaped and stamped, and he began to feel as if the top of his head was lifting off. Gradually he became aware that one or two men from the crowd had edged forward and joined the drummers in the centre and were writhing and wailing along with them, jerking their bodies to the rhythm of the beat. A thought came to him that he would like to join in, that it would provide relief from the strange pent-up sensations in his chest and the light-headedness that made him feel as if he could step up into the air and fly.

Then it happened, there was a fluttering on the terrace above them, the gauzy curtains were pulled back, and the goddess appeared in the window above the temple steps, her bell-skirt hung with offerings, her full breasts glistening, her high headdress glinting in the sun as she moved her head very slowly from side to side in order to see all the people down below.

A great groan escaped from the crowd. The cacophony of the drumming carried on, but he could not hear it: he could

only see her, her beautiful arms lifted in the gesture of blessing, and he wanted to go to her, to serve her in some way . . .
he plunged forward, past the warrior girls into the centre of
the square. Around him were other boys and men sweating,
and swaying with eyes shut. One had a knife and was slashing
his back and sides so that blood gushed out. Somehow it
seemed all right. It appeared to be what the goddess wanted.
He began to stamp his feet, and whirl on the spot, the fizz of
elation spreading from his chest to all his limbs, he began to
look around for something, anything would do, with which to
cut himself, to let some of the rising pressure out of his
body . . .

A hand landed on his shoulder and yanked him back
through the mêlée to the sidelines again. His friend was slapping his face and someone was pouring water over his head.
'Solon, what would your mother say if I brought you home
without your balls? Do you know what they were going to *do*
to themselves with those knives?' He struggled, but he felt his
body sagging down on to the dusty ground, held there by the
strong hands of his shipmates. As the water hit him and he
opened his eyes and focused on their faces, half concerned
and half amused, the ecstasy began to slip away, but still it
didn't seem such a terrible thing to do. If that was what she
wanted, then she should have it, didn't they realise? 'You just
don't understand,' he protested before he fell into the darkness of her ever-open arms.

In this chapter we have moved from the protective virgin Artemis
with her little dancing 'bears', via the athletic bull-leaping girls of
Crete, to the war-dances of the acolytes of the older form of Artemis
at Ephesus. In each of these there is an Amazonian element: at
Brauron, the virginity; in Crete, the gender-swapping clothing of the
leapers, and girls who look like boys; and at Ephesus, a ferocious

display of martial energy from warrior-priestesses. At Ephesus we stand right on the very edge of the 'dark' side of Artemis and the Amazons. Thus far there has been nothing *really* unpleasant associated with them, but in the next chapter we must step over that edge and face up to the worst that history can throw at us.

CHAPTER FOUR

The Medusa Face
of the Goddess

....

By now I was having to leave far behind my romantic image of the
two women grazing their horses at dawn. As I found out more about
the different versions of Artemis that existed throughout the ancient
Greek world and its fringes, I was coming across a side to Artemis
and her priestesses that is liable to make the most committed
goddess-worshipper blench, a face spattered with the blood of sacrifice both animal and human. Pausanias, writing in the first century
AD, describes a yearly holocaust offered to Artemis at Patrae. An altar
is made and surrounded by a circle of green logs. An approach is
constructed out of banked-up earth. The virgin priestess approaches
in a chariot drawn by deer. And then

> they bring and cast upon the altar living things of all sorts,
> both edible birds and all manner of victims, also wild boars
> and deer and fawns and some even bring the cubs of wolves
> and bears, and others full grown beasts. I saw indeed a bear
> and other beasts struggling to get out of the first force of the
> flames and escaping by sheer strength. But those who threw
> them in drag them up again on to the fire, I never heard of any
> one being wounded by the wild beasts.[1]

As Jane Harrison comments, 'even in the civilised days of
Pausanias the service of the Huntress maid was horrible and
blood-thirsty'. But the animal holocaust was itself a substitute for
human sacrifice. Indeed, in Euripides' play *Iphigenia in Tauris*,
Iphigenia is saved from the sacrificial death to which her father,

Agamemnon, has condemned her when Artemis puts a fawn in her place. Agamemnon needed a stiff wind so that his boats could get to Troy, and believed that Iphigenia's ritual death would persuade the gods to give it. But Iphigenia was in the service of Artemis and Artemis saved her in return for a promise that she would become a virgin priestess in her cult among the savage Taurians across the Black Sea in what we now call the Crimea. There, in the service of Artemis Tauropolos, Iphigenia was obliged to preside at the ceremonies in which wandering foreigners and shipwrecked sailors were sacrificed to the goddess. In his play, Euripides is discreet about the method of execution, but Herodotus is happy to supply the details: 'What they do is first consecrate the victim and then hit him on the head with a club. Some say that they then push the body off the cliff at the top of which their shrine is located, but impale the head on a stake; others claim that the body is buried in the ground rather than being pushed off the cliff, although they agree about the head.'[2]

Orestes, Iphigenia's brother, comes to the temple to steal away the sacred image of the goddess, and once the two of them have recognised each other, they steal it together and run away, taking it back to Greece. This image of the goddess was probably made of blackened wood, or it could have been a meteorite, conforming to the tradition whereby goddess-images 'fell from the sky', or it could even have been made of obsidian, the volcanic rock that had been used for blades and ornaments in the area since Neolithic times.

Some 10 kilometres north of Brauron, at Halai, a temple of Artemis Tauropolos has been excavated. This is the temple that Athene instructs Orestes to found in the closing scene of Euripides' play, and she goes on to demand that a special ceremony be performed: 'And establish the following custom: when the folk hold a festival to commemorate your rescue from slaughter, a sword shall be held at a man's throat and blood shall issue for the holy Goddess so that she may have honour.'

The play marks the time when the practice of human sacrifice had died out and was being replaced with less drastic symbolic action. Robert Graves speculates that: 'it is possible that the image at Brauron or Halai contained an ancient sacrificial knife of obsidian – a volcanic glass from the island of Melos – with which the victims' throats were slit'.

Yet another tradition claims that the sacred image ended up in Sparta at the temple of Artemis Orthia where it brought terrible bad luck to the devotees until an oracle advised that Artemis would be propitiated if her altar were drenched with human blood. A yearly ceremony of human sacrifice was performed until King Lycurgus banned it, and instituted in its place a competition in which boys were flogged in front of the image to see who could bear the most blows. Initially this was probably an initiation ordeal for boys who needed to grow up with a warrior's courage, although some scholars have suggested it was a pre-nuptial rite to promote fertility. However, later it became a sordid spectator sport in which boys sometimes died.

Artemis Tauropolos and Artemis Orthia were forms of the goddess in which a cruel aspect demanded blood and sacrifice, in both cases in the form of young males. That the priestesses of this bloody Artemis may have been 'remembered' in more civilised days as Amazons is possible, whether they were armed with the sacrificial knife or the flagellating whip. At the very least, the stories of these cults would have served to give a sharp edge to terrifying tales of gory practices in the primitive past or on the barbarian fringes of the Greek world.

THE OTHER WARRIOR-GODDESS

Surprisingly, cool Athene is also a goddess with connections to the Amazons, but while Artemis is definitely the women's goddess, Athene, although a virgin, belongs to the men. She is the original daddy's girl, reputed to have sprung fully armed from the head of

Zeus. She was the protecting deity of Athens and had one of the most beautiful temples in the world, the Parthenon, dedicated to her. She is normally portrayed as much more dignified than Artemis, in a long, flowing robe with a crested helmet on her head, holding her aegis (shield) with an image of snakey-haired Medusa on it, and sometimes her owl. She was Odysseus' helper throughout his travails, on Orestes's side against his mother in Aeschylus' play, and tends always to take the side of men against women – and even against the other gods.

However, Athene is not quite what she seems: there are many other versions of her origins, which point in very different directions, some of them directly to the kind of ecstatic and shamanistic practices that are suggested by the image on her shield. The most often quoted origin-myth is that she was the daughter of Zeus with Metis, the Titaness. Metis had tried to escape Zeus' advances by changing her shape, but Zeus caught her in the end and impregnated her. An oracle predicted that the child would be a girl, but that, if Metis conceived again, the child would be a boy who would depose Zeus, just as Zeus had deposed Chronos. To avoid this fate Zeus swallows Metis whole. Later while walking on the shores of Lake Triton he develops an agonising headache and howls with pain until Hermes comes to his rescue by fetching the blacksmith Hephaestus to prise open a gap in his skull, out of which Athene springs, fully armed.

Athene, then, is born of man not woman; she is a kind of masculinised woman, but unlike the Amazons she fights on the side of men, and sometimes against women. The question is how the male-supporting Athene comes to have the male-terrifying Medusa head on her shield. How did she steal the sexual power of the *shakti* and turn it against the female? Plato believed that Athene's origins were in Libya, that she was a version of the goddess Neith, and Herodotus tells us that Neith's virgin priestesses engaged annually in armed combat for the position of high priestess,[3] which gives them a distinctly warrior-like flavour.

Neith or Net was a war-goddess in Egypt, whose name means 'The Terrifying',[4] or, according to Barbara Walker, 'I have come from myself'. She was a self-begotten virgin armed with bows, arrows and distaff, and her symbol was the shield and crossed bows. There is certainly an Amazonian feel about her.

Under the name of Anath she was worshipped in ancient Egypt and the Levant where she had a particularly bloody reputation. She was a war-goddess to whom the blood of men was a fertilising substance. Her image was reddened with rouge and henna on the occasion of their sacrifice (which could either have been war or some kind of ritual bloodbath). Cuneiform tablets discovered at Ras Shamra in northern Syria tell us: 'Violently she smites and gloats, Anath cuts them down and gazes; her liver exults in mirth . . . for she plunges her knees in the blood of the soldiers, her loins in the gore of the warriors, till she has had her fill of slaughtering in the house, of cleaving among the tables.'[5]

This goddess Neith sounds much more like the terrifying Medusa than the cool Athene, and Robert Graves has a clever theory of how the two were combined. He suggests that Athene's *aegis* was originally the goat-skin chastity tunic or apron worn by Libyan girls (who may have been priestesses of Neith). This apron would of course cover and conceal the girls' pudenda, and could therefore be taken as a symbol of the female genitals, particularly when decorated with a snakey-haired face with a gaping mouth. This actually represents the *shakti*, the female sexual power. Athene *abstracts* this power from the body on to a shield and thus makes it safe for men to look upon. She tames that primitive terrifying 'female' power, and transforms it into a static, crystallised image which can be contained and contemplated.

There is another important clue here. The Libyan Amazons, who are supposed to have existed long before their more northerly sisters, lived on an island in the marsh Tritonis (Lake Triton is mentioned above as the birthplace of Athene). Diodorus describes theirs as a completely role-reversed society in which the women were trained as warriors whilst the men looked after the children and the house-work.[6] Therefore Athene's origins in Libya may connect her both with the Amazons and with Medusa and the Gorgons. The Libyan Amazons *could* have been priestesses or followers of Neith/Anath/ Athene in her primitive and bloodthirsty form before she was cleaned up to suit the Classical Greek taste.

At any rate, it would seem that the origin of the male-supporting, city-protecting Athene's power is the snake-headed Medusa, an expression of the raw sexual nature of the female that a man may not look upon directly. From a psychoanalytical point of view, it is true that few men can face the raw side of the female: the *yoni* or vulva may not be looked at directly because it is, symbolically, the gateway to the centre of the universe, the heart of reality, the place where we all come from and to which we will return. This terrifying route must be disguised before it can be contemplated.

Athene and Medusa balance each other out: Medusa is a connection to the Amazonian male-terrifying power, whilst Athene leads to the civilised and tamed version of that power which is directed towards the service of mankind. We can surmise that in the old initiation rites of the Bronze Age, boys may have had some kind of encounter with the Medusa and, having survived it, went on to become stable grown-up men who would relate to real women and the female principle with a mixture of respectful fear and confidence. In Classical Greece they tried to expurgate the power of that fear by sublimating it into a frozen image of Medusa on the shield of man-friendly Athene, and by diminishing the role of women and priest-esses in religion, which is one reason why it was reflected into the ferocious figures of the Amazons and their mistress, Artemis, making up her considerable 'dark' side.

ARTEMIS AND CYBELE, THE DARK SIDE

When I write about the 'dark side' of Artemis, I do not necessarily mean her bad or evil side but rather the aspects of her related to the ancient ecstatic cults that are so baffling and alien to twentieth-century people. The Amazons, of course, were associated with both the bright and dark sides of the goddess – with the dark side usually, but not always, manifesting itself under the name of Cybele.

Cybele ruled as Mother Goddess in Phrygia in western Anatolia, an area that reached to the Aegean coastline which we discussed in the previous chapter, from 750–546 BC, but was a presence on the continent long before that. The high-priests of Cybele castrated themselves during orgiastic rites, and were regarded as representatives of Attis, much as Christian priests are regarded as representing Christ. There are many variations of the myth, but they all revolve around Cybele's falling in love with the beautiful young man Attis, and have him being either castrated and/or killed along the way. In an intriguing version recorded by Diodorus, Cybele is a king's daughter who has been abandoned after her birth – as no doubt many unwanted girl children were. She is fed by panthers and other wild animals and then looked after by a shepherd's wife. She falls in love with the beautiful Attis, but when she becomes pregnant the king finds out that she is his daughter. He has both the foster-mother who saved her and her beloved Attis put to death and, mad with grief, poor Cybele flees to the wilderness and mourns. While she is absent, the country of Phrygia turns barren and the people pray for help. It will only be granted if Cybele is turned into a goddess and Attis buried.

This version of the myth has resonances of other myths in it – the baby girl fed by wild animals recalls Artemis and the pregnant woman's wanderings, Demeter, when she is seeking the lost Persephone. Also the father who rejects his daughter sounds very much like a patriarchal invader trying to extinguish the practice of inheritance through the female line.

Exactly how the cult was celebrated in Anatolia is difficult to know because there is little written about it, but in the second century BC Nicander of Colophon mentions 'the caves of Rhea Lobrine . . . the mystery-spot of Attis', and ancient notes added to the verse explain that these caves of Rhea Lobrine are sacred subterranean places where the worshippers of Rhea and Attis (Rhea was another name for Cybele, which came from Crete) who had emasculated themselves came to deposit their severed genitals.[7]

It is a cult very alien to our contemporary way of seeing and being. What kind of force could drive a man to castrate himself? Perhaps the clue may lie in the experience of fetishists and sado-masochists today. They seek a very fierce kind of sensual pleasure, accentuated to the point that it is inseparable from pain. We can guess that the trance induced by long periods of dancing to a repetitive beat would put Cybele's votaries into an altered state of consciousness, in which either their awareness of bodily pain would be numbed or they would slip into a kind of ecstasy in which all sensation, however painful, would produce pleasure. The sensations produced by self-mutilation must have been very powerful, perhaps a kind of very accentuated version of the kind of erotic pleasure that women feel in their whole bodies sometimes – the *shakti*, in other words. To become castrated was to become *like the goddess*, able to feel with her rather then desire her. The priests of Cybele, later called *galli*, had long hair and wore effeminate clothes, reminiscent of the Scythian Enarees, shamans who would also wear women's clothing and eschew masculine activities in order to acquire 'female' spiritual powers.

If the Amazons were originally priestesses of a cult of Cybele, perhaps an earlier version of it, then they might well have gained a reputation as mutilators and killers of men, even if the men who joined the cult actually did the mutilation themselves. All sorts of stories might be told about the mysteries of such a cult, given that the uninitiated would never have direct access to the truth. When the Indo-European invasions began, or as male priests began to wrest power away from the priestesses, perhaps women of these cults took up arms to defend their way of life or simply to guard the mysteries of their sanctuaries. Perhaps some of them were success-ful and thereby became more isolated from the common stream of life.

Cybele is normally portrayed in art with her moon, her cymbal, her tall hat and her musicians. She often has her lions next to her, and is sometimes accompanied by dancing votaries called Corybantes. Her followers would lose themselves in ecstatic danc-ing to the rhythms of drum and cymbal (the dance is discussed fully in Chapter 6) and it is possible that sexual union was involved, perhaps promiscuous mating while under the influence of the goddess. This ties in with the once-a-year promiscuous pairing that the Amazons are supposed to have practised. We need here to define what we mean by 'promiscuous sex', because our condition-ing makes it sound like a dirty and unworthy sort of habit. In fact, to have sexual intercourse while 'under the goddess' may rather have been seen as a holy and respectful act. There would be no possessiveness, no desire for personal gain, and the sexual energy aroused and fulfilled might result in the conception of a 'child of the god'. In fact, where there was no personal agenda, it is possible that both parents of the child would be considered divine since the woman votary would be transformed into the goddess at the time of the act of love.

A consideration of the etymology of Cybele's name leads us in some interesting directions: Barbara Walker comments that varia-tions of it, '"Kubaba, Kuba, Kube" – have been linked with the Ka'aba stone at Mecca, a meteoric "cube" that bore the goddess's symbol and was once known as "the Old Woman".'[8] Esther Harding develops this theme:

On this black stone is a mark called the Impression of Aphrodite . . . an oval depression, signifying the 'yoni' or female genitalia. It is the sign of Artemis the goddess of Untrammelled Sexual Love, and clearly indicates that the Black Stone at Mecca belonged originally to the great Mother.

The stone is covered with a black stuff pall called 'the shirt of the Ka'aba', and it is served by men who have replaced the 'ancient priestesses'. These male servitors are called Beni Shaybah which means the Sons of the Old Woman. The Old Woman is a very general title for the moon, so that the men who now serve the Black Stone are the linear descendants of the old women who performed the same duties in ancient times.[9]

The Amazons are directly linked to the black stone. Just offshore from modern Giresun on the Turkish Black Sea coast is an island that is associated both with the Amazons and with Jason and the Argonauts. On it are the ruins of an old temple – probably Byzantine, but maybe built on the site of something older. In his *Argonautica*, Apollonius Rhodius (296–260 BC) writes of this island:

– they went to the temple of Ares to offer sacrifice of sheep and in haste they stood round the altar, which was outside the roofless temple, an altar built of pebbles, within which a black stone stood fixed, a sacred thing, to which of yore the Amazons all used to pray. Nor was it lawful for them, when they came from the opposite coast, to burn on this altar offerings of sheep and oxen, but they used to slay horses which they kept in great herds.

I went to visit this island, but I hit upon a stormy day when little boys were playing escape-the-giant-wave on the foreshore and the boats that might have taken me out to the island were all heaving around in harbour. I drank lemonade while looking mournfully out at the island where the Amazons' black stone had been seen. I knew it was no longer there, but I would have liked to set my foot upon the island to see if there were any more intangible signs of the presence of the horse-sacrificing women or the ominous 'ravening birds' that Apollonius claimed haunted it 'in countless numbers'.

Instead I climbed the steep hill to the old fortress and looked down on the wave-lashed island: the clouds were still dark and lowering, but the sun had come out so that the whole scene was lit from within by a supernaturally bright light. The colours of the roofs, the trees, the sea and sky were all peculiarly intense, as if I had just climbed through a trapdoor and was looking out into an alternative world. I had been travelling round the area for days looking for Amazon traces – apart from some impressive fortresses that could have been built by anyone and the enigmatic figurines mentioned in the next chapter, there was nothing, no hard evidence at all. It had been frustrating. But two days later I saw the black stone.

It was a great lump of volcanic obsidian about 30 centimetres tall, 25 centimetres wide at the base, tapering to a point at the top. It sat, glinting balefully under harsh lights in a cabinet at the Istanbul Museum. Slivers had been flaked off it on all sides, but it was otherwise uncarved, magnificent and raw. I hung about it for ages, scrutinising it from all angles, wondering if it could be the 'Stone of the Amazons'. There was no helpful label saying what it was, so I presumed nobody knew. It was at the same time earthy, weighty and glamorous. Its facets gleamed and flashed as I walked round it. I wanted to get my hands on it.

This was the substance out of which some of the first mirrors in the world were fashioned, at Çatal Hüyük in Anatolia in the sixth millennium BC, mined from desolate mountainsides and craters, and it is easy to imagine that there once existed obsidian idols of the goddess that would arouse great awe in those who saw them glittering in the half-light of a shrine. Maybe they were deftly carved to evoke a figure or face, maybe they were left untouched and massive, to embody the most natural and chthonic aspect of the deity. They may have been suspended so that they turned and caught the light, seeming to come alive. They may have been considered very, very precious and required an armed guard, particularly if bands of marauding incomers with their patriarchal disregard for the Mother were about. After all, Orestes had come to Artemis' temple in the Crimea to steal such an image. Maybe those who guarded the idols were armed priestesses, Amazons, 'moon-women' to whom this 'stone from the moon' was sacred.

To me, the black stone was a connection to something very old and not human, something abstract, terrifying and yet absolutely essential to our lives. We try to pretend this level of reality is not there, but it is; and in the Bronze Age the moon-women knew it and valued it above everything else. I have a sliver of obsidian from Çatal Hüyük on my desk before me as I write, and I only have to pick it up and finger its sharp edges to feel the connection to that cold, ancient, abstract past.

DIONYSUS, THE WOMEN'S GOD

> Societies of raving women, maenads, and thyades, are no doubt also very ancient, even if direct evidence is available only from later periods. They break out of the confines of their women's quarters and make their way to the mountain. . . . An atavistic spring of vital energy breaks through the crust of refined urban culture.
>
> Man, humbled and intimidated by normal, everyday life, can free himself in the orgies from all that is oppressive and

develop his true self. Raving becomes divine revelation, a centre of meaning in the midst of a world that is increasingly profane and rational.[10]

Women, on the whole, find it easier to surrender to chthonic energies than men, to rave, to be 'taken by the god'. You can see this at any party where women and girls will get up and dance first while men hang self-consciously around the edges of the room. Men are more separate, while women have a natural sense of connection with each other and the natural world. This is why a priestess can *become* the goddess, feel the being of the goddess in her own body, whilst a priest has to act as a lightning conductor or bridge for the divine power. Unless of course that priest crosses the gender divide and becomes a 'female man' like the *galli* or the Scythian Enarees.

The god Dionysus is a kind of 'female man'. He is born as a 'horned child crowned with serpents'. At first Titans seize him and tear him to shreds. A pomegranate tree sprouts from soil where his blood falls, they boil him in a cauldron. He is brought back to life by his grandmother, Rhea (the Cretan Great Mother), and then reared as a girl in the women's quarters.

Dionysus is dismembered so that he loses his form and is then put back together differently (which is exactly what happens to a shaman at his initiation), and thereafter he is brought up as the opposite sex – in fact, becomes a female and is therefore able to experience the god in his own body, which is why he is the 'epiphany god'.

Walter F. Otto[11] suggests a Cretan origin for the name Dionysus and for central aspects of the cult. Burkert asserts that Greek tradition associates Dionysus very closely with Phrygia and Lydia, and also with Cybele, the Phrygian Mother of the Gods. There is therefore a strong link between Dionysus and the Amazon zones of the Aegean islands and coastline. Dionysus also has mythological links with the Amazons: he fights with Amazon queens from Libya to restore King

Ammon to the throne that the Titans had taken from him.[12] Opposed by Amazons on his return, he chases them as far as Ephesus where some take sanctuary in the temple of Artemis, while others flee to Samos.[13] Here he seems to be their enemy, and yet, with their horse-cult connections, they could be seen as his 'mare-headed maenads', who in the ancient rite would tear a boy-victim into pieces and eat him raw. There are many references to these horse-cult women in the myths.

Such terrible acts as the tearing to pieces of a human being during Dionysiac rites did happen, and Euripides' play *The Bacchae* commemorates them, and if you have ever seen a group of intoxicated women on the rampage you will believe it!

It was at the boss's leaving party, back in the early 1980s, when I had my experience of this kind of raving energy let loose. There were a lot of lively young women present and on this wild night when the booze was free, there was a reckless atmosphere in the air. Anything would go. There was one particular young man. He was blond, good-looking, talented and cheeky. He had once tied a secretary on to her chair with sticky-tape, and tonight she planned revenge. She had a whole sisterhood behind her, a sisterhood forged by months of working together, drinking together on girls' nights out with all the rowdy abandonment of the northern female.

We pursued him, caught him, and tore off all his clothes bar his Y-fronts (and there were those who would have had them off too); we then pushed him into a chair and tied him to it with Sellotape. Then we . . . well what could we do? We stood around hiccuping with laughter, caught in a sense that there were other things we could do but must not. The dangerous moment passed, we all collapsed in giggles, and let him go. He took it in good part – even enjoyed it, I think. But now our blood was up: we looked around for another victim and found him – an even better-looking young man, also tall, slim and blond. As ten or so drunken women swayed towards him he didn't just blench, he looked as if he would be sick or faint. There was no escape. He backed away, protesting. Being one of the older ones, I could see his protests were genuine and not in fun, so began to feel concerned. Three strong girls grabbed his arm and began to pull off his shirt. I felt slightly sick. What were we doing? What had possessed us? 'Hey, girls,' I said, in my best school-prefect voice, 'let him go.' They did, and gradually we all calmed down. Of course we would not have physically harmed either of the young men, but the desire to pursue, to overpower, to bend them to our wills, was very strong.

Dionysus had us in his power. Or, as we would have put it then, we were driven by drink. Dionysus is the god of wine, of intoxication, and loss of individual consciousness – and conscience – and the history of his cult is connected with the spread of the vine. Wine was not invented by Greeks; it was first imported in jars from Crete, but it is said that grapes grew wild on the southern coast of the Black Sea, one of the other 'homelands' of the Amazons.

Dionysus is a man-woman, and can operate as either gender, without losing his phallus or his womb-power. The Amazons too are borderline beings, like Dionysus: they are women with the power of women but they express that power in a masculine way. Horses may be one of the keys here: Amazons are often associated with horses – Lysippe, Melanippe, Hippolyta, all have the word *hippos* within them which means 'horse'.

Robert Graves says that Demeter herself was pictured at Phigalia as the mare-headed patroness of the pre-Hellenic horse-cult – horses were sacred to the moon, because their hooves make a moon-shaped mark – and believes that the myth of Demeter and Poseidon, in which the goddess turns herself into a mare to escape the god, records a Hellenic invasion of Arcadia: 'the early Hellenes . . . seem to have seized the centres of the horse-cult, where their warrior kings forcibly married the local priestesses and thus won a title to the land; incidentally suppressing the wild-mare orgies'.[14] By this interpretation the Amazons could be the native priestesses of a horse-cult, or their descendants, whilst the Indo-European mounted warriors are the invaders who come in and change the old ways in their favour.

There is another view: Lysias says the Amazons were the first to mount and ride horses; Apollonius Rhodius refers to the herds of horses they kept, partly for sacrifice. If they were part of the first or early waves of horse-pastoralist people, coming from the steppes, via the southern shore of the Black Sea, they may have been nomadic or semi-nomadic women (such as those whose graves were found in the Ukrainian steppe; see Chapter 2) who were good horsewomen and practised rites in which horses were sacrificed. Amongst Indo-European peoples horse-sacrifice is sometimes associated with sacred marriage – either the king or the queen engages in some kind of symbolic or ritualised intercourse with a horse, the beast representing the power of the land. When it is the queen who does this we might guess that originally she copulated with a young man who was then slain to fertilise the ground. The horse was a later, more humane, substitute.

Whichever of the above interpretations we favour, it does seem that the man-killing Amazons are an expression of the mood and conflicts of a particular time in our evolution, when men were taking religious power away from the hitherto all-powerful goddess and her priestesses. At this time the practice of human sacrifice was dying out and is remembered with a mixture of revulsion and excitement: the women who performed it embodying a deadly, terrifying, but also extremely glamorous power. This combination of ruthless cruelty and glamour is a particularly Amazonian quality.

In my trawl through descriptions of the practices surrounding Artemis in her many incarnations, the women's mystery festivals of Greece, and the cults of Cybele and Dionysus, many of the Amazons' attributes had emerged: strength and athletic power combined with erotic beauty (Crete); activities separate from men; armed war-dances; and man-killing in the form of human sacrifice. But most of these details came from reports written between the sixth and first centuries BC and the true Amazons were supposed to have flourished further back: in the Bronze Age, just before the time of the Trojan war in 1200 BC. Therefore I needed to find a way back to that time, and to do that I decided to try to find out more about the legendary city of the Amazons, Themiscyra.

Minoan snake goddesses
from Bronze Age Crete

Achilles slaying Penthesilea; Greece 540 BC

Amazon training horse

Hercules fighting an Amazon; Greece *c.* 500 BC

Part of the Bassae Frieze, Arcadia, Greece, *c.* 420 BC

'Our Lady of Sports' from Bronze Age Crete

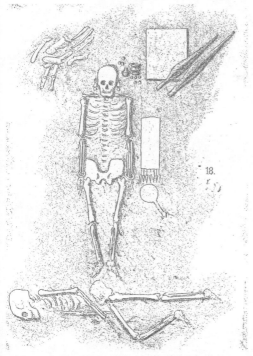

(*above*) Grave goods from 'warrior priestess' burial found by Jeannine Davis-Kimball at Pokrovka

(*left*) Burial of woman warrior and male servant found in the Ukraine by Count Bobrinsky in 1884

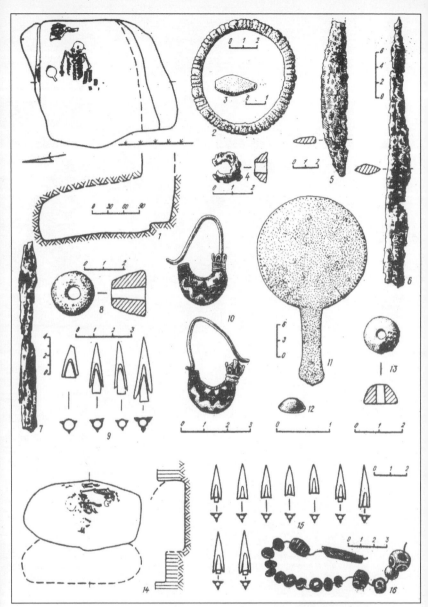

Goods from two women warriors' graves found by Elena Fialko in Akimovka

The costume of an Iron Age Scythian/Sauromatian woman warrior, according to Lyubov Klotchko. Note the leather cap with wooden ring, trousers of wool, linen or hessian, fur-trimmed tunic, snake bracelet and single earring

Statue of Artemis from the island of Lesbos;
Roman copy of Greek original from 5th century BC

(*left*) Woman or goddess on horse from Bronze Age Crete

(*below*) Female idols from Ikiztepe, Turkey; 3rd millennium BC

Gold and silver figurine of a woman,
Hasanoğlan, Turkey; 3rd millennium BC

The 'island of the Amazons' in the Black Sea off Giresun, Turkey, and author

(*above*) Snake bracelets from the Greek colony of Amisos – such bracelets are often associated with Artemis and the Amazons

(*left*) Breastless Cybele with her musicians; Phrygian, 6th century BC

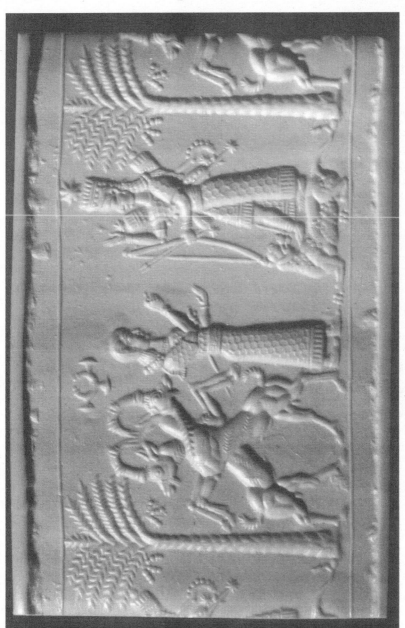

Cylinder seal of Ishtar/Inanna as war goddess, Neo-Assyrian, 7th century BC

'Lady with leopards' from Çatal Hüyük, sixth millennium BC

African 'Amazon' from nineteenth-century Dahomey

Maria Oranta dominating Saint Sophia's cathedral, Kiev

CHAPTER FIVE

The Hittite Sphinx

....

'In ancient times were the Amazons, daughters of Ares, dwelling beside the river Thermodon; they alone of the people round about were armed with iron, and they were the first of all to mount horses . . .' So wrote Lysias towards the end of the fifth century BC. Four hundred years later Diodorus embroidered:

> Now in the country along the Thermodon river, the sovereignty was in the hands of a people among whom the women held the supreme power, and its women performed the services of war just as did the men. Of these women one, who possessed the royal authority, was remarkable for her prowess in war and her bodily strength, and gathering together an army of women she drilled it in the use of arms and subdued in war some of the neighbouring peoples . . . she was so filled with pride that she gave herself the appellation of Daughter of Ares . . .
>
> This queen was remarkable for her intelligence and ability as a general and she founded a great city named Themiscyra at the mouth of the Thermodon river and built a famous palace . . .
>
> . . . she exercised in the chase the maidens from their earliest girlhood and drilled them daily in the arts of war, and she also established magnificent festivals both to Ares and to the Artemis who is called Tauropolos. Then she campaigned against the territory lying beyond the Tanais, and subdued all the peoples one after the other as far as Thrace.

The Turkish guidebooks will tell you that the River Thermodon is now called the Terme Çay and the Amazon city of Themiscyra once stood where you'll now find the little town of Terme on the Black Sea coast about 24 kilometres from Samsun. This is a lush, green and beautiful coastline, with temperate wettish weather like an English summer, where they grow tea and hazelnuts, but Terme is a nondescript place where there have been no excavations so far, so there is nothing for the Amazon seeker to look at except the glinting breakers of the moody Black Sea.

Except . . . I was sitting in the office of Samsun museum director Mustafa Akkaya, having a glass of the usual sweet black tea, feeling hot and frustrated, when he suddenly dipped his hand into his desk drawer and brought out a folder. Up to now, in the formal Turkish manner, he had been kind and informative, showing me round his museum, justifiably proud of the exhibits, being courteous to this British lady who had suddenly turned up. In the folder was the work of a British man called Keith Rowbottom who had lived in Samsun for some time. He had been an Amazon enthusiast too, and an artist, and had made plans with Mr Akkaya for an Amazon festival or conference – which had, sadly, never happened.

It was uncanny reading his proposal: he had been down almost the same routes as myself in his research, though from a masculine perspective. His accomplished and rather erotic art showed that, like Robert Graves, he had fallen somewhat in love with the Great Goddess, as men tend to do. But the interesting bit came when he mentioned evidence he had collected to support an excavation in the local area – there were stories, he said, of people turning up coins with bees[1] on them, an old fisherman who said he had found a city under the water, a student who claimed there was a 'queen's grave' in his garden. Keith had left Samsun to go to Izmir (ancient Smyrna and another 'Amazon' site) and Mustafa Akkaya had lost contact with him, so I was unable to confirm these facts with him. As a seasoned writer of book and television programme proposals myself, I guessed he may have 'talked up' some of this evidence in order to entice the possible financiers of the project. And yet . . .

Mustafa, a sensitive, cultured man with whom I had to communicate in French, also had a mild case of an 'infection' by the 'Amazon bug', although in his case it was fuelled understandably by the desire for more excavations on his patch. He took me on a tour of the archaeological sites of the area. Samsun is ancient Amisos, a Greek colony founded in the sixth century BC by settlers from Miletus on the Aegean coast (not far from Ephesus with its Amazon connections). We clambered up the hill just outside the town along with his sporty fourteen-year-old daughter, who wanted to practise her English. Bouncy and irrepressible in her teeshirt, tracksuit bottoms and trainers, how far she seemed from the Muslim women in their straight-up-and-down coats and headscarves, who are still in the majority in Samsun. She was clever and good at languages, so I guessed her life would be like mine rather than her mother's. She would go to university, travel, and have a profession. She might fit in a husband and children, although she might not, but she would not be financially dependent on a man – she would be his equal.

Amongst the finds from Amisos are a treasure trove from a rich grave of the first century BC, the Hellenistic period, an exquisite crown made of golden leaves, seahorses ridden by fierce-looking nymphs in helmets who were brandishing swords, and twining golden snake bracelets, reminiscent of the snakes that Artemis winds round her wrist, Athene wears on her aegis, and the Cretan goddesses hold with such insouciant sense of power and control. Suggestive images, but nothing at all decisively Amazon – not even any of the Greek vases that show affronted-looking Amazons and Griffons glaring at each other, which we had seen in museums on the other side of the Black Sea. But of course the 'true' Amazons who disappeared around the time of the Trojan war would have been much earlier than the period of the golden treasures.

With Mustafa, I visited the natural fortress of Tekkekoy 14 kilometres east of Samsun which had been used first by Palaeolithic hunter-gatherers and later by the Phrygians, and the third century BC citadel and rock tombs called Asarkale in the Kizil Irmak valley. There is also a mysterious brooding fortress made of giant blocks of stone at Dundartepe, also not far from Samsun, which is thought to be Hittite. This countryside seems very empty and silent to a person like me coming from crowded Britain, and yet there is a feeling of immanence about it, as if the ancient people were living very close by, behind a glass wall, which I have noticed in other places with a rich prehistory, like Symi or Crete or parts of Ireland. Beyond the coastal plain, as you go inland, there are the Pontus mountains, which are easily hopped over by plane, but in ancient times were a natural boundary that made the coastal area a secret and inaccessible coun- try. Large claims had been made by Amazon-enthused Internet sites that some of the places mentioned above were Amazon strongholds, but there is no hard evidence. However, there is one place so far exca- vated that *might* hold clues for Amazon seekers – the mound of Ikiztepe, near Bafra on the coast.

THE EPIPHANY IDOLS

The little 'idols' looked immediately familiar to me with their flat, innocent faces, round eyes and mouths, their arms raised in pleading or epiphany. They were clearly female because they had small pert breasts and a concave genital area, which looked as if it had been made with a thumb-stroke (see illustration). They reminded me of the Cucuteni goddess figurines I had seen in the museum in Kishinev, Moldova, and I wondered about a connection with the lands on the other side of the Black Sea.

A week before in Moldova we had visited the archaeological museum, which had just opened for the first time in years. Kishinev, with its leafy boulevards and French-style apartment blocks, had a raffish charm that made you feel democracy would take root more easily here than in the Ukraine. It cost 5p to enter the museum and we were entirely alone as we wandered through its shadowy rooms.

The encounter with the Tripolye and Cucuteni cultures was overwhelming: like meeting a new person who bowls you over with her charm and animation and instantly becomes a friend for life. Great pots 1 metre high stood unattended, decorated with crosses, snakes, swirls and spirals. It was impossible to resist the temptation to stroke them as we marvelled at the animation and sensuousness of their imagery. There were little altars with legs, in the shape of houses, tattooed and criss-crossed female figurines, a big-bottomed lady, a bird-faced goddess and a man with a flat beseeching face turned up as if to catch the sun. This was a culture that had time and security to make beautiful things, and had flourished in Moldova, Romania and the Ukraine in the fourth and third millennia BC.

When I got home I rushed to the London Library to look up the Ikiztepe excavation reports and was pleased that the archaeologists' findings confirmed my instinct. They had noticed a group of figures with common style: 'all have flat bodies, the faces are flat and round or diagonally oval-shaped. The mouth and ears have been indicated as round gouges. The nose is well-defined and protrudes outward. The ears are crescent-shaped and have three or more perforations for earrings etc. . . . these figures are seemingly alien to Anatolia, but are found in the Balkans'.[2] By 'Balkans' they meant Romania and Moldova in particular. The museum notes confirm that the people of Ikiztepe were not of Near Eastern or proto-Mediterranean origin, but from the same stock as the south Russian, Caucasian, Bulgarian and Romanian peoples of the early Bronze Age.

The implications of this seem to be that the settlement at Ikiztepe in the early Bronze Age, and perhaps earlier, had connections not just with central Anatolia but with the countries to the west of itself and across the Black Sea, and that these people were certainly goddess-worshippers.

And look at the little idol with her arms upraised (see illustration). It is the gesture of epiphany you see in many of the Cretan figurines, and in this gesture it is clear that the priestess *becomes* the goddess, takes on her power. Women who experienced this epiphany would know what it is like to have power coursing through their veins. There certainly would have been classes of women in this culture who *knew power*. But of course we cannot presume that religious power implied status or power in the material world.

Thus some of the settlers at Ikiztepe had come from across the sea, and were of a different racial stock from the people on the other side of the mountains. This was interesting, but it was even more interesting for me to learn that Ikiztepe, which would have been on the Black Sea coast at the mouth of the Kizil Irmak river in the Bronze Age, may have been a place called Zalpa which figures in Hittite writings from an early period. Now, although Terme is normally given as the site of Themiscyra, there is nothing to fix it exactly there and many scholars feel that if the Amazon city or cities existed, they could have been sited anywhere between Sinop and Trabzon, and still have fallen within the descriptions that the classical authors gave. Admittedly it was jumping the gun, but quite early on I started wondering if Zalpa could be Themiscyra. But, before we plunge into the esoteric controversies of the world of Hittite scholarship, we need to know a bit more about the Hittites themselves.

THE HITTITES AND THE HATTIANS

On my first visit to the archaeological museum in Istanbul I met a Hittite sphinx. It crouched, bulky, human-sized, in a shadowy corner, and it had *being* and presence just as surely as a cat does. At first I thought it was evil, then I realised it was just the unfamiliar smell that came off the creature, of a civilisation I knew nothing about. It held me in front of it for a long time; its empty eyes looked into mine. But what was it saying? What were the Hittites to me, or indeed I to the Hittites? At that early stage in my investigations into the Amazons I did not dream that the Hittites might provide a key to the riddle of the warrior women's identity.

And so to the beginning of a new riddle – which is perhaps what the sphinx was trying to make me understand . . .

The Hittites make themselves felt in Anatolia towards the end of the third millennium BC, when they appear in 'the land of the Hatti', who were the people already living in the central region of the country. Whether they came in one massive wave across the Bosphorus from west to east or in many smaller waves, they were of Indo-European origin and their language is an Indo-European language. If you look them up in the history books you will finds lists of kings with multi-syllabic names like Hattusili and Mursili, stories of battles and intrigues, lots of scholarly nit-picking about detail, but, as a people, they do not easily come alive like the Cretans or Greeks – they are as enigmatic as the sphinx in Istanbul Museum. Their power mounted from 1900 BC onwards and they grew to dominate nearly all of Anatolia before their empire collapsed around 1200 BC, though small neo-Hittite kingdoms survived for many more centuries in the south. I came to feel that the Hittites would be very important in tracking the source of the Amazon myths because the period of their rise and fall corresponds very much with the 'time of the Amazons'.

The Hattians are also very important to our story. They may have also been Indo-Europeans from an earlier wave of immigration, or an older native population, but they do have a very different feel to the Hittites. The best way to get a sense of this is to contemplate the grave goods found at Alaca Hüyük in central Anatolia, which would have belonged to the pre-Hittite Hatti people. There are delicate stat-uettes of stags and bulls, mounted to fit on to the ends of standards; other standard-models where groups of animals are ringed with twisted bronze or criss-crossed frames, stylised female figures made from bronze and silver, twin goddesses holding hands in gold, diadems, buckles, pins of gold . . . All in all, these grave goods have a flair and beauty almost equal to those of Crete. They certainly show that the royal families buried in these graves were rich, their craftsmen or craftswomen brilliantly skilled, and that they believed they would need all the badges of their royal status in the next world.

But these beautiful objects tell us nothing about gender roles – with the possible exception of the silver and gold statue of a woman found at Hasano lan: she is naked except for gold straps crossing over her chest, her eyes are shut, and her hands are placed over her solar plexus. She wears gold anklets and her small high breasts suggest youth or virginity. Her evident humility suggests that she is not a goddess. She could be a young priestess, ready for initiation, or the token of a rich young woman, perhaps a princess about to marry and asking that her womb be blessed with children. Or is she a warrior-priestess depicted in the moment she dedicates herself to the goddess? I would not push this interpretation too hard, but I mention it because it struck me the moment I saw the figurine that she looked like an athlete or warrior, and that it was her youth and strength that were being emphasised, not her fertility or womanliness.

At any rate, in the relationship between the native peoples and the incomers, various commentators have spotted a tension between the matripotestal Hattians and the patriarchal Hittites, a tension that was not easily or quickly resolved. For one thing the major deity in Anatolia in the early Hittite era was the sun-*goddess* Arinna. J.G. Macqueen remarks that 'she is the supreme deity of the Hittite pantheon: even the weather god of Heaven, the supreme male deity is subordinate to her'.[3] She is not just a sun-goddess, but a Great Mother Goddess, and Macqueen points out that, in Hattian myth, although the sun-god may be the titular head of the divine assembly, the prime mover always seems to be a goddess: 'She is one of the typical mother-goddess figures of the Eastern Mediterranean and Western Asia, and, as the mother of all things, she is the queen of all things. A male deity becomes her son, or, if he is her husband, assumes a subordinate position.' He believes that when the Indo-European Hittites came in, they quickly got their 'swashbuckling' weather god married off to the powerful Hattian Great Goddess.

The position of queen amongst the Hittites was unusual because she seems to have continued to reign after the death of her husband. Only after she was dead could the new king's wife call herself 'queen'. Macqueen argues that this means that there must have been a time (amongst the Hattians?) when the queen ruled in her own right. This is possible, of course, but it may instead refer back to a time when the queen was the 'king-maker' as in the sacred marriage rites where queen or priestess represents the goddess of the land with whom the king must copulate in order to win the right to rule, and indeed the power to do so.

Macqueen explores the etymology of the words 'Tabarnas' and 'Tawanannas', the respective titles of the Hittite king and queen, to prove that Tabarnas means 'husband of the queen': 'He holds his position simply because he is the "man" or "husband" of the queen. The predominance of the Great Goddess in mythology is only a reflection of the original situation on earth.' 'Tawanannas', on the other hand, means 'mother of the god', and is a linguistic relic of the earliest Indo-European incursions into central Anatolia, which took place not long after the beginning of the second millennium, according to Macqueen. He is suggesting that *her* title is much older than *his*.

THE QUEEN OF KANESH AND HER SIXTY CHILDREN

By 1900 BC Assyrian traders had established a settlement, or *karum*, for themselves just outside the central Anatolian town of Kanesh (now Kültepe). One of their main trade routes arrived here from Assyria and then continued onwards via Alaca Hüyük and Hattuša on the Black Sea coast (see Map 4). They brought with them goat hair felt, cloth, ornaments and perfume from Assyria and exported goods made of silver and gold. They also left behind them a mass of written records: cuneiform on clay tablets sealed within clay envelopes and fired. Kanesh was the old capital of the Hattians/Old

Hittites, and there is a fascinating story about its queen that also features a place called Zalpuwa (Zalpa) on the sea coast. Here is a fairly literal translation:

> The Queen of Kanesh bore in the course of a single year thirty sons. After this she said: 'What kind of an ill-omen have I borne?' She lined a basket with mud, then put her sons into it, and let them down into the river. And the river brought them to the sea in the land of Zalpuwa. The gods, however, took the children out of the sea and brought them up.
>
> As the years in between passed, the queen gave birth again, thirty daughters. These she brought up herself. The sons made their way to Kanesh.
>
> They drove the donkey(s) and, as they arrived in the place Tamar, they spoke: 'Here the hall has been heated and the donkey has mounted [the stairs?].'
>
> The men of the city replied: 'Where we come from the donkeys do that.'
>
> The children responded: 'Where we come from a woman bears only one child a year, but she had us all in one year.'
>
> The men of the town said: 'Once our Queen of Kanesh had thirty daughters all at once, but the sons have disappeared.'
>
> Then the sons said to themselves: 'Who are we still seeking? We have found our mother. Come let's go to Kanesh.'
>
> They went to Kanesh and . . . she [their mother] did not recognise them. And she gave her daughters to her sons.
>
> The older sons did not recognise their sisters. The youngest son, however, said: 'We do not want to commit such a crime as to sleep with them . . .'[4]

Apart from the mystifying line about the donkey mounting the stairs, the outline of the tale is quite clear. A queen gives birth to thirty boys, whom she casts into a river in a basket. The river in this tale is thought by most scholars to be the River Halys (now Kizil Irmak), in which case the settlement at the mouth of this river where the babies turn up, called Zalpuwa here, could be Ikiztepe. Volkert Haas[5] was reminded of the Greek myth of the Danaids, the fifty Amazonian daughters who murder their husbands, while Harry Hoffner[6] sees a stronger Amazon resonance in the theme of a woman who gets rid of her male children but preserves her female offspring.

As far as I can see, the only context in which this might be done would be by priestesses in a goddess-temple who would keep their girl-children and bring them up to follow in their footsteps, but might give away (or even kill) their sons. While of course one woman could not give birth to thirty children in a year, a group of twenty-five to forty women could. They would not all be boys, or girls, but it could happen that by a coincidence, which could be taken as an evil omen, nearly all the children born in one year would be male. And you can see how it might easily happen that one of the boys who had been sent away from the temple to be brought up elsewhere could grow up to meet his sister and have intercourse with her or even marry her, if she left the temple-service. In the old Hattian society this may not have been seen as a problem, but for the Indo-European Hittites such unions could have been taboo. Haas speculates that, in pre-Hittite Anatolia, brother/sister marriage may have been acceptable, but not to the Hittites, who are represented in the tale by the youngest son who sees the marriage to his sisters as a crime.

If the 'queen' of this tale was also the high-priestess of a goddess-temple in Kanesh, where sacred prostitution was part of the service, then it all falls into place. But how likely is it that there was such a temple? We know that such places existed in Mesopotamia and Assyria – Ishtar had temples at Nuzi, Nineveh and Carchemish, and it would be very unlikely that the Assyrian merchants who lived at Kanesh for several hundred years would not import some of their religious customs. That is if indeed the custom of sacred prostitution did not exist in Anatolia already. What would it have been like? Herodotus gives us a vivid picture of how such a temple worked in his own times at Babylon – and puts a prim patriarchal gloss on it:

> The most disgraceful Babylonian custom is that at some point in her life every woman of the land is required to sit in a sanctuary of Aphrodite and have sex with a strange man. It is not unknown for women who are snobbish because of their wealth, and who refuse to associate with the rest of the women there, to drive to the sanctuary in covered carts and stand there surrounded by a large retinue of attendants. The usual practice, however, is for a number of women to sit in the precinct of Aphrodite wearing a garland made of string on their heads. New women are constantly coming into the precinct to replace the ones who are leaving. Plumb-straight lanes run this way and that through the women, and the men they have never met before walk along these lanes and take their pick of the women. A woman sitting in the sanctuary is not allowed to return home until one of the strangers has thrown money into her lap and had sex with her (which happens outside the sanctuary). The man who throws the money has to say: 'I call on the goddess Mylitta to bless you' – Mylitta being the Assyrian name for Aphrodite. It can be any amount of money: by religious law she is not allowed to refuse it because it becomes sacred. The first man to throw money is the one she has to leave with; she cannot reject anyone. Once she has had sex with him, she has fulfilled her sacred obligation to the goddess and she is free to return home. Afterwards you can offer her as much money as you like, but you will not get her. Women who are attractive and tall get to go home quickly, while the ugly ones wait for a long time without being able to do their duty. In fact some of them wait three or four years[7].

We must remember two things: first, that Herodotus is writing from the perspective of a patriarchal Greek, to whom women are either wives or whores; and second, that the custom he describes may have degenerated since its heyday. But whatever the details, we must try to understand the meaning of such rites without letting modern conditioning get in the way.

Behind such temples in the Middle East, usually dedicated to Ishtar (see next chapter), was the idea that the sacred prostitute's role was to embody the power of the goddess, the *shakti*, in an impersonal way, meaning that the man who came to the temple would experience her as the goddess while they had sex and she would experience him as the god. When properly conducted, the rite would have a religious resonance that we cannot even dream of, so used are we to profanation of the sexual mysteries in pornography. For the man to encounter the *numen* of the female in this way, and for the woman to experience the divine masculine in her own body and soul, without any desire for possession on either side, would furnish the kind of experience that would be remembered for a lifetime.

This is an idea paralleled in Hindu and Buddhist Tantric practices. Philip Rawson[8] talks of Tantra being 'transmitted along a female line of power-holders; by ritual intercourse with them the initiation was diffused. Some scholars have identified them with a mysterious old sect called the Vratyas.' He points out that this kind of 'female transmission' would be entirely outside the caste system, and that such practitioners would be considered outcasts. The practices of the goddess-temples, when not decayed and decadent, might well have offered a similar kind of initiation into the mysteries of sexual power.

But to return to the story of the Queen of Kanesh. This story disguises a growing anxiety about the practice of promiscuous sexual relations even under a religious aegis. From the point of view of the temple-priestesses there was no problem, but from the point of view of the patriarchal incomers there was a big one: how would they know who had fathered any child? In the myths, the Amazons practise promiscuous sex to get children, girl children, in complete disregard for the notion of paternity that the Greeks valued so highly that they even implied that women contributed nothing to conception but the receptacle for the father's seed.[9]

At the very least, the story of the Queen of Kanesh, dating from the early second millennium, evokes a memory of a city ruled by a powerful queen who got rid of her male children, which is an essential part of the Amazonian ethos. Her behaviour strikes a note of unease in the patriarchal incomers who are not comfortable with the ways of the high-priestess-queen. And if there existed a group of women large enough to give birth to thirty children in one year, could these women and their strange practices be one of the sources of the Amazon stories?

THE MAGIC-WOMEN AND THE THRONE-GODDESS

The world of Hittite scholarship is not large and it is mostly German. There are several distinguished British scholars (quoted in this chapter), but the more speculative pioneering work is couched untranslated in weighty German tomes. Therefore I was profoundly grateful that Volkert Haas writes in a simple, lucid prose that I was able to get through without tumbling into deep sleep in the comfortable armchairs of the new British Library. His angle was immediately electrifying:

> The magic-women, who at the start of Hittite history, on account of their dangerous machinations and activities, were kept an eye on and driven from the courts, succeeded in the course of time in having even more influence and presenting themselves eventually as a class of priestesses. Their swearing-in rituals, which they collected, composed and compiled

themselves, were signed at the end with their name and place of origin and kept in the archives of the temples.[10]

My translation of *Zauberweiber* as 'magic-women' is not elegant, but I prefer it to 'sorceress' or 'witch', which both throw up unfortunate negative associations. Professor Oliver Gurney confirms that women were very prominent in the practice of magic in Hittite times, particularly sympathetic magic.[11] He translates the word used for these women as 'Old Women' or 'Wise Women', but points out that the Hittite term for them may be synonymous with the word for 'midwife'. In his study of the Hittite magical texts he has found thirty-two different 'Wise Women' involved, plus seven others who had different professions – three 'midwives', one 'doctor', one 'hierodule' (temple prostitute)[12] and two 'temple singers'. Both Haas and Gurney make the point that these 'magic-women' were often regarded negatively. Hattusili I is on record as expressing strong disapproval of the 'Old Women'. Significantly they tended to come either from Arzawa, which was the region near the Aegean coast that we discussed in the last chapter as an 'Amazon zone', or from Kizzuwadna, which was a Hurrian religious centre in the south-east and, as we will see later, the Hurrians gave women a very prominent role in religion.

Next in Haas's book I came across his translation of a very old text re-copied by a named scribe in the time of King Tudhaliyas in the thirteenth century BC. It may well have originated in earliest Hittite times, in the early part of the second millennium. In it, the king appears to be having a conversation with a 'throne-goddess':

Come, let us go to the mountains. You stand in the mountains. Don't become my people. Don't become my relative-by-marriage. Become my friend.

Come, let us go to the mountains. To you, I the King will give a glass dish and we will eat out of the glass dish. You protect the mountains. The sun god(dess) and the storm god have entrusted the land and my royal house to me to manage. I, the king, will protect my land and my country. Don't you come into my house. And I will not come into your house. To me the king the gods have ordained many years, and of the years there is no limit. To me, the king, the throne-(god/dess) has brought from the sea, power to govern and a carriage. They have opened the land to my gods.[13]

The skin on the back of my neck prickled. This king appeared to be very much in awe of this 'throne-goddess' who had given him both the 'power to govern' and a carriage. Haas reckoned that the place near the sea from which the throne-goddess brings these things could be Zalpa on the Black Sea. If this is the case, surely this 'throne-goddess' might belong to the same realm of female power as the Queen of Kanesh. Power in the text seems to be divided between the king and the throne-goddess. She rules over the mountains, and the king over the country, the kingdom of the sun-deity and the weather-god. The connection between throne-goddesses and mountains also comes up in Phrygian times when thrones are found in mountains. In Sumerian texts the throne is signed with the addition 'mother' and thought of as a mountain-goddess. Isis wears a throne on her head-dress in Egypt.

Clearly the king had to be 'adopted' by the goddess – he needed her to acknowledge him before he could have the right to rule. The time of this writing was a time of transition: the king appeals to the throne-goddess of this 'queendom' for a sanction to his power; he is frightened and resentful of *her* power and yet he needs it in order to rule.

I sat in the British Library fizzing with excitement: this all seemed almost too good to be true. If there was evidence here of an independent 'queendom' and it was situated close to Zalpa, which was in the area of Themiscyra, then maybe here was the Amazon homeland revealed. I sought out the Hittite language specialist Jill Hart at Oxford and begged for help. We met in the Oriental Institute coffee bar behind the Ashmolean Museum and pored over the relevant text together – or rather, Jill pored over it while I sat enthralled, hearing these words from more than 3,000 years ago for the very first time.

First Jill explained that the text does not say 'throne-goddess' every time that I had translated Haas's *Throngöttin*. Sometimes the Sumerogram used (Hittite includes both Sumerograms and Akkadian words) may just mean 'throne' without indicating either deity or gender of deity. Indeed gender of deity is never specified anywhere in the text, although you could presume that the 'sun-deity' is a 'sun-goddess' because we know that the principal sun-deity in these times was a goddess. This slightly took the wind out of my sails, but then Jill continued to translate the text which was about the rebuilding of a palace and the associated long life and well-being of the king. It continued, after the extract that I had read in Haas's book, with the king addressing the trees that he needs to rebuild his palace:

The lion slept under you, the panther slept under you, the bear climbed up on you. Now the storm-god my father put you out of harm's way. The cows grazed under you, the sheep grazed under you, but now the king has called the throne, my friend, from the boundary of the sea . . .

When the king comes into the house the throne [god/ dess] calls an eagle and says to the eagle: come on, I am sending you to the sea. But when you go, look into the green forest: who is there?

And he [the eagle] replies: I looked and the goddesses, the infernal, ancient female divinities are kneeling there. And the throne asks: what are they doing?

He [the eagle] answers: she holds a distaff and they hold full spindles and they are spinning the years of the king, and there appears to be no end or limit to them.

The phrase '. . . the king has called the throne, my friend, from the boundary of the sea . . .' was important because it linked the 'throne' once again with the sea, which could mean Zalpa and the Black Sea coast. The passage in which the eagle, sent by the throne to fly across the forest, sees that 'the goddesses, the infernal, ancient female divinities are kneeling there' struck a note of deep respect and fear for these ferocious female deities. I wondered if this might be one of the first references in writing to the Three Fates?

I left Jill believing that KUB 29 was a very old text that contained a conversation between an ailing king, insecure in his grip on power, and the throne-goddess or her priestess who had the power to give him back both security and health. I had to admit that this was no proof that Amazons had existed back in the early Hittite times of the Bronze Age, but there *did* seem to be proof that there was a caste of powerful priestesses/magic-women who were seen to have a hand in the making and breaking of kings.

On Jill's suggestion I wrote to Professor Oliver Gurney, now in his eighties and the acknowledged 'grand homme' of Hittitology, and asked his opinion on the position of Zalpa and throne-goddesses. He wrote back promptly, giving me chapter and verse and more on the subject: he said that while many scholars agreed that Ikiztepe must be Zalpa, others dissented. In particular:

G Steiner . . . has pointed out that this cannot be the Zalpa which was an important place in the old Assyrian colony period (1950–1750 BC) and was defeated by Anitta, since no palace and no Assyrian colony were found. He thinks the 'sea' is not the Black Sea, but the salt lake in the middle of the plateau. He thinks the Zalpa of the documents is Acem Hüyük on the east side of the lake, excavated by Nimet Ozguc. If he is right, you can't use the story of the Queen of Kanesh to support Amazons by the Thermodon.

However, according to the archaeological report of the 1978 season at Ikiztepe,[14] the pottery they found there belonging to the 'early Hittite' period is almost identical to ceramics found at certain levels of the Assyrian settlement at Kanesh. The 'early Hittite' period here means the twenty-first and twenty-second centuries BC – that is, just before the Assyrian colony period. Therefore it would seem that there was trade and travel between Ikiztepe/Zalpa and Kanesh *before* the Assyrians established their trade routes. It seemed to me that Steiner's objections were not strong enough to demolish the identification of Ikiztepe with Zalpa.

On throne-goddesses Professor Gurney had to be very technical, but bear with him, if you can, because it is crucial and fascinating:

> Starke, the most brilliant Hittitologist of the younger genera-
> tion, has done a detailed examination of KUB 29 1. Halmasuit
> (the word for 'throne') is sometimes written (gis)DAG, usually
> rendered 'throne'. Starke says this translation is incorrect: the
> ideogram means 'socle, stand' for a statue or other object. The
> name had previously been taken to be Hattic, with the suffix
> 'it' which in that language is feminine. Starke argues that the
> word is not Hattic but Hittite . . . and denotes some sort of
> symbol of kingship, not feminine possibly, but not certainly a
> statue.

Basically what Starke was saying was that the word in question does not actually mean 'throne' but 'stand', as in the foundation that supports a statue. In addition it had always been taken to be a feminine word from the old Hattic language, which is why it could be translated as 'throne-goddess', but he was arguing that it was in fact a Hittite word and not of the feminine gender. As far as Professor Gurney knew, Starke's view had been accepted. He also commented that if I had come across Haas talking about 'throne-goddesses' it must have been in an old book. He was implying that the view was now superseded by Starke's more accurate translation. Indeed, Haas's book had been published in 1977. He advised me to look up the Starke reference and read Haas's new book. I felt somewhat deflated and disappointed. I headed once again for the seductive armchairs of the new British Library.

As I waited for my books I visualised Starke as a dogmatic, nerdish chap with a mission to stamp out all the last traces of senti-mental Victorian goddess-worshipping tendencies amongst Hittitologists. Sure enough he dismissed the idea that 'Halmasuit' should be understood as the 'divinized royal throne, of Hattic origin and feminine gender' and claimed instead that it was never an ordinary deity but only an *'imaginäre Verkörperung und Symbol einer politischen Idee'*,[15] ('an imaginary embodiment of a political idea') – namely, the ideology behind Hittite kingship and the expansion of its hegemony in Anatolia in the early second millennium.

I opened Volkert Haas's fat new book[16] with anxiety and trepida-tion. If he no longer believed in throne-goddesses, then there was nothing to connect the Black Sea region at this time with powerful goddesses and their priestesses. I was on the edge of my seat as I struggled with the German:

The Indo-European incomers took over the institution of kingship from the native central-Anatolian settlers. . . . In pre-Hittite central Anatolia the kingdom of Zalpa took a dominant place. The kingdoms of Hattuša and Kanesh seem to have been in a dependent position vis à vis Zalpa. . . . In a remnant from old-Hittite palace-building ritual we find an exchange between a King of Hattuša and the Hattian throne-goddess Hanwasuit. It's clear that he has been legitimised as King of Hattuša by the highest gods, the sun-goddess and the weather-god, but that his power to govern and his insignias of rule, the Hulukanni ceremonial coach, he has received from the throne-goddess 'who comes from the sea', that means from the coastal town of Zalpa.

I felt triumphant: this learned scholar who had spent his life studying the Hittites had come out firmly in favour of the power of the Hattian throne-goddess. He actually states that, 'The Hattian throne-goddess Hanwasuit is the personification of the throne', and he had more of interest to say in telling the story of the king of Purushanda who, while surrendering to Anitta, gave up his insignias of royalty in the throne-room. He comments that 'in an earlier copy of the text, "throne-room" is written in place of "Zalpa"'. Therefore it would seem that the throne-room of the rulers of Kanesh was not in the palace of Kanesh, but in the town of Zalpa: Kanesh was their residence but their *coronation place* was Zalpa.

Here were two important points: Zalpa was a special, possibly sacred, place where the enthronement of kings was performed, and the insignias of royalty were kept, possibly by a caste of priestesses of the throne-goddess. Secondly there was a new gloss on the Queen of Kanesh story – that it indicated a period, in early Old Hittite/Hattian times, when a system of matrilineal succession reigned in the area of Hattuša and Kanesh. A priestess-queen, the Tawananna, ruled independently of the king and from her kinship group came the present king, who was not married to her. The post of king was therefore in the gift of the kinship group of the matriarchal Tawananna. Even Hattusili I legitimised himself through the title 'brother's son of the Tawananna'.

It seems Haas is suggesting that Zalpa was a centre of matriarchal power, where Hattian and Old Hittite kings had to come to be enthroned. The gift of royal power was in the hands of the priestess-queen Tawannana. It seemed to me that such a society could be the model for an Amazonian kingdom, because a later patriarchal people, hearing tales of it, might well feel that everything was topsy-turvy and reversed: a queen, not a king, in charge, and a caste of priestesses who hold the insignias of royal authority such as the throne and the royal carriage, and have it in their power to either give or withhold them from the king.

When Professor Gurney considered all this, he wrote, 'I must say the connection of Zalpa, Halmasuit/Hanwasuit, throne and throne-room look pretty convincing,' but, as the impeccable scholar, he was not *absolutely* convinced. He reminded me that no one has yet taken on Starke point for point over the meaning of Halmasuit. However, Jill Hart's research on my behalf suggests that they have made a good stab: Jill told me that 'Starke's rejection of the meaning "throne" has not been accepted in either of the dictionaries which covered the word later than Starke's article . . . I at least think that the old idea of Hattic origin is well-founded, and have not been convinced that "throne" is incorrect.'

Maybe this is why the Hittite sphinx smiles so smugly. The sex of the sphinx is ambiguous, and so he/she loves mysteries about gender. But before we leave this subtle battleground let us take a look at another Indo-European culture, the Celtic world of the early part of the Christian era. Here you will find suggestive tales about the role of women in relation to the crowning of kings. In the Welsh Mabinogion, King Math only retains his kingly power and indeed his life if he rests his feet in the lap of a virgin footholder all the time he is not away fighting. Clearly the virgin's lap is a kind of throne that keeps his feet from contact with the earth, and 'exalts' him as if he were on the top of a mountain. 'Lap' is also a euphemism for the vulva/vagina and 'feet' for penis, so that what the custom is really saying is that the king must be in a permanent sexual relation to the goddess of the land; she is his *shakti*. In cultures dominated by mother-goddesses, her son will often appear as a child in the goddess's lap, the place from whence he has come. This is the magical 'child of the virgin' who grows up to be a hero, such as Lieu in the Welsh tales. The king is the 'child of the virgin' in the sense that his father is understood to be the god. The many potent Christian images of Mary holding the

Christ child, Jesus, in her lap are the most recent version of this symbolism.

The idea that the goddess holds the power of kingship that will be handed over to the rightful king comes up in ancient Irish literature too. The goddess is depicted as the 'sovereignty of the land' and the king must sleep with her representative in order to win power over the land. 'Medb', as in Queen Medb/Maeve, means 'intoxicating one' and refers to a drink, 'the ale of Cuala', which would be given to the king by the priestess-queen to drink at his coronation. In Britain and Ireland we have the 'coronation stone' or 'stone of destiny' that the rightful king or queen sits on at their coronation and the tale attached to this stone, which was called the 'Lia Fail', is that it was brought to Ireland by the Tuatha de Danaan (the 'Children of Don', who may be related to the Danaans of Greece) and would shriek when the rightful monarch sat upon it. One legend, passed on to me by an old Welshman, has it that this stone came from the 'cave at the foot of the mountain' in which the death-goddess, Morgan, lived.

There is a vital point here: we are not talking about a golden age of matriarchy when women had power and men were subservient, but an era when women had specific magical and religious roles which they performed for the good of men and women equally. However, once they lost this power, the patriarchal people who took over interpreted the old ways as a topsy-turvy distortion of the 'natural order'. The story of the Amazons that has come down to us is one expression of this moment when the religious gender roles were shifting.

Was Zalpa in fact Themiscyra, the capital city of the Amazons? It is normally said to be on the Terme Çay river, not the Kizil Irmak, but there does not seem to be any hard evidence for this siting at all. If Zalpa was the place where the early Hittite kings had to go to be given the insignias of kingship, the enthroning place, it must have been associated with some pretty powerful female magic. If the 'throne-goddess' had a priestess who was a queen in her own right, and if she was served by a priestesshood of women who guarded the sacred symbols of kingship, then the place might well have acquired the reputation of an 'Amazon stronghold'. Diodorus' account is of a place *dominated* by women, where girls are trained to fight just as boys are; he does not claim that it was an all-female state. This might fit well with Zalpa, were it not that there is no mention in the Hittite writings of a war-like queen like the one described by Diodorus. However, if the women ever had to defend themselves and their sacred role, then they may have fought. Later in the second millennium, as the Hittite kingdom spread over most of Anatolia, Zalpa was lost to the wild Gasga people who inhabited the mountains near the coast. Whether the Zalpans were all killed or fled we do not know. It is of course possible that *this* was when Themiscyra was built somewhere else along the coast (Dundartepe near Samsun is a possible site) as a stronghold against the Gasgans.

One last complication is that there have been suggestions that the Gasgans were Cimmerians, warrior nomads from the other side of the Black Sea. Certainly the Cimmerians raided parts of Anatolia in the eighth and seventh centuries BC, including this area, and they may well have come earlier too and have had women warriors of their own who started the tradition of Amazons in this area. In fact, this variation has its own logic: it fits in with Justin's assertion that the Amazons originally came from Scythia and with the theory that the main waves of horse-riding Indo-Europeans came down into Asia Minor and Greece via the south coast of the Black Sea, thus avoiding the mountain route to Greece. If one of these groups had a female leader, and some women soldiers in her army, then maybe she deserves the title of Amazon queen. However, my money is on those power-possessing beings, the priestesses of the throne-goddess.

QUEEN PUDUHEPA'S LEGACY

Happily, there is one priestess-queen who has left a monument for us that bears witness to her status, strength and determination. That woman is Puduhepa, daughter of a priest and priestess from the sacred city of Kizzuwadna in south-eastern Anatolia, who married the Hittite king Hattusili III. Puduhepa had a very positive view of herself and her fertility. In a letter to Ramses II of Egypt she mentions that, with the help of her personal deity, she has produced both male and female children, causing the people of Hatti to speak of her 'exceptional vitality'. She took hold of the chaos of Hittite religion by introducing the pantheon of gods and goddesses from her own Hurrian background, in which women played a significant part. She was instrumental in the building of the rock shrine of Yazilikaya.

Yazilikaya was built just outside the city walls of Hattuša in the reign of Puduhepa's son, Tudihaliya, in the thirteenth century BC. After her husband's death she ruled alongside him for a time as coregent, which seems to confirm her connection with a matrilineal tradition. You can still visit this holy place today. High above the modern village, within an outcrop of rock, there is a system of natural galleries. Here the Hittite stone masons carved a procession of gods, goddesses and mythical beings, all engaged in an enigmatic ritual performance. The males and females are separated, which creates a powerful sense of polarity, and there are several divine couples: Teshub, the Storm God, stands with his feet on the necks of two mountain gods. Hebat, his wife, faces him wearing a high hat and standing on a panther; her son Sharruma, also on a panther, stands just behind her. Near the head of the procession of males is Shawushka, the Hurrian equivalent of Ishtar. She wears a high hat and a long kilt pulled up to show her lower torso, and to make clear her bisexual nature. She is half unveiled and winged. She has earned her place amongst the males as a goddess of war because of the high favour she stood in with Hattusili III who considered her his protector.

Shawushka is determined, ruthless, ready for war – and yet sexually female, capable of intercourse, of bearing children, uniting in herself the male and female power in equal proportion. She is an androgyne – and yet somehow the female predominates. Shawushka *looks* like an archetypal Amazon. Was she the next clue on the trail to find the source of their myth? To find out more about her and Ishtar, who also has an androgynous form, I had to turn my attention eastwards and backwards in time, to the 'land between two rivers' where civilisation was born – Mesopotamia.

CHAPTER SIX

The Source

....

Inanna/Ishtar has decided she will visit the Underworld. At first the guardian will not let her in. But she belabours the iron gates with her fists, she will not be denied. She enters.

So begins one of the most astonishing stories in world myth. It goes on to tell how the determined goddess, making her way down into the realm of the dead, has to pass through seven gates. Her sister Ereshkigal, Queen of the Underworld, has instructed that she appear before her stripped bare and crouching, so at each gate Inanna loses one of her items of fine clothing or adornment. When she finally comes to the heart of the Underworld she is undeterred: pulling her sister off her throne, she sits down in her place.

But the seven Anunnaki gods, the judges of the realm of the dead, condemn her to death for her arrogance and she is killed and turned into a stinking carcass of meat, hung on a nail. Her pride is completely humbled: Inanna is snuffed out.

But, with canny foresight, she had prepared her maid Ninshubar for just such an emergency and Ninshubar goes to seek help from the other gods. Neither Enlil, Inanna's father, nor Nanna, the moon-god, will help. But Enki will, and he fashions two little mourners out of the dirt under his fingernails and sends them off to ingratiate themselves with Ereshkigal and revive Inanna with the water of life. Because Ereshkigal is deep in mourning for her children she appreciates the mourners' sympathy and falls for their trick. Finally they manage to sprinkle Inanna with the water of life and she returns to her human form.

But the Anunnaki gods declare that she may not go scot-free: she must find a substitute victim who is willing to go to Hades in her place. She leaves hell with a crowd of wild and brutal deputies and the first person they meet is Ninshubar, her maid. The deputies want to grab her as Inanna's substitute, but Inanna will not have it – after all, Ninshubar has saved her life. They search all over and eventually come to the sheep-fold of Dumuzi, Inanna's young husband, and find him ensconced in fine clothes and enjoying himself instead of mourning. Inanna is filled with rage and jealousy and allows the cruel deputies to take Dumuzi away.

Inanna, by the way, is the Sumerian name of Ishtar (which is Akkadian) so we are dealing with a version of the same goddess Shawushka/Ishtar we saw at Yazilikaya with her wings, axe and pointed hat. She is a goddess of many aspects; however, feminist writers have tended to emphasise her 'good' ones, and glance over her warrior-goddess side. But battle to the Sumerians was 'the dance of Inanna' and the story above shows her as arrogant, greedy, proud, irrepressible and, ultimately, cruel. Volkert Haas enjoys himself painting a vivid picture of her wickedness:

> Ishtar, after the Mesopotamian tradition of the city of Uruk, is the daughter of the Skygod Anu and after another equally prevalent tradition, the daughter of the moongod Sin. She's the semitic goddess of sexuality and passion, uproar and battle; she is the godhead of wildness, chaos, disorder and menace. Just like the demons, she has no mother, husband or children. 'A whore is she', she sleeps with the dying, in order to kill them: to her lover Dumuzi she 'decrees year after year of crying'; the shepherd whom she leads astray 'sits now like a bird with broken wings in the wood'; she changes a herdsman into a wolf, so that his own herdboys hunt him down . . .[1]

Over time the goddess was worshipped as Sumerian Inanna, Babylonian and Assyrian Ishtar, North Syrian Astarte, and Hittite/ Hurrian Shawushka. She is sometimes shown with men's as well as women's clothes; she is thought of as both male and female, and one of her skills is to take away maleness from men and femaleness from women. Here is a Hittite Ishtar-curse:

> Then take from the men masculinity, power of procreation, and health; take weapons, bows, pipes and daggers and bring them into Hattiland. Lay the mirrors and spindles of women into these men's hands. Clothe them like women and put a hat on their heads. And take your goodwill away from them. From the women take away motherhood, power of love and sexuality and bring it into Hattiland.[2]

Usefully, Oliver Gurney gives us the magical ritual that will undo such a curse:

> I put a mirror and a spindle into the hand of the patient and he passes under a 'gate', and when he steps out from under the gate I take away from him the mirror and the spindle and give him a bow, and I say to him: 'Behold! I have taken away from you womanhood and have given you back manhood; you have cast away the manners of woman and you have taken up the manners of man.'[3]

Ishtar is the mistress of sexuality, and like a shaman she can take on the attributes of either sex. She is the protector of harlots, whether they are working in her temples as sacred hierodules, or out in the fields. The evening star is sacred to Ishtar, and is likened by an ancient poet to a harlot herself as she solicits the skies and lights up the land for the harlots out working below. Thus the harlots become incarnations of the goddess, and their pick-ups of her bridegroom Dumuzi.

Ishtar/Inanna seems to embody the element in women that a man cannot know or understand or own, the 'virgin' who is also a harlot, the wild, uncivilised, dangerous part of the female psyche. This part is in essence neither good nor bad, though it can become either. Joan of Arc might be seen as a 'good' version of it; the Dionysiac maenads tearing a man or animal to pieces, a 'bad' version. Lilith, Anath, Ashtoreth, the Morrigen, Skadi, the harmful one – all cultures have their deified personification of it. It rejects the normal feminine path of service to husband, children and society, and serves either a higher or a lower god. As Jacobson says of Inanna:

> In the epics and myths Inanna is a beautiful, rather wilful young aristocrat. We see her as a charming, slightly difficult younger sister, as a grown daughter (a shade too quick, perhaps, to see her own advantage), and a worry to her elders because of her proclivity to act on her own impulses when they could have told her it would end in disaster ... she is never depicted as a wife and helpmate or as a mother.[4]

This quality of inviolability and unavailability emerges in the goddess archetypes as the Mother Goddess begins to lose her universal power in men's eyes. It is as if as women began to lose their status and power in the outside world, and the goddess power also diminished, this power channelled itself into a form where it could not be challenged – that of a warrior-goddess in a warrior society. As a war-goddess we find her celebrated in both early and late myths. Thorkild Jacobson[5] quotes one chilling battle-hymn in her honour:

> When I stand in the front line of battle
> I am the leader of all the lands,
> when I stand at the opening of the battle,
> I am the quiver ready to hand,
> when I stand in the midst of the battle,
> I am the heart of the battle,
> the arm of the warriors,

> when I begin moving at the end of the battle,
> I am an evilly rising flood,
> when I follow in the wake of the battle,
> I am the woman (exhorting the stragglers);
> 'Get going! Close (with the enemy)!'

Sumeria in the fourth millennium might seem to be very far away from Athens in the fifth century BC, but this was a civilisation that in one form or another lasted for over three millennia, and whose goddess, Inanna, did too, although her name changes in different times and places. In early Sumer, from where her archetype came, women had considerable status and power – amongst the upper class they were socially and economically the equal of men. In the Dynastic era women were still held in very high regard: Sargon's daughter Enheduannna was a high-priestess of the moon-god at Ur and was known both as a remarkable woman and a poet who wrote two great cycles of poems to Inanna/Isthar. With the advent of the northern Akkadian influence, and the consolidation of urban life within its centralised authority, its temples and male priesthood, this power balance began to swing in favour of the male. Samuel Kramer quotes from the inscription of a 'reform document' of a king in 2350 BC that nicely evokes the change: 'the women of former days used to take two husbands, but the women of today (when they attempted to do this) were stoned with stones inscribed with their evil intent'.[6] From this it sounds as if women had once had the freedom to be polyandrous. Later, although men could take an extra concubine or two, women were expected to be faithful to their one husband. But Inanna the goddess at least managed to hang on to her sexual freedom.

The Babylonians retained her as Ishtar, absorbed the essence of Sumerian culture, and transmitted it throughout Assyria and Canaan, and via the trade routes, into Anatolia. Right at the end of the Assyrian trade routes on the Black Sea coast was the Amazon homeland,

Themiscyra. Here between the sea and the mountains messages from the Mesopotamian/Assyrian culture would flow in and eddy around. The matrilineal Hattian legacy would still remain in some form. The Hurrians too moved steadily westwards during the Bronze Age, and we know from the previous chapter that a Hurrian princess brought Shawushka's warrior-goddess image to Yazilikaya, the Hittite capital. So here in 'Themiscyra', wherever it was exactly, we have a receiving point for the image and maybe the rites of Ishtar/ Shawushka, the pre-Hittite matriarchs and queens, and the Hurrian priestess-oriented religion. Of course the same influences could be received in many other places in Anatolia and undoubtedly were, but here they would arrive and be trapped between the Pontus mountains and the sea.

Until as late as the fifth century AD, the Black Sea was popularly titled 'the Sea of the Amazons'.[7] Perhaps the old matripotestal ways lingered longer here than elsewhere, which may well be why stories of powerful and war-like women seem to have their source and homeland in this pocket of coastal land behind the Pontus mountains. But elsewhere in Bronze Age western Asia there were great cities dedicated to the goddesses who continued to have great clout even throughout patriarchal times, notably Nuzi near the Zagros mountains, Nineveh in Assyria, Carchemish in eastern Anatolia, part of the Hittite Empire, and Comana in Cappadocia.

THE GODDESS-CITIES

The north-Assyrian city of Nineveh was famous for its Ishtar-temple. The goddess was still known here by her Hurrian name, Shawushka, at the end of the eighth century BC. Her statue was thought to be therapeutic, and it was twice sent to Egypt to bring the pharaoh good health.[8] Shawushka/Ishtar is usually depicted as winged and often accompanied by lions. Sometimes she has clawed lion's feet and is standing upon her sacred mountain, or else the mountain is symbolised by her high horned hat. On cylinder seals she usually has rods appearing from behind her shoulders, which can be seen either as arrows or maces and green shoots. The wings and the claw feet both signify her origin as a goddess of the mountain people. In a haematite seal from Old Babylon around 1825 BC, amongst the storm-gods and demons there is a goddess who is a snake from the waist down, has wings and windswept hair, and bird feet. This is the wild aspect of Ishtar.

At Nuzi, a Hurrian city near the Zagros mountains, there was a temple of Ishtar/Shawushka where there were lion figures and lion-shaped vessels used for libations. Countless naked female figurines with exaggerated sexual characteristics have also been found plus a little androgynous ivory statue that is thought to represent Shawushka. She holds a battle-axe and wears a tall hat with curly horns of divinity, a cutaway coat and one upturned boot, and holds a Hittite battle-axe in her right hand.

Kubaba was the city-goddess of Carchemish on the eastern boundary of the Hittite empire. The foundation of the city dates back to at least the middle of the third millennium and it lasted well into neo-Hittite times in the first millennium BC. In the middle of the second millennium, Kubaba arrived in Anatolia via Carchemish and lived on in the Graeco-Phrygian Kybebe/Cybele. In Syria, Kubaba and Ishtar were fairly similar – Kubaba was associated with Ishtar's dove. Cybele is also originally double-sexed – there is a statue from Bogazkoy in which she is depicted as almost breastless, which is, as I mentioned in chapter one, one of the meanings of 'Amazon'.

The Victorian scholar A.H. Sayce thought that the Amazons were priestesses of these Asiatic goddesses whose cult spread from Carchemish along with the advance of the Hittite armies. She was served by a multitude of armed priestesses and eunuch priests: under the name of Ma, for instance, no less than 6,000 of them waited on her at Comana in Cappadocia. Certain cities, in fact, like Comana and Ephesus, were dedicated to her service, and a large part of the population accordingly became the armed ministers of the mighty goddess. Generally these were women, as at Ephesus in early days, where they obeyed a high priestess, who called herself the 'queen bee'. When Ephesus passed into Greek hands, the goddess worshipped there was identified with the Greek Artemis, and a high priest took the place of the high priestess.

> . . . we cannot explain the myth of the Amazons except on the supposition that they represented the armed priestesses of the Hittite goddess.[9]

And Adolf Holm in his *The History of Greece* embroiders on this theme: he thinks Amazons may be a 'poetical transformation of the priestesses of the goddess Ma at Cumana in Pontus, whose war dances gave rise to the stories of a nation of women practising warlike exercises'. However, Donald Sobol[10] points out that nowhere in the rites of Ma is there a record of armed priestesses, never mind the 6,000 who Sayce claimed waited upon the goddess at Cumana. Early scholars persuaded themselves that the relief on the King's Gate at Bogazkoy was a woman with a battle-axe, but it is now definitely proven to be a male warrior-god. Breasts emphasised on a statue do not mean it is female, just as lack of breasts doesn't necessarily signify maleness.

THE CYMBAL-CLASHING CORYBANTES

But it is worth lingering over the 'war-dances'. Callimachus, writing in the third century BC in his Hymn to Artemis, records that the Amazons, having set up an image of Artemis at Ephesus under an oak tree, performed dances around it: one a combat dance in armour, the other a circle dance – 'their feet clicked quickly, their quivers rattled'.[11] He may have been referring to dances from his own time that imitated and commemorated the original 'Amazon' ones. The people who performed the original dances would have been called 'Corybantes' as the ecstatic dancers of the Mother Goddess, Cybele. Cretan Rhea, who was close to Cybele in most of her aspects, had similar dancers called 'Curetes', and the two varieties of acolyte were often confused.

The Cretan legend was that Cybele's Phrygian Corybantes were summoned over to Crete to protect the newborn Zeus from his jealous father. They did the job by beating their shields with their swords so that the baby's cries were drowned, thus inspiring the Curetes to invent a noisy war-dance called the 'Pyrrhic' in honour of Rhea. Thus were the 'sons of the Great Mother' present at the birth of the 'Great Father', who was eventually to steal all her power. The Corybantes are also connected through Corybas, son of Jason and Demeter/Cybele, with the introduction of the worship of the Great Mother into Phrygia from Samothrace. And, most significantly, the shrine and sanctuary to the Mother at Samothrace was said to be founded by the Amazon queen, Myrina. Samothrace may turn out to be a key location in the search for the truth about the Amazons.

THE GODDESS OF SAMOTHRACE

Whilst Queen Myrina and her army were engaged in subduing some of the Aegean islands, she was caught in a terrible storm. She prayed to the Mother of the Gods to save her and her shipmates and her prayer was answered: she was washed up on an uninhabited island where she had a dream commanding her to make the island sacred to the goddess. She set up altars there, offered sacrifices, and named the island 'Samothrace', which means 'sacred island'. Later the myths say that the Mother of the Gods, well pleased with the island, settled her own sons, called 'Corybantes', there – who their father was is handed down as one of her mysteries celebrated on the island, not to be divulged to the uninitiated. The sacred area was declared a sanctuary.[12]

Samothrace is a rugged island set in the Aegean between the Greek mainland and Turkey (see Map 2), full of woods, waterfalls and towering mountains, little visited by tourists because of its lack of beaches and easy transportation, but with a strange, subtly powerful atmosphere, as if the island is holding its breath waiting for the mysteries to come back again. Samothrace was famous throughout the ancient world for its mysteries: a sequence of initiatory rites that offered candidates protection at sea, safety in danger and freedom from fear of death. People came from all over the Greek world and Asia Minor, and later from Rome, to participate in the ceremonies. They were mainly men, but the inscriptions on Samothrace do record some women – including two who donated buildings for the sanctuary. Alexander's mother, Olympias, was said to have been initiated here, which is intriguing since she is also associated with Dionysiac rites that included the carrying of a very large snake (see chapter two).

Samothrace was associated with two or maybe more male gods variously called Cabiri, Dioscuri or Corybantes, and with the Great Mother, who seems to have had attributes close to Cybele's. Together they were known as the 'Great Gods'. What their relationship was to each other we do not know. The Cabiri may have been, like the Corybantes, 'sons of the mother'. Nobody knows exactly what the rites were because initiates were sworn to secrecy, but archaeologists and classicists together have excavated what is left of the sanctuary, pieced together fragments of inscription and classical references to the place, and ended up with a jigsaw that so far does not quite fit, although it throws up some fascinating images.

Purity was very important in the rite; candidates had to tell the priests what was the worst thing they had ever done in their lives. After this there was some sort of ritual bathing (a drain has been found) to cleanse from sin, and then the neophytes were given a purple sash and a ring made of magnetised iron. The iron may have come from a lodestone on the island which was connected with power of the goddess. A demonstration of the powers of magnetism, for someone who did not know about the science of it, must have been very impressive magic. At some point there might be a wild, Corybantic dance with clashing cymbals and wailing flutes, both terrifying and awesome, and an epiphany of the mother, meaning that the goddess would become present in some form.

Susan Cole mentions three ithyphallic statues that were said to have stood in the shrine. Herodotus, himself an initiate of the Samothracian mysteries, said that the statues and the mysteries were of Pelasgian origin, the Pelasgians being one of the old, pre-Hellenic peoples. He said that a sacred story was told about them as part of the ritual, which suggests, according to Cole, that the mysteries were concerned with the meaning of sexual activity. Did the rites of Samothrace involve sexual intercourse with sacred hierodules, or was the sacred marriage shown symbolically? We do not know. It sounds as if these mysteries, like the Eleusinian ones, represent a kind of balance point in the evolution of religious practice, between the old goddess-worshipping rites and the new priest-run ways of the Classical Greeks and Christians, where the role of the female is reduced or sublimated.

Armed Corybantic dances are linked with the island by several authors. Nonnos, writing in the fifth century AD, reports that Kadmos, when he came to the island to be initiated, witnessed a dance of Corybantes in which they leapt about and beat oxhide shields with their spears to the tune of a double flute.

Strabo thought the Cabiri and the Corybantes were identical and defined them as 'a kind of inspired people ... subject to Bacchic frenzy ... inspiring terror at the celebration of the sacred rites by means of war dances, accompanied by uproar and noise and cymbals and drums and arms and also by flute and outcry.'[13] He thought that all the places where this sort of rite was performed, such as Samothrace and Lemnos, had something in common, presumably the worship of the goddess.

Wherever there was a centre of female power where the Great Goddess was recognised and embodied in an epiphany to the accompaniment of frenzied music from Corybantes, such as at Ephesus (examined in chapter three), or Samothrace, we find Amazon connections. At Lemnos too there were Corybantic rites in honour of the goddess Bendis who is described as a fierce huntress with two spears who receives human sacrifices, and it is here we find the Amazonian tale of the women who murdered their husbands.

The story goes that Jason and the Argonauts, along with Hercules, stopped at Lemnos on their way to find the Golden Fleece. They were greeted by a horde of armed women, ready to defend their island to the death. When a herald was sent ashore to explain that they came in peace, the women relented and Queen Hipsipyle explained that the women had been so ill-treated by their husbands that they had risen in arms against them and forced them to emigrate. In fact, about a year previously, the Lemnian men had gone on a sex-strike against their wives saying that they smelled obnoxious, and taken Thracian slave girls as concubines instead. The women had risen up and murdered every man on the island except Thoas, the king, whose daughter saved him by setting him adrift in an oarless boat.

Now the women, realising that their nation would die out unless they reproduced, invited Jason and his men to share their beds, and the men naturally agreed. Many children were begotten before Hercules strode into the capital city Myrina (named for the Amazon queen) and banged on all the house doors with his club, reminding the men of their task. They left, calling in at Samothrace on their way to be initiated into the mysteries.[14]

Robert Graves suggests that the story of the massacre of the men was a way for the patriarchal incomers to understand a gynocratic society supported by armed priestesses where men had no power. It could equally be that the Lemnian men had gone to war and all been slaughtered. The women's unpleasant odour, he suggests, may have come from working in woad, which was used by their Thracian neighbours for tattooing. Apparently woad has a nauseous and lingering smell. At any rate the tale seems a record of some sort of woman-only or woman-dominated society, although whether temporary or longer-lasting we cannot know.

There is one more intriguing pointer to what the secret rites of Samothrace may have been, from Lucian, writing in the second century AD:

> Attis was Lydian in origin, and was the first to teach the secret rites devoted to Rhea. The rites performed by the Phrygians, the Lydians and the Samothracians were all learned from Attis; for when Rhea castrated him, he left off the masculine form of life, took on a feminine appearance, put on women's garments and, travelling into every land, performed secret rites related to what he had suffered and sang the praises of Rhea.[15]

The Phrygians, Lydians and Samothracians were all known to practise the rites of the Great Mother and her son/consort. Cacophonous music and wild dance was usually involved: Cybele herself is often shown with musicians playing on flute and drum; she carries a tambourine or cymbal; and in Istanbul Museum you can see her female followers dancing – there are some marvellously abandoned and rhythmic figurines from Myrina in Lemnos. The orgiastic dancing might include the clashing of cymbals, banging of drums, shrieking and wailing and hollering, and, in some cases, self-mutilation amongst the men, in memory of Attis. Alternatively some of these dances may have been much more disciplined, as in the Pyrrhic dance of the Curetes in which they moved to and fro in measured time, nodding their crested helmets and striking their shields. It is easy to believe that anyone witnessing *women* dancing like this would be both impressed and terrified, and might well go home with stories of 'armed and ruthless women warriors'. But the Corybantes were normally presented as male. Could it be that they were sometimes self-castrated or eunuch men, wearing women's clothes? If this is the case, then they might well look very feminine. If such dances were experienced as part of a sacred rite or mystery initiation, the witness might well not be able to ask 'Were they men or women that I saw?' and would draw his own conclusions, sometimes thinking them men and sometimes women.

But war dances were definitely performed sometimes by real biological women. In Greece, from the fourth century BC onwards, professional dancing girls with helmets, shields and spears would execute so-called war-dances as solos, sometimes gracefully, sometimes as a burlesque, and sometimes 'with lewd gestures and motions'.[16] This was a degenerate form, in an increasingly patriarchal culture, of something that had once had real meaning and dignity, but it shows how deeply ingrained the idea had become of armed women performing dances that were both erotic and aggressive.

At the shrine of Artemis Limnatus in southern Greece votive tympana have been found, which suggests that some of the dances performed there by choruses of young girls were orgiastic (which does not mean that sexual intercourse was involved, simply that the votaries would become abandoned and possessed by the god or goddess). Lilian Lawler claims that the insistent beating of the tympanum was characteristic of such dances in order to induce the necessarily frenzied state. And in Sparta, women and girls would come to the shrine of Artemis and perform 'unrestrained ecstatic dances to the goddess, "wearing only one chiton"' – that is, scantily clad. At Ancyra in Asia Minor there were women's dances that were likened to Bacchic orgies, dedicated not only to Artemis but also to Athene. Pausanias mentions the early worship of Artemis in Elis being celebrated with a lewd dance of remote antiquity called the kordax, which later formed part of the Old Comedy performances at Athens.[17]

It is curious that two of the elements for which the Amazons were famous – war-like behaviour and unrestrained sexuality – are expressed in these dances, and they were clearly very widespread in Archaic Greece, and presumably also in the Dark and Bronze Ages. The thread to hold on to here is the idea of *war-dances performed by priestesses* (or by castrated male acolytes) *in honour of the Great Mother Goddess*. Undoubtedly these dances, in their early, undegenerate form, would have had a religious purpose; to raise a certain kind of energy that would then shift the level of consciousness of those present. These war-dances were sacred dances. If we follow the thread of sacred dance into the heart of Anatolia we may find other clues to the identity of the Amazons.

THE WANDERING DERVISHES

We know that in some phases of Cybele's cult, dances were performed as part of orgiastic rites in which her male devotees castrated themselves, but were there *other* forms of dance sacred to the goddess? We should consider that there may have been more to this dancing than clattering cymbals and shouting and getting in a frenzy. After all, Callimachus mentions that the Amazons of old did two forms of dance – an armed war-dance and a circle dance. At Samothrace there is a charming frieze dating from the fourth century BC of maidens dancing along hand in hand, and one of the ancient Hittite texts mentions a form of dancing that was done at the Kilam festival, which can be translated as 'turning' or 'whirling'.

Whirling has its home in Konya on the central Anatolian plain. It is now firmly associated with the Mevlevi dervishes, for whom it is a sort of physical prayer, a reaching out for union with the divine. It was supposedly 'invented' by the great saint, poet and mystic Jalaluddin Rumi in the thirteenth century, but of course every small child whirls naturally just for the fun of it, so it is more likely that the saint 'rediscovered it' when he was himself recovering from the loss of his friend and master, Shams-i-Tabriz, and was by all accounts gripped in a frenzy of grief. Today dervish dancers wear a tall felt fez and white dress with a full skirt that floats outwards as they whirl. Some people have suggested that the dervish tradition was started by the *galli*, the wandering followers of the Mother, who switched their allegiance to Islam when it appeared in the sixth century AD. But it actually seems that there are now two separate categories of dervish, in Persia anyway – the Islamic ones who are very devout religious men, and the independent ones who are tramps and wanderers. Intriguingly this second category sometimes wear the double-axe as a symbol, which has been associated with the religion of the Great Mother from Minoan Crete onwards.

I learned to whirl like a dervish in a dusty church hall in Chorlton-cum-Hardy, Manchester. I was taught by a man who'd been taught by another man who was a real dervish from Konya. The principle is simple: you stick your arms out to balance you and spin on the spot, using one leg as a pivot point and the other to push you round.

Once you get over feeling sick, which happens surprisingly quickly, it is a wonderful sensation – the silence of meditation combined with the exhilaration of flying – and afterwards you feel an intense warmth towards others. It is not like anything I have done before or since – a completely unique experience.

I decided to go and see it for real. We crossed the Anatolian plain in a blizzard at 15 miles per hour in an eerie snow-muffled silence in a bus full of heavy smokers. Arriving late in Konya, we were ushered right to the front in the sports stadium where the public performance is held. Tired and tense after hours on the icy road, we were dazzled by the dervish dancers, whirling like snowflakes in their white full-skirted robes, the tall tombstone hats on their heads, their faces rapt with devotion. This was part of a week-long festival held every December to celebrate the death of Jalaluddin Rumi, who lived in Konya and is loved by the Turkish people with an intensity we save for football and Princess Diana.

This was good but we knew there was more, that the 'real thing' would be happening elsewhere, in private. So we started to ask around, were passed from carpet shop to carpet shop, drank much sweet tea, ate *pide* (Turkish pizza) and finally were introduced to an unassuming man in a raincoat who shook our hands and invited us to attend the private ceremony at his house to mark the last day of the festival.

I sat at the back in my headscarf with the women. My husband was allowed to sit at the front with the men. We seemed to be the only Westerners there. While they chant the dervishes egg each other on, jerking their right arms into their chests as they sound the holy names of God, turning their heads from side to side, pumping up the rhythm to fever pitch. This is the *zikr*. Accompanying the chanting is heart-breakingly poignant singing from a blind man and the sound of the *ney* (an intense wavering sort of flute made from reeds) and drums. It is exciting and frightening to watch, the energy absolutely unrestrained. One boy of about fourteen sobs quietly throughout. Every so often a man or boy dressed in white with the tall hat rammed down on his head steps forward and begins to whirl, right hand cupped towards heaven, left pointing down towards the earth, skirt floating outwards like a lily flower. There's a tall man, calm and ethereal, then a red-haired boy who spins with complete abandon, holding nothing back. He whizzes on the spot like a Catherine wheel, often teetering on the brink of tumbling. When he stops his eyes are full of the light of paradise. It's terrifying and awesome. This is the burning mystical heart of Islam, as far away from rigid fundamentalism as you can get.

The *sema* done in private is a far more primitive spectacle than anything you will see done for a festival or a concert in the West, and many scholars feel it must have a pre-Islamic origin. Having seen it, I would agree. By three in the morning, I was finding the whole experience disturbing: it was stirring me up at a level too deep for comfort. I became aware of how powerful the effect of this kind of dancing can be. There is no doubt in my mind that if anyone had asked the young red-haired boy to castrate himself for the glory of God, he would have done it. The physical and emotional energy raised was uncomfortable for me, a Western woman used to the sublimation of such instinctive forces: I could see that in itself it was neither good nor bad, but could turn either way – into self-mutilation and violence on the one hand or into a glorious affirmation of divine power on the other.

Did the votaries of Kubaba at Carchemish or Cybele/Artemis at Ephesus perform something like the *zikr* and the whirling? In an intriguing little book called *Land of the Blue Veil* published in 1950, Allan Worsley, a doctor who worked in the Sudan for many years, tells the story of a special dance ceremony he was invited to attend. He had attended Sufi *zikrs* in the 'dervish city' in which he practised, but this was a secret dance, performed by women of easy virtue, which he would not normally have been allowed to see had he not been taken by a young *fille de joie* (his own euphemistic and non-judgemental words) whose life had been saved by his medical intervention. He describes how the dancing girls put on the end of their bootlace plaits a 'dollop of gum mixed with fat, the size of a walnut' which was to play an important role in the dance:

As she danced she made a curious sucking noise, something like that you make when you call an animal, or like the twitter of sparrows. Her naked breasts were arched forward by the throw-back of her head. As she slowly drew nearer to me, the chorus worked itself up into a crescendo of feeling. Higher and higher the tension grew until she was just about a foot away from me.

She now moved round me in a half circle, for all the world like some savage beast that hypnotises its victim before it strikes. Her hips began working in sinuous snake-like movements from side to side, yet round in circles at the same time.

The music, which had reached, as it were, a climax, now broke off into a shrill lu-lu-ing, in which all present joined: the joy-cry of zagharet, of Sudanese women, like the long sustained note of a prima donna. As the girl drew nearer and nearer, the movements of her hips intensified. Then suddenly, without warning, the music stopped dead, and at the same time she swung her head around sideways and forward, so that I received the full weight of her fat-ended curls in my face!

'That was a great honour, genaabak!' Zehnab whispered. 'She gave you the shebbaal.'

From the description it sounds as if this dance, obviously erotic, was in imitation of a snake, enchanting and then striking its victim, so that the dance enacts both orgasm and death in the same stroke. It is surely the kind of dance that the temple hierodules of Ishtar might have performed to prepare the men who had come to be initi-ated and remind them that orgasm is a 'little death'. It also sounds as if the dance had similarities with the Egyptian Raqs Sharqi, which also uses sinuous hip movements. The writer viewed it, understandably given the time and his gender, as a degenerate form of the *zikr*, but of course it may have actually been an *earlier* form of it. The woman performing the dance became the snake, and thus the embodiment of that raw Medusa-like sexuality that is so terrify-ing to men.

One of the meanings of 'Amazon' is 'moon-women' (in Armenian) and the Amazons in their 'moon-women' incarnation are not so much fighters as priestesses of Cybele, who was a moon-goddess. Esther Harding makes the point that the first forms of the moon deities were often animals – and later the goddess herself would be associated with that animal – Artemis with bears, Cybele with lions, Isis with the cow. The deepest level of female instinct was considered to have animal power: the ruthlessness of the lion, the fierce protec-tiveness of the bear, the maternal generosity of the cow. Of course as human females evolved, this primitive layer has been covered up, but it is still there ready to emerge if the occasion allows it. Watch the ferocity of a mother defending her child from harm, see the ruthlessness of women in business and politics – they are often harder than men.

The Greeks wanted to disguise and smother this level of elemental female power, but it cannot be smothered and so was incarnated in the tales of the Amazons and the Gorgons, who embodied sexual desire, violence and passion in a way that no domesticated Greek women would be allowed to do.

Cybele is often shown sitting between lions or riding in a chariot pulled by lions, Ishtar/Shawushka is often seen standing on a lion, and Artemis is connected with various wild animals. The lion or leopard is consistently found with goddess figures in Anatolia from the seventh millennium BC onwards. This association of the female with the savage feline force of these animals lasts right through to the Amazons who are sometimes depicted on Greek black-figure vases wearing lion-pelts and the Scythian woman warriors buried with lions' claws. To track down the significance of this link between the female and large felines we must visit the place where the earliest example in Anatolia was found, Çatal Hüyük.

THE GODDESS OF ÇATAL HÜYÜK

The low mounds of Çatal Hüyük stand in the Anatolian plain, swept by bitter winds in winter, broiled by searing heat in the summer. They are near the confluence of two rivers, within sight of the mountains from where the obsidian used for weapons and tools was brought. Here from 6800 BC (and possibly well before) up until 5700 BC, lived a sophisticated and stable community – a 'town' of 5,000 souls or more. These were people living on the threshold of the agricultural revolution, they may have already domesticated cattle and were beginning to grow various different sorts of plants for food.

They were skilled in the arts of making and modelling, created beautiful wall paintings, stone and clay figurines and elegant tools.

I visited Çatal Hüyük in midwinter when an icy wind blew over the plains. It was too cold to think, but not to sense that this was a place that had been inhabited for two millennia, albeit 8,000 years ago! As you walk around you can see the ghostly outline on the excavated rocks of the walls and floors of the little houses built right up against each other on the hillside and everywhere under your feet you find shards of pottery, slivers of obsidian, stones with holes in them which could have been goddess-idols. It is uncanny to pick up a fragment of brown-glazed jug handle and think that the last person who touched it did so 7,000 years ago or more.

When James Mellaart first excavated Çatal Hüyük in the 1960s he was amazed to find that over 50 per cent of the houses there appeared to be 'shrines' – that is, they were decorated with wall paintings and reliefs, bull's heads covered with plaster, and a large splayed-out figure that he interpreted as a mother-goddess giving birth. He believed he had stumbled across a 'priests' quarter' where the people specialising in religious rituals had lived, but later investigators, such as Ian Hodder, argue that we are talking here about a society in which the religious and the mundane were not tidily separated as they tend to be in urbanised settings today. The numinous world of the divine with its titanic forces and the everyday world of human endeavours may have merged with each other in a way that we find hard to grasp, so well insulated are we now from the basic acts required to obtain a living from the earth.

The site of Çatal Hüyük, in a marshy basin near the place where two rivers meet, made it a very suitable place for herding cattle, which may well be why it was chosen in the first place, but gave it another quality less positive – it was a breeding ground for mosquitoes. In 41 per cent of the skulls found at Çatal Hüyük there are traces of overgrowth in the spongy marrow space of the skull which is caused by falciparum malaria. Malaria, of course, produces fever and hallucinations, which would have eroded the barriers between the real and the imaginary, between the human and the divine realms, still further. In other words, it might produce a community particularly prone to mystical and religious experience.

Certainly my first encounter with those strange bull's-head-lined shrine rooms (in the Ankara Museum) produced an eerie sense of stepping into another realm, a powerhouse of dark Underworld energy barely contained by four walls. The people of Çatal Hüyük would have spent much of their daily life in contact with cattle, hunting or herding, minding, slaughtering, milking, breeding them, and then they brought these bull's skulls into their houses, covered them with plaster and stuck them on the walls. They also set other breast-shaped protuberances into their walls, embedding in them the skulls of boars or griffon-vultures, in the latter case so that the beak appears where the nipple should be. The same birds would be responsible for tearing the flesh off corpses laid out after death, after which the remaining bones were buried in the houses under the sleeping platforms. Unlike us, they did not feel the need to separate rigidly life and death, the animal and the human realms, the tame and the wild – they allowed the polarities to interpenetrate each other's realms in a way that feels very uncomfortable to the modern psyche.

THE MATRIARCH OF ÇATAL HÜYÜK

Several of the figurines from Çatal Hüyük show women with large felines. In particular there is the famous fat woman with large drooping breasts and enormous podgy legs seated with her hands on leopards at either side, her feet on skulls, possibly giving birth, who was found in a grain bin. When I saw her in the Ankara Museum they were preparing a special Çatal Hüyük exhibition and everything was in disarray. She sat in a glass case in a roped-off area. I climbed over the rope and edged towards her, hoping the builders would not notice. They did, but with typical Turkish courtesy chose to look the other way. I was immediately struck by how life-like the sculpture is: if someone at a sculpture class made it she or he would be much praised for their naturalism. There is nothing stylised or iconic about it. It seemed to me that this must be a model of a real woman, an older woman whose childbearing days were nearly over, thence her flaccid breasts and belly.

In the Rumi mausoleum in Konya, 50 kilometres from Çatal Hüyük, I saw her 'twin', a live twentieth-century peasant woman in oriental trousers, about 4 feet 10 inches tall with vast pendulous breasts and an enormous half-moon stomach. At her back her buttocks made a great shelf upon which her grand-daughter sat, snugly tied on. A daughter fast approaching her shape stood beside her. They emanated a fierceness and pride that made me careful not to bump into them. We women of Western Europe have utterly lost that sort of earthy female power and replaced it with an androgynous lightness of being.

Later, as I turned the image of the leopard-lady around in my mind, I wondered if she might be the matriarch of Çatal Hüyük, the 'priestess-queen' who watches over the great family of the tribe and protects them. She is a wonderfully solid, strong figure; I could imagine her presiding over the games or rituals of the people, awarding prizes, sentencing the guilty to punishment, embodying the connection of the female with powers of life and death, being the gateway both into and out of life. The strange flattened, open-legged wall-relief figure that Mellaart believed was the earth-goddess giving birth does not look much like a woman in labour, but it *does* look like the mantel of a gateway. For a parallel experience, stand behind the two 'birthing' stones at the Stones of Stenness in Orkney and look towards the hills of Hoy. The sensation that you are standing at a gateway facing into the body of the goddess, up towards her breasts, is very strong.

The fact that the leopard-woman has the sagging breasts and belly of an older woman who has borne many children supports the idea that older women were seen as the repositories of religious power in Çatal Hüyük. Her head has been reconstructed so we do not know what her expression was, but the modern reconstructor, after considering other similar models, has given her the impervious face and closed eyes of a person in a trance. Perhaps in her trance she merged herself with her leopards and skittered over the earth, sniffing the air to know where the wild bulls were feeding, where the hunters should make for on their next expedition. Or she may have been an oracle, communing with the gods and *devas* of the natural world to find knowledge essential to the survival of her people. Certainly she looks as if she was able to merge with the power of the wild, the power of the dragon, know it and speak for it. At Çatal Hüyük, in this community of people more mystical than most perhaps because half of them had malarial fevers from time to time, one could guess that *merging* was a most valued mode of being. But separation is necessary for development, as all good parents know; and the time would come when man would need to break away ruthlessly from the all-encompassing body of the Mother Goddess and strike out on his own.

THE LEOPARD-LADY AND THE AMAZONS

So what happens between the Neolithic Age in which the massive, motherly leopard-lady lives, and the Bronze Age, in which the Amazons and their legends are born? When man stops being primarily a hunter and takes up agriculture, his communion with the animals fades. Once he has tamed the animals he can afford to lose his empathy with them. He separates himself from them just as he separates himself from the Great Mother. He turns her into a dragon to be subdued or slaughtered; or he finds other ways of making her into the 'enemy'. The Amazons are a form of 'the enemy'. Hercules, the archetypal male hero, finishes subduing the animal monsters, including the lion, and then sets about subduing the Amazons, unnatural monsters in human form. The Amazons resist; they fight back bravely on behalf of the Great Mother and the leopard-women, but we know that they are going to lose. By the time the Bronze Age is over, this revolution in consciousness is accomplished and the stories of the Amazons are all that remain to remind us of the old order, of another kind of female power.

CHAPTER SEVEN

The Ghost-dancers

....

There was something about the way Morocco moved that I found completely entrancing. She was not beautiful, or young, and her body was well covered with easy-going flesh. She wore spectacles like those of my school scripture teacher, and her hair was caught back any old how. But when she swayed her hips in that sashaying way, when she shimmied her breasts so that they wobbled under her slightly tarty gown, and when she flashed us that candid self-enjoying smile, the whole roomful of northern ladies in their belly-dancing finery would have shimmied their way to hell with her.

I had come to the two-day oriental dance workshop near my parents' home in Macclesfield to find out about the Berbers from a woman who called herself Morocco (her real name is Caroline Varga Dinicu), having encountered her intriguing comments about them on the Internet along with sweeping claims from other sites about the connection between the Libyan Amazons and the Berbers and Tuaregs of North Africa. Morocco had been back and forth visiting them and dancing with them for thirty years. She seemed like the kind of 'authority' who might be able to tell me what I needed to know.

There were about forty women in that northern gym, women of every age and shape and size – a genial girl with boat-like hips sailing forth in an enormous pleated sparkly skirt, tough Scousers with firm fiftyish bodies in leotard tops, serious young women who worked in banks and universities by day and transformed themselves into sirens by night, bare-bellied, snake-hips snugly clasped by scarves and spangled belts, eyes kohled and ears heavily laden with jangling jewellery. I, in my faded black skirt and scruffy tie-dyed teeshirt, with an old scarf tied round my hips, looked drab and out of place, every inch the detached and embarrassed researcher.

But that was not really so. Years before, in Manchester, I too had learned oriental dance. I had snaked my hips and slammed my feet, flashed my eyes and awoken the serpent sexuality in my rather rigid television director's frame. So that now, ten years on, my body did not find it too hard to respond to the Middle Eastern rhythms blaring out of the PA system from Morocco's tapes. As we repeated hip-drops and figure-of-eights for the fifth time, the old elation began to rise in me: this was the secret that we always forget, that women have the power, we have it inside us *anyway*, whereas men have to strive like mad to get it or else steal it from us!

Oriental dancing, belly-dancing as it is sometimes called, against the will of its serious practitioners, is very, very old. Put simply, it is a dance in which women can enjoy and flaunt their sexuality. You can shimmy your bottom, your hips or your breasts, or any other part of your body that moves; you can swirl your hips round in snakey circles or figures-of-eight; you can stomp around looking haughty and untouchable, you can sway entreatingly, whirl lightheartedly. Men think it is for them, that the dance is put on for them to ogle, but most women do it for themselves – though of course being admired and desired may well contribute to feeling good. To see it danced in a Turkish restaurant on the Bosphorus shore, at an Eccles wedding, in a party atmosphere anywhere, is to taste the delicious froth of erotic excitement without having to drink it to its sometimes bitter dregs. Men can do it too after a fashion, though they will be more subtle though not less sexy than women, if they know how to use their eyes as well as their shoulders and hips. It is danced all over the Arab and the Muslim world in many different forms, but with the same underlying movements. Some say it was originally an initiatory dance for girls about to be married to teach them how to give and get pleasure from the sexual act.

Of course we often see it in the West in a pitiful degraded form, danced by women who do not really know how to move their bodies beautifully, but can only bump and grind. But then, it is generally

agreed that we in the West have never really known about the mysteries of sexual magic such as the Hindu and Buddhist Tantrics teach.
And yet every women can be a *shakti*, whether she lives in Rochdale,
Cairo or Bangalore. It's just a question of letting the snake into the
body . . .

THE AFRICAN AMAZONS

The only full account of the African Amazons is given by Diodorus of
Sicily, writing in the first century BC.[1] It is a coherent and detailed
picture of a war-like matriarchal tribe who lived, he states, many
generations before the Amazons of Themiscyra who were active until
the time of the Trojan war.

He claims that there were several races of women in North Africa
at that time who were 'warlike and greatly admired for their manly
vigour', including the Gorgons. But the customs of the particular
race of Amazons that Diodorus focuses on were that women should
be trained in the arts of war and required to serve in the army for a
fixed period, during which time they must remain virgins. After that
they would get together with men and have children, but live in a
society where the normal gender roles were completely reversed: the
women would deal with government and affairs of state whilst the
men would look after the children and housework, and in general do
what they were told by the women. When girls were born their
breasts would be seared off so that they would not be a hindrance in
warfare, which is why they were called Amazons – 'breastless'.

This tribe lived on an island called Hespera ('westwards') in the
marsh Tritonis, which is said to be near Ethiopia and the mountain
called by the Greeks 'Atlas'. They lived on milk and meat from their
herds because they had not yet learnt to grow grain.

The war-like Amazons subdued all the cities in their neighbour-
hood, founded their own city called Cherronesus (Peninsula) and
then, hungry for conquest, set out to conquer the Atlantians, a

prosperous and civilised people in whose land it is said the gods were born. Myrina, the Amazon queen, collected together an army of 30,000 foot soldiers and 3,000 cavalry who went to war protected by the skins of giant snakes, using as weapons swords and lances and bows and arrows, which they could shoot not only facing forwards but facing backwards too. They put the men of the Atlantian capital city to the sword before the rest of the inhabitants surrendered. Then Myrina behaved honourably, rebuilt the city, and helped the people in their struggle against the Gorgons.

The Amazons were near victory when one night some captive Gorgon women escaped and launched a surprise attack. They very nearly turned the tide and slaughtered many Amazons before they were butchered one and all themselves. Later, of course, when the Gorgons had recovered their strength and Medusa was their queen, Perseus subdued them finally.

Myrina then led her army in both Syria and Anatolia, reaching as far as the Mediterranean Sea, and founding many cities there including Cyme, Pitana and Priene. She seized the island of Lesbos and founded the city of Mitylene, calling it after her sister. Her last act was to found the sacred sanctuary of the Mother of the Gods at Samothrace (see chapter six). Eventually Myrina and her armies were defeated by an alliance of Thracians and Scythians, she was slain, and the remnants of her troops withdrew to North Africa.

Here Diodorus is quoting from another writer, Dionysius the 'Skytobrachian' ('leather-armed'), who composed a mythical romance about Amazons, Argonauts and so on, so there is no reason to take his account in any sense as historical. But it may yet contain useful clues about the origins of the Amazons and their myths.

First, the location of their African homeland is said to be in western Libya near the Atlas Mountain. 'Libya' referred to the vast vague area to the west of Egypt, and so far no one has traced anything that could be 'Lake Tritonis' but, if the Atlas Mountain is to be linked with what we now call the Atlas Mountains, we could place these ancient

Amazons in present-day Algeria near its border with Morocco. Diodorus reports that they are pastoralists who grow no grain, which suggests they would have been a nomadic or semi-nomadic people. The period referred to would be the Neolithic or very early Bronze Age. There is no archaeological evidence for women-dominated tribes in that area at that time, but once history begins to be written by Herodotus in the fifty century BC there are some intriguing, though by no means reliable, anecdotes about the area.

In one Libyan tribe, the Nasamones:

> It is the custom for each man to have a number of wives, but as in the case of the Massagetae, any woman is available to any man for sex; a staff set up in front of a house indicates that sexual intercourse is taking place inside. When a Nasamonian man gets married, first it is the custom for the bride to have sex with all the guests one after another on her wedding night; every man she has sex with gives her something he has brought with him from his house as a gift.[2]

Another tribe, the Gindanes, has women who tie on anklets for each man they sleep with, and the woman with the most anklets has the most prestige because she has had the most lovers.

Both these stories refer to a kind of sexual promiscuity that is usually associated with matriarchal customs in which the identity of the father of a child is not considered to be important and men do not 'own' women. But to Herodotus this is just uncivilised behaviour – 'their sex life is just like that of herd animals' – and indeed it is not in itself the kind of custom that denotes a society where women have power. But it does link up with the Amazons who practise promiscuous sex once a year in order to get children.

Even more intriguing is Herodotus' account of the ritual battles of the Ausees tribe, said to live around Lake Tritonis. They:

celebrate a festival to Athena once a year at which the unmarried young women of the tribe divide into two groups and fight each other with sticks and stones; the women say that any women who died of their wounds were not true virgins. Before they let them fight, they join together and dress up the prettiest of the current generation of young women at public expense in a Corinthian helmet and a set of Greek armour, mount her on a chariot and take her round the lake. . . . The Ausees claim that Athena is the daughter of Poseidon and Lake Tritonis, but that she got angry for some reason with her father and put herself into Zeus's hands, and he made her his daughter. That is their story anyway. They have intercourse with women promiscuously.[3]

Furthermore, Herodotus argues that the Greeks derive the aegis (shield) that is carried by Athena's statue from the clothes worn by Libyan women (see also chapter four). They wear 'tasselled goatskins, de-fleeced and dyed with madder, as their outer clothes' with thongs rather than snakes as the tassels on the edge. They have simply changed the name *aigeai* or goatskins to 'aegis'. He adds: 'I also think that the *ololuge* or cry of praise emitted during the worship of Athene started in Libya, because it is often employed by Libyan women who do it extremely well.' This is the 'joy cry' mentioned by Allan Worsley in his description of the Sudanese women's dance in chapter six, and the ululation still practised all over the Near and Middle East and North Africa by women who are either dancing or watching some sort of spectacle, to show their enjoyment and approval.

Herodotus loves to describe bizarre customs, particularly any that reverse the Grecian norms, and we cannot take any of it as objective truth; but the idea of the girls fighting in honour of their goddess is a suggestive one in relation to the Amazon myths because it could point to the kind of root practice out of which women's armed dances, such as those performed at Ephesus, might have come. If the best of the fighting girls formed a virgin priesthood serving the warrior-goddess, we would have a very promising source for the Amazons. Various feminist authors, following Plato, have suggested that Athene was a form of the goddess Neith, whose symbol was two crossed bows (see chapter four).

The idea in Diodorus' writings that the Amazon army swept through Anatolia to the Mediterranean and proceeded to found various cities, especially on the island of Samothrace, is probably a *post hoc* explanation for the strength of the goddess-worshipping practices still extant in Diodorus' time. The Corybantes were of course the dancing acolytes of the Great Mother, Cybele. This is the area where Cretan religious ideas had been sown most strongly and may have lingered longest.

MOROCCO'S JOURNEY

Morocco is an American woman proud to call herself an ethnic gypsy, though not at all pleased to go along with all the expectations that such a label may excite. She was struggling to make ends meet as a flamenco dancer when she went along to a belly-dancing audition by mistake and got hired because the resident dancer looked like 'a cross between Richard Nixon and a Christmas tree'. She fell in love with the Middle Eastern music and learned how to do the dance properly from the restaurant's clientele, coming as they did from the Arab and Turkic regions of the world. Morocco reeled off a list of the nationalities of her informal teachers (mainly grannies – she followed them into the Ladies and asked, 'Could you show me what you just did?') while she got into a see-through cobwebby dress for the afternoon's dancing: 'Egyptians, Algerians, Libyans, Moroccans, Tunisians, Lebanese, Syrians, Jordanians, Albanians, Turks, Greeks and Armenians,' she said. Strange, I said, it sounds just like a list of all the countries associated with the Amazons and lost female power.

In 1964 Morocco saw a Moroccan dance troupe perform in New York and was entranced. There is something about this dancing that reminds women of how they used to feel about their bodies before self-consciousness and comparisons with Kate Moss set in. She borrowed the air fare from her mother and set off in search of their teacher, B'shara. By plane to Casablanca, train to Marrakesh, then bus, jeep and, when that broke down, donkey to get to Guelmin. Finally there, she was walking across the square when she saw a young woman coming towards her. As they drew closer she had the strangest feeling that she was looking into a mirror: the girl coming towards her was her spitting image, with a skin tint perhaps two shades darker than her own. She pulled out a mirror and they both looked into it and laughed. The girl took her straight to her aunt's house – and it turned out that her aunt was B'shara of Guelmin, the teacher that Morocco had come to meet. B'shara welcomed her as a long-lost niece who had found her way home, she stayed a month, and was to return many times to learn about the Tuareg's dances from this extraordinary woman who was in fact the Guedra dancer to King Hassan of Morocco until her death from cancer in 1992. Guedra is a ceremonial blessing dance performed mainly by women.

The Tuareg are a nomadic people who inhabit the Sahara and Sahel regions of North Africa: you will find them in Morocco, Algeria, Libya, Niger and Mali. The word for a Tuareg of the noble class is 'Imajeghan', which an imaginative web-page weaver[4] claims is close to 'Amazon' and suggests they may be the descendants of the African warrior women whose story Diodorus told. The women go unveiled while the men always cover their mouth and nose in public with the end of their *tagelmouss*, a cross between a turban and veil. According to Morocco, the Tuareg have been a largely matriarchal people until very recently. The women own the tents, which means that they can decide where to live and close to whom. They usually also hold the keys to the boxes that contain the family's goods. She says that there is a complete acceptance, unusual in Muslim countries, that both men and women can take as many lovers as they like before marriage, and a sexually experienced woman is admired and has high status. There is an uncanny resonance here of Herodotus' comments about the Libyan women of the fifth century BC who wear anklets to show off how many lovers they have had. It is fine for women to be assertive, show off their strength in informal wrestling matches, and to choose a man. Marriages, because agreed on by both sides, tend to last and to be strong. Women continue to have platonic friendships with men. One Tuareg proverb says: 'Men and women towards each other are for the eyes and the heart, and not only for the bed.'

Lloyd Cabot Briggs, writing in 1960,[5] confirms much of what Morocco says and gives a vivid example of the sexual freedom the women enjoy: every so often the Tuareg of the Ahaggar Desert celebrate an *ahal*, a sort of courtship festival. Romantic music is provided by a noble lady *imzad* player (an *imzad* is a single-stringed violin) and male or female singers, and there is much badinage and entertainment before the official part of the evening ends and the women wander off, each followed by two or three admirers. Each little group settles down in a secluded spot and the girl talks and jokes with the young men who each take it in turns to whisper in her ear and transmit mute messages by writing on her palm. There are different signs for 'I want to be alone with you' and responses such as 'I love another' and 'Leave with the others but return alone'. When finally the girl is alone with the man of her choice they kiss, breathe up each other's noses nostril-to-nostril, and go as far as the girl wishes sexually. Briggs comments that women are held in such high respect that the girls are in no danger of being raped or abused, or of being forced to go further than they want to.

This is the culture of the 'blue people' who like to colour their clothes with indigo – the deeper the colour, the richer the person. They pound the indigo powder into the cloth with a stone (rather than dyeing it) so that it will rub off on their bodies and protect their skin from drying out. The men take care to use their *tagelmousses* to cover all the orifices on their faces, particularly in the company of strangers. They believe that evil spirits can enter the body through these openings. Women, according to Morocco, are protected by their magical ability to create life. Briggs favours a more down-to-earth explanation: the men are out in the saddle in hot dusty weather and need to protect their faces and throats with their veils. Whatever the reason, it is the kind of gender 'reversal' that would have pleased Herodotus!

Briggs says that the Tuareg bride retains full title to all her personal property after marriage, whilst her husband pays all the family expenses. But he claims that women cannot hold office or exercise much power outside the home: the tribal leaders are men, although chieftainship is passed through the female line, passing from an incumbent to his eldest sister's eldest son. A child of Tuareg parents inherits rank and privilege through the mother who retains her status even if she marries 'down', and yet a child will be known as 'the child of X', 'X' being the father's name. However, Francis Rodd, writing thirty years earlier in 1926, believed that the women did have a share in public life, but expressed it in a different manner to the men: 'They do not seek election to tribal councils. They enter them as by right and not in competition, but not even then do they order men about. Their function is to counsel and to charm. They make poetry and have their own way.'[6]

Rodd commented that the women of the 'people of the veil', as they called themselves, were 'respected by their men in a manner which has no parallel in my experience'. He tells with admiration of an example of the women's extreme bravery: 'in one engagement in Air the Kel Fade women led their men into battle, covering them with their own bodies and those of their children to prevent the French firing'.

Until recently, the Tuareg class structure was still fairly rigid – there being three levels: 'noble', 'vassal' and 'slave', the last being mainly Negro people. Tuareg men took slaves as concubines because they are 'less capricious and overbearing' than Tuareg women and 'because they have cool skins'. The advantage of the slave system for the women of noble class was that they were not overburdened with physical labour and could take time to educate the children, telling folk-tales containing tribal lore and teaching them the Tuareg alphabet which belongs to an ancient writing system called *tifinagh*. The Tuareg have a rich inheritance of poetry and song, which has been passed on mainly by the women of the tribe.

Briggs comments with some insight on the common assertion that Tuareg women of the Ahaggar, young or middle-aged, single or married, 'lend themselves freely to male guests'. He claims that this is a myth that has grown out of a misunderstanding about the women's sexual freedom before marriage. In fact, he believes that most premarital sex happens at the special gatherings such as the *ahal*, which exist to help young people get to know each other and find partners. Again there is a resonance with Herodotus, who regales us with the information that 'when a Nasamonian man gets married, first it is the custom for the bride to have sex with all the guests one after another on her wedding night; every man she has sex with gives her something he has brought with him from his house as a gift'.[7] If we look at this as a patriarchal custom imposed on women by men, it seems abusive to the women, but if we regard it as a matriarchal custom, designed to give young women a store of useful presents, then it takes on quite a different, rather light-hearted and festive quality!

It would be far-fetched to suggest that the Tuareg really are the direct ancestors of those Iron Age Libyans with their strange sexual customs which may point to truly matriarchal societies back in the Bronze Age, but information from both groups is useful in building up a picture of what a pre-patriarchal, matripotestal society may have been like. Once we get rid of any tendency to romanticise the 'matriarchal' past we can begin to get a sense of some very different patterns of sexual behaviour. The Amazon myths may have been the Greek way of trying to make sense of these old customs; they tended to associate, just as we do, political power with religious power and respect. But the Tuareg show that women can be deeply respected, given wide personal freedoms, and yet excluded from political power. And indeed we might wonder what real 'power' a modern woman has whose life is so devoured by her job, her childcare duties and her obligations as a wife that she has no 'time for herself' to sit and talk in the tent as the Tuareg women do.

But, Morocco says, the Tuareg 'matriarchy' is nearly gone. A twenty-year drought and bitter civil wars have forced nearly all the Tuareg to leave their tents which were owned by the women and live permanently in cities where the men own the houses. Then, as Morocco says in her New York drawl, 'the men take on the rooster characteristics of patriarchy'. Although the women are still respected, the influence of Islam has upset the balance: the anthropologist Susan Rasmussen, who has worked with the Tuareg of Aïr in Niger, recently reports that now 'the men say that "women tell lies and children's tales" while men tell history . . . women's possession songs are "not science" while the men's *ezzeker* songs praising God are derived from Sufism and are thus identified with the "science of the Koran"'. The Kel Ewey Tuareg of both sexes told her that women are afraid to touch the Koran and that menstruating women are not allowed to touch Islamic amulets. However, at the unofficial name-day ritual, the women give the child a name that is different from the one given by the father and *marabout* at the mosque the following day.[8]

The female power lives on as a ghost in some of the dances, like the Guedra, which is a blessing dance done principally by women. 'Guedra means "cauldron",' Morocco explained, 'a valuable thing for nomadic people who can only carry with them the most important things. It also means "drum" when it gets an animal skin stretched across it to play the heartbeat rhythm which is the basic rhythm of the dance. And Guedra is also what the woman who performs the dance is called – as long as she is doing it on her knees. When she stands up it is called something else.'

Morocco was careful to explain that this is essentially a woman's dance, although a man or a child may sometimes perform it with her. It usually happens at night and the whole point of it is to draw up peace and blessings from the earth and channel them out to the people present – and those not physically present too. The Guedra dancer wears a traditional women's garment called a haik, which is formed from one very long piece of material held in place at the front by two fibula pins of ancient design, and she starts the dance with her head covered. As she dances she flicks out blessings from head, heart and liver (the Tuareg believe the heart is fickle and that the deepest feelings come from the liver), gradually uncovering her head and passing into a rhythmic trance. It is a simple dance in which sincerity is all, accompanied by simple heartbeat rhythm and chanting, but it can last for hours, well into the night.

Morocco performed the dance that Sunday afternoon, in the gym of the posh health club near Macclesfield, watched by a crowd of women who had come for exercise and eroticism, not spiritual uplift. Morocco is certainly in touch with the true tradition; she is one of those who can still trail her fingers in the hidden stream of female power, but that afternoon the *baraka* (blessing) was not present, only the ghost of it. But you could sense what the dance would be like performed throughout a long cold desert night, and how you would feel the *baraka* spraying from the fingertips of the Guedra as she flicked it towards you, how you would absorb it and go home quietened, reassured and refreshed.

Morocco told us that she had often asked Tuareg people where their tribe came from and always got a similar answer: 'Long ago we used to live on an island in the sea and come over here to trade and sell our wares. But one day that island disappeared under the waves and we had to make our lives and continue our generations here.' I cannot help but remind you that, according to Diodorus, the Libyan

Amazons came from an island 'in the lake Tritonis' which is thought to have been on the western border between present-day Libya and Tunisia. There is also the earthquake that destroyed Santorini in the late Bronze Age and created tidal waves that may have hastened the end of the Minoan civilisation on Crete. Could the Tuareg have come originally from one of the Aegean islands where the Great Mother was worshipped, as she was in Samothrace, Lemnos and Crete? These islands are a long way from the African coast, so this must be an unlikely scenario, but I am haunted by Francis Rodd's assertion that the Tuareg women were 'respected by their men in a manner which has no parallel in my experience'. Where did that respect come from and will we ever find its like again, once it has finally died out amongst the Tuareg?

THE LAST MATRIARCHS

I missed talking to Eva Meyerowitz by a few months. When I had tried to contact her via her publisher a few years ago, after reading an article she wrote in *Spare Rib* magazine, I encountered those petty obstructions that sometimes for no particular reason rise up in the path of the researcher, with the result that I gave up and only tried again last year, when a most helpful person at Faber & Faber told me that, sadly, Eva Meyerowitz had died.

Eva found herself in Ghana in west Africa just before the Second World War when she and her husband moved there from South Africa. A sculptor by vocation, she gradually slipped into anthropology as she became more and more interested in the art of different African peoples. In 1944, while travelling alone in search of the ruins of a medieval city, she encountered the Akan, a people who still retained a matriarchal social system, and wrote four books chronicling the gradual decay of the matriarchal elements in this society under the influence of British rule.[9] Her *Spare Rib* article was about the Amazons: she had come across real Amazons in her travels in Africa.

The first paragraphs of *The Sacred State of the Akan* encapsulate the essence of matriarchy: 'The *Ohemmaa*, female king, or queen-mother as she is called by Europeans, is regarded by the Akan as the owner of the state; the *Ohene*, male king ... is appointed by the queenmother as the ruler of the state. ... The queenmother repre-sents the *Great Mother Moon-goddess*, the king the *Sungod*, and the state the Universe.'

Because of her identification with the moon, the queenmother wears silver jewellery and rides in her sedan chair on ceremonial occasions with a casket of silver dust on her lap, which she plays with and casts into the air for the delectation of the people. When she dies she is buried adorned with silver jewellery, and the eight openings of her body – eyes, ears, nostrils, mouth and vagina – are filled with silver dust.

The queenmother could marry whoever she wanted or simply take lovers and have children with them. Only her sons were princes and could succeed to the throne, not the sons of the king. In life she did not have to bother herself with administration, but took care of everything to do with women and their welfare. In the Akan state she had her own court in which she would deal with cases concerning women, and she was the king's legal adviser in cases of divorce, charges of rape or seduction. She could also pardon people condemned to death. She had her own stool or throne symbolising the creation or birth of the universe. In public she sat close to the king, but a step behind him on the left so that, in case of assault, the king could throw himself before her and shield her with his body, suggesting that at root she was the more valuable person.

In rank the queenmother was clearly above any of the royal wives (and the Bono kings had over 3,000!), having her own retinue of young and beautiful girls to walk before her in processions. But how did this embodiment of matriarchal power affect the status of women in the kingdom? Eva Meyerowitz describes the long complex festival that marked the rite of passage for girls into womanhood, called the *beragoro*. There was no equivalent for boys and the ceremony seems throughout designed to make the girls feel important and valued and to give them a sense of their own dignity. After ritual bathing in which some of the girl's body hair is shaved off and offered to the spirit ancestors to inform them that she has become a woman, the girl is freshly clothed in women's cloth and carried home to be fêted for a full five days and given presents by everyone. She sits in state, beautifully adorned; behind her, an old woman completes her instruction in matters of sex by whispering into her ear. However, remembering the rites of Artemis practised by girls at Brauron, we might feel there is an element of 'have a good time now because tomorrow you'll be a mother and live a life of sacrifice'.

Although the husband is master in the house, the law favours and protects women in many ways. Meyerowitz comments:

> If a man insults a woman, or gossips about her in a vulgar way, the woman may bring him before the queenmother's court, where he may be heavily fined. In olden days this law was often invoked by queenmothers who more than once inflicted the death penalty on a man for speaking in a deroga-tory way of a princess. The princesses, taking advantage of their protected status, did much as they liked and changed their husbands (and lovers) frequently.

However, British colonisation was not good for the women of Akan. The British overlooked the queenmothers and her female ministers and dealt only with the men. When their mistake was pointed out to them they tried to include the women, but it was too late: the men had learned to disregard the women.

There were no true Amazons in the Akan kingdoms. Young women did not fight as soldiers, though sometimes older women past menopause did. In Ashanti they fought as shock-troops to encourage the men and were buried with military honours if they were killed. In neighbouring Dahomey, however, within living memory there were 'professional' fighting women who were much closer to our idea of Amazons. The last of them fought against the French in the wars of 1894 and 1898, and in 1937 three of them were still alive. In 1900, the explorer-diplomat Richard Burton wrote about his encounter with them:

> They were divided into blunderbuss-women, elephant-hunt-ers, beheaders, who carry razors four foot long and the line, armed with muskets and short swords . . . All the Amazons were ex-officio royal wives . . . it was high treason to touch them even accidentally; they lodged in the Palace, and when they went abroad, all men, even strangers, had to clear off the road . . . Such a regime makes the Amazons, as might be expected, intolerably fierce . . . Their sole object in life is blood-spilling and head-snatching. They pride themselves on not being men, and with reason. The soldiers blink and shrink when they fire their guns, the soldieresses do not. The men run away; the women fight to the bitter end.
>
> In the fierce attack on the city of Abokuta (March 15 1864) several of the Amazons of my own regiment scaled the walls; their brethren in arms hardly attempted the feat.[10]

Although ostensibly 'king's wives', these 'Amazons' were obliged to live in celibacy and any woman found with a lover or falling pregnant was usually executed. It is intriguing to hear from Burton, who had no axe to grind on gender issues, that the women soldiers were much braver and more ruthless than the men. Possibly the sublimation of their sexual instincts into aggression might go some way to explain this, plus hormonal changes wrought by heavy physical training. But Burton himself had another explanation: 'The origin of this excep-tional organisation, is, I believe, the masculine physique of the women, enabling them to compete with the men in bodily strength, nerve and endurance. It is the same with most of the races inhabiting the Delta of the Niger, where feminine harshness of feature and robustness of form rival the masculine.'¹¹

Although Burton admired their courage he found the sight of these Amazons grotesque and unnatural. In his *Mission to Gelele, King of Dahome*, he describes two king's bodyguards:

> This dignitary is a huge old porpoise, wearing a bonnet shaped like that of a French cordon-bleu, but pink and white below, with two crocodiles of blue cloth on the top, and the whole confined by silver horns ... the Humbagi ... is also vast in breadth, and a hammer-head in silver projecting from her forehead gives her the semblance of a unicorn. As a rule the warrioresses begin to fatten when their dancing days are passed, and some of them are prodigies of obesity.

It seems few of the 'soldieresses' lived up to the lissom, epicene image of the traditional Amazon: 'I expected to see Penthesileas, Thalestrises, Dianas – lovely names! I saw old, ugly and square-built frows, trudging "grumpily" along, with the face of "cook" after being much "nagg'd" by "the missus".'

Burton had heard that in the time of King Gezo, who was the man who had raised the Amazons to their present position of importance in the middle of the nineteenth century, the bow-women were all young girls, 'the pick of the army and the pick of dancers'. Burton reckoned that about two-thirds of all the Amazons would actually be virgins – the other third having being married. They were kept separate from men at all times and 'never leave their quarters unless preceded by a bell to drive men from the road'. Burton makes a rather snide remark about the expression of their sexuality: 'as a rule these fighting *célibataires* prefer the *morosa voluptas* of the schoolmen, and the peculiarities of the Tenth Muse', by which Victorian euphemism I think he means they were lesbians!

Women's actual status in Dahomey appears to have been ambiguous. At the court women took precedence over men, and yet Burton observed that the warrioresses would say 'we are no longer females, but males', and a soldier disgracing himself was called, in insult, a woman. Certainly the girls chosen in adolescence by the king to be his celibate Amazon wives had no choice in the matter, and one can imagine that some of them at least were not pleased with their fate. In truth, the Dahomeyan Amazons appear more as a useful and flattering aid to the male royal ego than an expression of female power and independence, and Burton clearly felt they were an ugly aberration. Yet they prove that, psychologically and physiologically, young and older women can make good soldiers. That black African women may sometimes have bigger and stronger bodies than women of many other races does not weaken the essential point: if women do not put their energy into sex and reproduction they can be trained to be as ruthless and aggressive as the toughest man. We might well not want to be this sort of Amazon, but it is good to know we could be, if needs must.

CHAPTER EIGHT

The Last Amazons

....

The story of Penthesilea is a poignant one. She is the last *true* Amazon. Hercules has slaughtered or routed most of her sisters in the wars of Hippolyta's girdle, but a small band have escaped and survived long enough to make their way to Troy to fight on the Trojan side. Penthesilea launches herself against Achilles, that chilling embodiment of male pride and heroism, and fights him hard in hand-to-hand combat. But her Amazon courage is powerless against his consummate skill and power: he thrusts his spear through her breast and she staggers back dying. Bending down, he pulls back her helmet and, seeing her beautiful face, falls in love with her. Thersites, who mocks him for this piece of sentimental unmanliness, he flings to the ground so hard that he expires too.

The story is told in a long-winded poem of the fifth century AD by Quintus of Smyrna who got the details from a lost version of an epic by Arctinus. There are still other versions: in one of them Achilles is gripped by lust and violates Penthesilea's still-warm dead body; in another, Thersites is gouging out the eyes of the dying Amazon when Achilles stops him angrily and strikes him so hard that he smashes his teeth and sends his ghost to Tartarus!

The poignancy comes from the hopelessness of it. Penthesilea can never conquer Achilles: he is a killing machine and she is a brave, foolish, idealistic girl. The Amazon here is barking up the wrong tree: the *shakti*-power has flowed, into a dead-end channel. The time of the Amazons is over and the time of the male warriors has come, and there is nothing a lone heroine can do about it. The stories continue, of course, but they are always 'travellers' tales' of the variety: 'I know a man who knows a man who was in a spat in some godforsaken spot on the Black Sea, and do you know, when they went to despoil the corpses of the men they'd killed, every one was a woman? No, honestly, he swore it was true . . .'

There are countless other stories of warrior-queens and women fighters in the ancient world, most of which, for me, do not quite catch the spirit of the Amazons.

Telessilla, a warrior poet in the fifth century BC, rallied the women of the besieged city of Argos with war-hymns and chants and led them in defending the city against the invading forces. Arachidamia was one of a number of Spartan princesses who led female troops. She fought against Pyrrhus during the siege of Lacedemon in the third century BC. In the first century AD, Triaria, dressed and armed as a knight, accompanied her husband, Emperor Lucius Vitellius, into battle and fought at his side.

Zababi and her successor Samsi reigned as Arabian warrior-queens from approximately 740 to 720 BC. Both commanded armies containing large numbers of women. The magnificent Zenobia Septimia governed Syria from about 250 to 275 AD. Not for her the litter that was usual for rulers; she led her armies on horseback wearing full armour, and during Claudius' reign defeated the Roman legions so decisively that they retreated from much of Asia Minor. Arabia, Armenia and Persia allied themselves with her and she claimed dominion over Egypt by right of ancestry. Claudius' successor Aurelian sent his most experienced legions to conquer Zenobia, but it took almost four years of battles and sieges before her capital city of Palmyra fell. Even in defeat, Zenobia was triumphant: in the procession of conquered queens in Rome she rode in a war-chariot of her own design and was weighted down not only with chains, but also with glittering jewels.[1]

Some of these tales may well be true and reflect what a persistent 'aberration' the warrior women are within a wide range of societies. The most convincing reports tend to be of fighting women amongst nomadic peoples: Tomyris was queen of the Celtic Massagetae, a people close to the Scythians in their love of horses and war, mentioned by Herodotus as having promiscuous sexual customs, whose homeland was in what is now Iran. Cyrus of Persia encountered her when he was building his empire, and captured her son by playing a trick on him. When her son was released he committed suicide in shame, and this must have decided Tomyris to be completely ruthless. Herodotus tells us that the battle between her troops and those of Cyrus was the fiercest between non-Greeks there has ever been. Most of the Persian army was wiped out and Cyrus was killed too. Tomyris had promised him that she would 'quench his thirst for blood', so she searched out his corpse and, when she found it, shoved his head into a wineskin filled with human blood. Herodotus feels this is the most trustworthy account of Cyrus' death: it is certainly the most picturesque, and my own favourite too.

The tradition amongst nomad women continued long into well-documented historical times: sometimes it is the warrior aspect that surfaces, sometimes the theme of matriarchal sexual practices. When Ruy Gonzalez de Clavijo made an embassy to the court of Tamburlaine in the first years of the fifteenth century, he too came across 'Amazons':

Fifteen days' journey from the city of Samarcand, in the direction of China, there is a land inhabited by Amazons, and to this day they continue the custom of having no men with them, except at one time of the year, when they are permitted, by their leaders, to go with their daughters to the nearest settlements and have communication with men, each taking the one who pleases her most, with whom they live, and eat and drink, after which they return to their own land. If they bring forth daughters afterwards, they keep them; but they send their sons to their fathers. These women are subject to Timour Beg; they used to be under the Emperor of Cathay, and they are Christians of the Greek church. They are of the lineage of the Amazons who were at Troy, when it was destroyed by the Greeks.[2]

This report is describing a society not very different from that of the present-day Mosuo women of Luoshui in the mountainous region of south-west China. These people, of Tibetan and Burmese descent, practise a way of life that seems entirely matriarchal. The women never marry and never leave their maternal home, but they are free to bring any man they choose home to make love with him and have children. Boys share rooms in their parents' homes, while girls get their own rooms and are allowed to take lovers from the age of thirteen onwards. Children are always raised by the mother's family.

At the annual thanksgiving festival the young women get dressed up in their exquisite embroidered silk jackets and elegant braided wigs and set off determinedly to flirt and choose a man for the night. They avoid Chinese suitors like the plague, knowing that they will want to marry, which feels like slavery to these women. That's the story, anyway. To me it sounds almost too good to be true, and I suspect that the details may have been honed to make a good splash in the magazine where I came across it. I am not accusing the journalist of distorting facts, merely pointing to the human tendency to smooth out and omit details that don't fit the big picture. I suspect this has happened when many travellers report sightings of 'Amazonian tribes' – they round off the picture to make them sound like the archetypal Amazons of Greek legend.

As I mentioned in the Introduction, many people think that when you talk of 'Amazons' you are referring to tribes from South America who live in the rain forest or on the banks of the River Amazon. In the Elizabethan era it was believed that, after Penthesilea's death, the Amazons emigrated from Asia to South America, and thereafter many missionaries and explorers were keen to find their homeland there. In fact, explorers did find 'Amazonian' tribes living there who seemed to have all the characteristics of the Greek variety, which is where the confusion has come from. In his account, written in the seventeenth century, the Jesuit Cristobal de Acuna describes how, as you travel down the River Amazon and follow a tributary flowing north, you come eventually to a mountain called Tacamiaba, a barren peak constantly buffeted by the winds. Here live the Amazons.

These women live together in isolation and protect them-selves without any help from men. However, at certain specific times of year they are visited by their neighbours, the Guacaris. When the latter arrive, the Amazons run for their weapons for fear of an ambush. But as soon as they recognise their friends, they all hurry down to meet the boats of the newcomers. Each woman takes a hammock from a boat and goes to hang it up in her home. Then she lies down and awaits the men. A few days later, the Amazons' guests go home, returning without fail the following season. The girls that are born of these unions are raised by their mothers. They are taught to work and to bear arms. As for the boys, nobody knows exactly what becomes of them. I have been told by an Indian who, in his youth, went with his father to one of these assignations, that the following year the Amazons hand back to the children's fathers any males to whom they have given birth. But, as a rule, it is thought that they put these male children to death. I cannot be certain.[3]

The putting of the male children to death often crops up, in a curi-ous reversal of the common practice in patriarchal societies (which continues today in China and India) of exposing girl babies whose value is felt to be less than that of boys. One way for a woman to raise her value is to become an honorary man, which is a prize awarded to certain girls in the northern mountains of Albania even today. Life is tough in this barren, poverty-stricken region and the ancient tribal laws known as *Lek* still hold sway. A 'sworn virgin' is worth six bags of gold pieces or twelve oxen, exactly twice the value assigned to ordinary married women. Where necessity or inclination demand it, women can choose to become 'sworn virgins', to wear men's clothes, do the hard agricultural work, and carry the clout of the 'man of the house' in every way. They may not marry or have children, but they get to sit in the bar, drink raki, smoke and become 'one of the boys'. At weddings they will sit with the men, not the women, and it seems that the men really do accept them as their own.

Journalist Julius Strauss[4] who visited the region in 1997 met forty-two-year-old Lule, a 'sworn virgin', who had been born into a family of ten sisters and one sickly brother. Her mother had asked her to take over the family when she was fifteen, and in her village she is treated as an equal by all the other men. 'She behaves like a man, smokes and drinks like a man and we respect her as a man,' said one fellow in the local bar. Under the Soviet regime she worked as a tractor driver, but now she freelances as a welder. Lule herself said: 'My sisters always considered me to be a boy. I didn't want someone to rule me. . . . But I certainly wouldn't recommend it to my nieces. It's a tough life.' Her sisters serve her raki and coffee and look after her as if she were a man.

In Monoklisia, a Greek town near the Bulgarian border, once a year in December the men and women swap roles: the men stay at home, do the housework and mind the children, while the women, in a caricature of male indolence, go to the café to play cards and backgammon, drink ouzo and coffee. After a wine-rich lunch they parade through town and elect themselves a queen for the day, finishing off, in an echo of the ancient Thesmophoria, with hours of ribald songs and storytelling over a meal of roasted cockerel (never hen). Local tradition has it that the town was an Amazon stronghold in antiquity, and indeed our Trojan heroine Penthesilea was supposed to come from an area of Greece called Thrace, not far from Monoklisia. On the other hand, some people call it St Domna's Day, and say that it is a Christian festival honouring midwives and female fertility. Patricia Storace visited the town on the day of the *Yinaikokratia* (women-in-power) festival with a male Greek friend, Yiannis, and found that the tables really were turned:

> A woman comes forward carrying a bowl of water and a sprig of basil, and with gleeful malice splashes Yiannis with the drops clinging to her plant, in a deadpan parody of a typical Orthodox priest's blessing and assumption of moral authority. 'Why do you splash me?' Yiannis asks, a shade of hurt in his expression. 'Because you are a man ... polluted,' she says, 'and you must be purified to enter.' She winks at me, having a high time mocking the theology which defines women as physically and morally imperfect, and evoking in particular the prohibition against women entering a church during their menstrual periods, a routine prohibition for a woman of her generation. As a girl baby, she would not have been baptised close to the sanctuary as a boy baby could be.[5]

But once again, occasional masculinity, along with its privileges, is awarded to women to keep them quiet in their customarily subservient role. The Monoklisia custom exists to let off steam (and attract tourists, writers and film-makers?), but it certainly does not point these women out as inheritors of the Amazon strength. To find the true inheritors of the Amazon spirit we must look elsewhere.

INHERITORS?

It is mainly lesbians who have tried out the 'separatist' life of the Amazons in various sorts of Utopian communities, whether rural, political or fictional. The Amazons were, not surprisingly, a source of inspiration for the idea of the 'Lesbian Nation' which grew up in the 1970s. Monica Wittig defined Amazons as 'women who live amongst themselves, by themselves and for themselves at all the generally accepted levels: fictional, symbolic, actual . . .'

But the idea had been explored much earlier, at the beginning of the twentieth century, by two lesbian women called Renee Vivien and Natalie Barney. Barney was a tall striking woman actually called 'L'Amazone' by her contemporaries, and she and Vivien decided to travel from Paris to the island of Lesbos in the Aegean where Sappho the female poet had educated a group of girls (who were not at all Amazonian) in order to create an ideal all-female community. However, they discovered no traces of Sappho or her school on the island and decided eventually to found an Academy of Women in Paris, a place more conducive to their plans.

They were the first of a long line of groups of women who were to find that the ideal that read so appealingly in books like Marge Piercy's *Woman on the Edge of Time*, of an egalitarian, decentralised, communal and nature-respecting society run by reasonable and peaceful women, did not transfer itself easily into reality, possibly because aggression was labelled as a negative, male quality that was not allowed to be expressed openly. It then proceeded to flow into underground cross-currents that would build up and erupt in a violent and destructive way. I know whereof I speak, having worked in several women-only groups, in which I would often come to long for the straightforward self-assertion of the male. But the true Amazons did not have this problem: they expressed their aggression openly – as they could, because they were 'equal to men' physically and did not have to subscribe to a sentimental view of female nature.

In the final analysis, the Amazons did not and do not work as a role model for Utopian feminists or lesbians because of the Amazons' direct, 'masculine' tendency towards violence. Admittedly that violence is aroused by the need to defend themselves from male depredations, but it is there just the same and most ideologically sound feminists deplore it.

Who really are the inheritors of the Amazon spirit? Or, to put it another way, where did that female power, that *shakti*, go, what channels does it flow into now, in the last days of the second millennium?

Here it is very easy to be sidetracked into considering every story of fighting women or of an aggressive or original woman living in an unconventional set-up, or to plunge into sub-sociological ramblings about Lara Croft and Red Sonya, but I want to avoid all these things, entertaining though they can be. Female soldiers won't really do because modern warfare does not put women into face-to-face combat. Being in the army is not enough to qualify as an Amazon, neither is being a strong, determined woman – of whom there are very many awe-inspiring examples nowadays. It is something more subtle and yet more radical, to do with the deliberate crossing of gender lines with the aim of using energy differently, what Florence Bennett, in her 1912 book, charmingly refers to as 'the oriental idea of sex confusion'.

The Sorcerer's Crossing is a curious book purporting to give a true record of the training and initiation of a young American woman into the secrets of a South American Indian tradition of sorcery. At a key point in her training, Taisha Abelar's teacher, Clara, tells her that all over the world women are reared to be at the service of men: 'It makes no difference whether they are bought right off the slave-block, or they are courted and loved,' she stressed. 'Their fundamental purpose and fate is still the same: to nourish, shelter and serve men.' Taisha protests that this is not always true but Clara insists that it is, and that when a woman sleeps with a man he leaves 'energy lines' inside her body and henceforth can collect and steal her energy. The sorcery practices that Clara teaches Taisha are designed to win that energy back.

You do not have to take the above literally to see the point: sexual intercourse starts processes that use up women's energy – whether that energy goes into making a relationship, or conceiving and nurturing a child, or into more subtle affairs. Women in our society are still usually conditioned to please and support men. Unmarried women past a certain age, particularly if they are celibate, are pitied and looked down upon because they cannot 'catch' a man. Yet it is important to distinguish the argument of this book from the classic feminist position that takes a resentful view of this situation: the 'woman warrior' in Abelar's universe does not indulge in self-pity, neither does she reject men; she simply learns to save her sexual energy and use it for exploration of the unknown: 'to evolve is an equal if not a greater imperative than to reproduce'.

Later in Taisha's training a new teacher, Nelida, teaches her a surprising lesson about the source of female energy: '. . . she lifted her skirt and spread her legs apart. "Look at my vagina," she ordered. "The hole between the legs of a woman is the energetic opening of the womb, an organ that is at the same time powerful and resourceful."' At first shocked and embarrassed – 'the area around her vagina seemed to radiate a force that if I stared at it made me feel dizzy' – Taisha gradually calms down and recognises the truth of what Nelida has said: 'Showing me her nakedness had done something inconceivable to me; it had soothed my anguish and made me abandon all my prudishness. In one instant, I had become extraordinarily familiar with Nelida. Stammering pitifully, I told her what I had just realised. "That's exactly what the energy from the womb is supposed to do," Nelida said cheerfully.'

The sexual energy that most of us put into erotic encounters and their concomitants is stored by these sorceresses and put into a sustained effort to cleanse the doors of perception and travel into inconceivable worlds. To do this, the 'warriors' – both male and female – have to be 'impeccable'; that is, to give up utterly self-importance and be capable of steady, continuous efforts of self-discipline.

When Nelida pulls up her skirt she is doing what the scowling, vulva-exposing Sheila-na-gigs sculpted in hidden corners in British churches are doing, what the naked goddesses of Babylonia, Assyria, the figures from Crete and India with their forceful breasts are doing – embodying the *shakti*, the power that brings the world into being, clothes it, animates its creatures, and gives them forms and names. But we must take care to remember that, although women embody this power, they do not *own* it. Perhaps this is the mistake that Amazonian societies have made: of thinking that either sex can own this power, and deprive the other of it.

We have traced back the idea of Amazonian female power through the Hittites and Cretans, their priestess-queens and sacred hierodules, back into the more eastern lands where the androgynous Ishtar, goddess of love and war, ruled; and we saw how, in order for civilisation to advance, the male side of human nature had to organise and order the wild chaotic energies of the female side. Mind had to master body, and Christianity with its image of a human body nailed to a cross, was the religion that best expressed this necessity. But now it seems that, in order to evolve further, we may have to go back and rediscover the body and the female and learn to handle this *shakti*-energy rather differently. This is what the 'sorcerers' mentioned above are doing. But let us hope that this will not mean a return to some kind of grotesque matriarchy where women rule like queen bees and men must either be drones, mothers' sons, or castrated priests.

In 1985 Jenny Lewis was in hospital after a radical mastectomy for breast cancer when she received a letter from a friend. 'Dear Jenny,' it said, 'now you are a true Amazon.' The letter broke through Jenny's paralysis, terror and confusion, and made her determined to survive. It also made her find out about the Amazons, following something of the same track as me, but as a poet, not a head-banging researcher. She talked about how the 'powerful, outward-going energies of our tribal ancestresses are often subverted to the whims of a patriarchal culture in which women have been taught to feel shame for their sexuality and distaste for female behaviour which is non-submissive'. She tapped in, as many writers and poets have done before her, to the Amazon in the psyche of mankind. She recovered her spirit of resistance and is still, thirteen years later, in remission. She wrote her book *When I Became an Amazon* in celebration of her discovery and recovery.

The Amazon

We came over the ice
of the Cimmerian Bosphorus,
5 thousand of us running in unison
at a steady pace, leaving freezing
trails of breath behind us.
We were robed in furs against
the bitterness of winter,
our minds and blades
sharpened for vengeance.
The blizzard rang against our shields
as we leaned heads down
into the biting winds.

On our backs we carried staves,
ropes and rolls of canvas
for constructing rough shelters
when we stopped at night
to camp. Dog sleds flanked us
to the left and right, transporting
food, weapons and supplies
of the deadly poison with which
we tipped our arrows.
Those at the back carried spears,
knives and axes. In front, the archers
who could unleash winged death
in an instant. And all our strength
and all our javelins, and all our dreams
and lives were pledged to victory—
and keeping free

the spirit of the Amazons.[6]

Maybe it is through the sorceresses (or should we call them 'magic-women'?) and poets that we can still contact the spirit of the Amazons today.

SO, WHO WERE THE AMAZONS?

As you enter the cathedral of St Sophia in Kiev, the first thing that catches your eye, after you get used to the gloom, is the gigantic figure of a woman looking down on you from the cupola above the altar. She stands, glittering in mosaic, knees slightly bent, her piercing eyes following you wherever you go. Her arms are raised in the gesture of epiphany or blessing, and she wears a golden cloak over a blue robe and a red belt, signifying her sacred lineage. She is radiant with power. When the Tartars invaded Kiev in the eleventh century and stormed into the cathedral to destroy it they encountered her and, backing away, left the building alone. When we ask the female guide on duty about her somewhat prominent position, she says, 'But of course, she is the goddess of our city!'

She is in fact Maria Oranta, the virgin mother of Jesus, but she has no baby in her arms and her son, Jesus, and his archangels are lost up in heaven above her, so that you have to crane your neck to see them. She has the position of power; it is her presence that fills the cathedral, she is the warrior guardian of the city of Kiev.

A millennium and a half before this virgin warrior, Mary, was created by an artist who was certainly aware of the old *shakti*-power, in the steppes on all sides of Kiev, Scythian and Sauromatian warrior women would have roamed, standing guard on their camps and settlements or rallying to fight a threat from a tribe from the forest steppe in the north. These women fought alongside their men-folk, doing so out of necessity, so that they and their children and their homes would survive. Some of them were also priestesses, who could perform the rituals that held the tribe together and bound them to their gods and goddesses. These are the sort of women whose graves the three women archaeologists I visited have examined and pondered over. Significantly, it took women to lead the search to find women warriors – or, rather, to begin the slow uncovering of the truth about gender roles in the past.

Travelling further back in time we encountered the other Amazon prototypes – the war-dancing priestesses of Ephesus or Samothrace, the bull-leaping girls in their codpieces, the king-making matriarchs and magic-women of Zalpa/Themiscyra, the ebullient Hurrian Princess Puduhepa who revolutionised Hittite religion. We entered the great 'goddess-cities' of Anatolia and the Near East where the power of the *shakti* was understood and celebrated, whether by sacred prostitutes or armed priestesses or castrated men-women, or androgynes. The linking of these goddesses to wild animals, particularly lions or leopards, took us right back to the old lion-priestess from Çatal Hüyük in Neolithic times.

From the seventh millennium BC onwards, as civilisation was gradually evolving, the struggle to tame this wild 'female' power continued, until finally in Classical Greece the battle was won and we had the dazzling beginnings of democracy, and the modern state with its enshrinement of the freedom of the individual. Reason conquers mystery, male conquers female, and the image of the Amazon blossoms brilliantly, representing that which must be loved and lost, admired and then wiped out, attractive and compelling though it may be.

The Amazons are a memory of a kind of female power, the nature of which we have almost entirely forgotten. But the memory is coming back. As I have studied their image, it has changed, as if I was looking at a negative in a developing dish that never stops developing, which is sometimes clear and lucent, sometimes fuzzy and opaque. I have come to realise that they are not what they seem to be, but something else that manages to be both potent and elusive. It is very unlikely that a race of women *exactly* like Herodotus' or Diodorus' Amazons existed, but I have satisfied myself that all the components of the myth existed in different times and places, and if you piece all these fragments together they make an image close to the Amazon archetype. Whether she be Penthesilea or Antiope or Xena, the Amazon is powerful, deadly, glamorous and free.

The hero *had* to crush this female monster – whether she took the form of a dragon or an Amazon, it was all the same. It was a step that had to be taken, and that brought many good things with it, but, as with all progress, something was lost along the way. It is what was lost that this book is about. Because sometimes, when the time is right, we have to go back and retrieve what was discarded or rejected and bring it back into consciousness again. Maybe this time round we will do something different with it. The enormous interest in the Amazons suggests that we have got to such a point.

Notes

....

1 ESSENCE OF AMAZON

1. Diodorus of Sicily, Book IV, 15–16.
2. Apollodorus, Book II, 5.9.
3. Camille Paglia, *Sexual Personae*, Yale University Press, 1990.
4. D.J. Sobol, *The Amazons of Greek Mythology*, Barnes, New York, 1972.
5. Sarah B. Pomeroy, *Goddesses, Whores, Wives and Slaves*, Robert Hale, London, 1975. Much of the information about life in Classical Greece comes from this excellent book.
6. Mandy Merch, 'The Amazons of Ancient Athens', in *Tearing the Veil: Essays on Femininity*, edited by Susan Lipshitz, Routledge & Kegan Paul, London, 1978.
7. Apollonius Rhodius, Book II, 1173.
8. Victor Ehrenberg, *From Solon to Socrates*, Routledge, London, 1973.
9. John Boardman, *The Eye of Greece*, ed. D. Kurtz and B. Sparkes, Cambridge University Press, Cambridge, 1982.
10. Dietrich von Bothmer, *Amazons in Greek Art*, Oxford University Press, Oxford, 1957.
11. Homer, *The Iliad*, 3:176, translated by Martin Hammond, Penguin, Harmondsworth, 1987.
12. Hesiod, *Catalogue of Women*, quoted by Mina Zografou in *Amazons in Homer and Hesiod*, Athens, 1972.
13. Printed in Anne Baring's and Jules Cashford's *The Myth of the Goddess*, Viking, London, 1991.
14. George Thomson, *The Prehistoric Aegean*, Lawrence & Wishart, London, 1949.
15. Spelt variously as Šaušga or Šawuška. I have chosen to be phonetic.
16. A.H. Sayce and Adolf Holm.

2 THE SECRET OF THE STEPPES

1. Herodotus, *Histories*, Book IV, 113, translated by Robin Waterfield, Oxford University Press, Oxford, 1998.
2. Hippocrates, *De Articulis*, Section 53.
3. Hippocrates, *Airs, Waters, Places*, xvii.
4. Herodotus, Book IV, 64.
5. Hippocrates, *Airs, Waters, Places*.
6. Elena Fialko had started by looking at 112 burials of women with weapons, but excluded those graves that had been robbed or only had a couple of arrowheads to signify as weapons. Neither did she include those in which the woman's goods might have got confused with those of a partner buried next to her. This left ninety-five, of which seventy-seven were in the steppe areas, and thirty-six had their gender confirmed by anthropologists. The others were counted female because of the 'mixed inventories' they were buried with. Thirty-four were the main burial in their *kurgan*, though most of these mounds were not very big.
7. Elena Fialko only counted as a warrior a woman buried with more than one arrowhead because a single one could have been used as an amulet or in a necklace and would not necessarily signify that the woman was any kind of fighter.
8. Hippocrates, *Airs, Waters, Places*.
9. Timothy Taylor and Tatiana Miroshana.
10. Discussed in Miranda J. Green, 'Images in Opposition', in *Antiquity*, vol. 71, December 1997.

3 ARTEMIS, BRIGHT AND DARK

1. Sue Blundell, 'Who Are the Amazons?', *Classical Association News*, August 1998.
2. Vincent Scully, *The Earth, the Temple and the Gods*, Yale University Press, New Haven, 1979.
3. Scholiast on Lucian, pp. 275, 276 (Rabe).
4. Carlos Castaneda, *The Eagle's Gift*, Penguin, Harmondsworth, 1982.
5. Who all but one murdered their husbands.

6. Walter Burkert, *Greek Religion*, Basil Blackwell, Oxford, 1985.

7. Arthur Evans, *The Palace of Minos*, vol. IV, i, Macmillan, London, 1921. There is now some argument about the authenticity of this figure, but the point also stands without her.

8. St Paul – Holy Bible, Acts 19.

9. Herodotus, *Histories*, Book I, 173.

10. Mina Zografou, *Amazons in Homer and Hesiod*, Athens, 1972.

11. Florence Bennett, *Religious Cults Associated with the Amazons*, Columbia University Press, New York, 1912.

12. W.R. Lethaby, 'The Earlier Temple of Artemis at Ephesus', *Journal of Hellenic Society*, vol. 37, i.

4 THE MEDUSA FACE OF THE GODDESS

1. Pausanias, Book VII, 18.12, translated by Jane Harrison in *Mythology*, Harrap, London, 1925.

2. Herodotus, *Histories*, Book IV, 103, translated by Robin Waterfield, Oxford University Press, Oxford 1998.

3. Ibid., 180.

4. Jessica Amanda Salmondson, *The Encyclopedia of Amazons*, Paragon House, New York, 1991.

5. Quoted by S.H. Hooke in *Middle Eastern Mythology*, Penguin, Harmondsworth, 1963.

6. Diodorus of Sicily, Book III, 52, 4–53.

7. Marten J. Vermaseren, *Cybele and Attis*, Thames & Hudson, London, 1977.

8. Barbara Walker, *The Woman's Encyclopedia of Myths and Secrets*, Harper & Row, New York, 1983.

9. Esther Harding, *Women's Mysteries*, Rider, London, 1971.

10. Walter Burkert, *Greek Religion*, Basil Blackwell, Oxford, 1985.

11. Walter F. Otto, *Dionysos: Mythus und Kultus*, Frankfurt, 1933.

12. Apollodorus, Book III, 5.1.

13. Pausanias, Book VII, 2.4–5.

14. Robert Graves, *Greek Myths*, Penguin, Harmondsworth, 1966.

5 THE HITTITE SPHINX

1. For the connection of bees with the Goddess, see Hilda Ransome, *The Sacred Bee*, Boston, 1937.

2. U. Bahadir Alkim, *Ikiztepe: The First and Second Years' Excavations, 1974–5*, Ankara, 1988.

3. J.G. Macqueen, 'Hattian Mythology and Hittite Monarchy', *Anatolian Studies* vol. 9, 1959.

4. My translation from the German of Heinrich Otten, *Eine altheth-itische Erzählung um die Stadt Zalpa*, StBoT 17, Harrossowitz, Wiesbaden, 1973, with additional help from Jill Hart in checking the original Hittite text.

5. Volkert Haas, *Magie und Mythen im Reich der Hethiter*, Merlin Verlag, Hamburg, 1977.

6. Harry Hoffner, *Hittite Myths*, Georgia, 1990.

7. Herodotus, *Histories*, Book 1, 199, translated by Robin Waterfield, Oxford University Press, Oxford, 1998.

8. Philip Rawson, *The Art of Tantra*, Thames & Hudson, London, 1978.

9. Sarah B. Pomeroy, *Goddesses, Whores, Wives and Slaves*, Robert Hale, London, 1975.

10. Haas, *Magie und Mythen*.

11. Oliver Gurney, *Some Aspects of Hittite Religion*, Oxford University Press, Oxford, 1977.

12. See discussion of temple prostitution below.

13. KUB 29 1 kol. 1 10–25, '*Keilschrifturken aus Boghazkoi*'.

14. In *Anatolian Studies*, vol. 30, 1978.

15. F. Starke, in *Zeitschrift fur Assyriologie*, vol. 69, 1979.

16. Volkert Haas, *Geschichte der Hetitschen Religion*, Brill, Leiden, 1994.

6 THE SOURCE

1. Volkert Haas, *Magie und Mythen im Reich der Hethiter*, Merlin Verlag, Hamburg, 1977.

2. Quoted in ibid.

3. O.J. Gurney, *The Hittites*, Penguin, Harmondsworth, 1981.

4. Thorkild Jacobson, *Treasures of Darkness*, Yale University Press, 1976.

5. Ibid.
6. S.N. Kramer, 'Poets and Psalmists' in *The Legacy of Sumer*, ed. Denise Schmandt-Besserat, Udena Publications, Malibu, 1976.
7. Claudian, *Against Eutropius*, 11, 263–64.
8. Gernot Wilhelm, *The Hurrians*, Aris & Philipps, London, 1989.
9. A.H. Sayce, *Hittite Religion*, The Religious Tract Society, London, 1892.
10. D.J. Sobol, *The Amazons of Greek Mythology*, Barnes, New York, 1972.
11. Callimachus, Hymn III, To Artemis.
12. Diodorus of Sicily, Book III, 55, 8–11.
13. Strabo, Book X, 3.7, quoted in *Samothrace – the Ancient Literary Sources*, Princeton, 1959.
14. Apollonius Rhodius, Book 1, 1–607.
15. Lucian, *De Dea Syria*, 15.
16. Lilian B. Lawler, *The Dance in Ancient Greece*, A & C Black, London, 1964.
17. Ibid.

7 The Ghost-dancers

1. Diodorus of Sicily, Book III, 52–5.
2. Herodotus, *Histories*, Book IV, 172, translated by Robin Waterfield, Oxford University Press, Oxford, 1998.
3. Ibid., 180.
4. www.net4you.co.at/users/poellauerg/Berber/Berber.html.
5. Lloyd Cabot Briggs, *Tribes of the Sahara*, Harvard University Press, 1960.
6. Francis R. Rodd, *People of the Veil*, Macmillan, London, 1926.
7. Herodotus, Book IV, 172.
8. Susan Rasmussen, *Spirit Possession and Personhood among the Kel Ewey Tuareg*, Cambridge University Press, Cambridge, 1995.
9. Eva Meyerowitz, *The Akan of Ghana*, 1951; *The Sacred State of the Akan*, 1958; *The Divine Kingship in Ghana and Ancient Egypt*, 1960; *The Court of an African King*, 1962, all Faber & Faber.
10. Richard Burton, *Humanitarian*, vol. 16, 1900, p. 118.
11. Richard Burton, in *Transactions of the Ethnological Society of London*, vol. III, 1865, p. 405.

8 THE LAST AMAZONS

1. Jessica Amanda Salmondson, *The Encyclopedia of Amazons*, Paragon House, New York, 1991.
2. *Embassy of Ruy Gonzalez de Clavijo to the Court of Timor*, Hakluyt Society, 1859.
3. Cristobal de Acuna, *New Discovery of the Great River of the Amazons*, 1641.
4. Julius Strauss, *Daily Telegraph*, 6 February 1997.
5. Patricia Storace, *Dinner with Persephone*, Granta Books, London, 1997.
6. Jenny Lewis, *When I Became an Amazon*, Iron Press, Manchester, 1996.

Glossary

....

Anatolia

The central plateau that makes up most of modern Turkey, bounded by the Aegean Sea in the west, the Mediterranean in the south, and the Black Sea in the north.

Antiope

Amazon princess, given as a war-trophy to the Athenian hero, Theseus. She bore a son, Hippolyte, and fought against her sister Amazons when they came to Athens to retrieve her.

Artemis

1. Greek virgin goddess, huntress and mistress of the animals, she protects all young and wild creatures and women in childbirth. Often said to be the Amazons' goddess.
2. In an earlier, more primitive version, Artemis is a Great Mother Goddess worshipped at the temple at *Ephesus*.

Athene

The warrior-goddess who protects the city of Athens. Wise, grave and pure, she is the counsellor of heroes. Carries an aegis (shield) with the snakey-haired Medusa on it and wears a crested helmet.

Bronze Age

The period of time between the *Neolithic Age* and the *Iron Age*, before the making and use of iron was commonly practised. In the Amazon zones, this falls between 3000 and 1200 BC.

Çatal Hüyük

An 8,000-year-old settlement on the *Anatolian* plain near Konya, it is one of the earliest 'towns' in the world. Famous for its shrines decorated with bull's horns and its goddess-figurines.

Corybantes

Dancing and singing acolytes of the goddess *Cybele*.

Crete

Large island situated in the Mediterranean Sea equidistant from mainland Greece and the Aegean coast of Turkey. A major centre for trade since *Neolithic* times, and home – in the *Bronze Age* – of the *Minoan culture* in which women played a central religious role, and delicate and sophisticated artwork was produced.

Cucuteni culture

Artistically brilliant *Neolithic* culture centred in Moldova and western Ukraine.

Curetes

Dancing and singing acolytes of the Cretan mother-goddess, *Rhea*. Often confused with *Corybantes*.

Cybele

The Great Mother Goddess of Phrygia whose roots reach back to Kubaba of Carchemish in the *Bronze Age*. She was taken to Rome in 204 BC where she was popular for several centuries. She was served by self-castrated priests and by her *Corybantes*.

Demeter

The Greek goddess of the fruitful earth, mother of *Persephone*. Their separation and reunion formed the basis of the *Eleusinian mysteries*.

Dionysus

The god of wine and ecstatic self-abandonment. His female followers were known as *maenads*.

Dorians

A people who invaded *Crete* and Greece around 1200 BC bringing *patriarchal* customs with them.

Eleusinian mysteries

A ceremony of initiation lasting several days in which a profound secret was revealed and which was said to liberate the initiates from fear of death. The myth of *Demeter* and *Persephone* was its central theme.

Enarees

Scythian shamans who dressed as women, lost their male sexual potency, and practised as prophets and clairvoyants.

Ephesus
Goddess-city on the Aegean coast of Turkey where the great temple of
Artemis once stood.

Galli
The self-castrated priests of *Cybele*.

Guedra
Tuareg dance of blessing performed mainly by women.

Hattians
The native peoples who lived in northern *Anatolia* before the *Hittites*
moved in. They seem to have had *matrilineal* customs.

Hellenes
A name used for the Greeks. Hellen was the common ancestor of most
of the Greek tribes.

Hercules
Dorian super-hero, son of Zeus, who had to perform Twelve Labours,
including the theft of the Amazon queen's girdle. His Greek name is
Herakles, but I have called him Hercules because this is the most
common usage nowadays.

Herodotus
Greek historian, often called 'the father of history', who lived in the fifth
century BC and wrote vividly about the life and customs of places in
the Greek Empire and beyond, which he had either seen himself or
heard about. It is very difficult to disentangle fact from fiction in his
work.

Hippolyta
The Amazon queen whose girdle was stolen by *Hercules*, thus triggering
a war in which many Amazons perished.

Hittites
An Indo-European people who came to *Anatolia* at the end of the third
millennium BC and whose empire lasted nearly a millennium.

Homer
Author of the great epics *The Iliad* and *The Odyssey*. He was writing in the
eighth century BC about the Heroic Age, which was thought to have
ended with the fall of Troy around 1200 BC.

Horse-pastoralists
Horsemen who lived by rearing animals that they would herd from summer to winter pastures and back again.

Hurrians
A people who moved westwards from the Zagros mountains into *Anatolia* in the second millennium and whose religious genius had a profound influence on *Hittite* culture.

Ikiztepe
Bronze Age settlement near the Black Sea coast in Turkey, which may have been the site of the ancient *Hattian/Hittite* town of *Zalpa*.

Inanna
The earliest name of the Great Goddess in Sumer.

Indo-Europeans
Name given to all the peoples who moved westwards from an Asian heartland (where this is exactly is still much disputed) into Europe and who share a common root-language. *Hittites*, Greeks and Celts are all Indo-European peoples.

Initiation
A religious ceremony that marks an individual's rite of passage into a new role or state of consciousness.

Ishtar
Babylonian goddess, called the Queen of Heaven and the Mother of Harlots. At her temples, men would come to be sexually initiated by priestesses.

Kurgans
Large grave mounds found all over the European and Asian steppe-lands.

Lara Croft
Athletic, pneumatically breasted 'virtual' warrior-woman heroine.

Lemnian women
The women of the island of Lemnos who murdered their husbands after the men rejected them for smelling bad.

Maenads

Female followers of the god *Dionysus* who would dance themselves into an ecstatic frenzy at his festivals, sometimes tearing animals to pieces with their hands and teeth.

Matriarchy

A social system in which women hold the central governmental power.

Matrilineal

Refers to a society in which descent is traced through the female line and children belong to the clan of the mother.

Matrilocal

A social system in which a man moves into his wife's home community when he marries.

Matripotestal

A word coined to express a society in which women have significant power, although not necessarily power of government.

Minoan culture

The culture that flowered in *Crete* in the later *Bronze Age* in which the snake-goddess and the bull-games flourished.

Moldova

Small, newly free republic situated between the Ukraine and Romania.

Mycenae

City in the plain of Argolis in Greece which gave its name to the culture that developed in the late *Bronze Age* in mainland Greece, celebrated by *Homer* in his epics.

Myrina

African Amazon queen who founded cities in Asia Minor and was shipwrecked on Samothrace where she set up the shrine and sanctuary of the Great Goddess.

Neith/Net

Egyptian war-goddess whose symbols were a shield and crossed bows; possible ancestor of *Athene*.

Neolithic Age

'Stone Age' period before the skills of metal-working were discovered. In *Anatolia*, it ended around 6000 BC.

Parvati

The goddess-wife or *shakti* of Shiva in the Hindu Pantheon.

Patriarchy

Social system in which men hold the central, governmental power.

Penthesilea

Amazon queen who fought Achilles at Troy and was killed by him.

Persephone

Beloved daughter of *Demeter*, snatched by Hades, the god of the Underworld, and only restored to her mother on a part-time basis after *Demeter* has turned the world into a wasteland.

Puduhepa

Dynamic *Hurrian* priestess and queen, wife of *Hittite* king Hattusili III. She helped organise and strengthen *Hittite* religion.

Red Sonya

Glamorous and skilful warrior-heroine from film of the same name.

Rhea

Cretan mother-goddess.

Sacred prostitution

Practice in which men go to the goddess-temple to be initiated into the sexual mysteries by a priestess.

Sarmatians and Sauromatians

Semi-nomadic people who replaced the *Scythians* in the steppe-lands of what is now the Ukraine in the fourth and fifth centuries BC.

Sauromatians

(see previous entry).

Scythians

Horse-pastoralist people who inhabited the *steppes* north of the Black Sea from the eighth century BC until the *Sauromatians* and *Sarmatians* replaced them.

Shakti

Within the Hindu tradition the word can refer both to the actual consort of a god, or the power she embodies. I have extended its use to cover that power when expressed by goddess, priestess or warrior woman.

Shawushka
The *Hittite/Hurrian* name for the bisexual war-goddess.
Steppes
The flat grasslands (now largely planted with cereals) that stretch from China and Mongolia down to the Ukrainian Black Sea coast.

Tank girl
Punkish, aggressive cartoon character with woman-warrior attributes.
Tantra
Hindu and Buddhist system in which sexual energy is aroused and transformed in order to bring about heightened states of consciousness.
Themiscyra
The capital city of the Amazons according to the ancient authors, thought to be on the Black Sea coast in present-day Turkey, perhaps near Samsun. The River Thermodon may have been the River Terme Çay, which flows through the little town of Terme.
Thesmophoria
Women's mystery festival in Classical Greece in which pigs were sacrificed and the women engaged in bawdy celebrations.
Tuareg
Nomadic people who inhabit the Saharan regions of Africa. Sadly, they are now being forced to give up their nomadic ways and settle in towns, which means that their *matripotestal* customs are fading.

Xena
The warrior-princess heroine of the television programme of that name. She is strong, intelligent, and high-principled, and also has magical powers.

Zalpa/Zalpuwa
Hattian/Hittite city in the *Bronze Age*, in which a caste of 'magic-women' or priestesses possessed king-making powers.

Index